THE NEXUS

THE WATCHER SERIES BOOK TWO

ROBIN WOODS

Second Edition

CONTENTS

Epic Books Publishing

Editors Edition 1: Katie Isaacs & Alexis S.
Editors Edition 2: Beth Braithwaite & Tamar Hela

Cover Design by Vera Walker.
French Coven Crest illustrated by Vera Walker.

Summary: After fleeing home, Ali Hayes settles into her studies to become a Watcher. When a surprise informant reveals the French Coven's unprecedented use of resources to locate her, it becomes apparent that there's something about her not even she knows.

[FICTION-YOUNG ADULT, FICTION-PARANORMAL, FICTION-VAMPIRES]

Paperback ISBN-10: 0985454202
Paperback ISBN-13: 978-0-9854542-0-3

"Prefer et obdura: dolor hic tibi proderit olim."
–Ovid

Be patient and strong;
someday this pain will be useful to you.

PROLOGUE—PROPHECY

October 2nd, 3:00 A.M.
Private Archive in the London Library

Despite the chill, the air in the library was dusty and stale. Gabriel sat in the creaky booth in the far corner of the building, pressing his thumbs into his temples. He strained over his notes, haunted by an elusive feeling. Something was coming, and he hoped to find a clue as to what it was.

There was a flash of movement, and Gabriel's Durateus dagger was instantly at the throat of his uninvited guest. The veins on his arm stood out like ropes as he blinked, shocked by the identity of the intruder.

Bowen sat calmly on the bench with hands raised in surrender, his blond hair glinting in the light from the wall sconce. Not a hint of aggression was in his posture. "I came in peace," he reassured. "Please, you will want to hear what I'm going to say."

Gabriel eased back into his seat, still poised to fight. "I did not sense you."

"I, unlike my brother, can mask my presence. It's beneficial at times," he admitted, tipping his head to acknowledge the powerful Slayer sitting so close to him.

Gabriel's jaw flexed, and his dark eyes narrowed. Finally, he nodded for Bowen to continue.

"I," he paused. "I don't know if, by some miracle, she is with you and hasn't been seen. But I..." another pause, his face tormented, "feel compelled to protect her."

Gabriel's body was stone—no reaction. Bowen's fierce blue eyes were fastened on him, analyzing every breath. Gabriel knew Aleria was being hunted and wondered if this was a trick to see if Bowen was getting close, to see if he was in the correct city. But Gabriel's gut told him to believe Bowen.

"We are protecting her," Gabriel acknowledged.

"All of your training facilities are under surveillance. My brother is obsessed with finding both her and Joshua. My mother is supporting the effort with unprecedented resources."

"Why?"

"My brother simply wants Joshua dead," he said with a shrug. "But there is something else with Aleria. I believe she is important. You are familiar with the exile of the Devourer? When he was banished from our realm?"

Gabriel nodded.

"Seven Watcher families were responsible—all royalty in their own lands. In order to reverse the banishment, my mother needs the blood of specific members from each family." He hesitated. "And a member of the Lux."

Gabriel shifted uneasily in his seat, not liking what he was hearing. "Specific members? The Lux?"

"People with specific genetic traits, like a warrior from the Van Heerden family or a Polyglot from the Sato family..."

"What does this have to do with Aleria?"

"We have a partial copy of one of Ahijah's personal journals.

He was the Old Testament prophet who originally warned King Solomon to cease consorting with pagan women or be punished by God. In later journals, he prophesied about every aspect of the Devourer's banishment and..." He closed his eyes as if wanting to shut out the next two words, "his return." His mouth was pulled down in the corners. "I don't want to return to the old ways, but I will not betray my family."

"Is not speaking to me a betrayal?"

Bowen exhaled harshly. "Besides the surveillance, I haven't told you anything you didn't already know." He struggled for a moment. "I have to protect her," he said, shaking his head.

"What makes you think the prophecies have something to do with Aleria?"

His gaze bore into Gabriel. "How many girls have you known with lavender eyes? As I have said, I only have part of the manuscript, but what I do have..." His thoughts became more fragmented as he spewed out his ideas. "She fits. Eyes of amethyst. Humble life. She was to unite what was once divided —that could be your Concilium. And her nightmares. I don't know about the rest. I don't have access to your archives."

"But she would have to be from one of those families."

"What if she is? What if her ancestors fled to America during the French Revolution? Many were believed to have perished at the guillotine, but what if..."

Gabriel sank back in his seat, weighted down by the possibilities, his thoughts racing. *A surviving member of the Lux?* The hope of having a seer amongst the Watchers again was invaluable. *But the threat of having Aleria captured.* He could not allow himself to finish the thought. The world would be plunged into chaos if the Devourer was ever to return.

Bowen slid an envelope across the table, and then vanished without a word. It was filled with surveillance photos—they had found the public front for the London academy, the actual academy, and most importantly, the secret satellite campus forty kilometers outside the city where the Concilium had Aleria.

He quickly shuffled through the pictures one more time; they had images of everyone except Joshua and Aleria. Then he realized that there was also a single slip of paper with the title of Ahijah's journal, *The Nexus*.

With a phone pressed to his ear, Gabriel was out the door in seconds. Though he had left two other Slayers on campus, he still felt as if he had abandoned his post.

Gabriel gripped the phone hard. "Uriel, wake Sebastian and Raphael. Leaving the city; be there in thirty. Prep transports. Zero ripples."

1

SIGNUM ACADEMY

"You're acting awfully cavalier about my pain," I scolded in mock irritation.

He tried to stifle his grin. "Cavalier?"

"You know, indifferent, offhand, uncaring, thoughtless, *condescending*. You need another synonym or two?"

"No, I know what it means. I just wanted to see how many you could come up with. Five is quite impressive for such a mentally challenged person."

"Urgh!" I tossed my book at him.

Peter ducked and let out a roar of laughter.

"Not all of us were born with the foreign language gene. You're impossible." At some point, I started getting genuinely upset. I popped out of my seat and began thrusting my books into my bag.

"No, no, no, no. Sorry, sorry. Please sit back down. I promise to help."

Glaring at him through narrowed eyes, I measured his sincerity. "Fine, but I've reached my teasing limit today." I exhaled hard and sprawled back onto the sofa. I started to laugh, feeling a little stupid for my tantrum, even though it was partially justifiable. Peter had been teasing me *a lot* all day.

He settled back onto the other couch again and was fanning the pages of the book I'd flung at him. His light brown hair was sticking up all over the place in a serious case of bedhead. His skin had grown pale without the help of the California sun. He had used to spend so many hours in the pool playing water polo that he had radiated a golden glow even in the winter. Now, his natural blond streaks were almost gone. Our relocation to England had altered him dramatically.

"You know you are remarkably good at most of this stuff," he said. His expression was earnest.

I sighed, feeling conflicted, but appreciating the olive branch. "Not as good as you, genius boy."

"Everyone has their strengths and weaknesses."

"And Sebastian seems to know mine. This is my own personal hell—not one, but *two* foreign languages. I think my head may spontaneously combust one of these days." I dramatically reclined, pressing the back of my hand to my forehead.

"Hey, you wouldn't have to conjugate anything in Latin."

"Or French."

"Don't worry, I would write a nice epitaph for your tombstone. Something like:

> *Here lies Aleria Hayes.*
> *She has seen better days.*
> *In Latin and French, she was no good.*
> *Too bad she never understood."*

"I'd better not combust if that's the best you can come up with."

"I was on the spot."

"And poetically gifted you are not."

We both laughed. Bad poetry aside, Peter kept me grounded. He'd been a close friend for over three years, but here in exile, he was my best friend. Besides Joshua, he was now the only person in my life who'd known me for more than a few months.

While I pondered in silence, he grew thoughtful.

"You ever get homesick?" he asked, raising his dark brown eyes to meet mine. It was the first time he'd voiced that question.

It'd been four months since we'd fled here to protect our families. Of course, the parental units were under the impression that we had earned scholarships to an exclusive academy in London. They didn't know that the academy was actually not in London and was run by the Council, which was part of the Concilium of Watchers. Nor did they know about vampires and their conflict with the aforementioned Watchers and how we mere mortals had been swept up in the middle of it.

"Yeah, sometimes, but we're always so busy that I don't really think about it that much." I frowned. "I guess that makes me kind of heartless, doesn't it?"

"I've always thought you were a little heartless." His eyes widened, and he put up his hand before I could react. "Sorry. No more teasing, really."

"It's fine. I was just being a baby." I paused for a beat. "No comments; I know I just opened myself up *again*."

He laughed.

"It's going to be hard being away for the holidays, isn't it?" I questioned. I thought about my thirteen-year-old brother, dressing up in his Halloween costume, stuffing his cheeks with too much turkey at Thanksgiving, opening Christmas presents with religious zeal—all without me.

If we couldn't solve some very serious issues with the French coven, it would never be safe for me to go back. I would have to "die" in an accident while abroad and disappear.

I studied Peter for a second and felt miserable. He'd been kidnapped and used as a pawn to control me, thrust unwillingly into the vampire world, nearly dying because of it. Well, he actually *had* died in surgery for about sixty seconds.

"Yeah, it'll be hard to be away, especially at Christmas."

"Do you regret it? Choosing to come?" My voice sounded thicker than I'd wanted it to.

"Sometimes."

My heart clenched, and guilt flooded in. I tried to be still and not react.

He rolled onto his stomach and gathered a throw pillow against his chest, resting most of his weight on his elbows. "But I know it's better I'm here. I just couldn't risk my family. Part of me is really excited. I love learning about all this, and I actually like England. I can't wait to be a Watcher out in the field. It's this whole world that I would've never known about." He paused thoughtfully, and seemed to be chewing on what he had said. "No, I don't regret it. I like this life."

My heart started beating regularly again, and I tried not to exhale in a noticeable gust. I didn't want him to realize I'd literally been holding my breath, awaiting his answer. I looked at the antique grandfather clock next to the entrance of the common room. "It's 5:40. We'd better get changed. Sunset is in twenty minutes. We're supposed to be in the mat room by 6:10."

"I guess the break is over." He stood, stretched, and let out a long groan. "Time to get our butts kicked."

"Speak for yourself. I plan to do the kicking."

"See you in thirty. I—" He cut himself off when we heard someone frantically running down the hall.

Gentry emerged, visibly shaken, her red hair wild and skin

so pale it was almost translucent. "Meeting in room 110 right now; grab anyone else you see. Go now," she commanded, then sprinted down the hall.

Peter and I looked at one another for a split-second, then simultaneously sprang up and ran to the stairs. I could hear Gentry behind us as we sped down the last hall. The large classroom was already full. All faculty, staff, and students—about twenty in total—were abuzz with nervous energy. Peter found a seat in the front.

I surveyed the room for a place to sit. Leslie motioned to me from the back and slid over to make room for me on the table where she was sitting. When we'd first met, I'd wondered how she could possibly be a Watcher in training. She appeared to be more supermodel than stealth. The whole leggy, blonde thing had really intimidated me, though she was nothing but welcoming. She and Gentry had helped me adjust to life in the Watchers.

I shuffled through everyone on my way to the table. It was so tall I had to jump a little to seat myself next to her. Leslie looked at me; instead of giggling from my lack of grace getting up there, her grey-blue eyes were apprehensive. A horrible feeling gripped my stomach. I nudged her shoulder with mine, and she smiled thinly at me while we waited.

Sebastian entered the front of the room like a gust of wind and stood before us. Gabriel and Joshua arrived behind him and positioned themselves to the side, both leaning against the wall. Sebastian's shirt was misbuttoned and his tweed jacket rumpled. I'd never seen him with even a hair out of place.

He launched into the briefing: "I am ordering an immediate evacuation of this facility. You have thirty minutes to pack your things. Bring only what you can carry. Destroy anything personal that you are not taking with you. Pull hard drives if you cannot take the computer. Leave nothing that can be traced.

"Three days' worth of clothing will be required. You will get wet leaving here, so wrap anything that needs to stay dry." He surveyed the faces in the room, but it seemed like he looked at me a split-second longer than everyone else.

Out of the corner of my eye, I could see Gabriel staring at me with a peculiar expression, but I kept my focus on Sebastian, wanting answers. Gabriel's eye contact made me realize that Joshua had kept his gaze *away* from me, without wavering. He had stayed focused on the front of the room. *Am I imagining this?*

I wasn't surprised when Ian, one of my classmates, raised his tattooed arm and started to ask a question. He was never afraid to make extra inquiries, even if that meant having someone irritated with him. But somehow, his cool factor and intelligence seemed to keep his constant questioning from getting annoying. "Sir, why do we need—"

Sebastian held up his hand and exhaled noisily. "We have lost contact with all of the other academies in the last three hours. Four experienced Watchers have gone missing; they are presumed dead after the message we decoded from one of them. We are out of time. Go now. No more questions. Meet in the basement. Leave the lights on, so it appears to be business as usual."

With that, he left the room. Everyone seemed frozen for a moment, reeling from the information. Then, with a purpose, everyone erupted from the room.

I lingered for a few seconds as the last few rushed off. Reality seemed to slow and sounds became indistinct and hollow as though I were trapped under water. In this daze, I was only vaguely aware of Gabriel stepping out with a grim expression. When I realized I'd lost sight of Joshua, I started to leave the room.

Then, suddenly, he was behind me and gently caught my arm. He turned me to face him, holding both my arms firmly. "I need you to promise me something. Can you do that?"

I nodded mutely, still feeling numb.

"When we evacuate, I won't be with you. You need to stick with Gabriel. No matter what. Don't leave his side."

"I can't ask him to babysit me. Everyone needs—"

"Promise me." His green eyes blazed into mine.

I wanted to argue, but I couldn't. I couldn't shake the feeling that I was somehow involved in what was happening. "Okay," I agreed hoarsely.

He pulled me against his chest and kissed the top of my head. "You should go pack," he said as he released me. Then I started to turn and head for the door. "Ali, wait." He looked at the door warily, then grabbed my wrist and spun me back towards him.

He took my face in both hands and kissed me urgently. I wrapped my arms around his waist and pulled him as close to me as humanly possible. A calm pulsed through my body as his cool lips moved with mine.

"Sorry, but you'd better get packing. I'll see you in a few minutes."

"Love you," I murmured.

"I love you, too," he breathed. His eyes were warm, but his expression was fixed with worry.

I turned on my heel and dashed up the stairs, then barreled into the postage stamp-sized room that I shared with Gentry. We'd only known each other a short time, but she was already a trusted friend. I'd seen her briefly in San Francisco the day I'd moved to England.

We looked enough alike that she had been one of the decoys for my extraction. All it took was a pair of sunglasses, temporary hair dye, and a curling iron. Even my parents would've had to do a double take. Having Gentry around was kind of like being able to have my friend Kaela with me; somehow, she always knew how I was really feeling, even if I put up a brave front.

When I entered, she already had most of her things packed; I'd thought I was efficient until I had started rooming with her.

"You're done already?" I asked, knowing the answer. I started putting my things in the oversized Ziplocs she'd left on the dresser for me.

"Of course, darlin'. *I* didn't feel the need to hang about after the meetin'," she teased in her adorable Irish accent.

"I didn't 'hang about,' Gentry."

"Sure ya didn't. You *needed* to talk to the hot vampire. I get it." She winked and started forcing the air out of some of my bags, sealing them, and loading them into my backpack for me.

My romantic relationship with Joshua was a secret. It was becoming increasingly hard to keep it that way since everyone in school was being trained to be observant. I think most dismissed it since Joshua and I'd known each other all our lives. They expected there to be a close relationship. Gabriel had had it figured out since the beginning, but he'd always turned a blind eye.

I put on some dark clothing that would dry quickly and sat on my bed for a moment, trying to think of anything I might've missed. "Gentry..." I hesitated, wondering if I should ask.

"Time is a tickin' here. What's on your mind, love?"

I sighed. "Was it just me? Or did both Gabriel and Sebastian...never mind." I remembered my journal. That would have been disastrous to leave behind. I reached under the mattress to procure it and sealed it in a bag.

A funny look twisted itself across her face. "Now that ya mention it..." Her words hung in the air.

"I didn't mention anything. It's fine," I said, shaking my head as I stuck a knife in my boot.

"They both looked at you more than the rest of us. I'd disregarded it, but..."

I sighed. "Which means that they think Bowen's coven is most likely to blame." I dropped my head into my hands.

"Time to go, love," she prompted, then strapped on her backpack. I agreed and did likewise. We left our room for the last time and navigated our way to the basement.

Gabriel appeared with a pack over his shoulder and a canvas bag in his hand. He unlocked a door marked "Storage" with a brass key, then ducked into the room for a moment to light a torch on the far wall.

We all strained to see inside. Instead of an industrial room lined with shelves and stacked with dusty boxes, the large space was empty, with ancient-looking stone walls befitting a castle. A murmur went through the room as we looked at one another in surprise. Gabriel opened the canvas bag and handed Ian a compact electric lantern as he motioned him into the room. As each of us filed in, he handed us a lantern.

The room was cool and smelled like some of the medieval cathedrals I'd visited while heavily disguised on my days off. The odor resembled dust, wax, incense, and a hint of iron. Joshua arrived with an oddly shaped pry bar and an ornamental-looking metal object about the size of my hand. He tossed the fancy metal item to Gabriel, who walked over to a decorative design chiseled into the wall. He pressed the object into the center of the design, and it fit snugly. Then he proceeded to twist it clockwise.

The sound of sliding stone rumbled beneath us, followed by a clank, as if something had unlocked. Everyone instinctively moved to the edges of the chamber. Joshua bent down and lodged the pry bar into a deep groove that must have appeared after Gabriel twisted what I then realized was a key. I expected him to try to lift the stone, but instead, he pulled it down like a lever, and the entire section of the floor sank down a few inches. Gabriel twisted the key counter-clockwise in the wall, and a mammoth stone in the ground slid to the side. Only blackness could be seen beneath.

Joshua stepped into the gaping hole in the floor and disappeared. I listened for him to land, but there was nothing. *Of course, he's a vampire, so that doesn't mean anything.*

Light began to glow from the opening. Joshua called up, "Okay, I'm ready."

Gabriel walked to the edge of the hole and looked down. "Good." Turning to us, he spoke quietly. "Toss Joshua your bag, then follow. He will help steady your landing. Quickly, go."

One after another, members of our group disappeared through the opening. Within a couple of minutes, I turned and looked around. It was my turn; only Gabriel was left. He motioned me towards the entrance with an open hand and a grin. He seemed to enjoy the adventure of this much more than anyone else, or maybe he just wanted it to appear that way to me.

There was some murmuring drifting up from below. It sounded muted, like the others were in a passageway a little farther away from the room beneath me. I peered over the edge —there was about an eight-foot drop down to a stone platform of some sort.

I dropped my bag and sat down at the edge, dangling my feet into the hole like a small child. At that moment, I felt like I was five years old, sitting next to my mom on the piano bench, wishing I was big enough to reach the pedals.

Sliding off the ledge, I hit the ground hard enough that my feet tingled. Joshua steadied me when I arched backwards. If he hadn't been there, I would've toppled off the ledge onto my head. I noticed that we were essentially alone and that everyone else had moved down the hallway because the room was quite small. He gently kept hold of my arms and projected his voice to Gabriel. "Is that it?"

Gabriel peered down at us. "Yes. You ready?"

Joshua shrugged, and then looked at me with the same concern he had shown earlier.

Then I realized we were missing someone. "Where's Sebastian?"

Gabriel nodded to Joshua and disappeared from view.

Joshua kept his voice low. "He wants everything to appear like business as usual. I am going to escort him to his weekly meeting with the Concilium in London as I usually do when Gabriel isn't attending. Well, it will look like we are heading that way from Signum's main campus. We have an alternate exit plan."

I opened my mouth to say something, but he squeezed my elbow and glanced towards the passageway. All within a second, I slumped my shoulders, set my jaw in protest, then exhaled in defeat. I already knew he wasn't leaving with me. He looked towards the murmuring, gave me a quick grin, kissed my forehead, and jumped up through the opening above with ease.

"Take care of her," Josh said overhead.

Gabriel reappeared, and I scrambled off the platform. At that moment, I realized we were actually in a tomb, and it was the entrance to a network of catacombs. Shelves were carved into the south wall where bones rested, crowded together. Gabriel landed on the lid to the crypt and strapped on his pack. As the ceiling started to close, I looked up and watched Joshua until the room went dark. Gabriel handed me the lantern I'd left on top of the crypt, and then urged me forward.

The last expression on Joshua's face—the worry—and something else, was burned into my vision while my eyes adjusted to the darkness. Sensing the urgency, I caught up to Gabriel, his presence making me feel better. But the other part of me kept thinking about the sound of that sliding stone sealing us into the catacombs—sealing us into a tomb.

2

FOUND

Quiet fell over the crowd as soon as Gabriel and I entered the next chamber in the catacombs. There were twelve students—including myself—three Slayers, and three of the Watchers who taught classes.

Gabriel always commanded everyone's respect. He was head Slayer and a born leader, who was very physically imposing at 6'4". He spoke openly with me, which was not the norm for him. He was usually the quiet warrior; but when he did speak, people listened. Of course, the jagged fishhook-shaped scar on the left side of his face didn't hurt the image.

Gabriel addressed everyone. "I will take point. We need six teams. Leaders, I want each of you to have two students with you at all times. Let's move out."

Peter had already moved to my side. Gabriel acknowledged him as our third. We started moving towards the next chamber with considerable speed, bearing in mind the darkness and the uneven ground. I glanced back. Gentry and Leslie were right behind us with Uriel, the second Slayer.

We walked and walked and walked, for what seemed to be

forever, passing chamber after chamber of petrified remains in an unending network underneath the suburbs of London. Gabriel proceeded with utter confidence. Without him, I would've gotten hopelessly lost within a few minutes.

As we moved forward, a sense of urgency continued to push at me, and I tried to not let it overwhelm me. It was bad enough being in creepy passageways filled with forgotten bones. We entered one large room after another with exits spiraling out like spokes on a wagon wheel, but Gabriel always knew exactly which one to take.

Finally, we came to a different kind of hollow where there were no carved-out cavities for remains, and the far wall was a grey brick archway that reminded me of a trip to Rome I'd taken with my parents during sophomore year. I could hear running water in the distance.

We ducked through the archway and proceeded down a long tunnel towards the sound of the water. The walls were not as reflective as the previous carved, natural stone. This type of rock seemed to devour the light from my small lantern. I glanced at it, hoping the battery life was very, very long. We had already been walking for hours.

I shivered. The temperature felt as if it was dropping with each step as we neared the water. With the echoing sound of the droplets, I realized that we must've been headed for a rather large cavern.

We exited the passageway, and I saw I'd been correct; we entered a huge room and stood on a large terrace. A little ways off from us, it sloped down to a series of stairs, which descended into a huge pool of midnight water. The reflection of our lanterns looked like yellow stars. A similar platform was on the far end of the room about one hundred yards away. Circular ducts on the walls spilled water into the main pool.

At water level, there were a few half-submerged tubes keeping the pool from overflowing. I figured this was where we would get wet, but prayed we were going to use the stairs on the far side and not have to go into one of the tubes containing water.

Gabriel's voice startled me, as I hadn't heard anyone speak in over an hour. "Take five and prep yourselves to go into the water. We will be heading to the stairs on the north side." He pointed to the stairs mirroring the ones we were on. There was an audible sigh of relief in the crowd. *So I'm not the only one having claustrophobic thoughts about the prospect of crawling through water-filled ducts.*

I sat down on the frigid ground and pulled a granola bar from my pack. Leslie gazed at me longingly, so I handed her a spare one. She smiled and eased down next to me. It was a small slice of heaven to be off my feet.

I looked over at Gabriel. He'd pulled some type of laminated blueprint out of his bag and was examining it. I rubbed my eyes with the backs of my index fingers, wishing I could lie down, but with all of us sitting on the platform, there wasn't much room left.

Ian asked, "What is this place? It seems like we're really deep underground."

"We are," Raphael, the third Slayer, answered. "The Romans started building an aqueduct system here when they occupied this area. This is channeling an underground river. We will start ascending towards the sewer system soon."

Great. Sewers. It was hard to keep from sighing. I gritted my teeth and determined that I would keep a good attitude, even if we had to go through the sewers. I shivered at the thought.

"Time's up," Gabriel's voice echoed.

Peter stood, offered me his hand, and hoisted me onto my

aching feet with a groan. I resealed my bag of snacks and secured my pack as I moved toward the water.

Gabriel waded in silence, not making so much as a splash. He waited at the bottom of the steps, the water to his waist.

I hesitated for a moment. The water was as black as coffee. I half-expected some creature to rise from the depths and pull me under. Clenching my jaw, I descended the steps and tried not to let my teeth chatter.

When I reached the bottom, we moved forward. I kept my arms up to keep as dry as possible, but the bitterly cold water was already at my chest. We reached the other side and sloshed up the steps, continuing into the next chamber. To my relief, the air in there was much warmer than the water, so I felt a teensy bit better.

After another five minutes of walking, our entire group reached a huge junction of eight passageways with approximately ten feet between each of them. We were about to continue to the passageway on the easternmost wall when I stopped dead in my tracks, simultaneously grabbing Gabriel's arm.

He whipped his head towards me. I peered at him through terrified eyes, frozen with fear. He looked toward the tunnel we were about to enter, and his eyes widened as if he could hear or sense something the others couldn't.

He abruptly turned to face everyone and made some hand signals I could see out of the corner of my eye. I sensed some movement; they must have signaled a reply. The group moved over three tunnels on the eastern wall, and all lanterns were snuffed out. Everyone was so silent it seemed as though the passageway was empty.

My legs felt rooted to the ground as I remained in the junction with Gabriel and Peter, my eyes glued to the mouth of the cave we'd been about to enter. Gabriel put his hand on my shoulder and started leading me to the passageway next to the one I was staring at and stopped a couple of yards into the tunnel.

We took off our packs and quietly placed them on the ground. Gabriel drew his Durateus sword, and I sorely wished I had something more than just the throwing knife in my boot. Finally, we cut our lights, faced the junction, and waited.

All I could hear was the drip, drip of water and the beat of my heart. After a few minutes, we heard movement, but it was faint. Suddenly, the junction was filled with silvery-blue light. The source of the noise wasn't far off like I'd initially thought— it was simply the whisper-quiet steps of vampires. The light stopped moving, and they fell silent. Shadows of men lined the walls.

"This way," a gruff voice echoed through the tunnel.

The light started to dim as the vampires filed into the passageway from which we had originally come. I counted the shadows as they slid down the walls: seven...eight... nine... ten... I wondered how many I couldn't count. If we had been in the junction, we would have been slaughtered. There was no way we could have fought against that many vampires, even with three Slayers.

Then I was hit with a presence so strong, I didn't realize for a moment the ground was swirling up towards my face. I felt like my bones went soft and the air was liquid. I couldn't breathe. I was jerked to a stop right before my cheek met the stone floor. Gabriel hoisted me up and pinned me to his side with one arm. My head bobbed back, and I looked up into his face. There was just enough light filtering from the junction that I could see an outline of his features. He gently shook me and nodded his head.

I realized he wanted me to explain what had just happened. I slowly mouthed, "Tier-ran," almost unable to form the syllables with my lips.

His mouth thinned into a hard line, and he shifted his weight, leaning slightly towards the entrance. What looked to be a single light moved closer to our location. I wondered if the smell of the sewers was enough to mask our scent if they had a vamp with a heightened sense of smell with them.

A voice boomed from a few yards away, "Sire?"

Silence.

"Sire?"

The light retreated from the entrance. "Coming," Tyran replied, his voice sounding reluctant.

We waited. I could feel Tyran's presence fade and wondered if he could feel my presence as well. Obviously not as strongly as I felt his, or he would have stormed into our tunnel.

My incapacitated reaction distressed me. Was it because I'd felt safe for all these months? Had the connection grown stronger? In my memory, I could still feel his body pressing down on me, his teeth plunging into my neck. Any time I thought of Tyran, Bowen's twin, a sense of overwhelming dread snaked through my body and made me feel ill. To me, he represented all that was evil about vampires.

After we were sure the vamps were far enough away, we joined the rest of the group again, but I was so wrapped in thought, I hardly noticed the remainder of the journey. My feet moved robotically beneath me. We eventually emerged from the sewers into a basement, and then traveled through several electrical tunnels, which dumped us into an underground garage.

Three vehicles were parked in the corner. One of them was a small tour bus like the ones at an airport. Over half of our group boarded the bus, and Raphael took the wheel.

Uriel got in the driver's seat of a taxi with Leslie and Gentry in the back. Gabriel opened the back of a delivery truck for Peter and me. I looked through the front window as well as I could and watched everyone depart in different directions.

The lights of the city faded away as the night wore on, and we drove in silence. I wished my clothes had dried. I'd thought I'd chosen clothing that would have dried more quickly. My fingers and toes felt almost numb, and I wanted to change out of my wet clothes, but there was no way I was going to attempt it with Peter in the back with me.

He moved closer and put his arm around me. I flinched.

"Are you okay?" he whispered.

"Yeah, sorry."

"You're shivering."

"Sorry, my mind was somewhere else. I guess I'm still a little freaked about our close call."

"Yeah, I don't care to ever see him again either."

I nodded in agreement, but fell silent. I couldn't shake the feeling of Tyran's presence. The heat from Peter's body started to help me relax, and my shivering dissipated. I pulled in a deep breath and scrunched my nose; the truck smelled like old cardboard with a hint of diesel exhaust.

I sucked in a short breath, and Peter squeezed me a little. "What?"

"I forgot to e-mail my parents and the girls this morning," I replied.

"Me too. It was a busy week, and now…"

I shrugged. "I've written them every Friday since we've been here. I hope they don't worry. I was going to send the pictures of that day trip we took to Windsor."

"I'm sure they'll assume you're busy and not running for

your life from a bunch of blood-sucking vampires." He leaned his head on top of mine.

"Yeah, I'm sure you're right." I closed my eyes and tried to let my sudden homesickness go. I took in another breath and felt sleep rush for me.

I knew I was dreaming, yet I didn't wake. I stood in front of an ancient stone structure fronted by countless steps. They were bathed in flickering amber light, cast from fires in massive granite bowls lining the stairs. I felt drawn to the top. I climbed the worn steps towards the precipice; there were a hundred stairs or more. It seemed like I was walking in slow motion with warm breezes swirling around me.

I reached the summit of the incline where a thick coat of ashes swirled and muffled the sound of my footsteps. Fires in large golden receptacles threw off a feverish heat that caused sweat to trickle between my shoulder blades. The focal point was a grand stone altar centered on the platform, and behind it were gargantuan pillars. I couldn't see beyond the pillars because there was a wall of churning black smoke.

Then, a presence I'd never felt before blotted out all my other senses, but there was a trace of something that rang familiar. I looked at the rear of the platform, and the immense figure of a man stepped through the smoke, walking towards me before stopping next to the altar. His hair was the color of flax, and his shoulders were broad. He wore an ornate golden breastplate embossed with the head of a horned calf over his abdominals, and two owls with mighty wings spread over each side of his chest. There were some other shapes and symbols that I couldn't see clearly.

He removed his armor and dropped it to the ground. It landed with a heavy clank, despite the blanket of ash. An enormous scar blazed across his chest. It was silvery, like it had been there for a very long time. I moved my gaze to his face and saw he was looking down at me, his eyes shockingly blue. His features were beautiful—and cruel. His greedy expression made my blood run cold.

His body shuddered slightly, and I gaped in amazement as magnificent black, feather wings spread out behind him. They looked slick and wet. Droplets of dark liquid splattered on the ground beneath his wings. I stumbled a couple of steps backwards when I identified the substance. His wings were drenched with blood.

I wanted to run, but I couldn't move. I tried to draw air into my lungs to scream, but he already had me by the throat.

He whispered my name, and I struggled wildly, grasping at his hand and trying to tear it away from my throat. I scratched at his face, but he readjusted his grip, so I was unable to pull in enough air to do more than take a shallow breath. He grabbed my wrist.

I could feel the heat of his breath, and he whispered in my ear again. "Aleria, I'm coming for you."

I woke in terror, screaming his name, though he had never told me what it was. I was disoriented, and it took me a moment to realize that the van wasn't moving and I was pinned to the floor. Peter was holding down my right arm and clutching his face with the other. I searched his face and found his eyes filled with both alarm and concern. I looked to my left, and Gabriel was holding my other arm, his expression as concerned as Peter's.

I took a deep breath and relaxed my body when I realized I was still fighting them. Once they recognized I was conscious and in control, they released me. I sat up, still a little confused.

I asked, "Peter, did I?"

He nodded. His jaw was tight.

My stomach twisted, and I felt horrible "Let me take a look at it, please."

He backed away from me and sat down, obviously angry. "I'm fine, don't worry about it."

I didn't like that at all. Then I realized that Gabriel still hadn't made a peep. I studied him, and the horrified expression remained. "Gabriel, what's wrong?"

"The name you screamed…" He didn't finish.

Peter and I looked at one another and back to Gabriel.

"What about it?"

Instead of answering me, he asked another question, "What were you dreaming about?"

I recalled the nightmare with as much detail as I could. The more I said, the more I didn't like Gabriel's reaction. I repeated the name I had been screaming a moment before.

Gabriel winced.

With an audible shake in my voice, I asked, "Gabriel, who is Moloch?"

He answered slowly through downturned lips. "The Devourer."

3

100

G abriel returned to the driver's seat and resumed course. We all sat in silence for a long while, lulled by the movement of the vehicle. I rested against the side of the van, folding and unfolding my hands in my lap. The name *Moloch* was nagging at me. I'd heard it or maybe read it somewhere, but whenever I seemed to get close to its significance, my mind would shift and it would elude me.

I glanced over at Peter. A small trail of blood seeped from the scratches I'd gouged on his face. I sighed, feeling horrible again, and crawled over to my bag, rummaging through it for the first aid kit I'd packed. Pulling out some alcohol wipes, gauze, and a bandage, I slid across the floor towards him. There was a change his posture, almost a recoil, as I approached. Smiling weakly, I waved the supplies.

He nodded consent, but it was very apparent that he was still angry. He looked away, avoiding my gaze.

"Peter, I'm so, so sorry, I..." I furrowed my brow and dipped my head.

He turned his head towards me, and I gazed up at him. He

had a wounded expression; he moved his jaw like he was going to speak, his lips about to part, but then he reconsidered and remained quiet. The energy between us was all wrong.

I finally whispered in a thin voice, "I would never hurt you on purpose."

His eyes rolled towards the roof of the van as he allowed me to dab at the scratches with the alcohol.

He didn't wince or react; it was as if I wasn't touching him. I couldn't figure out what was going on in his head. His breathing was slow and steady—and infuriating to me. Obviously, I had hurt more than his physical body somehow. I didn't know why his being upset with me vexed me so much.

I placed the bandage over the deepest gash a little harder than necessary and abruptly got up and headed toward the cab. Several boxes were blocking the cab, so I haphazardly crawled over them, collapsing them a little. I wasn't sure how Gabriel seemed to get back and forth with ease. I finally reached the passenger seat and plopped down with a *harrumph*; the old vinyl seat whooshed under me and released a smell I could only describe as old.

Peering into the back, Peter had pulled a black beanie over his head, obscuring his eyes. I couldn't tell if he could see me or not, because his stoic expression held no indicator. He'd reclined on the floor with legs stretched out in front of him, crossed at the ankles. His left arm was around his torso and his right hand over his heart.

I couldn't stand it, so I closed the sliding door behind the cab. After a while, Gabriel broke the very loud silence. "Is Peter asleep?"

"Sleeping...sulking. What's the difference?" I grumbled without looking over at him.

He cleared his throat, but it was the kind of clearing you do when attempting to cover up a chuckle. I felt irritated by the strangled noise and darted my eyes in his direction. Sure enough, he had a crooked grin on his face that tugged at his scar.

"Gabriel, aren't you the strong, silent type?" I huffed.

He sucked in some air between closed teeth and let out a single laugh as he glanced in my direction.

I exhaled in a gush. "What?"

"Nothing." He shook his head, amused.

"Well, obviously you have some great insight, O Powerful Keeper of All Knowledge," I responded melodramatically.

He chuckled outright this time. "Time. Just give him time."

"I didn't mean to scratch him," I said, half angry and half bewildered.

The words hung there, and Gabriel didn't comment. No comfort given. I'd rarely felt the need to fill silence with speaking, but my mind was screaming and going in a hundred different directions. Peter being upset at me was the last thing I could handle.

"Everything was normal just an hour ago. Is he really that mad? I just don't get it. I've never seen him be so infantile."

Gabriel raised his eyebrow and quietly said, "Time, gracious one. Maybe you should look at things from his perspective."

I nodded and folded my arms across my chest. "Sure thing, Atticus." But my *To Kill a Mockingbird* reference only made him chuckle again. *Yes, I am being ungracious! Case made. Fine.* Then I felt humbled. I felt like Gabriel knew something I didn't, but I decided to let it go.

Suddenly, something occurred to me. "Hey, where are we going anyway?"

"Holyhead. From there, we will sail to Dublin."

"How long to Holyhead?"

"We will be in Gloucester within twenty minutes. We need to pick up a package. Then, it will be about four hours."

I batted my eyes. "A midnight cruise and a trip to Ireland—what more could a lass like me ask for?" I said as lightly as I could, desperately trying to shake my sour mood.

"Home to the motherland, eh?"

"Half of me, anyway. My dad is full-blooded Irish."

"And your other half?" he asked.

"Ugh, after meeting the evil twins, do I have to claim it?"

"French…" His voice drifted off, I could see his wheels turning. "Do you know when your family originally came to the U.S.?"

"I'm not totally sure. It was a long, long time ago. I've heard two stories, but I'm not sure which, if any, is true."

I reflected for a moment about my great-grandmother. I could still smell the honey and milk lotion she used to rub into her delicate skin. I looked a lot like her. All of my most striking features were hers: my curves; my dark hair, and my porcelain skin. But the most important feature we shared was our eyes: a rare genetic quirk—lavender eyes. One in millions of millions, they said. I twisted the Claddagh ring on my right hand; she'd given it to me the last time I'd seen her alive. I had never seen her without it.

Gabriel's voice cut into my thoughts. "Lost you there for a moment."

"I'm sorry." I shook my head and rubbed my eyes. Then I drew in a deep breath. "My great-grandmother lived to be one hundred years old. I used to spend some time with her each summer up in Ashland, Oregon.

"She was strong, and there was something about her. Towards the end, she told me some stories. She said our family came here during the French Revolution, that we were royalty and being hunted by evil. It was weird. I made some comment about humanity being evil sometimes, and I'll never forget what she said: 'This evil was not born of man.'" I stopped my story briefly and remembered the fierceness in her eyes. It had terrified me; they seemed to flash when she said it. Whatever this evil was, it had been very real to her.

Glancing at the road, I continued. "I asked my grandmother about it and she said Nana was delusional. She said our family did flee from France, but it was because they were Huguenots fleeing religious persecution. That our family had been here for fifty years before the revolution. I don't know wh—"

I completely lost my train of thought when I looked over at Gabriel. I was so absorbed I hadn't realized that he'd pulled off the road. He was scrutinizing me with utter seriousness. I looked doe-eyed and shrugged my shoulders.

"Now what did I do? Or do I just have something horrible hanging from my face?"

His jaw flexed. "Did you ever do any research? Or follow up?"

"A little. I logged onto that ancestry site and tried, but there were some name changes or something. I didn't get further than Nana. None of the names I had matched anyone on record. So, I didn't really think about it much after that."

We sat in silence for a couple of minutes, the car still idling. Then there was something at the edge of my memory—a name coming to the surface.

"You know, there was a name I never checked." I chuckled humorlessly to myself. "When my great-grandma passed, I went up with my mom to help clean out her house. I found a book of poetry with a name written inside that I didn't recognize. Paper had been glued over the inside cover, but it was so old that it came apart. I found a photo hidden under the paper."

"What was it?"

"It said 'To Rosemond Le Clair'. I thought it was a beautiful name. The picture of her was when she was young, probably around my age. I was surprised at how much I look like my great-grandmother. I have her eyes. She was with two men in the photo, and there was something familiar about both of them. I asked my grandma if she knew anything about the picture or the documents, and she said she didn't know anything. Said my great-grandma had things she shouldn't."

Gabriel drew in a deep breath, then exhaled slowly and pinched the bridge of his nose. Then he murmured something like, "That bloody vampire was right."

He pulled out a phone. I started to ask something, but he held his finger up, so I leaned back in my seat and waited patiently. I might have had the liberty to harass Gabriel from time to time, but I knew when it was important to take orders.

"Sebastian. Yes...yes...no. As planned. No, it was necessary. It appears he may be right. We cannot wait. I need to retrieve it now. We need to know what is in that prophecy. No, we cannot wait. If we have a problem they may go after it too. No...no. As is. I know. I will. Yes, be well." He hung up and looked intensely into the distance. It seemed as if he had made some sort of decision, and then abruptly pulled back onto the road.

Periodically, I looked at him to see if it would be safe to ask him what all of this was about, but his body language seemed to say, "Ask and lose a limb."

My head swirled with so many questions that it made my stomach queasy. *Who was right? What prophecy? What couldn't wait? And what did all this have to do with me?*

I had the ominous feeling that the night was just getting started.

4

SHOES

We arrived in Gloucester and parked the van near an active railway station. There were groups of revelers everywhere headed home after a Friday in the pub. After stashing our bags in a locker, we took a cab to a location a couple of kilometers away. We got out in front of a tattoo parlor.

Once the cab was out of sight, we walked a few doors down to a still bustling pub nestled between two other businesses. It was a four-story building, the bottom floor faced with wood paneling and painted black, the name painted gold in a Celtic-looking script. Lace privacy curtains obscured the view into all the upper rooms. People sat at outdoor tables, rapt in conversation. Many were speaking too loudly from either excessive drinking or a humming in their ears from the music. The establishment smelled of ale, stewed meats, and cigarette smoke.

Peter and I trailed behind Gabriel as he entered. His head swept back and forth as he scanned the crowd for threats; I did the same, but didn't see any. The patrons seemed like normal people who were laughing and telling secrets on any given weekend. A very loud lady spilled her drink on another woman's ugly floral shoes. That caused a stir. A skinny, awkward guy was hitting on a blonde way out of his league. It all seemed ordinary.

Gabriel circled to the edge of the bar closest to a hallway leading to the back of the building. A heavyset man with greasy skin and a bad case of bed-head drooped over the edge of a stool; he seemed to recognize Gabriel and held up a finger over his lips for a split-second. I would have missed the gesture if I hadn't been looking at him so attentively.

The man then stood as quickly as he was able with a heavy limp and trudged behind the bar. He pulled out a shoebox and slid it towards Gabriel. The man nodded as acknowledgment of the exchange, and then lumbered off in the opposite direction.

Gabriel tucked the package under his arm and indicated that we should follow him to the back exit, the opposite of the way the other man had gone. The whole exchange, from the moment we walked in the door, was less than fifteen seconds. But those few seconds robbed me of all the peace I'd managed to muster up since my dream. It wasn't safe here. I glanced back over my shoulder at the crowd and wondered why it wasn't safe. A vampire? A familiar? Who?

We moved quickly down the hallway and out the back door. Gabriel took an abrupt left and headed down an alley at a trot. We came to the back door of the tattoo parlor in front of where we'd been dropped off. He confidently walked into the shop. We entered a small, rundown office that stung my nose because of the overwhelming smell of rubbing alcohol.

A tiny, compact woman, inked seemingly everywhere save her pixie-like face, looked up. She had abundant hair with intense purple streaks that fanned out in an amazing display; it swayed like feathers when she stood. Before she could say anything, Gabriel made a couple of signs meaning "stop" and "silence."

She nodded and, without speaking, lightly walked to a William Blake painting in the corner of the room. I recognized it as the *Michael Binding Satan* that had been in my school textbook last year. It was creepy, like most of Blake's paintings. I shuddered. She pulled the thick, black frame away from the wall and stuck her hand behind it. Then she drew out some keys and tossed them to Gabriel. He snatched them out of the air without so much as a jingle. *How does he do stuff like that?*

She pursed her lips in a smile and led us towards the front of the building. We walked through a worn door into a hallway that had cracked and peeling paint in three different colors. A burgundy curtain was at the other end of the hall, separating the storefront from the back of the building. I could hear the busy electric needles in the front humming away, along with the sharp breaths and low moans that accompanied pain.

The tattooed girl rolled back the carpet runner on the floor and stuck her finger into a recessed hole, extracting a black, iron loop, and heaved a little. A door popped up. She placed her left hand on the edge to help ease it up quietly, and then opened it wide. I looked into the entryway and saw nothing—dark as black velvet. She pulled a couple of glow sticks out of her pocket, cracked them, then tossed them into the abyss. A dull, yellow light emanated from below. There were more than a dozen grey, stone stairs disappearing deep underground. There wasn't enough light to see beyond.

Gabriel motioned for us to descend, and to my relief Peter took the lead. Part of me wanted to make a joke about the spooky tunnel to ease my nerves, but we needed to keep silent.

I started to reach out to touch Peter's shoulder. I was so close

I could feel the heat of his skin, but I snatched my hand back. If he had shrugged off my hand, I didn't think I would have handled it well. When I was halfway down the stairs, I turned and looked back up at the entrance. Gabriel had the tattooed girl's hand in both of his and cradled it there.

They looked at one another for a long moment, with an expression that said volumes. Her bottom lip quivered even though she had a faint smile pulling at the edges of her mouth. They touched foreheads, and Gabriel started to turn to follow us. There was some serious history there. I had to squelch my curiosity and scamper down the rest of the steps before he caught me gawking.

By the time I got to the bottom, Gabriel was behind me and the door at the top of the steps was sealed shut. The tunnel ran parallel to the street; I couldn't see the end either way. It was only a few inches taller than I was, so the guys had to bend down. Peter and Gabriel picked up the glow sticks as we started to walk to the left, and I fell in between them, Peter at the rear. I wished I had the flashlight out of my bag.

My arm brushed against the wall, and I winced. Rocks stuck out of the rounded walls and ceilings, some flat, some jagged. Of course, I managed to find a pointy one. *New resolution: no more creepy underground passages, catacombs, or sewers.* With my luck, I'd run into a mutated race of mole people bent on ruling the world, and I'd be their first human sacrifice.

I sighed and continued groping my way through the darkness, continually tripping over unseen obstacles. I wondered if this might've been an escape tunnel during one of the world wars. I was afraid to speak since Gabriel hadn't said anything yet. Could vampires hear us all the way down here? We had to be at minimum two stories underground. My apprehension grew as we padded over the dirt floor. I could taste the dust we were kicking up.

There was a huge pile of rubble on the ground that I stumbled over. I mildly twisted my ankle—it smarted, but I could tell there was no permanent damage.

Gabriel touched my arm lightly and motioned overhead. A large stone protruded from the ceiling.

It would have taken me out, for sure. I exhaled, smiling in thanks, but he had already turned. I couldn't see if Peter was stumbling as much as I was. He did have a light, though.

The lace from my shoe caught on something, and it pitched me forward. Peter latched onto the back of my shirt before I completely face-planted. He hauled me up a little, and then held my elbow while I freed my lace from some kind of metal debris that was twisted like a skeletal hand where the ground met the wall. He might not have been speaking to me, but he was still looking out for me.

We walked for several more minutes, then came to a halt. A warped, rusted metal ladder led upwards. We climbed up through a hole that was so small, my back scraped each time I reached up for the next rung. Dust filtered down on me from above as Gabriel squeezed through the opening—how, I wasn't sure. We stopped, so I assumed he had reached the top.

Heavy stone slid out of the way, and then we emerged into the night air, I expected to pop up through a manhole cover, but when I glimpsed stairs leading downward, it was apparent we weren't at ground level at all. We came out on a raised brick platform and were about one-story up. Then I realized it was the veranda in front of a grand church. It had huge columns across the front, and we had come out of one.

Gabriel pushed back the heavy, stone cover plate where we'd emerged to cover the tube leading back to the tunnels.

We entered the church through a sturdy wooden door darkened with age and laden with black wrought-iron embellishments. The lobby was perfumed with incense, so I speculated the church was Catholic, or maybe Orthodox.

Gabriel marched directly to a clothing donation box in the far corner. He rummaged through it and tossed some items at us. Both Peter and I started altering our look. I pulled on a canvas, charcoal button-down shirt and wrapped a black and lavender scarf around my neck. Then I tucked my hair into the black newsboy style hat Gabriel had given me.

The germaphobe in me didn't want to think about whether these clothes were clean or otherwise. Not that any part of me was remotely clean right now. I would keep my dreams of soaking in a hot tub for once we reached safety. For a makeshift outfit, I actually looked pretty good. Peter looked borderline homeless; his sweatshirt was very worn, and his baseball cap was beyond distressed. Gabriel quickly pulled on a beanie and cable-knit sweater, and we were out the door.

We took another cab back to the train station where we picked up our bags, and Gabriel gave us a crash course in stashing IDs. In the cab, he'd opened the all-important package we'd picked up at the pub. There were three sets of new IDs and papers for each of us. I wondered how long this backup plan had been in the works. We each left a set at the station in different lockers.

I tried hard to remember the information that'd just been dumped on me by repeating things in my head. It had to be pushing midnight when we hopped on a train going north. My legs ached and pulsed with my epic level of tiredness. Consequently, I wasn't being very good at monitoring my surroundings for threats.

Trying to keep awake, I lazily looked around. The rhythmic

sounds of the rails started to lull me. A woman with a baby carriage sat at the other end of our car, softly murmuring to her infant. My eyes drifted to her shoes, weird black wedges with raised velvety roses—ugly. Then my mind sluggishly came to a realization. Her outfit was different, her hair was different, and the baby carriage was new, but it was the woman in the pub who'd been doused by the drunken lady. I wasn't sure how, but I knew she wasn't human and felt oddly drawn to her.

My heart started hammering. I took a deep breath and yawned to attempt to calm myself down. Gabriel was seated across from me, but I couldn't catch his eye. He was intently looking into the next train car. I couldn't see what he was examining from my angle.

Peter was seated on my right between the woman and me. I tried not to look at her too often. I wanted to say something to alert the guys. *Think, stupid, think!* I forced myself to remember overheard conversations about codes and tactics. We hadn't gotten to any of this in class yet. I finally decided to start an obviously fictitious conversation with Peter. But it needed to be real enough that if the ugly shoe lady knew who we were, she could be fooled.

I angled my body a little towards Peter and took his hand. I spoke softly enough that it seemed I wanted privacy, but loud enough so Gabriel could hear. "Sweetie, are we meeting with the others at 2:00 tomorrow?" I squeezed his hand and thought *possible threat on your two* over and over.

He ran his other hand through his hair casually, "Ummmm. Yeah, two o'clock." He was playing along, but I couldn't tell if he knew I wanted him to look to his two o'clock.

"I can't believe Rachel is going to be forty next week. Can you imagine having little kids at that age? It must be exhausting." *Fortyish woman in the corner with a kid!!!*

Gabriel shifted, and I could see him looking at her reflection in the opposite window. He scratched his face with two fingers —translation: *Yes*. My stomach sank. There wasn't a baby in that stroller, was there? I prayed it was empty and not filled with something terrifying.

My hands started getting sweaty, but I didn't release Peter's hand. Peter leaned in and whispered, "Start strapping your bag on. Now giggle." I did.

"Oh, you are bad," I laughed and pushed him a little, knocking my bag to the floor. I groaned and picked it up, swinging it over my shoulder.

"And you're not?" he retorted. He tickled me, and when I pushed him, he slid something out of his side pocket and into his hand. The train started to slow. Gabriel hitched his thumb in his pocket and turned his body slightly away from the woman.

When the doors opened, he counted down with his fingers. When he got to one, we sprinted off the train onto the deserted platform, Peter in the lead. The doors slammed shut behind us.

Peter pulled me forward, but I frantically looked back past Gabriel and saw that the woman had managed to get off the train too. I had to have been right; she was too fast to be human.

She had shed her innocuous-looking coat and stood on the edge of the platform like a warrior goddess dressed in black leather. *What is with evil vampires and their penchant for leather, anyway? Cliché much?* And why hadn't Gabriel sensed her?

She had some gun-like contraption in her hands that didn't look welcoming. Within two seconds of exiting the train, I heard a metallic click followed by a whooshing sound behind me. I looked back again. She had fired at Gabriel.

A net was flying through the air, but instead of weights, it had horrid-looking eight-inch spikes at its edges. It hit Gabriel with such force that it knocked him a couple of feet into the tile-covered support column and locked him in place. The net made a winding sound and tightened, trapping him. He had spikes through his shoulder and thigh that pinned him to the post. It looked like the net was cutting into his skin. He fought to breathe, but still managed to yell, "Ruuunnnn!"

The moment the vamp confirmed Gabriel was incapacitated, she launched herself towards me. I ran for another few steps, but was conflicted. Gabriel had ordered me to run, but I was better off with him. Deliberately disobeying, I went with my gut and circled back. Freeing Gabriel was our best bet, and leaving him wasn't really an option anyway.

Just as I spun to my left, she seized my backpack and swatted Peter into the nearby column. I wriggled out of my bag, but not fast enough. She immediately grabbed my wounded arm and twirled me around to face her. I cried out in pain when her thumb dug into the gash I'd received from the rock in the tunnel.

Then she promptly lifted me off the ground with ease and held me by the throat. I clutched at her arm to keep from choking. I kicked, but my feet could not find purchase on anything; she was too tall. I couldn't claw her face either because of her giant, spidery, long, freak arms. I was so angry. My face was turning red from the exertion.

She coolly looked at me as I flailed, as if we were sitting across from one another at tea. She cocked her head to the side and examined me, her golden, brown eyes penetrating.

The moment I wondered where Peter was, I heard a tremendous crack that echoed through the terminal. She shuddered and dropped me. Then there was another cracking sound, and her head bent forward. She stumbled a couple of steps. Peter was behind her and had hit her so hard that his retractable, steel baton had bent. At that moment, I realized that was what he'd slid into his hand. He hit her in the back of her thigh. Her leg bent in an unnatural way, and she fell forward. I glanced at Peter; his lip was bleeding, and he had some scrapes. Otherwise, he looked okay.

We needed to free Gabriel and the sword strapped to his back. I fumbled with my boot, pulled out my knife, and bolted to him. He had loosened the net, but in doing so had opened a gaping wound in his shoulder. I started sawing at the cable next to his right hand to free his good arm first. It was coated with some type of metal alloy that made it almost impossible to cut.

I heard Peter hit her again and again, but without a sword, there was no way to keep her down for long. The original skull fracture was probably healed by now. I freed Gabriel's hand. He was able to get the knife out of the sheath on his hip. He started to cut his bonds too. After I released the rest of his right shoulder, we were moving much more quickly.

I got to his left shoulder. "What do you want me to do? Cut the net so you can pull it all the way through, or..." *Please don't make me pull it out the other way. Please, please.*

"The net," he breathed, "but start on the leg. I will do the shoulder."

"Okay," I replied and immediately started to sever the cord.

Peter's voice rang out. "Uh, guys. I'm running out of things to break and uhhh..." He was backing towards us. She was already on her hands and knees. He jumped in the air a little as he hit her in the head again. Her arms slid out from underneath her, and she hit her chin on the cement, but within two seconds, she started moving again. I felt like we were in a scene from *The Terminator*. No matter what we did, the cyborg kept coming.

We sawed through the net connected to the spikes at the same time; enough was cut away that Gabriel would be able to get out. It was just a matter of pulling his shoulder and leg free.

He pulled his shoulder out as if it was nothing. Action movie heroes should've taken notes from this man.

I sidled up next to him. "Lean on me. I'll steady you. Take some pressure off."

He was obviously in serious pain because he accepted my help without objection. I cringed as he stepped forward, freeing his leg. He steadied himself and sucked in a sharp breath. Then, with my help, limped forward until he towered over the vamp. His left arm hung limp at his side.

He looked at Peter. "Flip her." Peter kicked her over onto her back so we could see her face. Gabriel reached to the small of his back, pulled out a Durateus dagger, and artfully flipped it around. "You are not going to enjoy this."

She looked at him defiantly.

He balanced on his good leg and drove the dagger through her heart with such force I could hear the blade enter the concrete. She was paralyzed and powerless to do anything with the dagger in her heart; completely unable to speak. Her face twitched in what I imagined was an evil grin; she could only infinitesimally move her face. Unnervingly, her eyes were smiling.

He pulled the dagger out of her heart and then drove it through her sternum. It kept her pinned to the ground and slowed her recovery. We had maybe five minutes.

"Who is your sire?" he demanded.

But she didn't answer. I blinked. This was not the question I expected him to ask. *Who are you? Who sent you? Did you signal them? Why would you ever wear those ugly shoes?* I had a dozen questions for her, but not *that* one.

Gabriel reached between his shoulder blades, unsheathed his Durateus sword, and held it, ready to take her head. He raised the sword.

She gasped a sound that could have been, "Stop."

"I'll ask again: who is your sire?"

"Belenus," she whispered in an eastern European accent. I sensed no deceit. I swallowed hard. That was the last name I expected to hear. I felt disbelief and betrayal at the same time, even though I shouldn't have.

"Did he send you?"

She tightened her lips into a thin line, probably calculating what would get her out of this alive. "It was him…and not him." Vague, but I thought I could figure this out.

"What were your orders?"

She exhaled and looked away. Gabriel pressed the tip of the sword into her neck. She gritted her teeth and spoke through them. "There's bounty. Set for a century," she gasped. "Proof of death. Any Slayer or traitor who works with Watchers. They want the girl alive. If she is killed, they kill the one who ended her and everyone they have sired."

"That is a steep penalty."

She cackled. "Enjoy what life you have."

"Why do they want her? What do you know?"

"Don't you know? They are waking the gods. All of them. The Oneiroi already here." She laughed again, but it took on a crazed intonation. "They going to bring Source back. She will be his sacrifice." She broke her glare from Gabriel and added, "We will feed on your children."

She started sputtering things that didn't seem sane or make sense, but when she looked at me and used the words *harvest* and *innocence ripped*, my stomach squeezed into my throat.

Gabriel had heard enough. He pulled out his phone and took a picture of her. There was a flash of his sword, and then there was silence, but I could still hear her cackle echo in my ears.

He brought out a small bottle and sprayed her with something that looked like anti-freeze. After he was done, he tossed a lit match on the body. It went up like dry weeds in a California summer. The flame was a ghastly greenish color, and it put off an intense amount of heat. After two minutes, only ash and the smell of soot were left.

"What was that?" I whispered.

"I'm not sure. I told the new R&D team I would test it." Gabriel shrugged with one shoulder. "I would call that a success." He looked at the bottle with approval.

Peter and I looked at one another with blank faces.

I took a second to field dress Gabriel's wounds while we waited for the next train. Using a shirt from my bag, I tightly wrapped his leg. We didn't want to leave a blood trail—or for him to bleed out.

We took the train and got off one stop later and hobbled to a nearby parking lot. The keys Gabriel had picked up from the tattooed lady were for a car. We managed to get to it without any more excitement.

We headed north. Peter drove, and I crawled into the back-seat. The shirt I had tied around Gabriel's leg did the trick, but blood had soaked his shirt to the waist. I brought another shirt out of my bag and piled it on his shoulder from the back seat. We twisted the seatbelt around so it would help keep pressure on the wound until we got to the mystery location. Gabriel said we would stop in an hour or so and to get on the M5 for now. He wanted to put some distance between us and Gloucester. I couldn't have agreed more.

All I wanted to do was sleep. I was done. *Finis.* Dreams or not, I was going to sleep. I ached all over, my right arm burned and itched for some reason, and the blisters on my feet decided to invite friends. The last thing I heard was Gabriel saying that one of us was going to get to practice stitching. I kept my groan internal.

Drawing in a deep breath, my thoughts went to Joshua. I pulled my locket out from underneath my shirt and held it in the palm of my hand while rubbing the ridges on my North Star charm. I pretended to be safe in Joshua's arms and fell asleep in moments.

5

WOUNDS

I woke when the car came to a halt, and heard someone get out. I sat up and peered between the front seats to see the clock. It was still dark out—1:00 A.M. It seemed this day... night...*whatever* would never end. Someone was rummaging through the trunk. *Must be Peter.*

I fixed my eyes on Gabriel; he was very still. I spoke softly enough so that I wouldn't wake him if he was sleeping. "Gabriel?"

"Yes," he replied, his voice thick.

"How are you?" I leaned up between the seats so I could look at him. He was gravely still, holding his left arm, his mouth pulled down at the corners. At that moment, Peter returned.

"I think the question is, how are you with a needle?" Gabriel asked without moving or opening his eyes.

"Better than I am," Peter said before I could open my mouth.

"Yeah," I agreed, sounding disappointed. "Yeah, I am."

"It's very domestic of her, isn't it?" he teased, with a gleam in his eye.

"Apparently, you want stitches too."

Peter grinned. "Okay, killer," he said, then he cringed a little because of his busted lip.

Gabriel opened his eyes and swiveled his head towards Peter. "What do we have?"

"Uh, she stocked enough supplies for a small nation."

"Good," he breathed.

Peter glanced down the road. "Where do you want to do this, Gabriel? We don't have much room in here."

"You see the dirt road bordering the hedge row across the street?"

"Yeah."

"Follow it. Safe house at the end of the road. Everything appears to be clear."

I realized this stop was not only to check on supplies, but to make sure we weren't followed one last time. Peter ran to the driver's side and tore down the road, the tires spitting debris up behind us. He parked so Gabriel's side was closest to the front door. The small stone house had small slit-like windows and heavy shutters.

"Unscrew the bottom of the porch light; there is a key inside. Security pad inside the door...." He started to make an "L" sound, then stopped, thought for a moment, and spurted out some numbers: "5-2-9-5-2-4-5-6-6."

Peter and I unloaded within minutes while Gabriel rested in the car. It was a studio style cabin with a separate bathroom. The decor may have been a couple of decades out of date, but the security equipment wasn't. I walked around and flipped on all the lights to figure out the best place to stitch up Gabriel.

Peter helped me drag a recliner into the kitchen and set up the supplies. Twenty-five percent of the curriculum first quarter had been medical training. At the time, I thought it excessive.

Unfortunately, now I saw why it was so essential. Going to a hospital would've been suicide for all of us.

We helped Gabriel out of the car and inside. Once Gabriel was settled, Peter went over to the electronic equipment and started flipping switches.

After everything was sterilized, I cut open Gabriel's shirt and pant leg and gasped. His arm had looked like it was hanging limp because the spike had broken his collarbone, and when he had thrashed trying to escape, the wound had gone from half the size of a golf ball to the size of a baseball.

It'd been over an hour, so the blood had already started clotting. After cleaning and irrigating the wounds, I investigated what was happening with his collarbone. It was pushed deep into the muscle, and it appeared like the muscle was healing in a crazy pattern around it. I bit my lip and tried to come up with a plan. I didn't see any way around cutting him.

"Peter, I'm gonna need you."

"I'm all yours. Security system is up and running."

I took a few deep breaths and decided to make Gabriel eat a few bites of something and take antibiotics. He grumbled, but complied.

While Peter finished washing up to play nurse, I carefully filled a syringe with a painkiller. I figured Gabriel was about double my weight, so double the dose. I went to stick him in the shoulder, and he weakly grabbed me with his right hand.

"Antibiotics okay. Painkillers not," he rasped. His face was slick with sweat, and he was a sickly pale color.

I swallowed hard and tried to respond confidently and not sound petrified. "Gabriel, I have to give you something. I have to set your collarbone. There's a lot of damage—"

"Need to stay alert in case we need to evacuate."

Peter helped me out. "Gabriel, I figured out the security

equipment. If anyone or *anything* approaches, we'll have enough time to carry you out if we need to." But Gabriel didn't look convinced.

"Okay. I have a local anesthetic I could use."

"No."

"A half dose of local," I bargained. *Please!*

He exhaled in a manner that would probably have been exasperation if his breathing hadn't been so shallow. "Accepted."

I promptly stuck him with a needle and proceeded. I started moving the bone into place. His back arched a little and his eyes rolled wildly upwards. I gritted my teeth and continued. He'd been pale before, but there was no comparison to how he looked now. He barely made a sound. Perspiration started running down his face and soaking what he had left of his shirt. So I made a decision. I was going to flat out sedate him. There was no logical reason for him to suffer like this; I hadn't even finished setting the bone.

"Peter, can you come over here and hold this clamp like this for me?"

"Yup." He replaced my hand.

I walked behind Gabriel so he couldn't see what I was doing, filled another syringe, and stuck him. He slurred something at me, then he was out.

"You realize he is going to kill you when he wakes up, right?" Peter said.

I shrugged. "He can get in line." I didn't want to think about how true that statement was.

I took it slow and steady and remained calm. I finished setting the bone, then I concentrated on basic suturing principles in my head over and over: 1. Eliminate and close dead space, 2. Support and strengthen, 3. Minimize bleeding, 4.

Reduce chance of infection. Somehow, repeating a numbered list helped me to focus and not panic.

It was like Peter could read my mind—when I needed anything, he was already handing it to me. If I wasn't sure, he discussed the options with me. I concentrated so hard that I was clueless as to how much time had passed. I used every bit of training and instinct I had, and I honestly felt good about my work. Maybe I had missed my true calling.

When Gabriel started to stir, I gave him the painkiller I knew he wouldn't let me give him if he had been conscious.

"You're an artist," Peter complimented.

"Mmmm. Thanks for your help."

"Always." He pulled me to his chest and gave me a hug.

My eyes teared up, mostly from exhaustion. I was running on nothing at this point. As nonchalantly as I could, I pulled away to wipe my eyes before tears tumbled down my cheeks.

"Are you doing okay?" I asked him. "Did you hit your head when she knocked you into the pillar?"

"Just minor bumps and bruises." His face had a scrape, and his lip was pretty swollen.

"You sure? No concussion? I want to make sure you wake up in the morning."

He smiled again. "I'm sure."

"Do you mind if I get a shower?" I asked.

"Sure. Afterwards, I will bandage your arm."

"Huh?" I looked at the arm that'd been itching. My sleeve was crusted with dried blood and stuck to my arm. "Seriously bad day."

"Understatement," he replied as he sank into the couch.

The shower was the first moment of privacy I'd had since we left London. Dawn was not too far off, it was almost unbelievable that it'd been only ten hours ago.

My thoughts fluttered from one thing to the next in rapid succession. I thought about what my great-grandmother might have known. Of our trek through the catacombs. Of the girl with the tattoos. Of what the vampire assassin had said. Then, I wondered what Gabriel almost said the security code was... something with an L.

Too many images were pulsing through my head. I wanted to talk to Joshua more than anything right then. It felt like I hadn't seen him in a week, and my heart ached.

I picked up the pace so Peter could shower. The three-inch gash in my arm was still bleeding. After dressing, I entered the living area holding a gigantic pile of tissue to my arm.

"You want me to look at that?"

"Go ahead and clean up. It started bleeding again."

He didn't argue and disappeared into the bathroom. I sank onto the remarkably comfortable couch. I must've dozed off because I was startled when Peter sat down next to me, smelling of Ivory soap.

He gently took my arm and removed the clump of tissue. "I think we can glue it."

"Sounds good." I tried to keep a pleasant look on my face, but it felt like my face was made of heavy clay. He grabbed the medical adhesive and patched me up.

"And with that, milady, I bid you goodnight," he said, then collapsed on the bed nearest the front door.

I veered to the other bed sitting heavily, and groped through my bag pulling out my lip balm. Paper was wrapped around the tube—a note in Josh's handwriting.

> You will forever be my Miranda—
> Your Ferdinand

"My bounty is as deep as the sea,
My love as deep; the more I give to thee,
The more I have, for both are infinite."
—William Shakespeare

I smiled and dragged myself under the covers, thinking of Joshua and our secret names for one another. I allowed silent tears to pour down my face and soak the pillow—no sobs, no sniffles; just an abundance of tears. I wasn't crying over any one specific incident. I just needed to let go. *Worst day ever.*

Was it weak of me to want my mom and dad? I even wanted to see my punk little brother and my friends from home. I tried to get my mind off the immediately impossible. Sebastian had said I might be able to see them this summer. My last thoughts were hopes that Joshua was safe, and I fell asleep for the third and final time that night, holding onto my scrap of paper.

I woke to the sound of rain pelting the rooftop. Faint light filtered through the tiny windows, making the room a greyish-blue color. I would still be wearing shorts in California in October, but not here. I rolled onto my side and felt the glue on my wound pull, so I rolled onto my back. I wondered what time it was.

The sound of the calm breathing of deep sleep was drifting over from Peter's bed. I decided to check Gabriel and make sure his dressings didn't need to be changed. My feet protested as I stood. In my hand, I still had the poem Joshua had slipped into my bag. I read it one more time, then put it back around my lip balm.

I shuffled over to Gabriel and dropped onto one knee, gently pulling up the edge of the dressing on his leg. It looked good. Minimal bleeding after I had closed him up, but the leg was the easy part. I raised the bandage on his shoulder. It was weeping clear fluid, but didn't appear to be infected. I wanted to put a new dressing on it, but I didn't want to wake him. Super Slayer healing abilities or not, sleep was key.

When I stood, I realized he was watching me, his expression far away.

"How are you feeling?" I asked.

His eyes flitted down to his leg, then his shoulder, and then back to my face. "I have seen better days, doc." The edge of his mouth twitched upward.

"You're gonna have some pretty cool scars to show off to the ladies." I winked.

He let out a single chuckle. I opened some new bandages and pulled up a chair. Then I peeled off the old dressings and replaced them. When I put the last piece of tape on his shoulder, he gently placed his hand over mine and held it to his chest. I met his gaze.

"Thank you." His eyes were glossy and kind.

I nodded my head.

"But."

My posture deflated.

"Never, ever knock me out again."

I twisted my lips to the side. "Um…only if you can promise never to get hurt like that again." I paused when he furrowed his brow. "Unless, of course, you would like me to lie to you. If so, then yes, of course, I will never do it again," I promised with a fake smile.

"Honest as always," he said, and I couldn't tell if he was approving or disapproving.

I had a knot of emotion lodged in my throat, and debated

saying something, then changed my mind. I slid my hand out from underneath his and asked something else. "On a scale of one to ten, how is your pain level? *Be honest.*"

"I can endure it."

An irritated sound escaped my mouth.

A groggy voice drifted from the bed. "I can't believe you let her off that easy."

"Do not think that any grace I afford her extends to you." His eyes smiled.

"Teacher's pet."

I was tempted to call out, "Bitter, party of one," or "He obviously likes me more than you," but I refrained. The fact was, he *had* let me off easy, and I wouldn't want to be ungracious again. So I simply said, "Go back to sleep, eavesdropper."

Gabriel looked towards Peter's still unmoving form. "Peter, you up to driving some more?"

"Absolutely," he responded, though he didn't move.

"I can drive, too," I offered meekly.

"I would rather have you secreted in the backseat, a little more out of sight."

I didn't say anything. I understood, but didn't like it.

"Where are we headed anyway?" Peter inquired.

Gabriel got the same faraway look I'd seen on his face earlier. "To see Winslow. We head to York."

"Can we stay here a while and rest?" I was thinking more about *him* resting.

"There will be some downtime there. I want to get there well before sunset."

"On it," I replied.

Gabriel was still in pretty bad shape. He needed help dressing, but he was able to get into the car with only Peter's help. It was going to take about three hours to get to York.

Moments before we were out the door, Gabriel asked me to confirm my great-grandmother's name and made one phone call. I knew he was out of it if he had to ask me something twice.

We were on our way to see someone Gabriel didn't seem keen on visiting. The way he was acting about my ancestry made me feel like I had a stone in my stomach, and I really wanted to talk through everything that'd happened in the last twenty-four hours. I sighed, sat back, and tried not to grind my teeth.

It occurred to me there was one thing I could do while out of sight in the backseat. I pulled a piece of paper out of my pocket. I had written down the security code to the house. Terrible of me, but I wanted to know what started with an L. I started writing down phrases of words I could spell on a keypad with the three sets of digits. My friends and I had figured out what all of our cell phone numbers had spelled. It was kind of hilarious.

So this, of course, assumed that the whole thing was a combination of words and phrases.

5-2-95-2-45-6-6

LAWLAGJON

LAXKAGKON

LAY KAHKOM

LAZLAHLOO

Nothing seemed to jump out at me; maybe Gabriel had a friend named Laxlagkom who meant a lot to him. I shoved the paper back in my pocket and watched what I could see of the scenery out the window.

6

WINSLOW

W e made good time; even with detours, back roads, and the drizzly English weather, we pulled into town in only four hours. I was relieved that we still had hours of daylight.

We drove by York Minster. The mammoth cathedral overpowered everything in the landscape. It was truly beautiful. Ironically, I'd always wanted to visit this place. We parked in a small lot next to some tourist shops then started walking —slowly.

Gabriel placed his right hand on my shoulder to help keep the pressure off his leg. As we walked, I spied something in the window of the shop we were passing and stopped.

"I'll be right back," I said, starting to pry Gabriel's hand off my shoulder.

"You are not leaving my sight."

I rolled my eyes and pointed up. "Sunlight." I pursed my lips. "Well, sort of. You—er—Peter can watch through the window, and I'll stay within a twenty foot radius. Scout's honor."

He begrudgingly nodded in agreement and let go.

With speed, I bought snacks and a gift for Gabriel, then walked back out to the street with my new treasure behind my back.

I grinned widely. "Here you go, *old man.*" I handed him an overpriced wooden cane with a carved head. It was an angel straining under a globe, its wings wrapped protectively around it.

He looked at me blankly.

"You can sharpen the end and stab something with it when you are healed up," I said as I pushed it at him. Peter was doing his best to keep a straight face.

Gabriel still didn't say anything, but I thought there was a hint of amusement in his eyes—if I looked really, really hard. He accepted the cane, and our pace picked up considerably. I was also less worried that he was going to pull open the stitches in his thigh; he was already leaning on the cane much harder than he had me.

We entered an area called The Shambles. Gabriel led us to a bookseller in the heart of the area. We paused, facing the front door. Gabriel reached for the knob, then dropped his hand. He paced, or rather, hobbled back and forth for a minute with that faraway look again. I didn't know which was worse: seeing him injured or seeing his internal turmoil. I wondered if anyone else had ever seen him like this.

His jaw flexed, he fixed his face with determination, and he walked in the door while we trailed behind him like ducklings. Inside there was a mixture of new and used books. The ten-foot ceiling seemed to sag onto the oversized bookshelves, making the room seem heavy. The place was much larger than I would have guessed from the outside.

Halfway down the left wall was a steep staircase with a tarnished brass chain roping it off next to an accordion-style gate. A black door with thick, wavy glass was in it—probably an elevator.

I realized there was an awkward-looking boy with thick glasses and a weak chin watching us from behind the counter. He held a small volume to his chest and gently stroked it as he peered at us.

"May I help you?" he chirped.

"Winslow," Gabriel replied with no emotion.

The boy walked to the wall and pressed a prehistoric looking intercom. "Mr. Clark, there are people here to see you."

A very polite voice responded, "I'm afraid I can't come down at the moment. Please do what you can to help them, Stephen."

Gabriel shook his head. "Tell him we are here to see the special collections."

The boy relayed the message. There was a long silence, but no answer. As we all stood there, the quiet became very loud. The wind picked up outside, and rain droplets started to pelt the window.

Finally, I heard the groan of an elevator. We watched the floor of the lift drop to ground level through the distorted glass. I was able to make out a towering figure. He slid the pocket door out of the way, and then the gate. His head was in a book as he entered the room.

When he looked up, he stopped short. He and Gabriel stood fifteen feet apart and stared at one another, both unmoving like tall trees on a still day.

I took a long moment to observe the person who had Gabriel so rattled. He was a lofty man with broad shoulders and a wiry build. He looked like someone who'd once been athletic, but had spent too many years bent over books. His mousy brown hair was short, and his small almond-shaped eyes were enlarged by gold-rimmed spectacles. His nose was sharp, and his mouth wide and thin. But all of this was overshadowed by the burn scars. Pinkish-silver scarring twisted its way down his neck and disappeared under the high collar of his shirt. His right ear and sideburn were distorted by the injury.

Over a minute ticked by—an excruciatingly *looooong* minute. It didn't look like Gabriel or Mr. Winslow Clark were going to move from their frozen state. I cleared my throat—nothing.

I finally walked forward towards Winslow and offered my hand. "Hello, I'm Aleria...this is Peter." I hooked my thumb in his direction.

Mr. Clark took my hand, but didn't shake it for a full three-second count, his eyes still fixed on Gabriel. Then the look of shock and whatever else it was melted from his face. He fastened his eyes on me, and kindness warmed his features.

He sounded befuddled—and a little embarrassed—when he finally replied and shook my hand. "I'm so sorry. It is very nice to make your acquaintance."

Then Peter shook his hand.

"I think you know Gabriel." I glanced back at him.

"Um...yes, of course." Mr. Clark offered his hand, but it hung in the air. He finally dropped it to his side. "Yes, well. Why don't we head up to special collections then, and see how I can help you?"

He ushered us towards the stairs. He opened the door to the tiny elevator and motioned Gabriel inside by himself, then unclipped the chain blocking the stairs and waved Peter and me upwards.

Gabriel had said we were going to have some downtime; I prayed it wasn't going to be filled with this type of tension the entire visit. I reached the top of the first flight of stairs to discover a room almost mirroring what was below—floor to ceiling books.

Mr. Clark caught up and took the lead. We followed him up to the third floor. When the elevator groaned to a stop, we watched Gabriel hobble over, his arm straining against the makeshift sling.

This room was half the size of the other floors and smelled like rain and sweet biscuits. A window was ajar in the back, hence the smell of rain. Again, weighty bookshelves lined the walls, but the space was furnished with leather couches with lots of gold studs, intricately carved wood tables, and sturdy wooden chairs. It was a place for research and study.

The far table was covered in open books and dog-eared texts. Along with the remains of some tea, a plate with crumbs, and a neatly folded napkin. The sight of the food made my stomach grumble. I remembered the snacks I'd picked up in the gift shop. It was all I could do not to drop my bag and tear into them like a crazed raccoon indulging in a camper's groceries.

Winslow ushered us to a sitting area. Peter and I took the couch, and Gabriel and Mr. Clark took the chairs opposite one another.

Gabriel finally spoke. "What do you know of the Lux?" he asked, his tone civil—just barely.

Winslow cleared his throat and seemed to think for a moment. "They were prophets or, I should say, *prophetesses* ordained by God. They were some of the Watchers' most powerful allies and a weapon of sorts until they vanished in 1793 during the Reign of Terror in France. Vampires used Robespierre's rampage to try to flush out and capture the last of them, but ended up killing all of them instead."

"They weren't Watchers?" I asked, surprised.

"Not in the beginning, but they eventually joined the Seven." I opened my mouth to ask another question, and he instinctively understood. "The Seven were just that: seven families all with special abilities who made up the core of the Watchers. Six of them are still part of the Concilium today. Others have earned their way on, but the Seven had something unique to offer."

"Like?" Peter asked, leaning forward.

"Many of the Abacha family are empaths. They can tap in and feel the emotions of others. So they can sense anger or disdain and so on. Imagine the tactical advantage of being able to detect deceit?" He sighed. "When we lost the Lux, we lost a valuable advantage."

I wanted to ask what the Lux's special ability was, but I didn't get the chance.

Peter said, "Why do you call them the Lux? Didn't you say they were a family? Or is that a name?"

"They were, but the gene was carried through the women, so their names would always change. It helped them keep their identities secret. Lux simply means light, but if memory serves, there was more to it. I believe Lux is a shortened version..." He paused. "It has been so long since I've thought about any of this, I'm afraid I am a little rusty. It's a great history, but not really relevant anymore; they were exterminated."

"Winslow, we need access to some of Ahijah's work," Gabriel requested, his tone softer than before.

Winslow pressed his thin lips together. "All right, that can be done." He hesitated a moment, and then got on his feet. "Follow me, please."

He showed us to the corner of the room nearest the back of the building. He stood in front of one of the bookcases; the center shelf had eight pewter, circular embellishments pressed deep into the wood of the shelf. He turned four of them in different directions, each making a very faint clicking sound like a combination lock—which was exactly what they were.

When he turned the fourth one, a whirring sound was expelled like pressure being released, and the bookcase pulled into the wall and slid two feet to the side. Clever—no scuff marks on the floor this way.

We followed him through the doorway. Faint lights cracked to life once we entered. He pressed something on the back of the bookcase, and it closed us into the room.

The room was extremely narrow, maybe five feet wide, and ran the length of the entire building. It was like those hidden rooms where they hid slaves in America or Jews in Western Europe. Immediately inside the door, temperature and humidity displays glowed on some electronic equipment.

There were oxygen tanks with masks and long tubes at the base of each bookcase. "If you start to feel lightheaded, put a mask on and turn the yellow knob. Delicate balance in here." I expected leather-bound books, but there were scrolls and stacks of individual sheets of thick paper instead. "B.C. is at the far end," he said as he made his way down the long hallway-like room.

I started to feel lightheaded. I stopped to use the oxygen and immediately felt better.

Mr. Clark was saying, "Ahijah had written hundreds of pages on sheets of papyrus. The largest collection is here." They stopped in front of a section.

Gabriel uttered the words: "The Nexus."

Mr. Clark's fingers fluttered back and forth over the shelf as he scanned for the document. "Ah," he said at last. He pulled out a wide, flat box and read something attached to the top. "It looks like someone started to translate this in..." He cocked his head to the side. "1793."

They headed back towards me. I bobbed my head as they passed, acknowledging my status as a total lightweight. Gabriel actually grinned. It was the first smile I'd seen on his face since the train station.

Mr. Clark placed the box on the desk by the entrance. I turned off the oxygen and joined them. He pulled a heavy volume out of the box. "A codex: rare for this early in the period."

I must have made a face, because he explained.

"It's a papyrus book developed by the ancient Egyptians. Most of the writings at this time were still on scrolls."

I smiled and nodded.

"It is much too delicate to remove from the room. Ah, here. I have a portable unit. It will take too many hours to translate this in here." Donning a pair of white gloves, he removed the book from its container and placed it into a rectangular box that looked like it belonged on a space station.

He explained that the box had U.V., humidity, and temperature protections. It was also equipped with holes with gloves attached to be able to handle the document from the outside. The box itself was tall, but it had an adjustable platform in it so you could move the book up to the glass to read it, then down to have room to turn the pages. Kinda ingenious and way better than spending hours in the special room.

Mr. Clark looked at a monitor to make sure no one was in the study, then pulled a lever to open the doorway. We exited, and I took a deep breath, ready to be out of the hidden room.

"How much of the book was translated?" Gabriel asked.

"There should be a copy in here. Once documents are translated, a copy stays with the original." He started shuffling through parchment. "That is quite odd." He frowned. "The first section was translated. Three copies were made, but no destination is listed. All of these documents are considered restricted. As far back as the Middle Ages, we have kept logs on where they are. Very peculiar." He picked up the storage box.

I peered through the glass at the ancient book. Without looking away, I asked, "May I turn to the first page, Mr. Clark?"

"Winslow, please. And, yes, of course, but go slowly. If there is any resistance, please stop, and I'll take over."

I slipped my hands into the gloves and carefully opened the cover. The first page was blank, so I turned another page. I didn't recognize the writing at all: a Middle-Eastern-looking script with all the words to the right margin. I had to assume it was read from right to left. "What language is this?"

"It would be Hebrew," he replied as he moved towards me. He examined the page, his eyes squinting with concentration. "A rare dialect, or maybe coded. How quickly do you need this?" he inquired, craning his head towards Gabriel.

"It takes precedence over everything."

"Yes, yes, of course. I suppose you wouldn't have come without..." As the words floated out into the room, the awkwardness that had started to recede returned. It was an acknowledgment of the elephant in the room.

Of course, I wanted to ask, "And why wouldn't he want to see you?" But I bit my tongue, forcing myself to wait for the right time.

Winslow walked to his desk with its piles and grabbed some books, writing instruments, and pads of paper, then returned. "Haven't your charges completed their training in Hebrew yet?"

"No, they have only been in the program for a few months."

Winslow raised his eyebrows in surprise. "Really?"

"Special circumstance," he answered with no other explanation offered.

Winslow went over to the book and peered into the case, the corners of his eyes crinkled like straw. He carefully flipped through every page of the codex. "Ancient Hebrew. It has been a while. I don't think this is a code, but I believe Ahijah had some sort of shorthand. It will take me some time." He immediately started scribbling on his pad of paper.

Gabriel hobbled to the corner of the room and pulled out a phone. He had a brief conversation that was so whispered, I couldn't hear a thing, despite listening as hard as I could. Then he made a second call. I heard him say, "Did you make any progress?" He was looking my way.

I quickly looked at the books in the case next to me and tried to look casual.

More hushed words, something about lines and connections, and then he said, "Go and physically get the records if you need to. Tomorrow then." He glanced at me again, and then hung up. After this, he went over to the box with the translation in it and began to carefully examine the parchment on the table. He grabbed one of the pads of paper and started writing.

I walked over to Gabriel and looked over his shoulder. "The translation is in Latin?" I said, but it sounded more like a complaint.

"Yes. None of our documents were in English until the twentieth century."

"Translating the translation. Fun," I stated, deadpan.

"Go ahead and relax. I will call you if you can help with something."

"Okay. We should check your dressings again soon."

He nodded and returned to deciphering. He glanced at Winslow for a split-second, and something grim shaped his expression. His eyes hardened, and his jaw tightened ever so slightly.

Peter and I were pretty useless at this point, unless it was to boil water for tea or arrange some scones on a plate. Peter took the opportunity to sleep. I was too agitated to do the same. There was too much tension between Mr. Angry and Mr. I-don't-know-what. It didn't seem like Mr. Winslow Clark was angry or bitter like Gabriel. Maybe resentful? Or guilty? He definitely seemed to bow to Gabriel, although that could simply have been out of fear. I certainly wouldn't have wanted to make Gabriel truly angry.

I decided to take advantage of being in a room full of books and read. I hadn't read anything for pleasure since setting foot in England a few months ago. I ran my fingers along the books lined on the shelves, waiting for one to speak to me. There was a case of classics, both new and old. Austen, Brontë, Faulkner, Lewis, Marlowe, Shakespeare, Tolkien...hundreds of them. Then a bell went off in my memory. I went back to Milton and pulled *Paradise Lost* off the shelf.

I started perusing "Book 1." I came across a name on line 391. My heart started to hammer. It was that familiar thing that had been nagging at the edges of my memory when I'd had my dream. Moloch. I strode over to the table and picked up a spare pad of paper and a pen and started writing down pertinent lines. Anything having to do with Moloch.

Then I came to another name I'd heard somewhere. *Dagan. Dagan. Dagan.* A sick feeling slowly worked its way up from my stomach. My knees felt weak. The captain of Queen Agrona's Royal Guard was named Dagan. I'd only seen him for a fleeting moment in the warehouse where I'd been held captive. Could this be a coincidence? How could it be? Both connected to the French coven? I feverishly wrote down every reference to both of them that I could.

I wanted to talk about my findings, but it didn't seem to be the right time. There were references I didn't understand, so I decided to research everything first. "Winslow, do you have a Bible commentary up here?" I asked.

He pointed to the other side of the room. I went over and spent the next hour explicating and cross-referencing the passages I'd copied. The *Paradise Lost* conversation had to be saved for the near future.

Winslow and Gabriel worked diligently on the text, always standing on opposite sides of the table. It was as if they were children having a fight. They kept the table between them for safety as they circled back and forth in their awkward dance.

Winslow reached to the middle of the oversized table and the side of his shirt came untucked, revealing more burn scars. His skin was the texture of dry mud in the California desert. He caught me looking and quickly tucked his shirt back in. I could feel my face flush with embarrassment. I didn't mean to gawk, but I had. I'd never seen scarring so bad. The scars must have covered half of his body or more.

A short while later, I noted the time on the clock. It was 4:00 P.M., and I was starving. I wanted more than just snacks. "Should we get some food?"

Gabriel looked up from the parchment, bleary eyed and obviously on a different train of thought. He looked at the grandfather clock swinging the seconds by.

"We have two hours of light left," I said, rising to my feet. "I can go get something."

"Yes, we need food. No, you are not leaving my sight," Gabriel replied.

"I'll send Stephen to fetch something," Winslow offered.

Stephen was sent on his way and returned with enough fish

and chips to feed twice as many people as were present. I drowned mine in malted vinegar and lemon. I ate so much I had to lean back in my seat. Stupid. When I finished, I noticed how awkwardly quiet it was. It was killing me. I looked at Peter, and he bulged his eyes and shrugged his shoulders. I tried to prod him to speak, but he shook his head with a you-are-crazy-if-you-think-I'm-going-to-say-something expression.

Bottom line: neither one of us felt comfortable attempting a dialog. The strain in the atmosphere and all the food in my belly made me feel exhausted. I wished I had somewhere else to go. I wished I could go home—like home-home with my parents.

It was late. Sleep was in order, but Gabriel had this strange, dogged determination, or maybe obsession, at this point. Winslow looked almost beside himself. I wondered if we were going to be here all night. I looked at Peter, put my fists to my temples, then splayed my fingers like my head was exploding. He mimed a gun to his head. Obviously, something was important here, but I was bored out of my mind. I was tempted to try to sleep on the couch, but the way Peter had been complaining about his back since his nap made me reconsider.

I heard a chair shove back on the floor and hushed voices. I whipped my head to look at Gabriel and Winslow. Gabriel was leaning across the table in a menacing fashion, the fingertips of his right hand pressed onto the table. Winslow had scooted back in his chair, but he leaned forward. He wasn't backing down. A snarl of words went back and forth and finally erupted. Winslow stood.

Gabriel replied to something, "...it is life or death for someone."

"How could this piece of disconnected history impact us today?" Winslow scoffed.

"It does not matter how. Sometimes you just need to follow orders," Gabriel spat back.

Winslow jerked like he had been hit. "I do follow orders."

"Not always."

"It has been fifteen years, and you…" Winslow dropped his shoulders.

Gabriel's eyes were burning with hatred. I'd never seen that look on his face. He stood abruptly and hobbled to the elevator.

I popped up, mouth open to ask him where he was going. Before I could speak, he pointed his cane at me.

"You stay here!" he yelled, and he slammed the door.

My mouth snapped shut. The elevator disappeared below. A minute or so later, we heard the chime at the front door.

After the shock wore off, Peter and I looked at one another, then at Winslow. The grimace etched on his face melted away, as he slowly lowered himself onto the chair.

Glancing at both of our questioning faces, he drew in a long, deep breath and stuck his fingers under his glasses to rub his eyes. He seemed a million years old at that moment. Or maybe his burden was a million pounds. When he exhaled, he met my gaze. "I am responsible for the death of his sister."

I didn't know what to say.

"How?" Peter finally whispered.

"I was her Keeper." *She was a Slayer too.* "Gabriel told me she wasn't ready for field training yet. I did follow orders. We were out one evening. Dinner…with our newly formed five-person unit. All of us were there: Keeper, Slayer, Scout, and two Watchers. We anticipated her finishing her training within a few months, so we were already running simulations, in-house only." He seemed to drift off in thought.

"So you weren't doing field training, then?" Peter prompted.

"No, celebrating something. It seemed the perfect evening. It was March. It was still quite cold, but there is something about the anticipation of spring. The air was crisp and clear. The stars were ablaze. I remember thinking they were smiling down on us that night. Laylah…" He smiled. "Her enthusiasm was infectious." He shook his head. "We ate at a pub a few blocks from the training center. We stayed out late, and when we left, it had clouded up and began to drizzle—a bad omen, I guess.

"We walked back with speed, but we witnessed a purse snatching and immediately realized it was a neophyte…er, a new vampire. It's common. Many commit petty crimes for money, especially if they don't have a Sire to guide them, to show them how to make money and be inconspicuous. But that wasn't the case this night."

"It was a trap?" I asked.

"I'm not sure. It seemed like we interrupted something… bigger. We think the vampires may have been targeting people. Stealing information to target them later, maybe the runners for an older vampire. There were a rash of home invasions, all the crime scenes had a lack of blood, and all the victims' bank accounts were drained. The vampires seemed surprised we were there."

"So what happened?"

"Laylah took off like a shot; she was fast. All of us pursued her into an alley. It was narrow and opened up into a courtyard at the end. We rounded the corner and saw she had already seized the boy; she had a dagger buried in his back, but she was holding him up like a shield because there were four of them. All appeared to be recently turned. We engaged. Took them all out. And then…" he squeezed his eyes closed.

"One of them wasn't dead?" Peter asked.

"No, something from above. A bottle...heavy...glass... fell and hit me, shattering the joint at my shoulder, cracking the tip of my humerus, and cutting into the rotator cuff. I fell forward, slicing my hands on the broken glass. It was some type of accelerant. Alcohol maybe. And I was covered in it.

"I searched the roofline and watched a shadowy figure drop from stories above. It was instantly apparent that he was an old vampire, maybe an Ancient. He was powerful enough. His eyes were almost black and matched his dark-hair. He had large, silver rings etched with symbols on the ring fingers of both hands. Within seconds, both Watchers and the Scout—Rogers, Smith, Evans—were lifeless on the pavement. I screamed at Laylah to run, but she tried to get to me. He seized her from behind and held her by the waist. She struggled, but despite her strength, he was unmoving. I had never seen a vampire that strong.

"He looked me straight in the eyes and said, 'I've never had Slayer,' before he sunk his teeth into her. Her body writhed and then went limp." Winslow's voice became hoarse.

"I struggled to get off the ground, and at that moment, I heard a metallic click behind me, and then I was on fire. I yelled out as I watched him savor killing her. I was powerless to do anything.

"Afterwards, the dark-haired one strolled past me, whistling. I heard the other one chuckle as I laid there smoldering. They assumed I was dead. If it hadn't started to rain, I would have been. One of the Watchers had dialed the training center. They traced the call and found me. That was it. I survived."

"Did you ever find out who they were?"

"A vampire by the name of Breton. Blackthorne, the head of the Conclave, had a detail in town tracking him. He was a rogue loosely allied with the French coven. He was friends with some of Queen Agrona's Royal Guard. Well-connected. It didn't matter though. He was not long for this world. Once identified, he had twenty-four hours."

"Gabriel?" I asked.

"Yes." He ran his finger from his temple, down his cheekbone, and fish-hooked it upwards.

"That's who scarred his face."

"A constant reminder of his sister and her killer every time he looks in the mirror. Just as I have these scars." He waved over most of his body.

"Did you find the other one?"

"I never saw him. He was behind me the whole time. No one was tracking him. No cameras picked him up. A ghost."

"I'm sorry." I didn't know what else to say. But all of this made an incredible amount of sense now. "Did you and Gabriel ever talk about any of this?"

"I was in the hospital for months. My lungs were damaged, and I was unable to speak. By the time I had recovered, Gabriel had put in for reassignment and moved back to America."

"And you haven't seen him since?" I asked.

"No, I have not. All correspondence returned."

"Ouch." Peter cringed.

"It is what it is," he stated matter-of-factly. "Ultimately, I am responsible. I was her Keeper. I have to live with that."

I wondered how many people he'd told about this. Was he as quiet about his past as Gabriel?

"It is late. I need to get back to work, and both of you should get some rest." He stood up and shooed us into an adjoining room. "A place for wayward travelers."

"Thanks," I said as I entered the room. There were two sets of bunk beds and one queen-sized bed. Each had clean sheets and blankets folded on top.

"You know where the water closet is."

"Thank you."

"Yeah, thanks," Peter added.

As Winslow left the room, I grabbed his hand for a moment and squeezed. He didn't stop, but returned the gesture. Once we had the room to ourselves, I claimed the bottom bunk in the corner.

Peter let me clean up first. When I emptied my pockets, I found the paper on which I had been trying to decipher the code LAY LAH. It was an option. I conjectured what the last three digits were. Would Gabriel have used such an easy code to crack? Of course, who knew what the last three digits were?

Peter and I didn't talk. I didn't know if we were too tired or too overwhelmed by Winslow's story. My heart was heavy for everyone involved. I realized this whole side trip was torture for Gabriel. I wondered if I would be able to help him in any way. She was the only family he had left. This led me to think about my family again. I went to sleep wanting home, wanting my family, and wanting Joshua.

7

FENCES

I woke to the sound of rain again, and there was only a hint of light. I rolled over and tried to return to sleep, but it was no use. I finally resigned myself to getting up. I shuffled to the bathroom, eyes mostly closed, and went through my morning routine.

When I returned to the bedroom, I realized that Gabriel was asleep on the queen-sized bed. He was still in his clothes from yesterday, feet hanging off the end of the bed since he hadn't bothered to kick his shoes off. Or maybe he'd needed help getting changed, and Peter and I had been comatose. The pile of clean linens were under his head. I grabbed the blanket that was next to him, gently spread it over him, and tiptoed out the door.

The other room was much lighter due to the large windows on the backside of the building. I went to the table near the stairwell to make some tea. I was startled when I realized that I wasn't alone. Winslow's long, gangly body was smooshed onto the tiny couch; he looked like a Great Dane trying to fit on a much too small cushion—legs awkwardly dangling off the side.

He was hugging his notes. I wished I could take a peek at them. Gabriel's strange intensity had made me curious.

I turned on the electric kettle, wishing I had my mom's French press and some coffee. A wave of homesickness hit me for the second time since we'd arrived in York. Distracting myself, I gnawed on a day-old scone and made my tea.

I wandered over to the enormous back windows and found there was a four-foot-deep balcony outside that ran the length of the building. It looked like I'd have to climb through the window to get onto it, and part of me wanted to climb outside and be alone, even though it was pouring.

A minute later, the rain stopped and no one was awake, so I slid the heavy window open and leaned out. The chilled outside air felt like a little bit of freedom, so I decided to risk a few minutes on the balcony.

I grabbed my sweatshirt and managed to slip through the window without spilling my tea. Then, all it took was moving a flowerpot off of a pedestal and I had my private little retreat. I leaned against the wall and sipped my tea. I felt like Simon in *Lord of the Flies*, after he'd found the bower, his paradise hideaway. I just prayed that the savages wouldn't come for me.

The city was quiet. Cars weren't allowed in The Shambles, so the vehicles I heard were far enough away to be a whisper. I closed my eyes and wondered what my friends were doing back home—probably getting ready for bed. The Sadie-Hawkins dance would only be a week away. I wondered who each of them had asked. Going to a dance seemed like a different lifetime—a different world.

I thought about my possible paths with the Watchers. Most worked full-time, and being a Watcher was their life. Some of them worked as assets or resources and weren't assigned to a specific coven. They got jobs in the real world and worked as support for specific Keepers within the Concilium. That was my goal. That was my ticket to attend college in the states with some of my friends, to be able to spend some time with my family. Sebastian said something about them "winning" a trip to a location that had been secured so I could see them.

I did like life with the Watchers, but anything can be handled for a few seasons. My end game was to not make this my life. I knew there must be some way to balance normality with the supernatural. I had told Joshua my plans, and he said we would make it work. There hadn't been a cloud of worry on his face.

I heard the bedroom door rattle like it was opened in a hurry. It was Gabriel; I could hear the cane thumping on the floor with a few urgent steps. I started to lean down to pick up the teacup I'd placed on the ground.

"Ali," Gabriel barked. "Aleria!" he thundered before I had a chance to open my mouth. "Ali!" It sounded like he was yelling down the stairwell.

"I'm right here," I said as calmly as possible, though I felt shaken by his tone.

His angry face appeared around the window. "I told you not to go anywhere."

My eyes were wide and bewildered. "I didn't; I'm right here. I didn't even go downstairs." I tried not to sound defiant, but I didn't like being yelled at. I climbed back inside.

"These rooms." His tone was harsh. He swept his good arm back and forth indicating the bedroom and research room.

Matching his tone, I shot back, "I didn't mean to scare you! I'm sorry, but I didn't do anything wrong." I wanted to storm off, but I couldn't leave the designated rooms. "You are making me feel like a prisoner!"

I stormed into the bedroom and realized Peter had somehow slept through all the raised voices. So, for his sake, I barely resisted slamming the door so hard it would crack the plaster. Peter was on his side hugging a wad of blankets to his chest. His mouth was wide open, drool pooling on his pillow.

I threw myself on my bed, and in doing so, conked my head so hard on the top bunk, it rattled my teeth. And then my nose started to run from my time outside. There was no tissue in sight, so I picked yesterday's shirt off the floor and used it. My frustration was so overwhelming that I promptly picked up a pillow and screamed into it. Childish, but it did make me feel better.

I curled up in the fetal position for a few minutes, but I was so angry, my heart wouldn't stop racing. I decided to go and have a few more words with Gabriel while I still had enough ire to do it. He was already mad, so I had nothing else to lose. The tension between Gabriel and Winslow was unbearable, and it was going to end before they gave me an ulcer.

Rolling out of bed, I was careful not to hit my head this time, and returned to the other room. Gabriel glared up at me from his seat, his face still red, and I'd thought he might have felt bad for yelling at me. I drew in a deep breath and steeled myself, determined that I was going to say everything on my mind.

"This thing here," I pointed back and forth between Gabriel and Winslow. "It needs to be resolved. I know these are monumental things you need to work through. But you need to do it. This anger and guilt and whatever else is crippling both of you."

Both of them sat up straight. Gabriel looked like he was a bear about to rear up on me. Winslow looked shocked. I heard Peter come in behind me.

Gabriel stood and started to speak. "Do not—"

I cut him off. "No. You don't get to disagree here. If I step out of line at all, even something like calling Peter a baby," I whipped my head around. "Sorry, Peter."

He put his hands up not wanting to get sucked into this. "No prob."

I turned back to Gabriel. "Whenever I have one tiny misstep and you go all Atticus on me and call me on it...tell me to look at it from the other person's perspective. And then you act like this? Now it's your turn. I know everyone has their thing, and yours is your sister. But you need to get over it. Hear his side of the story. Walk in his shoes. I doubt she would've wanted you to carry this around for fifteen years."

"Ali—" Winslow said.

"No, you need to get over it too. You are a KEEPER, for Pete's sake! You can't rise through the ranks any higher—save being on the Council! And you are HERE, guarding books?! You're here to punish yourself, aren't you?" I paused for a brief moment, staring him down. He didn't deny it. "Time limit is up. Fifteen years is long enough. Any objections to a confab?" I raised my eyebrows, daring them to challenge me. "It's settled then. You two will talk or..." I didn't know what to threaten them with. "Or you'll be sorry." *Lame.*

I grabbed Peter's arm and started dragging him across the room towards the window. I snatched the blanket off the back of the couch and shoved it against Peter's chest. I opened the window, pushed at Peter to climb through, and I followed. I looked at both of them. "Now start talking," I ordered and slammed the window shut, realizing too late that we had no way back in without help. I clenched my fists. Way too much adrenaline. When I turned, Peter was looking at me blankly.

He twisted his mouth to the side. "Looks like I missed something."

"Uh, yeah, Captain Oblivious." I smiled, yet was still clearly overwhelmed.

"Wow," he said and clutched his chest like I had shot him.

"I'm sorry." I stuck out my lower lip, covered my face, and walked over to him. I leaned into his chest, and he wrapped his arms around me. I groaned. "And the morning had started out so well..." and went to hell in about three seconds.

"I can't say being stranded on a cold balcony without breakfast would be my first choice."

I pulled away and plopped onto a pedestal. "Gah!" I shook my fist in the air. "Food! I forgot food. Well, I remembered the blanket," I offered.

"True...Ummm... You called me a baby?" he asked.

"Yeah, sorry. It was in the van after I scratched you."

He shrugged. "Hmpf, I was. Don't worry about it."

"Thanks."

"You wanna fill me in?"

"Sure." I pivoted around and peeked in the window. Gabriel and Winslow were talking. They both had defensive postures, but their lips were moving. I wished I were better at lip reading. I turned back to Peter and started talking.

I told him everything about the morning, including how homesick I'd been feeling. He said he felt a little homesick, but with his parents' divorce and all the tensions there, it was actually nicer to be away. And then he said something I had never considered. He said since he was always going back and forth between households, he didn't get homesick that easily.

We'd been so busy the last few months, I'd forgotten how much I liked talking to Peter. I mean, *really* talking.

It had been a long time since I had spied through the window. Gabriel and Winslow were still speaking, but their body language was completely different. It was open. They leaned towards one another and were actively listening.

"It looks good in there," I commented to Peter.

"Good, one more minute of that tension between them, and I was ready to stake myself in the head."

"Me too."

He laughed, then winced when his smile pulled at his split lip. I gave him a pouty face in sympathy.

Another hour or so passed. It was getting rather cold. Peter and I were now squeezed onto one pedestal instead of two and had the blanket wrapped around both of us. But we refused to knock on the window to ask admittance. A few raindrops started to fall, fat ones that slapped the ground loudly. The smell of wet brick filled the air. I wondered how much longer they would talk. Finally, I heard the squeak of the handle being turned and the window opening.

We jumped up and almost ran back into the building. The heat of the room flushed my face, and my nose began to run again. I sniffled and noticed Peter's was doing the same thing. I looked around. Gabriel was leaning on a chair nearest the window, but Winslow was nowhere in sight.

"Where's Winslow? Dead and stuffed in a trunk some-where?" I quipped, hoping it wasn't too soon.

He grinned. "He went on a food run. Thought you guys would be starving."

Peter said, "Yes!" before Gabriel had finished his sentence and started towards the bedroom. "I'm going to get dressed now that I'm not held captive on a balcony by a crazy woman."

"Cute. You know you're lucky to be hanging out with a girl at all."

"You're a girl?" he volleyed back and shut the door before I could reply.

I turned and faced Gabriel and waited. He didn't seem angry anymore.

"Are you speaking to me?" I gave him my best innocent look.

"You did what you needed to do. I may have been," he paused.

I wanted to say a jerk, but I refrained.

"Overzealous."

"Overzealous," I repeated.

"Yes. I apologize."

I smiled. "Accepted." I waited a few moments before asking, "How did things go with Winslow?"

There was a very pregnant pause. "We will continue to repair what once was." *Diplomatic.*

"Good," I said, feeling even better. "No cane?" I realized.

"How did you put it? Super Slayer healing powers?" he replied.

"Yeah, but I might need to add a *duper* to that."

He laughed. "All right, super-duper Slayer healing powers."

"Can I check your shoulder?"

He sat and let me examine it. I was amazed. "I should be able to take the stitches out soon. Your leg wound is so much cleaner; I could probably do those now. I can't believe it. Seriously, that's a week or two of healing in two and a half days."

"Sounds about right—we heal in about twenty to twenty-five percent of the time."

A short time later, Winslow returned with the food and a proper sling for Gabriel's arm. The whole vibe in the room was infinitely better.

Now, all I wanted was to figure out what Gabriel was so focused on uncovering. Though, if I was truly honest with myself, a large part of me feared it.

8

LUX CASTA

G abriel and Winslow had been getting along brilliantly since their talk late in the morning. So after eating, I finally felt comfortable asking about what we were doing in York.

"Gabriel, I have a question. I understand that this document is important for some reason, but why? Why are we here now? I feel like there is something I'm not catching onto. Or maybe there is something you aren't telling me. I mean, this whole thing started too fast. The evacuation, Gloucester, our trip here."

"I thought you said you had a question," Peter teased. "I think that was a dozen or two."

I lobbed a crumpled piece of paper at his head.

Gabriel pursed his lips and thought for a moment. "How about we look through some of the items we have translated, and you can tell me."

I did not like the sound of this and wasn't sure why didn't he want to tell me outright. "Okay…"

Gabriel motioned to Winslow, palm upturned, entreating him to begin.

"Yes, yes, right. The entire codex is called *The Nexus*, but that is only one part of the journal. The bulk of it is about the Lux. It seems the text is broken into several sections. The first is a general description of the Lux themselves, the second describes some members of the Lux who seem to have additional abilities, the third one gives specifics on a single person called the Nexus, the fourth through sixth sections seem to be three possible paths, and the last section may be on a different topic. We have only gotten through the first three. And we may not be able to translate everything. Ahijah used a rare dialect and abbreviations, but we can get the spirit of what he wrote about."

"So what exactly are the Lux?" I asked.

"As I said before, they were prophetesses or Seers. They were called 'Lux' or light, because they were the lights that guided the Watchers. They gave them great hope, kept them on track. Ahijah states that they were of royal blood. They had the ability to interpret dreams and had unparalleled intuitive abilities. But this is what we didn't know: they were special. All of them have had a special ability to resist vampire mind control."

"Wait a second," Peter interjected. "Mind control? Did I miss a day of class or something?"

Gabriel fielded this one. "No, we just have not caught you both up yet. All vampires have varying degrees of mind control abilities. Sometimes it is called compulsion, glamouring, mesmerizing, enchanting, and so on. But it is all the same thing: mind control. If you look directly into vampires' eyes, they have the ability to hypnotize you. Those with minimal abilities can hold someone in place against their will. Others with more skill or ability can actually probe minds, alter memories, or plant new ones. They can make you forget that anything happened and cover their tracks. People have run-ins with vampires often; they just do not remember."

Winslow continued, "So you can see why having a Seer who cannot be controlled would be valuable. The only other people known to resist compulsion are Slayers."

I nodded. "Ummm, would the Lux know vampires were trying to control them? Like," I hesitated, "would they feel it and be able to resist it when they concentrated? Or would it be like it never happened?" I felt the blood drain from my feet and hands.

"They would probably feel it, especially if it were a powerful vampire—an old one."

I nodded, but I didn't trust my voice. Had I ever told anyone I'd resisted Tyran's attempt to compel me? Or Queen Agrona's herself? I forced myself to look at Winslow. I could feel Gabriel watching me.

Winslow's voice was steady. "Behind Slayers, Seers have always been the top target of vampires. Many started carrying poison in case of capture. Others had their minds picked apart by the On—"

Gabriel cleared his throat.

"Oh, yes, yes. Sorry. The journal." Winslow paused and gathered his thoughts. "So, as you know, Lux means 'light,' and, as I said before, I thought there was more to it. There is. A select few are called the Lux Casta, meaning 'pure light.' The pure ones had the gift of foresight, usually through dreams."

"So their dreams foretold the actual future?" Peter excitedly asked.

"A possible future perhaps. There aren't many details on this part. I don't know. Or it could be..." He kept conjecturing for a few minutes, but my mind drifted. Gabriel's voice brought me back.

"So, you worked on the third section. What do we know about the section discussing *The Nexus?*" Gabriel requested.

"Sorry, I haven't digested that information." Winslow looked at his notes and adjusted his glasses. I walked around in back of him and followed his finger as he read. "The Nexus will be a member of the Lux Casta. So, she will be a Seer with the ability to resist compulsion and so on. But it actually gives two words in the Hebrew: one meaning 'light,' while the other one is closer to *accendo* or *accendere*. My research says it is to 'kindle, set on fire, light; illuminate; inflame, stir up, arouse.' It sounds like she will cause a stir, hmm."

I gave a weak chuckle.

He continued, "Of course, the original was a little more poetic, but here's what it boils down to. It says: 'In a new age, a presence will unify that which was once divided.' This could be any time in the future, and as for what was divided, who knows. It could be anything. Then it gives seven specific descriptors:

"'Of humble life and noble origins of thee derive.' So obviously, she would have royal heritage, but she wouldn't have been raised as part of the aristocracy.

"'Weighted with dreams of a Seer.' Now, all of the Lux Casta had dreams, so the fact that dreams are mentioned again would indicate they were of importance. But the term 'weighted' is a word that can also mean troubled or even tortured.

"'Lamps of amethyst.' Common word for eyes, like Solomon used in Song of Songs in the Bible."

I looked at Gabriel. I couldn't help myself. I struggled to swallow.

"'Vision of dark and light.' This could literally mean color blind, but I am more inclined to think it was her complexion, maybe fair skin and dark hair or vice versa. Again, multiple writings of the day would use these words regarding appearance.

"'Pure heart able to withstand, never to be bent.' I think this is self-explanatory. Someone who always stood for what is right, one who would not bow to the will of others or to peer pressure. The context indicates a strong sense of justice.

"It called her, 'A marked star that will appear when the need is great.' Or maybe the word is 'discovered,' not appeared. The context isn't clear on this one. She would have to have all of these traits. I supposed that would have weeded out most every-one. Too bad we lost them all to Madame la Guillotine."

"You said there were seven?" Gabriel asked. "Didn't you only give six?"

"Oh, yes, yes. She would have been untainted."

I looked at him, confused.

"A virgin," he added bobbling his head.

I felt light-headed. I reached for the chair next to me, pulled it out, and slid down onto it.

"So, the marked star thing." I could see Peter on the edge of an epiphany. "When we read *The Crucible* and studied about the Salem Witch Trials, they would physically examine suspected witches for things like moles, an extra nipple, or birthmarks. Could that be the mark it refers to?"

"Yes, I suppose so. Yes, absolutely." Winslow seemed delighted at Peter's interpretation.

Peter laughed. "Ali, you so would have burned at the stake with your little tramp stamp," he prodded.

Out of the corner of my eye, I saw Gabriel lean forward a little.

"You have a tattoo?" he asked, gently rubbing his injured shoulder.

"No, I don't. I have a birthmark. Peter just jokes that it's a tramp stamp to torment me."

"She gets all weird about it. I only saw it because she wore a bikini to the beach when she thought it was going to be just the girls."

I looked at the floor, refusing to make eye contact with Gabriel, but I could feel his eyes on me. He gently said my name, and I knew I got a defeated look on my face. Winslow was still clueless to Gabriel's suspicions. And Peter obviously didn't think I fit something in the criteria, even though he had outed my birthmark. Winslow and Peter were talking to one another, but all I could hear was the beating of my heart.

Gabriel said my name again.

I looked at him pleadingly, my brows pinned together. He held my stare. I slowly stood and turned my back to him, then stuck my thumb in the waistband of my pants. I just stood there. The moment he saw it, everything would change.

Suddenly, the room was silent. It seemed that Winslow had finally caught up. I revealed the small birthmark on my lower back just to the right of my spine. It was in the shape of a perfect, pink artsy star.

Winslow murmured, "Oh, dear one," under his breath.

Peter cut in. "No way. You and Robert."

There it was, the reason he'd discounted everything.

I sighed. "No, Peter. That was part of the reason I broke up with him. He kept pressuring me. We never..." I didn't need to explain further.

"He totally lied," he said, the sting of guy code betrayal on his face.

I wanted to die at that point. I prayed for lightning to strike me down. As if on cue, Gabriel's phone rang. I knew from the expression on his face it was the call he'd been waiting for.

He repeated, "Are you sure?" multiple times. Then he said, "Burn the evidence. No one is to know, that includes the Concilium."

He hung up, but before he had a chance to say anything, I announced, "And there is our confirmation, people." I got up and started to walk to the bedroom. I wanted to be alone.

"She knew, Ali." I stopped and leaned against the doorframe face first, pressing my forehead to the wood. I gripped the trim with both hands. "Your great-grandmother. She changed her name three times before the age of thirty. As did her mother before that, and before that. Uriel found a trail leading all the way back to France. You are a Countess."

"Humpf," was all I could manage.

Bewildered, Peter asked, "Ali? Why are you so upset? You are royalty. You have super powers."

Tears pricked my eyes. "Peter, it means I can never go home." My voice broke on the last word.

There was only silence. I glanced at Gabriel one last time before I shut the door. His eyes were closed. I walked through the back room, my despair so heavy it was choking me.

When I reached my bunk, the sobs welled up. I buried my face in the pillow, though I doubted it muffled my reckless cries. I cried and cried.

And cried, until I felt like I'd run out of tears.

My breath was jagged. *I'm lost*, I thought. I was mistaken before—*this* was the worst day ever. Yesterday I'd had a future of my choosing ahead of me. I'd had free will. Now, it felt like fate was laughing at me.

Nana, why didn't you prepare me for this?

I woke some time later from a dream I couldn't remember. I didn't hear anyone else in the room. I walked woodenly to the door and opened it. Winslow was gone. Peter was asleep on the couch, and Gabriel was in a wingback chair.

"Guys," I said softly. I rubbed Peter's shoulder.

He squinted up at me. Then Gabriel stirred.

"Thanks for giving me privacy. Please go get in bed. I want both of you to be able to walk tomorrow." I was glad the room was dim, because I could feel how puffy my face was. The boys sleepily lumbered into the bedroom, but I couldn't handle following them.

I wandered to the back windows. There was a deluge of rain coming down. It was storming so hard, I couldn't see the building behind. Liquid air. I opened the window and stepped out into it. My clothes were plastered to my body within seconds. I started to shiver, then my teeth started chattering, and then my knees started shaking so violently I thought I might topple over.

Yet, I remained outside in the downpour. Thankful that I could feel something besides the gaping hole in my heart. I stepped forward and looked over the edge of the balcony. For the tiniest fraction of a second, I thought about jumping. Then, I felt embarrassed that the idea had even occurred to me. I didn't know what to do, literally or philosophically, now or in the future.

A half hour or more had gone by, and my core temperature was dropping to the point of hypothermia. But I couldn't will myself to move.

"Ali." I turned to see Gabriel through the open window.

"I should come in."

He held up a towel. "See, intuitive," he said, making a sad attempt at levity.

"Ha ha." I climbed through the window, and he wrapped the towel around me with his good arm and held me tight.

"It will work out, you know."

I was too choked up to reply.

He led me back towards the bedroom. "There are dry clothes in the bathroom, best I could do. Change and get to bed. We will worry about this in the morning. Okay?"

I nodded, wet tendrils of hair sticking to my face. There was a giant t-shirt and boxers folded on the counter. I did as asked. I crawled into bed and prayed for good dreams, but I wasn't that lucky.

I was dreaming that I was flat on my back and needed to get up. I rolled onto my knees and noticed my palms were scuffed by tiny, sharp pebbles. I flicked them onto the ground and rubbed at my stinging skin. It was then I realized that I was on the rooftop of a tall building I didn't recognize.

The sound of cars drifted up from below, and I followed the sound. I was startled when a figure hunched at the edge of the building came into view, but when I focused, it was only a gargoyle glaring at the city below.

A wicked wind kicked up and drowned out the sound of traffic. I turned around a few yards short of the edge and looked back towards the roof-access door.

Fear froze me, my heart beating painfully hard. Tyran was on the roof with me, walking towards me with deadly determination. He had a slender dagger in his right hand, and it seemed as if I were watching him in slow motion.

I stumbled backwards a few steps to get away, but then reached the guardrail. There was nowhere left to go—trapped.

He reached me and grabbed the back of my hair, turning my face up to look at him. A cruel smile twisted across his perfect face, his blue eyes cold.

He bent down and whispered in my ear. "Are you broken yet?" He raised the razor sharp blade and placed it above my heart. Then he pushed the blade into my flesh until the hilt stopped it.

I looked at him, somehow surprised. "You killed me." Then everything went black.

I woke and silently tried to suck in a breath. It felt like there was no oxygen. I clutched my heart. *He killed me! He killed me!* I screamed in my head.

I squeezed my eyes shut, and tears streamed down my cheeks.

"Ali?" Peter's voice. Covers rustled, and then he was shaking me.

I still couldn't draw breath to answer.

"Ali? Are you okay?"

I gasped, finally getting air.

A light turned on. It must've been Gabriel.

A sob came out. "He killed me. Tyran killed me."

Peter put his arm around me. "It's just a dream. It'll be okay," he cooed. "It'll be okay."

I'd felt myself die. I sank into Peter's embrace and met Gabriel's eyes. "I don't know if I'll ever be okay again."

9

REUNION

I didn't have the will to get out of bed. I felt empty. Vacant. Void. Like everything I was had been wiped away. I rolled over. The beds the guys were using were stripped again. *Must be leaving today.* I had to use the bathroom, but I didn't want to get up. I stayed in bed for as long as possible.

Eventually, I slid one leg off the bed, then the other, remaining in an awkward L shape for a few more minutes while I summoned the energy to sit upright. I shuffled to the door and was about to open it when I heard the exhaust fan rattling in the bathroom. *Occupado.*

I stood next to the closed bedroom door, leaning my forehead on the wall. The plaster was cool and smooth. I didn't want to open the door and have an unnecessary conversation. I could hear the deep tones of Gabriel's voice and Winslow's soft, polite ones.

I wasn't really paying attention until I heard Winslow ask, "Are you going to tell her?"

Gabriel answered, "I do not know. Would you want to know

your future? Would you want to know what was going to happen to the people you care about?"

"Difficult. But yes."

"And we do not know for sure it is him."

Winslow's voice was strained. "Do you know the details about Moloch? What he did to the sacrifices? Why he wanted untainted ones?"

I tried to press my ear against the door, but accidentally tapped the door handle. I chastised myself, then went ahead and opened the door, since it was obvious I was up.

They both looked at me pleasantly—and warily.

"Morning," I acknowledged, though I didn't say "good." My voice was hoarse from all the crying and probably from the standing in the rain like a lunatic.

"Oh, I got you something," Winslow chirped. He motioned toward the table with the kettle and tea supplies. There was a new French Press, a pouch of coffee, and a small carton of cream resting in a bowl with half-melted ice.

I walked over to the carafe and ran my fingers over it affectionately. "Thank you." I got all choked up; my emotions were still so close to the surface. My mouth twitched in a smile for a second at the gesture. I could've started bawling again. "I was homesick yesterday. This helps."

After I'd made coffee, I forced myself to sit at the table with them. I leaned my head on my knees in between each sip of coffee while I listened. Honestly, it was hard being social at all; I guess I was more zombie than participant, but then again I wasn't in the fetal position in bed—I wanted to be, though.

Gabriel and Winslow talked about the journal a little more. It was agreed that Winslow would finish translating the other sections and hand deliver the notes at a later date. Gabriel feared anyone getting their hands on it.

Gabriel hinted that there might be a mole in the Watchers. But I'd already gathered that from his side of the conversation with Sebastian in the car—the conversation that had led to us changing course and coming here.

I remembered something I had asked him the day before that he'd sidestepped. "Gabriel," I said.

"Yes," he answered, more gently than usual.

"Yesterday, I said it seemed like you'd kept something from me..."

His lips grew thin.

"I... No, *how* did you know we had to evacuate? How did you know we had to find this book?"

He leaned back in his seat, then glanced over at Winslow, who peered back at him questioningly. I didn't think he knew either.

"I had a visitor in the middle of the night. He brought news that you were in danger. He had a page of the translation and recommended finding out if you were, well, who you are."

I nodded my head and realized Gabriel hadn't said who had visited him. Was he being deliberately vague? Or did I not know the person? My voice was quiet. "Who warned you?"

He was silent for about a minute, and he rubbed his temples while he deliberated over something. Any other day this would have driven me crazy, but today my emptiness gave me patience.

"Bowen warned me," he finally answered.

This was the last thing I would've guessed—like *ever*. I opened my mouth to ask something, but nothing came out. I was literally speechless. I didn't know how to feel about this information. Happy, sad, angry. What? Should I have felt betrayed that Gabriel hadn't told me? Thinking back to the evacuation meeting, both Sebastian and Joshua must've known. I finally managed, "How?"

"It does not matter," he said, shaking his head. "But it seems that he does genuinely want to protect you. Though I still would not trust him."

"Who is Bowen, if you don't mind my asking?" Winslow inquired.

"One of the vampires in love with her." Gabriel said it in an odd way, like he was trying to cheer me up by joking, but he had a melancholy undertone. Then he looked at Winslow and added, "I think you would know him as Belenus."

"I thought he died around 300 BC?" Winslow asked. "That was the first time Watchers had instigated an uprising to overthrow a ruling class vampire."

Of course he would know that. Winslow seems to be the ultimate history nerd.

"Yes, he was assumed dead, but he obviously escaped. There is a good chance he went dormant to escape his pursuers," Gabriel replied.

"Wasn't it his wife who was resurrecting the blood rituals again, trying to bring back the Devourer?" Winslow asked.

His wife. I'd never thought of him being married before. In over two thousand years, I suppose he could've had many wives.

Gabriel affirmed this thought: "Yes, she sacrificed hundreds in the hope of returning him to this realm before she was killed in the uprising."

And the forces of evil are rallying once again to bring him back.

"An odd coupling," Winslow mused. "Belenus was known as a healing god, and she…" His thought was never completed. He looked pensively at me. "A little bit of a subject change. Aleria, did you know that you were different? I mean, did you feel special deep down? That your life would never be normal? That you never quite fit in?"

I gazed back at him and blinked. "I think you just described every teenager on the planet."

He chuckled. "I suppose so."

"I don't know. I...I'm adjusting."

Peter finally came out of the bathroom causing us to pause in our conversation—it was the perfect time to escape.

"If you'll excuse me, looks like it's my turn." I headed to the shower.

After bathing, I put on my still damp clothes from the day before and shivered. I caught my reflection in the mirror and stopped to examine the bruises from the ugly shoed vamp. They were now in full bloom around my neck and looked terrible, but they didn't hurt that much. When I came out of the bathroom, Gabriel sat in the corner looking over some maps, while Peter packed up the last of our stuff, including mine.

Before I could do anything to help, Winslow pulled me aside and talked to me in hushed tones. He spoke of Laylah and the fact that I reminded him of her, of my relationship with Gabriel, and of some cautions and advice about my future. I could feel the importance of everything he was sharing with me and accepted it readily. There was so much I didn't know. I knew he was trying to encourage me, but the information was crushing and overwhelming, making me feel even more alone.

After our conversation ended, I sat silently and waited. We were planning on heading out in a few minutes when the intercom sounded—Stephen's voice announced someone who wanted to see special collections.

Gabriel turned to him. "You expecting someone?"

Winslow drew his shoulders upwards. "No, no. You were the first in years to show up here."

"Years..." Gabriel ran his hand through his hair and walked back and forth.

Winslow pressed the button on the intercom. "Please inquire as to who would like to see them."

There was a pause. "A Mr. Akhar, sir."

"Who is Mr. Akhar?" I whispered.

Gabriel glowered. "Phineas Akhar."

There was an instant lump in my stomach. Phineas was the raven-haired Watcher who hated me. He'd been dispatched to watch for vampire activity around me, before I'd even known that vampires existed. The only good thing he had ever done, as far as I was concerned, was send for Sebastian, Gabriel, and Joshua. If he hadn't, I would probably have been dead—or worse.

My mind drifted to the attack in Bowen's apartment and to Tyran. Then all rational thought seemed to stop. I could hear them talking, but I couldn't force myself to listen. Thoughts of Tyran striding forward in my dream and sliding that blade into my heart overwhelmed me.

I was pulled out of my trance when Gabriel gently took my elbow, pulled me up, and ushered me into the other room. I followed, still dazed. He sat me beside to Peter, then walked over to the door and shut it most of the way. He leaned against the wall next to the entry. We listened and waited.

There were sounds on the stairs. Then, "Ah, Mr. Akhar. How may I help you?" Winslow asked cordially. He was good. I would never have suspected anything.

"Yes, I have been ordered to acquire this collection from you."

I could hear paper rustling. "I'm afraid, sir, that this particular collection is very old and cannot leave the premises. It needs to be in a temperature-controlled environment and such."

"Mr. Clark, I'm afraid this is an order from the top."

"*I'm afraid* that without a signed order from *every* member of the Concilium, none of Ahijah's journals will go anywhere. They have been marked restricted. I'm sure you knew that."

"I'm sorry to have bothered you. I will get my papers in order." His words were polite, but his tone was tinged with frustration.

When the sound of feet on the stairs grew quiet, Gabriel peeked through the door. He nodded and opened it the rest of the way. We slowly drifted into the other room and waited until we could hear the bell at the front door.

Winslow pushed the intercom button. "Is our new friend still down there?" He asked.

"No sir, he left. Headed north."

"Thank you, Stephen. Please let me know if he returns."

"Yes, sir," Stephen answered.

Gabriel rubbed the back of his neck. "Do I need to ask what series of journals he was looking for?"

"I'm afraid not. He wanted Ahijah's entire collection," Winslow answered.

"So they are on the trail, but don't have specifics," I said.

"Who signed the order?" Gabriel asked.

"Blackthorne and Rousseau," Winslow replied.

"It looks like the Conclave isn't sharing information again. What a surprise," Gabriel said.

Winslow got an earnest look on his face. "Too bad *The Nexus* codex was separated from the rest of Ahijah's journals and misfiled. It would take years to sort through all the documents to find it."

"Thank you," I responded to his collusion.

"Of course, dear one. No one needs to know who you are

until it's time." He looked at Gabriel. "I will finish the translation and get it to you or Sebastian personally."

"If you cannot get to one of us, call this number. I will send Joshua for it." Gabriel handed him a small slip of blue paper.

"The vampire that has caused the stir amongst the Concilium? You would trust him with this?"

Gabriel looked at me when he replied, "Yes, I trust him with my life and hers."

We gathered our few possessions and headed out the back door of the bookstore. Now that Gabriel only had a mild limp, we were able to navigate the streets quickly. We were a block from the car when Peter grabbed my arm and shoved me into a store. I tripped on the threshold and almost fell into a stand of tacky souvenirs.

As I spun around and was about to get angry, he clamped his hand over my mouth and pulled me behind a rack of novelty sweatshirts. His eyes bulged at me, and then towards the window. I peered outside between the shirts. I was shocked to see Phineas. He was talking with intensity on the phone and didn't appear to be happy.

"Where's Gabriel?" I mouthed.

"Next door," he returned.

The elderly storekeeper with shaggy eyebrows glared at us in our hiding spot. I settled onto my knees; it looked like Phineas was going to be there for a minute. He rested against the glass in the front window as he listened.

Peter leaned in and whispered, "How are you today?"

"Good," I mumbled.

"I don't know if I would be." He took my hand, and I suddenly felt awkward. He was too close to me. "If...you need to talk. If you need me. You know I'm here for you. Right?"

I suddenly flashed back to when he had kissed me on the

cheek months ago. I wrote it off as nothing, but there was the slightest edge in his voice. I hugged him and gave him the friendship pat on the back. "Thank you," I murmured and pulled back. I looked through the rack again. Phineas had disappeared.

Peter moved closer to the window. "I don't see him." He casually stepped outside, keeping mostly hidden, and looked both ways. "He's about a block down. He just turned the corner. It's clear. Come on."

Darting after him, I glanced back at the old man who was still glaring at us. I wondered what he must have thought, with all our scrapes and bruises, hiding in his store. Gabriel emerged from the adjacent shop. I wanted to make some quip about being out of his sight, but I wasn't up to joking about anything.

I felt like a free radical bouncing around—no place to call home and everything around me getting damaged. I wondered if I should simply disappear. *It might be better for everyone.* I gazed at Peter and Gabriel. Both of them had almost died because of me—more than once. Joshua too. The hopelessness I'd felt the night before returned.

I followed the boys back to the car. We climbed in, and there was a blur of travel down highways, side streets, and country lanes, over a body of water, and eventually to another safe house. Twenty-four hours later, we boarded the DART in Dublin, Ireland, headed to the city center. Finally, we took a cab to a location within an area called the Temple Bar District.

We entered a pub through a backdoor, emerging behind a line of older gentlemen at the bar watching their beers. We slid past them into a hall and entered a room marked "Private." Inside, there was a spiral staircase behind a panel. I followed Peter up the steps.

Two flights up, we entered a narrow room with an eerie glow because the bottom window had been painted over with green spray paint. Some boxes were piled all over and some bedrolls heaped in the corner. My spirits dropped. I'd thought we were meeting up with some of the others, but it looked like we would be holed up here instead.

I started to take my bag off my shoulder when Gabriel said, "This way." He pulled back another panel and revealed a passageway.

I looked into the passage, and then at the room I was standing in, confused at how this was possible.

Gabriel explained. "It is an illusion. The way the buildings butt up to one another. We were able to put in a bridge that you cannot see. We can get to the adjoining building without being seen."

I was astounded at the network the Watchers had built. I couldn't fathom it. We went through and came out in a small living room in the other building. Gentry and Leslie were curled up with their noses in books.

Gentry shot out of her seat and yelled, "They're here!" Then she ran over to us with Leslie on her heels. They both grabbed onto me and held tight. When they released me to hug Peter, I almost toppled over. Sebastian entered the room and hugged me, his beard tickling my forehead.

We must have looked beat-down. Gabriel's arm was still in the sling, Peter still had a split-lip and scratched up face, and I had the horrible bruising around my neck.

"I'm glad you're safe," Sebastian murmured.

I was hugged and greeted by everyone who filed into the room. It looked like everyone had made it. But I didn't see the one person who I wanted to see more than anyone else. The feeling of loneliness surged inside me.

And then there was a cool hand on my lower back. I turned and buried my face in his chest. I squeezed him so hard; it was like I was clinging to him for my life. He held me there, chin on top of my head, rocking ever so gently, while rubbing my back. He continued to hug me until I pulled away. I didn't care if we embraced for too long in front of the others. I needed him now more than ever.

Sebastian started speaking to the three of us. "We need to debrief, but we'll give you a chance to clean up." He called over to Leslie and Gentry. "Ladies, would you show Aleria to her new room?"

"Absolutely," Leslie replied, her eyes aglow. She looped her arm through mine and pulled me towards the hall.

I didn't want to leave Joshua's side—and honestly felt a little panicked—but allowed myself to be pulled away.

Walking down the hallway, Leslie beamed. "You are going to be even more in love with me than you already are!"

Gentry agreed. "I have to admit, she had a wee bit of fun on your behalf."

She let out a little excited squeal. We climbed the staircase to another floor and proceeded down the hall. She swung open a door and said, "Duh duh du dahhh." I couldn't help but smile. She was being such a dork. She pulled me into the room when I didn't move quickly enough.

"I got to shop for you! And you have a room all to yourself this time." I made a sad face at Gentry, but on the inside I was more than thrilled. Not that she wasn't a great roommate, but the thought of my own space was bliss.

The room was double the size of the one I'd shared with Gentry. Cabinets ran halfway down the wall on the left and a full-sized bed was nestled in the corner. A small desk resided under the window, and to the right, was a cozy sitting area with a red velvet captain's chair and a very old floral couch. The artsy touches in the room could have only come from Leslie.

Gentry spoke first. "Well, love, the room came with the furniture, but we got everything else. I took her to some secondhand stores, and she went a little crazy. She found an entire bolt of fabric for a few pounds and—"

Leslie interjected, "I remembered you always said you wanted a canopy bed when you were younger."

The fabric she'd found was a deep red and cut it into four panels. She'd tied them together in a magnificent swirly knot, and splayed them out from the ceiling over the bed like a mosquito net. Then she'd strung white Christmas lights along the fabric and clear across to the other wall, framing the window. It was beautiful. Shabby chic perfection.

"You did this for me..."

"Aye, and that's not the least of it." Gentry walked over to one of the cabinets and opened it while tucking her red hair behind her ears. "Since I'm your body double, she made me try everything on. They'll fit brilliantly." Probably a dozen outfits were neatly hanging for me.

I walked to the bed and plunked down, feeling overwhelmed. "Thanks, guys. You are awesome."

"We arrived three days ago, so we had some time. Everything has been at a standstill. The way people have been actin' around here, we figured you'd had a rough time of it. And lookin' at you..."

"Nah, near-death experiences. I scoff at them." I tried to laugh, but I still couldn't. I paused. "How were your travels? Did everything go smoothly?"

"Not exactly. When we got to the train station in Slough, Uriel recognized a familiar of the Italian coven. She had been assigned to them for a few years. So we ended up flying out with Sebastian and Joshua."

"Aye, and Joshua knew something went amiss before Gabriel

failed to check in. He sort of went mad late that first night. He said something was wrong, and you were in danger. He paced back and forth like a wild thing caged. I don't think he slept a wink 'til we got a message late the next morning."

Oops. I hadn't even thought about check-in when I sedated Gabriel.

"It was a bad day," was all I could say.

"Where'd you disappear to after the initial evacuation?" Leslie asked.

"We were sent to check out a lead Gabriel had. There wasn't much action after that. A lot of waiting."

There was a knock at the door. I opened it to Joshua, and the tenderness he had in his eyes made my breath hitch in my chest. I ached to reach out and touch him, but instead I opened the door wider so he could see I still had visitors. His posture straightened slightly.

"Sebastian would like to see you in a half hour. You have a little more time to clean up if you want."

"Umm, yeah, that would be good. Will you be there?"

"Yes." He gave my arm a little squeeze and disappeared down the hall.

"Well, love, we should let you get ready. Shower is across the hall, two doors on the left. There's a cabinet in there with towels." She pulled open a drawer. "Your toiletries are in here."

"Thanks. Where are your rooms?"

"We are at the end of the hall across from one another."

"Who's next to me?"

"There was some shuffling yesterday. Now you have Gabriel on one side and Uriel on the other."

"Are you serious?" I asked, giving them a withering look.

Leslie pursed her lips and suppressed a smile. "Yup. Michael and Raphael are down a floor, each next to an entrance."

"They're staying? Since when do four Slayers stay in one place? I thought it was a fluke they were all in London at the same time."

"T'was, but somethin' happened. They're here for now." Gentry shrugged and opened her pale-green eyes wide. "Sebastian hasn't breathed a peep."

"Alrighty then. Okay. I better hit the shower before I run out of time."

"Bye, love." Gentry gave me a peck on the cheek as she left.

"Glad you're okay. See you later," Leslie said as she gave me a sideways hug and headed down the hall.

The shower helped me clear my head. I made a list of the things for which I needed answers. Maybe it was brazen of me, but I wanted to use the Watchers' information to do just that.

When I was dressed, I stepped into the hall and realized that I had no idea where to go. I stood there and looked one way, and then the other. It seemed like this floor was mostly housing, so I decided to go downstairs. I ended up in the living room where we had originally entered. I found everyone. Gentry, Leslie, Peter, Ian, and all the other trainees were gathered around watching television.

"Would one of you mind pointing me in Sebastian's direction?"

"Sorry, love. Down the hall, the other side of the stairs. You'll run into it. I can take you, if you'd like," Gentry offered.

"Thanks, I got it."

I turned and headed towards the debrief, determined that the information would go *both* ways in this meeting...

...but I was also afraid that I wouldn't like the answers I got.

PARADISE LOST

The hall creaked with age as I ambled down the worn wood floor. The door to the meeting room was ajar, spilling warm light into the otherwise dark passage. I knocked.

"Come in, child," Sebastian's gravelly voice beckoned.

"Hi." For some reason, I felt like I was being called to the principal's office, even though I knew I wasn't in trouble.

The overstuffed room was lined with wall-to-wall chocolate-colored bookcases; small sconces with amber lights illuminated each one. It was dark yet inviting, putting me at ease.

Sebastian, Gabriel, and Joshua were seated in a circle of furniture in the corner, mismatched pieces from different genres: a slipper chair, wingback chair, loveseat, and wooden armchair. I maneuvered through some boxes and random bits of furnishings to get there.

There were five seats total. The armchair and a space on the loveseat were open. I hesitated. I wanted to sit next to Josh on the loveseat, but headed to the armchair instead. I started to sit, when Sebastian said my name. I stood erect and looked up at him, a little confused.

"Go ahead and sit on the couch; I'm not blind. I appreciate both of you having discretion, but with all that's happened, and all that's going to happen..."

Part of me thought he was trying to trick me into admitting something, but he was always straightforward. I started to get a little nervous. I looked at Josh, and he shrugged his shoulders, so I moved to the couch.

"Is Peter coming?" I asked.

"We finished a few minutes ago," Sebastian answered

"Oh." I was surprised for the second time.

"I wanted to start with the train station. Gabriel told me that even though you defied his orders to flee, you kept your head and never panicked."

"I suppose. I felt panicked. I guess I just trusted my gut," I explained, sounding really hesitant.

"How did you know the woman was a vampire?"

I bit my lip, almost embarrassed. It seemed so superficial. "I didn't. It was her shoes. They were really ugly, and I'd noticed them in the pub earlier. She'd changed her clothing, but not the shoes."

He continued to ask question after question. We went through everything step-by-step in excruciating detail. When we got to Gabriel's questioning of the evil Euro-vamp, I still had a question. "Gabriel, why did you ask who'd sired her? I expected 'Who sent you?' to come out of your mouth."

"Simple. I did not sense her. There has been only one other vampire I had not sensed."

"Bowen," I stated.

"Yes. I wanted to see if there was a connection. If she was being truthful. But he has not used the name Belenus in centuries, and she was not that old. If she had been, there would have been no way Peter could have held her off that long with the weapons we had at hand, even with the surprise blow to the head."

"Do you think she was telling the truth?"

"Maybe. She may have simply used an older name to make a point. He was worshipped as a god back then. A deity is a little more frightening than a younger vampire. She was most likely trying to make herself appear more formidable."

Sebastian asked, "When Gabriel questioned her, what do you remember her saying?"

"A lot of it was gibberish to me. She seemed like she wanted to scare me—specifically me. General doom and gloom stuff. Threats to humanity, bounties on our heads, death to all slayers. Blah, blah, blah. Oh, they aren't allowed to kill me. I'm to be captured. Something about waking the gods. Then there was a name I didn't know. The Onerous are here? The On…er something or other."

"The Oneiroi," Sebastian offered.

"Yes, that was it. Who are they?"

"It's not important right now. Anything else?"

"Besides the evil cackle? Ummm, oh…" My stomach fell again at some of the words she used. "I didn't catch everything, but she looked at me. Said they were going to harvest me for the Devourer. That he would rip my innocence away, and with it he would…" I couldn't remember. I'd stopped thinking straight at the 'innocence ripped' part. I picked up a throw pillow off the empty chair and hugged it to my chest.

Gabriel finished the phrase. "He would be able to *see* all."

"What does that mean?"

"I still have more questions." Sebastian started to steer the conversation away.

That sick feeling in my stomach came back. "I'm sorry, but no. Sir, I don't mean to be rude, but isn't this about my future?

Why won't you answer me? Who are the Oneiroi? What does 'seeing all' have to do with me?"

The room was uncomfortably silent. I could hear everyone breathing. I was playing nervously with the tassel on the pillow. I didn't realize that I was destroying it until Josh put his hand on mine. He kept my hand in his and rested it on top of the pillow.

Sebastian finally spoke. "The Oneiroi are from Greek mythology, Ovid's writings, and some other works. Some say they are sons of Nyx or the night; in other works, sons of Hypnos, the god of sleep. There are three brothers: Morpheus, Icelos, and Phantasos. They have the ability to infiltrate and influence dreams."

"So why did she say they are here?" I asked.

"Because three vampire brothers assumed those names during the Middle Ages; they had the same gifts. Their favorite prey was Seers. Phantasos would alter the physical world of the dream, setting the stage for his brothers. Icelos could cause mind-bending nightmares. Morpheus liked to appear as someone they knew and feed them lies. When all three worked together, they could alter a vision to the point that the Seer believed it was truth. We lost Slayers and Watchers because of false information," he explained

"So they *just* feed them false information? You said 'prey.' Not that the false information wasn't bad." I was trying so hard to make sure I clearly understood what he was saying.

"No, they drove some to madness. A mind can only take so much, and never being able to sleep…"

My throat felt horribly dry. "Do you think they could do that to me?"

"Honestly, we don't know. We are hoping that since you're of the Lux, you can resist them. If they are, in fact, back."

Gabriel added, "Or at minimum sense what they are doing and know it is not to be believed."

"But they can't invade your mind without some of your blood. They have that limitation, according to our archives."

I tried to cover up the terror I was feeling inside by joking, but it came out too forced. "Note to self—don't let them drink my blood. Isn't that a general rule for all evil vampires?"

"All evildoers would be good," Sebastian winked.

"I think I understand the Oneiroi part now, but the 'bringing back the gods' comment she made?"

"The raising of the Ancients, the oldest of the vampires that pre-date Christ. They used to play gods and have worshippers. They were incredibly powerful. Many of them have gone dormant for one reason or another. Some have slept for centuries."

"Are there very many of them?"

"We think less than one hundred, but we don't have an exact number. Vampires existed for fifty years before the Watchers were *officially* founded. The Sentinels didn't record anything. And many of the earliest records have been destroyed," Sebastian said.

This was the first time I had heard the term *Sentinels*, but I had to pick a question from the million racing through my head. I decided to stick with the paper trail.

"Destroyed by vampires?"

He swayed his head slowly from side to side, weighing the question. "Some. Disasters took others. The burning of Rome in 64 A.D., the Great Fire of London in 1666, and so on."

"Mmmmm." I nodded.

Sebastian asked about Winslow and my reaction to the prophecy. It reminded me of my *Paradise Lost* questions. When he finished with his line of inquiry, I pulled out the folded piece of paper from my pocket. I waited for a natural transition to ask. Once Moloch was brought up again, I did.

"I was wondering, while Gabriel and Winslow were translating, I did some reading." I paused, trying to choose the best words. "I found something in a piece of literature, and I can't help but wonder if this is the same Moloch?"

"What were you reading?" Sebastian asked quizzically.

"*Paradise Lost*. I copied some excerpts starting at line 381. It says:

> 'The chief were those who from the Pit of
>   Hell Roaming to seek their prey on
>   earth...
> Abominations... cursed things... And with
>   their darkness dare affront his light.
> First Moloch, horrid King besmear'd with
>   blood.
> Of human sacrifice, and parent's tears, their
>   children's cries unheard, that passed
>   through fire...
> Of *Solomon* he led by fraud to build. His
>   Temple right against the Temple
>   of God...
> To do him wanton rites, which cost
>   them woe...
> Of Moloch homicide, lust hard by hate...'

And it goes on. Is this writing about the same Moloch you are talking about?"

It got quiet again, that same awkward silence that meant I was onto something. When they didn't answer right away, I added more. "And there was another familiar name. Maybe it's nothing, but a little further down in the text, Milton used the name Dagan. Isn't he the captain of Queen Agrona's guard?" I still remembered the look he gave me when we were in the warehouse.

I didn't wait for an answer.

> "It said: 'Dagan his Name...
> Rear'd...dreaded...
> He also against the house of God was
> bold... God's Altar to disparage and
> displace...
> Their wandring Gods disguis'd in brutish
> forms...'

And it continues on a little. Is Dagan an Ancient?"

Gabriel answered almost reluctantly. "No, Dagan is not an Ancient; he is something else."

"Something else? I don't understand. What is he? He didn't seem human."

Sebastian and Gabriel looked at one another. I looked at Joshua to see if he might know. He frowned and shook his head, indicating he didn't.

Gabriel made an impatient sound. "He is an angel."

"A fallen one," Sebastian added.

I blinked. "Really?" I didn't know what to think about this. "So some of what Milton wrote about was true?"

"Some," Sebastian confirmed, matter-of-factly.

"So there are angels really running around on Earth?"

"Yes."

"And this one's evil and in league with Agrona?" I asked.

"Yes, since the age of Solomon," he said.

"And Moloch? Is he an angel too?"

"Yes."

That explains the wings in my dream.

"And they sacrificed people to him?" I looked at Milton's lines again. "Sacrificed *children* to him?"

"Yes," Sebastian answered.

Gabriel shifted in his seat and added, "He was the one they worshiped in Solomon's time. He was the one that Agrona fell in league with. He is the reason the tribe was cursed. He, in essence, was the first vampire."

"But it says they burned the sacrifices." I tried to understand.

Gabriel rubbed along his scar. "They were burned, but the sacrifices were first brought to a series of chambers by the priests. There were four rooms total. The outer chamber, that the public could see, was where they burned the sacrifices at the end of the ceremony. The second chamber was where the priests would do the cleansing rituals and bathe them. Then the offering was brought to the third chamber, where the priests would cut them and leave them to their god. Moloch would feed on them. Afterwards, the body would be taken back out to the fires in the first chamber, shown to the crowd and burned for the final part of the ceremony."

My throat felt strangled. "Were they alive?" I could hardly say it. "When they burned?"

"He took the life of the children," Sebastian answered.

I grieved for the children for a moment. I was sickened that someone or something could do something so horrible. Then I realized Sebastian's words were being picked carefully. The children, not all the sacrifices. "Wait. Some were still alive?"

Sebastian pursed his lips. "Aleria, I think this is enough for tonight. You should get some sleep. All of us should."

"Sir, who was still alive?" My heart started beating really hard. "What aren't you telling me?"

Joshua squeezed my hand. I wasn't sure if it was for reassurance or to reign me back.

"Moloch drew power from the sacrifices. If they were pure, he gained more. That is why he demanded children and...virgins."

My palms were sweating. "Wait. You said there were four chambers. What about the fourth one? What happened there?"

Sebastian answered, but he was reluctant. "No priests were allowed in the inner-most chamber. Girls of age, who were found to be pure, were brought to the door. They say—" He stopped, like he caught himself.

"They say what, Sebastian? Please, just tell me."

He let out a very controlled breath. "They say the screams could be heard for miles. After Moloch was done with them, they would be taken to the fires. Their bodies appeared to be branded with symbols afterwards. Some were given to the fires still alive..." His words trailed off.

"No one knows for sure what happened to them," Gabriel said softly.

"Sure we do." I whispered, "Bad things. Very bad things."

It was quiet again.

"And this is what Agrona wants me for. I'm the key to all of this. I'm the sacrifice to bring him back. To unleash him once again. So children can..." I couldn't say it.

"Moloch isn't in this realm. There is no fourth chamber," Sebastian said firmly.

Almost to myself, I murmured, "But there is blood to flow and fires to burn. He said he is coming for me." I let out a morbid laugh. "He wants to see all. He needs a Seer to be sacrificed—one of the Lux. He wants my power. I understand now..."

I got up and walked to the door. I turned and looked at their haunted faces and added, "I can't help but think the world would be safer if I didn't exist. If there was no way he could return."

Then, after a long pause, I added, "Maybe one of you should just kill me."

With that, I left the room.

I heard my name, but I just kept walking.

11

CONTROL

M y thoughts were scattered as I paced back and forth in my room. I didn't want to go to bed, because bed meant sleep, and sleep meant dreaming, and dreaming meant nightmares. I didn't want any of this.

For a while, the glamour of my new life had felt exciting, but now that fate seemed to be stealing my free will, I bucked against it. I'd probably cried more in the last few days than I had in my entire life. And now, Sebastian seemed to look at me differently. Maybe it was my imagination. I didn't want my being the Nexus to change who I was.

It all came down to this: I hated not feeling in control.

Still fighting sleep, I crawled on top of my desk to look out the window of my dark room. There wasn't much of a view, but I could see part of the alley and the street it spilled onto. There was a streetlight where the alley met the road. I sat, mesmerized, watching the rainfall in the glow of the light. The occasional car whooshed by, scattering the puddles on the ground.

My head started drooping, but I still fought it. I squinted at the clock again when it was 3:30 A.M. Sighing heavily, I decided to toss in the towel. My left leg had fallen asleep, and the pins and needles stabbing sensation was a painful reminder that I'd been sitting there for too long. Maybe not having a roommate was bad. I crawled into bed and pulled the covers over my head for protection. My body felt heavy, and I was out in minutes.

<hr/>

Terror woke me. It was pulsing through my limbs and threatening to burst my heart. I felt like throwing up. So I tumbled onto the floor and crawled to the trashcan. I heaved, but nothing came up. Soaked with sweat, I hugged the can in abject misery.

There was a soft knock at the door. "I'm okay," I rasped. "Sorry if I woke you."

"It's me," Joshua whispered. "May I come in?"

I paused. I didn't really want him to see me like this—not that he hadn't seen me in a worse state before. Somehow, it felt different now. This hole inside me was eating away my hope—eating away part of me.

"Are you okay?" he asked.

Only a sob came out.

"I'm coming in." He entered silently, scooped me up from the floor, and cradled me. My arms were in a ring around his neck, with my head resting on his chest, swaying slightly until I calmed.

After a few minutes, he sat on the bed, keeping me on his lap. "Do you want to talk?"

I deflected the question. "Did you hear me?" I wondered, my voice muffled in his shirt.

"I felt you; I can't explain it."

"It was just a stupid dream," I sighed.

"Night terror, more like," he replied.

"Humph...terror. That seems to be my destiny."

He placed his index finger under my chin and raised my eyes to meet his. "Ali, don't do that. You know it won't always be like this."

"No, I don't. It's not safe to see my family again. And I might go crazy from the dreams, or get captured and die a horrible death. I have no future; there's nothing left."

There was a flash of hurt, but he swallowed it. "I—"

I put my hand over his mouth. "Please, just hold me."

He made a show of clamping his mouth shut, then pulled me tighter. I rested my head on his shoulder again, my forehead on his neck. We sat there for a while, then I slowly moved my head and rubbed my nose up and down his neck, breathing him in, followed by my lips, lightly, barely touching his skin.

When I got to his ear, my kisses became more assertive. I drew his earlobe into my mouth, and he let out a little gasp. I wanted him more than I ever had before. I suddenly felt ravenous, and I violated our number one rule when alone—no kissing on the bed.

I eased off of his lap and stood in front of him. I ran my hands up to his neck and grabbed his hair. I tilted his head back and kissed him. Something broke loose in me; I lost all control. I straddled him and pushed at him so he would lean back. He did, and I followed him down, my lips never leaving his. Our breathing became more labored. My kisses grew more urgent.

"Ali, please stop."

I didn't. He rolled me off of him, but our lips didn't part. We were on our sides facing one another. I hooked my leg over his thigh and pulled him closer. I moved to his neck again, mixing my kisses with bites. I ran my hand up under the back of his shirt.

"Ali, I..." He started to pant.

I looked in his eyes. They were glowing the most brilliant green. I should've stopped; part of me wanted to, but I couldn't. I kissed him again. His fangs had unsheathed. I could feel their prick on my lip and could taste my blood.

He moaned and threw his head back and gulped at the air. "Ali, please stop. I am begging you," he said between gasps of air.

And I should have. "Why?" I whispered back.

He rolled on top of me. Desire burned in my belly. I was shaking. He kissed my neck, and I could feel the scrape of his fangs against my flesh.

Then he reached over and hit the wall with a loud thump. Almost instantly, I heard the squeak of hinges, and there was a knock on my door.

Joshua seemed to vanish.

Gabriel, voice heavy with sleep, asked, "Aleria? You okay?"

"Yes." I rolled my eyes and cringed. "Just a dream."

"Would you open up, please?"

I walked angrily to the door and opened it. I tried to fix my face with emotions other than the ones I was feeling. I opened the door wide. "Sorry to wake you."

"You sure you are okay?" He looked past me into the room, though it appeared empty.

"Yeah, fine."

"And your lip?"

"Oh." I dabbed at it. "I must have bit it," I lied.

"If you need me." He looked at me earnestly.

"Goodnight. Sorry." I closed the door and pressed my forehead against it. It smelled like stale furniture polish. I didn't want to turn around. I knew I was in for it.

When I did, Josh was there—seething.

He whispered, but it might as well have been a yell. "What is

wrong with you? I could have hurt you! I could've killed you!"
His voice cracked. "What are you thinking?" His hands were
clenched into hard balls. It looked like he wanted to shake some
sense into me, but he never touched me. He stood waiting for a
response, not allowing me to avoid the question.

"I don't know," I stammered. I hung my head to avoid eye
contact.

"I don't get it. Do you want me to hurt you? If you do, you
better damn well not make me your executioner!"

And with that, I was suddenly alone. I felt like he'd ripped
my heart clean from my body when he left, or maybe he'd
ripped out my lungs because I felt as if I could hardly breathe.

New sobs started to well up from some part of me I didn't
know existed, violent and convulsive. I collapsed onto the bed
and was barely able to stick my face into a pillow to muffle the
first wails. I must have sounded like a wounded animal.

Now I had ruined the only thing that was keeping me teth-
ered to this world.

And I loathed myself.

12

DOWNWARD

The day was a torment. I wanted desperately to apologize to Joshua, but he was nowhere to be found. His basement room was empty. I searched the building over and over. I finally asked Gentry, and she told me she thought he'd left with Gabriel before dawn and wouldn't be back for days. No goodbyes—just gone.

I guess I deserved to live with the consequence of my behavior. Even if I could've called him on the phone, I doubt he could've really talked. I spent most of the day in my room. After dinner, I went to see Sebastian. The lights were on in his office, but he wasn't there. I decided to wait for him. I sat on the loveseat and drew my legs up to my chest and rested my chin on my knees. I felt spent, both physically and emotionally, dead like a burned-out sun.

Sebastian finally returned. He seemed startled. "I'm sorry, Aleria. I didn't know you were waiting to see me."

I looked at him with intensity. He put the pile of papers down on the desk and eased himself onto the chair across from me.

I had his full attention. "Would they have found me?"

"I'm sorry, who?"

"Queen Agrona. If I hadn't gotten pulled into all of this already." I made a sweeping motion with my left arm around the room. "Would they have found me?"

He leaned back in his seat and scratched his perfectly manicured beard, the light catching the silver streak on his chin. "Your great-grandmother never told you anything, correct?"

I looked at him through heavy lids. "No. I realize now she hinted at it, but my grandmother always shut her down."

"It's almost a certainty. Apparently, the Lux had some sort of training program. Once the dreams and visions had reached full strength, you probably would've reached out for outside help. And medical facilities are often monitored. People with your sort of abilities are often misunderstood. That's how the Watchers have recruited many Seers, and how vampires have picked them off or turned them." An odd look passed over his features like a fast-moving cloud.

"What?"

His hand returned to his beard, and he combed through his whiskers with the tips of his fingers. He thought for a moment. "A curiosity."

He stood and walked with heavy steps to his desk to pick up a well-worn leather book with tattered ribbons poking out. I thought it might be a journal. He returned, sitting next to me this time, and thumbed through it.

He drew out an old photograph wedged between two pages. He handed it to me upside-down. The name "Frank" was scrawled in careful lettering on it. I recognized my great-grandmother's handwriting. I turned the photograph over and couldn't believe what I was seeing.

It was the exact same photo of my great-grandmother when

she was about my age that I'd found in her things. She was with two men. Looking at the picture again, I still thought there was something familiar about both the men. They looked to be slightly older, maybe twenty or so. Her face still had the roundness of youth, but theirs were more defined.

I looked up at Sebastian with eyes wide and confused. "How do you have this? This is Nana."

"And someone named Frank," he commented.

I stared at the image. Their faces were serious, in the style of most photographs from that era. One man had his hand on her arm; there was gentleness and affection in the set of his hand.

"Who are they?" I asked, pointing to the young men.

"According to the journal, they were best friends." Sebastian pointed to the dark-haired one on the left. "He was secretly assigned to train and relocate her after the last members of her family were killed. Her mother took a suicide pill when her capture was imminent. It's all here. How he felt about her, that his family had been entrusted with protecting the last of the Lux, a fact that was kept from the rest of the Concilium. All of her cousins had been hunted down and killed. This was the only photo taken of the three of them."

"The name Gabriel called in—Rosemond Le Clair—was that her real name?"

"It was the name she was given at birth. I'm sure her family changed their names regularly to protect themselves."

A thought occurred to me. "If I may ask, why do you have his journal?"

He smiled softly, his eyes crinkling in the corners. "He was my grandfather on my mother's side. I'd only read pieces of his writings. When you returned from York and Gabriel revealed her name, it sounded familiar and reminded me of the journal. I spent last night reading it. That is probably why you looked so familiar when I first met you." He tapped the photo. "There is a strong resemblance." He thrummed the journal with his fingers. "I believe you can see the irony of your ending up in my care."

"Almost like fate." I shook my head.

"Full circle."

"Frank," I said, when a memory surfaced.

"What about it?"

"That was a nickname for my great-grandmother. When I was really young, I remember her being called that. She said it was because she was often too frank when she spoke."

Sebastian looked at the photo, his thoughts far off for a moment.

"Has your family always been in the Watchers?" I asked.

"My mother's side, yes. They were one of the original twelve families; they settled in England centuries ago. My father was a military strategist who was rising through the ranks quickly. He was in the American Navy and stationed in London when he was targeted by a group of vampires who wanted him to plan some raids.

"An asset intercepted a message, and my mother was dispatched to warn him. He didn't believe her—until she helped him evade his would-be kidnappers. Two years later they were married and the Concilium was glad to have him."

"A strategist. Isn't that what pulls you away from your duties as a Keeper?"

"Yes. My time is divided. I have always worked with Slayers who needed me, more as a sounding board and a conduit to the Council, rather than as a trainer. Neither Michael nor Gabriel has ever needed a Keeper."

"Are your parents still alive?"

"No, they passed years ago."

"Have you ever wanted to do anything besides this? Being a Watcher?"

He stood and placed the journal on his desk and sat back in the chair across from me. "No. I suppose I've been blessed. I feel called to what I'm doing. Just as I suspect you feel drawn to the Watchers and to your heritage of the Lux."

I rubbed at a jagged spot on my thumbnail and looked down. "I guess I am. Were any of the Lux ever turned?" I asked, feeling a little guilty I didn't want to make being a Watcher my life's work.

"No, they never turned or captured anyone from your line."

"So, my mom and grandma have never had strange dreams—not like the ones I've had. Nothing prophetic. Did it used to skip generations?

"Rarely."

I nodded. "Where did Gabriel and Joshua go?"

"To help you. To get some information about the Lux. To help you control the dreams. And the visions, when they begin."

"I keep thinking things are going to get better. But they don't."

"They will. Don't lose heart."

I let my breath out in a gust.

He moved next to me and took my hand, gently pressing it between his thick palms. His hands were warm. "Aleria, you are of great value. And about yesterday, I never want to hear you speak of dying like that again. The good you can do far outweighs any risk."

My voice began to tremble. "I just don't like the feeling that I have to be protected all the time. People getting hurt for me —*because* of me. I just…" I forced back the tears. "I just pictured my life differently." I pulled my hand away. "I'll be fine. I just need to process all this. I'm sorry. I gotta…" I quickly stole from the room and raced to mine. I hated being this emotional. I hated not being able to laugh it off or make a joke about it. I hated that I couldn't seem to suck it up and move on. I felt like pieces of me were flying apart and disintegrating so that I would never be able to put them together again. I hated feeling weak. I hated me for the first time in my life.

A short while later, there was a knock on my door. I didn't answer. "Aleria?" It was Sebastian's voice. He knocked again. "I know you are in there."

I rolled off the bed, reluctantly opening the door a few inches.

"Are you all right?"

My mouth turned down in the corners. "Thanks for checking on me. I'll be okay. I just need some time alone."

"My door is always open to you."

"Thanks." I quickly shut the door before I got emotional again.

I spent the next two days in bed. Leslie dropped some food off the first day, Gentry the next. I managed to choke down some water, but the food went to waste. On the third evening, I heard my door swing open with force. I didn't move—at all. It could've been Hades himself coming to drag me to hell. I didn't care.

A warm hand cinched around my wrist and pulled with such force, I was standing in one movement.

"All right, biscuit, enough is enough." It was Uriel in her Aussie, take-no-crap mode.

I went limp and started to fall back onto the bed.

"Oh no, you don't. It's time. And, it smells horrible in here."

She smelled me. "Ugh...you smell horrible, like dirty sweat socks came to die. Okay, missy." She threw me over her shoulder and started walking down the hall. I didn't fight. Her long, blonde locks tickled my cheek and smelled like some type of melon. She walked into the bathroom and flipped on the shower. She didn't wait long enough for the water to warm before I was dumped on the shower floor, clothes and all. It was all I could do not to scream out from the cold. I glared up at her.

"Okay, doll, start scrubbing or I will. And I promise you won't like it if I do it. You have fifteen minutes."

"Fifteen minutes 'til what?" I asked through chattering teeth.

She wagged her eyebrows. "I'm taking you out."

"You mean I can actually leave the building? I thought I had a life sentence."

"Awwr. Such a sourpuss. I've never seen this side of you. Fourteen minutes." She abruptly slid the curtain shut. I heard her tell Leslie and Gentry to strip my sheets and pick out some clothes. A couple of minutes later, she tossed a clean towel over the bar. "Twelve minutes. Chop chop."

I shrugged off my wet clothes and hung them on a hook. I took my time fingering the conditioner through my hair, trying to get the mass amounts of tangles out. There was a giant matted knot on the back of my head from all the hours of tossing and turning in bed.

My body ached from inactivity. My teeth felt thick from the lack of brushing, so I gargled some hot water to get rid of the feeling, but it didn't work much. And then I started to steel myself to the idea of going out.

The moment I stepped out of the shower and into my towel, Leslie entered the bathroom. "Okaaaayyyy, right this way." She wrapped a robe around me, ushered me down the hall to her room, and sat me on a stool in front of the vanity, my back to the mirror. Gentry arrived with a shoebox full of grooming products and a fist full of bobby pins. "Do you want to be a blonde or a redhead?"

For some reason, this surprised me. "Uh, either. Whatever you think is best."

"Definitely red. You need a little fire in your belly again."

I sat silently, their empty vessel to mold. They worked quickly to pin curl and wig cap my hair. Then they had me pull on a form-fitting black shirt with scrunching on the sides before crowning me with a wig.

Gentry handed me a short brown suede skirt. I looked at her. "I have leggings and boots. You won't freeze. Promise," she told me.

She'd read my mind. I nodded and started pulling them on. The boots went all the way up to my knees. Leslie added black liner and smoky accents to my eyes and a pale pink frost to my lips. They spun me around to look in the mirror. The whole process had taken less than fifteen minutes. I felt like I was looking at a stranger. With a few strokes of a makeup brush, they had even altered my jaw line and sharpened my nose. I sat in awe. I hadn't had any training in disguises yet; obviously, they had.

"So, love, you like?" Gentry asked.

I nodded and leaned toward the mirror and touched my face like it was a mask.

"Aye, you can't believe it's you."

I nodded again.

"We know. And yes, we are that good." Leslie grinned.

"And that's kinda the point," Gentry added.

I sat back down and waited as they worked their magic again on themselves. And then Uriel was at the door.

"She ready?" She tipped her head at me.

"Aye, physically. She's still a little away in the head," Gentry answered.

"Good enough for me. Come on, doll." She guided me out the door. I looked at them questioningly.

"We are going to see a band you'll be mad about. Playing a couple of streets over."

Once we got to the stairs, Uriel pulled ahead. We went down them and came out through the bottom floor of the building. I realized that though I'd been there for days, I'd never known how to get out. The bottom floor was a pub, reminiscent of the secret entrance we'd used last time.

When we stepped outside into the crisp evening air, I noticed that on this street, the bottom floor of most of the buildings were businesses, many of them pubs, with laughter echoing out their open doors.

It was Saturday night. Loads of people were hanging out. The smell of fish and chips made me start salivating. My senses were coming back to me, and I realized how desperately hungry I was.

The night sky was clear, and I couldn't remember the last time I'd seen so many stars. Back home, the heavens always seemed hazy at night. I didn't recognize any of the constellations; it was like a different sky than the one I'd grown up with.

Leslie and Gentry looped their arms through mine and kept me moving forward.

"Guys, I'm starving."

"It's alive!!" Leslie announced, dramatically channeling Dr. Frankenstein.

"Aye, the creature speaks."

I rolled my eyes.

Uriel commented, "They have food at the pub we're headin' to. Let's keep moving." Her voice was relaxed, but it seemed she didn't want to spend too much time on the street with all these people. We moved casually, yet purposefully, to the venue.

The pub was crowded with patrons. Someone was smoking vanilla tobacco near the door, and I found it comforting. It flooded my thoughts with memories of my grandfather smoking his pipe in the evenings. Once inside, the clank of glasses and excited rumblings of conversation overwhelmed me a bit.

"Are we even going to find a seat?" I asked Gentry.

"Taken care of." She thrust her chin towards the back corner. There was a huge booth with people in it.

At second glance, I recognized Ian and Peter with some of the others. Ian, one of the other recruits who'd fled with us, was also incognito. His normally strawberry blond hair was darker and gelled into spikes, and his clothing covered all of his tattoos.

Peter had a beanie on his head, a goatee, and a jacket with a fairly high collar. We got to the table, and I couldn't help but smile at his facial hair. He looked so different. I slid into the booth next to him. We were in the angled corner so our knees touched, but were positioned so we could look at one another.

He stared at me a moment, then leaned in to speak. "You look different. I mean, really good—but different."

"I could say the same."

It looked like the band was almost set up. A waitress snaked through the crowd to our table. I ordered a giant plate of fish and chips, knowing that I'd probably regret eating greasy food, but I doubted any would go to waste with this crowd. When dinner arrived, I devoured half the food like a hyena gorging itself. Peter and Gentry both poached their fair share.

The band started playing. Gentry and Leslie were correct: I loved them. Their music had a magical quality—I felt as if all my anguish was melting away as I listened.

Something welled up inside me. It made me want to live. Not just to live—to fight—to live well. As Thoreau would say, "to live deliberately...to suck the marrow out of life."

I looked at everyone in our group with new eyes and was overwhelmed by the feeling of family. *This is home now.* Peter and Gentry were whispering to one another and laughing, with a surprising amount of affection. Leslie was closing her eyes, allowing the music to envelop her. Ian drummed on the table with the beat. Uriel bobbed her head slightly as she sat alert, watching the crowd, probably for threats.

The band finished their first set. Recorded music replaced the live while the musicians gathered at the end of the bar. I was still quiet, but my outlook was infinitely better. I enjoyed being the observer. It was nice seeing everyone having such a great time, like the stress of the last week could be wiped away.

The band returned to the stage a short time later. I leaned back, ready to savor the final set. Uriel tilted forward slightly and nodded her head. I looked towards the door. Gabriel was moving through the crowd towards us; he was no longer limping, and he had shed his sling. You would never have known that a week ago I had been stitching him up.

I strained forward to see if he was alone, but I couldn't tell. Uriel got up and met him a couple of yards away from the table. They talked in one another's ears; their body language was pretty relaxed. They'd been speaking for the length of a song when Joshua ducked around them.

He took Uriel's seat on the end, with Peter and Gentry between us. When he looked at me, I placed my hand over my heart and mouthed the words, "I am so, so sorry."

He smiled his warmest smile and mouthed back, "Forgiven."

I smiled back at him with unguarded affection, sparks swirling around inside me. Then I caught myself and broke the eye contact. I hadn't asked Sebastian if we still needed to keep things under wraps. When I looked back at him, he was still watching me, his eyes soft.

A few tables were pushed aside near the band, and people started dancing. The next thing I knew, Leslie was tugging at me to get up and dance. Soon, most of our group was up. Uriel didn't seem very happy, nor did Gabriel. Both stood sentry on opposite sides of the pub. Joshua stood next to the booth.

It felt good to dance. There was a freedom in it I hadn't felt in a long time. I danced with the girls, then with Ian who was surprisingly good. At one point, he spun me around and dipped me with such ease that I felt like I was a great dancer, only to realize a moment later that I wasn't, when I danced with Peter. I made a mess of his feet.

It was one of those nights that I realized was magical while it was happening. The ones when you wish you could hold all the imagery and feelings inside forever to relive it over and over. It was perfection.

I caught Gabriel out of the corner of my eye tapping his wrist. Then, I felt Joshua next to me. I thought he was going to pull me off the floor, but he actually started to dance with me. He leaned down.

"Gabriel wants us out of here in two."

"Dance with me for one and a half?"

"Of course."

I started thinking about the last time we'd danced. It was my birthday, and he'd saved my life for the second time in two days. I wrapped my arms around his waist and rested my head on his chest. The song ended, cheating me of thirty seconds. I grabbed my jacket along with everyone else, and we spilled onto the street. Uriel took the lead; Joshua and Gabriel dropped to the rear. As I exited, I caught Peter's eye. He looked at me with the oddest expression, like I was a stranger.

I pushed his shoulder and said, "What?"

A smile flickered on his face like flame in wind. "It's nothing," he replied. But he wrapped himself in silence and looked into the distance.

I hooked my arm around his, concerned. "You sure?"

Another fleeting smile. "Uh, yeah. Just tired, I guess." He rubbed his chest like he was suffering from acid reflux. After a long pause, he seemed to remember I was walking with him. "Um, you okay?"

"Getting there. Better, I—" I stopped short.

"You?" Peter prompted.

"I'm…I don't know," I said, as I gently hip checked him. "Just tired, I guess." We walked arm in arm, but we didn't speak.

Our building came into view, and I stopped, an odd sensation slithering over me. It looked like Phineas was standing near the entrance. I whispered his name, looking fixedly ahead.

"Phineas? Where?" Peter asked. He sounded confused.

I didn't understand the question. Phineas was right there. Suddenly I felt cold, like icy fingers were running over me from crown to toe; then like the breath was being pressed out of me, and I wasn't sure if my legs would hold me.

Grabbing at Peter, he swiveled around to face me. I clutched his shoulders, vertigo seizing me. His hands were on my waist, steadying me.

I looked past Peter to the building. Phineas was both there and not there at the same time. The edges of him were ragged, and the light was wrong. I was seeing him in daylight. He wasn't in front of our building. But I recognized the building. It was one block over with stained glass around the door; we'd walked past it twice this evening.

Then it hit me: I was having a vision. It started to fade, so I concentrated with everything I had. It came into sharper focus, but it became painful. I gasped.

I started describing what I was seeing in between laborious breathes. "Phineas...waiting for someone...looks nervous...or angry...Someone on a motorcycle pulling up... all in black..." It started to fade again.

Part of me realized Gabriel was telling Uriel to get everyone inside. When I refocused, a new wave of pain sunk its claws into me. I did my best to stifle the whimper.

"He doesn't know...maybe..." I couldn't speak through the pain.

Of course visions would hurt. I recognized the next sensation. My vision narrowed into an ever-shrinking tunnel, and I felt my legs give out. I was losing consciousness—everything went black.

I started to wake. For a moment, I want to feel sorry for myself. I wasn't safe in my dreams and now I wasn't safe while I'm awake. But I was determined to fight. I'd hit bottom; now it was time to suck it up and move on.

The last thing I remembered was Peter pitching forward, keeping me from hitting my head. I realized I wasn't alone, and I wasn't exactly sure where I was.

My eyes fluttered open, just as I felt a cool hand pushing wisps of hair back from my face; my wig was gone. Bobby pins were pressing into my scalp on the back of my head. I was on my bed, and Joshua perched on a chair next to me. I could hear murmurs in the sitting area.

"How—" My voice came out as a squeak. I cleared my throat. "How long was I out?"

"Half hour." Josh's brows were pinned together. "How are you feeling?"

The world started to spin when I sat up. I rubbed my temples. "I'll be okay in a moment."

My eyes drifted to the sitting area. Gabriel and Sebastian were watching me. They seemed too big for my little room.

I swung my legs around onto the floor, and my head felt all loopy again. I wondered if I was going to feel this bad every time I had a vision. Josh moved next to me on the bed and put his arm around my shoulders. I rested my head on him. "Thank you." It helped my dizziness dissipate, like there was a fixed point in the room. "I saw Phineas," I said.

"Where?" Sebastian asked.

"Here in Dublin. One street over." I tried to remember everything I had seen. "He was waiting for someone. It was during the day. A person on a motorcycle pulled up, dressed all in black, but it was a vampire, in some kind of daylight gear. The visor on the helmet looked like the glass in Tyran's car. He handed Phineas a metallic tube; it looked a lot like the stainless steel cigar holder my dad has. I couldn't hold onto the vision after that."

"You said, 'He doesn't know,'" Gabriel prompted.

"Oh, my first impression was that he didn't know it was a vampire. But maybe he did. I'm not sure."

"Anything else?" Sebastian asked.

"I don't think so, but I couldn't tell *when*. I have no idea if this happened already or if it is going to happen."

"We haven't seen him in town yet," Sebastian stated.

"Yet, you sound like you expect him."

Joshua gave me a little squeeze. "We saw him while we were

away. We just missed him in Paris, and we ran into him in Belfast."

"And he was in York," I added.

"Yes, it seems he is gathering information on the Lux, too. But Blackthorne claims he didn't send him."

"Do you think Blackthorne is lying, or do you think Phineas is acting alone?" I wondered aloud.

"That remains to be seen," Sebastian answered. "Much of what caused the schism in the Concilium has been healed, but there's still friction. I fear there will always be discord between the Council and Conclave. Members of the Conclave still call for an extermination of all vampires."

Gabriel altered the subject. "We managed to locate a journal that was passed down between members of the Lux. It has methods on how to control the visions and dreams."

"And maybe how to keep from passing out like a lame-o?" I rolled my eyes at myself, feeling like a wimp.

Sebastian chuckled. "I don't think you could ever be accused of that. I think I'll take my leave. Get some rest. We will start your new training in the morning." He gave me a sympathetic smile as he moved to the door. Of course, the sympathy made me feel worse.

"Good night." Gabriel nodded and stealthily moved towards the door, then closed it behind him.

Joshua and I were alone. We sat in silence for a few minutes, listening to one another breathe. I pulled the remaining bobby pins from my hair, and it fell in spirals around my shoulders.

Joshua kissed me on top of my head. "I should probably let you get some more rest."

"Actually, ummm. I would like to talk. If that's okay?"

"There is talking that needs to be done," he acknowledged, hesitantly.

I stood wobbly-legged and moved to the couch; he followed. I sat with my back against the armrest and pulled a blanket over my lap so I could sit cross-legged. Now that I could finally talk to him, I didn't know how to start. I repeatedly tried to begin, but couldn't.

He had mercy on me and initiated the conversation. "I'm sorry I left without saying goodbye."

"You have nothing to be sorry for." I shook my head. I couldn't believe he was apologizing to me for *anything*.

"Als, I've always understood you. Our whole lives we've been on the same wavelength. You've never baffled me like most women. But, I'm confused now. I can't figure out what's going on in your head. No judgments, I promise. Please just tell me what you're thinking."

"I'm so, so sorry. I have this galaxy of regret from what happened before. It wasn't fair. I totally lost it." I struggled for a moment. "I'm not gonna lie. Part of me wanted to die. Past tense." I gave him a weak smile. "But, I do honestly feel like everyone would be safer if I just disappeared. And when I say everyone, I mean *everyone*—in the world. Without me, Moloch can't be raised."

He pursed his lips, not liking what I'd said, but he allowed me to continue.

"Then, there is this other part of me that feels like I'm always being punished for being good. Whether it's for not doing drugs at a party or not letting my ex into my pants. And now, if I am captured because…" I felt embarrassed even saying this. "Since I have managed to stick to my convictions and actually remain a virgin, I get to die an extra horrible death. Maybe I was trying to seduce you. I don't know. I mean, why do I try? What is the incentive to be good? I don't know the purpose anymore." I could feel my lip trembling. "I'm lost," I said in a whisper.

"You need to do what you think is right, what your conscience will allow. Do you really want to alter your beliefs because of someone else?"

I hated admitting he was right. "No," I pouted.

He scooted forward until his leg was against my knees and tucked a strand of hair behind my ear. "Your code of honor. Your goodness. That's part of who you are. Part of the reason I love you. Why I've always respected you."

I acquiesced with a sigh.

He smiled faintly. "I guess it's my turn to help you find your way." He picked up the North Star charm hanging from my neck. "I seem to recall being rather lost not long ago. Someone really amazing helped me find my way. I may have a ways to go, but I know where the path is."

I let out a solitary laugh. "Don't feel too amazing right now."

He cupped my face. "You are, and I'm thankful every day for you."

"Even when I'm a total pain?" I teased.

"Well, almost every day."

"What if…"

"There are always going to be 'what if's.'"

"No, but what if I'm captured? I—"

He cut me off. "Then your job will be to survive, no matter what happens. You keep breathing. Keep fighting. I *will* come for you," he said with deadly seriousness, keeping my face between his hands.

"I don't want you to sacrifice yourself for me. Ever."

"I would never leave you. Never give up," and he shut me up the only way he could have at that point: with his lips.

My lips parted slightly as he kissed me. My body relaxed and I allowed him to help me forget my worries with a tenderness I had never before experienced.

SOMETHING ELSE

My heart was pounding. The air around me was cool and spiked with something metallic. I made several strained attempts to open my eyes, but dark liquid was clouding my vision. Then I realized I couldn't move. A man's face was close, his breath on my face. He was holding me. No, supporting me.

I blinked until the moisture cleared. Terror jolted through my body when I realized I wasn't being held by a friend—it was Tyran. I tried to move my arms, but they felt hollow. I sucked in air to scream, but only a gurgling sound came out.

"Shhh. You're safe now," he cooed. Not Tyran. Bowen.

I relaxed a little. But I was still horrified; there was blood on his face, his shirt, and even in his hair. And the look of anguish on his face. I was so confused. I gasped for air again. He had a tormented expression as the word "sorry" slipped through his lips. His eyes started to glow as his fangs unsheathed. He took a hesitant breath and then he went for my neck.

A scream erupted as I grasped my neck. My hands felt slick. I reached for the lamp in such a panic that I got tangled up in the cord and pulled it off the desk, smashing the bulb. I yelped. Now there was glass all over the floor, and my shoes were in the closet. I rolled to the other side of the bed and was about to get up when the overhead lights flipped on.

"You okay?" Gabriel asked.

I looked at my hands and wiped at my neck. It was just sweat —a lot of it. I squeezed my eyes shut and took a deep breath, my nostrils flaring. "I'll be fine."

"What were you dreaming about?"

My lip trembled. "You don't want to know."

"Actually, I do," he pressed.

"Bowen had me. There was blood all over him. I think it was mine. He said he was sorry. Then, he went for my neck. It was so real. I thought..."

"You thought it was really happening."

I nodded. "And I can't tell if it's a warning or just a plain old nightmare. Do all my dreams have meaning now? Obviously, something has changed recently. Or will I still have normal dreams?"

"We will find out. We brought a lot of material back. Hopefully there is something in it. Would you like me to stay for a bit?"

I hesitated. "No, it's okay."

"And by that, you mean you would like me to, but you do not want to ask for help. I do not mind."

I sighed. "You need sleep too," I weakly protested, as I crawled back under the covers, leaving the broken bulb cleanup for morning.

He picked up the extra blanket draped on the end of my bed and headed for the sofa. "And I will get some." He tossed the blanket down and flipped off the light.

"Thank you," I whispered.

"Any time," he replied.

I curled on my side and hugged my extra pillow. I tried to sleep, but all I could see was Bowen's bloody face. *Why was he saying sorry? Sorry you're hurt? Sorry I hurt you? Sorry I have to eat you—now let me twist my handlebar mustache?*

I looked over at Gabriel. A small amount of light filtered through the crack between the curtains and bathed him in a bluish light. I wondered if he was going to be stuck being my personal bodyguard for the rest of my life. And that brought up another question.

At barely a whisper, I said, "Gabriel, are you still awake?"

"Umm hmmm."

"When we were escaping through the underground and I sensed Tyran: Is it normal for it to be so strong?"

"Yes and no. All vampires have a bond with those they feed on—a blood bond. I suppose it is a safeguard. If their prey gets away, it is easier to find them. Or they can find those they have sired. Vampires do live by a code, and they are responsible to mentor those they have turned or to destroy them. But they have to know how to use the link. From what we understand, they can also shut it off." He got quiet.

"So what is the 'no' part?"

"I have never seen or heard of any vampires that can impact someone they have bitten the way it impacted you."

"It was like a wave hit me or a pulse. I don't know how else to describe it."

"Tyran and Bowen seem to have abilities I have never seen in vampires. All of them have individualized, heightened talents." His voice sounded far off. He seemed to be deep inside his own head. "But, when I fought Tyran a few months ago..." He became quiet again.

I waited and finally prompted him. "When you fought him?"

"You have only interacted with three vampires. You need to understand that when most vampires see a Slayer, they retreat. The only ones who stand a chance against a *seasoned* Slayer are the Ancients. Slayers do fall in battle, but there are usually multiple vampires or some advanced weaponry as you saw the other night."

"I thought Tyran did so well against you because he's so old."

"He *is* old. He is an Ancient; he pre-dates Christ. Even then, we should have been equally matched. And I was slowly losing. There is something else about him."

"Do you have an educated guess?"

"Not one I am willing to share at this time."

"Gentry and Leslie said Joshua knew I was in trouble when we were attacked in the train station."

"Yes, when you gave him your blood, you were linked. He had never fed on living blood before. He is just figuring out how to tap into the connection. There are things we do not know how to teach him. Things only another vampire would know. Some things you have to experience; the book learning will only go so far."

"So you think the connection will get stronger?"

"I do not know. Joshua is another abnormality; his abilities are well beyond his years. That is one of the reasons I know something is different about Tyran and Bowen. I have made several trips to Eastern Europe with Joshua to clean out a hive of feral vampires that had been ravaging a village. He has taken out with ease multiple opponents much older than himself."

"He's always been really athletic. He was first-string in multiple sports," I offered.

"That is some of it, but there is something more. I just do not know what it is," he said. His tone of voice had some finality, like the subject was closed.

I decided to ask another question on the other topic nagging me. "Do you think Phineas is a threat?"

"I do not know. I know he has no love for vampires."

"Yeah, his foaming at the mouth every time a vampire is mentioned or Joshua is around him makes that quite apparent."

"Yes, he has a certain *intensity* about him," he agreed.

"That's a tactful way of putting it. I would have said he was *acrimonious*."

He chuckled. "Pulling out the big guns, eh?"

I paused for a moment. "What happened to him? What made him so bitter?"

Gabriel exhaled slowly. "His parents were transporting some prototypes to a unit in the Ukraine several years ago. Phineas was a teenager at the time. There was an ambush, and his parents were killed, along with Rousseau's niece, Neka. She was a young scientist who'd helped develop the project. She was also the Akhar's god-daughter."

"Both his parents at once." I thought for a moment. "I guess I would be a little bitter too."

"Umm hmmm. His father was tied to a tree and tortured a few yards from the car. Helen and Neka were burned to death in the vehicle. All we recovered were bone fragments amongst the melted metal and glass."

There was a giant knot in my throat. "You think he watched them die?"

"Yes." His tone was solemn.

I didn't have anything else to say. It seemed nothing was simple anymore. I still didn't particularly like Phineas, but now I had a window into his behavior. I could be a little more tolerant. My thoughts flitted like moths from one topic to another. I must've fallen asleep shortly after.

When I woke, Gabriel was gone. The blanket was folded neatly on the couch. A sharp beam of light from the gap between the curtains sliced my room in half. My sleepy eyes tried to focus on a piece of lint swirling in the light. It would almost land on my desktop, only to be sucked up into the current again. I felt like that sometimes, being caught in a current, desperately trying to stay in the light. I sighed. I'd slept well the second half of the night, probably because Gabriel had stayed with me.

I didn't know what to expect from my day. After cleaning up the broken light bulb shards on the floor, I went through my morning routine. I still felt a little off from the last few days, though I was excited at the prospect of getting training for my dreams and visions. I went straight to Sebastian's office; I looked at him nervously while I sat perched on the edge of a seat.

He grinned at me. "Child, you look like you're at the dentist's office."

"I can't help it."

"We are going to work on some focusing techniques and relaxation exercises. There's nothing to worry about."

"That's going to help?"

"According to this," he tapped a well-worn book, "yes."

We spent the next few hours going through several exercises. It was amazing how tired the relaxation methods made me. Sebastian explained that the Lux were able to have lucid dreams and to search for information they needed. They could also tell the difference between prophetic dreams and "normal" dreams, as I put it.

The information also indicated that as I grew in strength, I would be able to hold onto visions for longer periods of time without them taking such a toll on me. But until then, I needed to either let the visions go or risk passing out again.

I told Sebastian it would simply depend on what I was seeing. In my mind, it was worth knowing that there were some shady interactions going on, like the one where the vampire had given Phineas the metal tube.

Classes resumed for all of the recruits, and thus my days became regimented. Sebastian individualized my curriculum, though. I ended up with a ten-hour day with little break. I was elated that I no longer had to go to language classes, for the time being.

> 8:00 A.M. – History and Mythology
> 9:00 A.M. – Surveillance and Evasion
> 10:00 A.M. – Private Seer Tutoring
> 12:00 P.M. – Lunch
> 1:00 P.M. – Weapons
> 2:30 P.M. – Study
> 4:30 P.M. – Physical Training
> 6:00 P.M. – Dinner

Gabriel and Sebastian came up with another safeguard. People on the run rarely stay in one place for very long, so it was also decided that every week or two, we would travel for the sole purpose of having me pop up somewhere on the grid in continental Europe.

Sources said the vamps were using facial recognition software tied into bank ATMs and traffic cams, so we were going to manipulate this. Our first trip was slated for the following day, November 1.

We were given a prototype from Research & Development to test. I was kinda excited to try it. They called it a VSAD, Video Surveillance Avoidance Device. The name was not overly creative, but it worked. The prototype was a scanner of sorts, where a recon device with cameras and an electromagnetic (EM) detector would be rolled down a street. It could be mounted in a car or on a cart. The information would then be downloaded to a handheld device that looked like an MP3 player.

Once the information was compiled, I could walk down the street and see all the cameras' blind spots while holding the device in the palm of my hand. I would know exactly when to look down, change direction, or turn my head to elude detection. The handheld unit could also be used without the recon unit, but I would have no idea which way the cameras were facing. Instead of a cone appearing on the screen showing the angle of the video feed, a large circle showing the entire EM field would be displayed.

R&D had already done some field-testing in a controlled environment. Now it was time to test it in a real scenario. They had chosen downtown Munich. There would still be tourists for cover and lots of escape options. A retired Watcher named Claus had opened a shop in the underground mall not too far from the Glockenspiel, one of the big tourist attractions. We would be able to use it as a staging area.

Gabriel had sent Uriel and Ian ahead to manually survey the area, just in case. They had made a map of all the cameras. Sebastian would monitor everything when we made our run.

Tomorrow would certainly be different. I was both excited and nervous. As I went to sleep, I kept thinking about Gabriel's words from the night before. Both Bowen and Tyran were something different—*something different.*

14

EASY

It was the day of the test; I woke up before my alarm. *Stupid nerves.* I was ecstatic about my first real outing since the night at the pub. Leslie arrived at my room at 5:00 A.M. sharp with the makeup kit and other supplies.

"You ready for this?" she asked, assessing me.

My palms were sweating, so I wiped my hands on my thighs. "I think so...little apprehensive."

"You'll be fine. Two Slayers, a Keeper, and an almost full-fledged Watcher to help. And knowing Gabriel, an army of German Watchers. It'll be cake."

I looked at her warily.

"No, not just saying that. I really think it'll go well. And if the VSAD works as well as the tests, we'll all be in better shape."

I nodded.

"You," she pulled out a wig, "get to go blonde this time."

"You sure? My coloring isn't really ideal for blonde."

"No, but I got this great product." She pulled out a glass container of liquid makeup. "Looks really natural, even when it's altering the complexion or going over prosthetics."

"You are the master."

"Well, my apprentice, let's get started." She smiled.

She aptly attached a nose that had a subtle arch in it. She put a sticky wax over my brows so she could put a prosthetic over them that changed the shape of my lid and brow and was embedded with blonde eyebrows. When she added the false lashes, my eyes looked as though they were set differently.

After she applied makeup over everything, she handed me a tube of lip-gloss with a wand applicator. "Put this on."

I did, then yelped thirty seconds later. "Holy crap! It feels like bees are stinging my lips! What in the heck is in this?"

"Beauty is pain," she giggled, a little too readily.

"You could've warned me," I complained, my eyes bulging.

She fanned a piece of paper at the tears welling up in my eyes. "Don't ruin my work. It's a lip plumper. Very popular in Hollywood right now. No need for collagen injections."

"I think the injections might hurt less," I whined.

She handed me some clothes. I looked at them with disapproval and asked, "Really?"

"The German fashion sense is a little different. You'll look like a native...promise."

"Yes, Obi-wan."

She cocked her left brow. "Okay, I have everything you need for your exit disguise. I labeled each bag for you in the order you should put them on. Do just as we practiced last week. Easy peasy."

"Thanks, Leslie." I latched onto her, and she hugged me tightly, not letting go until I did. "You're a really good friend."

"Hey, don't be sounding like you're not coming back. You're part of our family now. You know I love you too much for anything to happen to you."

I gave her one last squeeze, then shot out of the room with

my bags before I became more sentimental. I dropped them near the back door and headed down to the basement to say goodbye to Joshua.

"Wow, it really doesn't look like you—at all."

"Good." I let out a relieved huff.

"Sooooo...I'll see you tonight?"

"Yup. That's the plan. Back a few hours after dark." I ran through our timeline. "Eighty-minute commercial to London. Three hours from London to Munich on the private plane. Be there by lunch. Three hours in Munich. Five to get back. And an extra hour for incidentals."

"Let's pray there are no incidentals." He pulled me in and wrapped me up in his arms. He pressed his cheek to my forehead.

"Yeah, that would be nice."

"I feel like I've hardly seen you in the last couple of weeks," he sighed.

"You haven't. Sebastian has had you going out every night, and I'm exhausted from my long days. You must be tired now. Weren't you out on surveillance all night?"

"Yes, ten hours. We tracked some vampires all over the city. They don't appear to be hostile, but we'll keep watch."

"Do you know who they are?"

"No, but we got pictures. Running them now. Not associated with the French or Italian covens. That's good news, in any case."

I squeezed him a little tighter. "I gotta go. I have two minutes to get upstairs."

"Okay." He kissed my forehead. "I'm not going out tonight. I'll stay with you until you fall asleep."

"Mmmmmm. Sounds like a plan." I tilted my head back and gave him one soft kiss and then jetted up the stairs.

Within ten minutes, we were off, ready or not. *Fake ID? Check. Disguises? Check. Nervous-wreck-posing-as-a-have-it-together-teenager? Check.*

I pushed my nerves down so far I could have sworn my toes were going to burst, but maybe it was my imagination. Everything went according to plan. We were in Munich in time for lunch, and I was starving—and ecstatic to find that German food was fantastic.

Gabriel and Ian installed the VSAD recon unit into a vehicle. Ian proved to be very good with the technical stuff. I guessed it made sense. He was always tinkering with music equipment. I thought that in another life he would have been in an indie rock band touring Europe, living on cigarettes and one-minute noodles.

I waited with a disguised Gabriel in the warmth of a café while Sebastian and Ian drove down the street. Uriel was already in place near the bank ATM where I was to pull out some money.

"Do you think it's going to work?"

"I have no doubt," he said decisively.

"Really? Not afraid it will transmit my location instead of helping me avoid detection? And that a hoard of leather-clad henchmen with laser guns will flood the streets and carry me off to an undisclosed location?"

"Just drink your coffee." He rolled his eyes at me. I was pretty sure that was the first time he'd ever done that with me.

"What? My keen wit and realistic assessment of the situation making you jealous?"

Gabriel grinned just as his phone chimed. We headed out to meet at Claus's store.

Once there, I carefully removed my disguise, cringing as it peeled every single peach fuzzy hair off of my face. A Watcher by the name of Elsa met us there. She picked up the IDs that we'd already used. She was going to continue to use them and lead our foes in the wrong direction. After I'd used it, I was to hand her the new ATM card in a brush pass on my way to Uriel.

We went over the plan one more time. It was so simple I was tempted to follow Gabriel's example and roll my eyes: walk down street, get money, brush pass, meet Uriel, new disguise on, and get out of Dodge.

This time through, I found out there were literally a dozen Watchers in place to report what happened after our departure. I wondered what they knew about me.

It was much colder in Germany, so it wasn't going to be hard to hide my face. I pulled the hood up on the grey sweatshirt I was wearing under a black wool coat. I wrapped a green scarf around my neck, covering my mouth.

Ian came in with the handheld VSAD and said, "It was flawless. It picked up a camera Uriel and I had missed on the plan we drew up. Someone had a camera outside of their window in a personal residence."

There were words of approval expressed by everyone, but I remained quiet. I knew what I had to do, but I was suddenly getting nervous again.

Gabriel turned to me. "You ready?"

"Always." I winked.

He plugged earphones into my ears, and then connected them to the VSAD. "I will be able to speak to you this way, and it completes the illusion. Give us a two-minute head start, then go. Ian, you are thirty seconds behind her." Gabriel put something in my pocket and disappeared out the door.

I watched the second hand sweep around the blue face of my watch. It seemed to go mockingly slow the second time around. I left the store and headed to the stairs at the corner closest to the Glockenspiel. I walked at a medium rate, one that said, "I have purpose, but am not running for my life."

The VSAD was amazing to watch—a bird's eye view of the streets with color-coded cones appeared. They even showed the movements of sweeping cameras. I wasn't sure how that was possible, but I was watching it. When I got to the bank, I tried to put my ATM card into the machine. However, I missed the slot, and my card popped out of my hand onto the street.

When I bent over to get it, a man stooped down to help. He was middle-aged with crooked teeth and a distinguished amount of grey in his sideburns. He handed me the card, clamped between his index and middle fingers.

"Thank you–I mean, *danke.*"

"Ah, American, vonderful," he said cordially in a thick accent.

"Um, yeah..."

"Don't usually see many your age this time of year."

"Oh, yeah. My dad's here on business. He let me come this time."

"Please, I must say you have beautiful eyes."

"Oh, thank you." He pressed in a little closer than I was comfortable with.

I heard Gabriel over the ear bud. "Get rid of him."

I'm trying!! "I guess I should get back to this." I motioned to the ATM.

"It vas nice meeting you." He smiled again and wiped his bottom lip with his thumb. His watch was loose; I noticed he had a small tattoo the size of a quarter on the inside of his wrist.

"Thanks again." I waved the card and turned my back on him to use it. I watched him in the bubble mirror. He lingered for a moment. It seemed as if he was trying to read over my shoulder.

"Vell, enjoy your stay. Vonderful country," he finally said, then disappeared from sight.

I pulled down the scarf so that my mouth was in view of the camera too. The machine spit out my Euros, and I turned on my heel towards the hotel lobby where Uriel was waiting for me, just two blocks away.

I made it about four steps when I felt it coming on. "Oh, no," I whispered. "Not now. Not now." I breathed to myself, forgetting that Gabriel could hear me.

Cold slithered down my body, and my lungs constricted. I continued to walk, but I could hardly see where I was going. I heard Gabriel order Ian to break cover and get to me.

Tyran stepped into my frayed vision, his cold eyes taking pleasure in something. He grabbed me, digging his fingers into my arms. Hands went up to push him away, but they weren't my hands.

I was inside someone else. The hands were female—long and slender, and on the middle right finger was a beautiful ring with stones of green and purple in a large silver setting that reminded me of a nebula in space.

Tyran whispered into her ear, "How does it feel to *fail?* All this work to protect her, and for naught."

I tried to let go of the vision; I could feel my legs about to give way. I could barely move forward. Then, in the vision, I realized there was a knife in her hand, and she thrust it into Tyran's chest, missing his heart.

He scowled at her, then his eyes started to glow, and I watched his fangs unsheathe like they had that terrible night last June.

"Don't worry. It'll be quick, but it won't be for your friend. She will suffer." His fangs pierced her neck, and I could feel every bit of it. He made a sound like she tasted good, and my stomach turned. I was actually thankful when I felt myself begin to pass out and pitch forward. I'd experienced everything she had—I'd felt death.

Right before I passed out, I heard Ian say, "Miss, are you okay?"

I tried to respond, but I don't think my lips moved. In my peripheral vision, I noticed the man from in front of the bank, and then, everything went black.

15

A WASTE

At first, I heard muffled voices, and then they became more distinct. The air was close and hot, and my body was curled into a ball. I went to straighten my legs and couldn't. Utter terror struck me. I opened my eyes, but it didn't matter because it was pitch black.

I was inside of something—something small. The walls or sides were cool to the touch, the surface felt like laminated paper. The temperature made me think it might be made of metal. Pressing on the walls, I tried to leverage my weight and push it open.

When it didn't budge, claustrophobia hit me, and I started to hyperventilate—there wasn't enough air. I squeezed my eyes shut and slowed my breathing. Freaking out wasn't going to help me. I considered screaming, but for some reason my hesitation to make noise won over—so I kept quiet. My mind searched for a good reason I could be in here, yet I couldn't think of one.

Feeling around, I checked to see if I had anything to help. The VSAD was gone, so I went through my pockets and found the item Gabriel had slipped into my pocket—a phone. I flipped it open and used it to look around. A seam was a few inches down from the top, running all the way around; it had to be a wardrobe trunk.

Suddenly, I swayed from a smooth movement, so I listened. A ding rang out, and then a faint clunk, maybe an elevator. A bump, the sound of metal, and another ding.

I went to the phone book on the cell. Gabriel had programmed in the number of his current cell. I made sure it was on silent. I pressed the phone against my forehead as I thought of what to type. I decided to keep it simple.

"Help" was all I inputted.

Then I noticed I didn't have any bars—no reception.

Now it felt like we were going down. Definitely an elevator...another ding. I lurched forward inside. The moment bars appeared on the screen, I hit send.

I waited.

And waited.

And after a few more excruciating minutes, a reply appeared, but not the one I wanted.

Two simple words: "Hold tight."

It was hard not to scream; the claustrophobia was getting worse. What sounded like a crowd of people became louder, but I couldn't understand anything—everything was in German. I was jerked to a stop with such suddenness that I let out a grunt.

I typed another message: "About to freak out."

The voices grew louder. I was being moved and lurched to the right, then the left, then the right, too abruptly to actually be traveling. Then I was moving again.

There was a terrible crash, and my head smacked against the side. It literally felt like I'd hit a wall. I was jostled by another shove. Arguing? More harsh sounding voices followed by a muffled popping sound, and a beam of light cut into the darkness. I sucked in a sharp breath of air and tried to make myself as small as possible when I understood a bullet had just punched its way through the trunk.

I struggled for breath, trying not to hyperventilate, but my panic was growing. I was helpless—fish in a barrel had more of a fighting chance.

I typed: "Shots fired!" and hit send.

At the very least, I wanted to warn Gabriel about the gun, which was pretty much the only information I knew in my current situation. My mind raced with questions: *How long was I unconscious? How did I get in here? What happened to Ian? Why am I only hearing German? Why is Gabriel not here?*

I was being moved again, but the ground was uneven. There was another type of sound...whirring...and clanking. A voice boomed over the background noise. It was a little ways away.

"*Alle Raus! Beeilt euch...schnell, schnell!!!* (Hurry, hurry! Everyone!!...Quickly!!*"

I could only pick out one word. I knew *schnell* meant hurry up or fast or something close to that. They stopped moving me again.

All of the background noises quickly died off. I carefully maneuvered myself around and pressed my eye against the bullet hole. A stainless steel table blocking was most of my view, but beyond it I could see several men.

One of them spoke; it was the same voice I had heard a moment ago: "*Sprichst du Deutsch?* (Do you speak German?)"

"No," a tense voice replied. It was Ian.

"Vef stopped your Slayers. You can't hold us off forever. It vill be dark in a couple of hours. Leave her to us; ve vill spare your life."

Now that he had spoken in English, I recognized his voice

too: the man with the crooked teeth from in front of the bank. Then what he'd said clicked. *"Stopped your Slayers?"* My heart started racing.

"Not going to happen," Ian responded with deadly seriousness.

"Vef no reason to harm you if ve get what ve came for," Crooked Teeth cooed.

"Step any closer, and you will meet the fate the last group of your men did," Ian threatened.

"Yes, but now there are only the two of you."

Who else is with him? What happened to the rest of them? It occurred to me that Ian didn't know I was conscious. I knew I could help if I could only get out of this thing. I softly patted the side of the trunk with my palm. Almost immediately, I heard someone pop the latches, and then open the lid.

I gulped in the fresh air and squinted at the harsh fluorescent light. We were in a galley-style, commercial kitchen with two butcher-block islands dividing the long room. Large, black rubber floor mats covered the brown tile at each cooking station.

A man with blood spattered on his white dress shirt offered me his hand. Ian was next to him, dressed in a burgundy hotel uniform with gold cording. I looked at Ian for approval, and he nodded.

The man helped me step out of the trunk, but it was on a bellhop trolley that rolled away from me before I could get my footing. I stumbled forward into the man; he grabbed me by the waist and spun me around behind him, then protectively held his ground.

The men across the room took advantage of the distraction and moved forward. I saw a flash of movement from Ian before I heard a thud. I looked around my protector to see one of the aggressors unmoving on the ground with a knife standing like a pillar in his chest. Six were left. They didn't move.

"I have plenty of knives. Stay back," Ian ordered.

Crooked Teeth raised his hands and smiled. "There are too many of us. Please, no more blood needs to be spilled."

The man to his right raised a gun with a silencer and aimed it at Ian. His finger slid to the trigger, and his eyes narrowed. Ian wasn't looking at henchman #2. I stepped out from behind the man guarding me and shoved Ian to the side.

A pop sounded, and Crooked Teeth tried to push the gun down to alter henchman #2's aim, but he was too late. It felt like something bit my right arm. I grabbed the wound. Ian shoved me behind him. After the stinging in my arm stopped, I examined it. The bullet had grazed me, leaving not much more than a deep scratch.

Crooked Teeth screamed a string of words at his men. *"Ihr Idioten, ich bring euch mit meinen eigenen Haenden um, wenn ihr was passiert!* (Harm the girl and I will kill you myself! Idiots!)"

They backed off and glanced at each other nervously. All guns were holstered and knives drawn instead—*great*. We were at a standoff.

At best they couldn't shoot us—*well, anymore*. In the movies, scenes like this seemed to go at a deafening pace, but this was horribly, painfully slow, the tension unbearable. I wondered why we hadn't yet made a move towards the door on the other side of the room.

Slowly, the aggressors split into two groups. Two stayed, blocking the main exit. The others went to the far side of the island and divided again, Crooked Teeth staying directly in front of us, by the break between tables. The others moved to the other side of the room. Ian and I backed up until we hit the wall.

I didn't see a way out of this. I closed my eyes and prayed. It was the only thing I could think to do. We needed divine intervention. I said the word "please," almost inaudibly as I had done so many times in the past.

When I opened my eyes, I looked towards the door just in time to see Gabriel's right arm lock around the neck of one of the men blocking the door. The man's feet dangled, his toes occasionally scratching at the ground while his face blossomed into a deep purplish red.

Gabriel had an AR-15 in his other hand, the barrel pressed firmly against the other man's temple, his head now pinned to the doorframe. He turned white, and his weapon clattered to the ground. I looked as Crooked Teeth whipped his head towards the noise, taking in all 6'4" of the Slayer holding his men captive.

At the same moment, one of the three men at the end of the room launched himself towards us. Ian met him a couple of feet away, and for the first time, I realized he was wounded, blood seeping from his side. Despite that, he grabbed a mop, hit the attacker in the chest with the end of it, stunning him, then hooked it under the guy's arm and flipped him onto the floor so hard his head bounced on the ground. The man moaned and stopped moving. Ian kept him immobilized by keeping his boot on the man's almost nonexistent neck.

Crooked Teeth looked shocked, his gaze moving between Gabriel and me. He licked at his thin lips nervously.

Gabriel's voice was calm, as if he were speaking over the Sunday paper. "Do you know *what* I am?"

Crooked Teeth flexed his jaw and answered through his teeth, "*Ja.* (Yes.)"

"You know *who* I am?"

He nodded, and I could see his mind racing. He looked greedily at me again.

"Then you know you won't get out of here alive unless I will it." Gabriel pressed the AR-15 into door blocker #2's head a little harder; the man inhaled sharply, emphasizing Gabriel's point.

"Vef more men on the way," Crooked Teeth said.

"And so do I." A wicked little smile curled the corner of his mouth. "All of you move to the far side of the room and get face down on the floor." He released the man he had at gunpoint, but kept in his arm the man who was playing the part of a ragdoll. He whispered something into his captive's ear.

The man looked pained and said, "*Zwei.* (Two.)"

Crooked Teeth screamed at Gabriel's prisoner. "Tell him nothing; you know zee consequence."

Gabriel asked his next question aloud. "Who sent you?"

After a long pause, "*Die Königin,* (The Queen)" the man in his arm croaked. Crooked Teeth was growing more furious.

"How many more are coming?"

Crooked Teeth actually answered, "Efryone. It is inevitable." Then he reached into his coat and grabbed for his pistol.

Before he had a chance to get it clear of his clothing, a shot blasted through the room. Blood appeared on Crooked Teeth's forehead as he toppled over. The way his coat, scarf, and tie loosed themselves and flapped in the air made him appear like he was falling apart, like a tower of sugar cubes had been knocked over and spilled across the floor.

I was still reeling from how loud the gunshot had been, and from watching a man get shot in front of me, when I became aware that the other men were already on the ground with their arms zip-tied behind them.

Ian grabbed my arm. "Police are on the way, and we don't want to mess around with law enforcement in this country."

I nodded and followed Gabriel and Ian to the service elevator. "Let's hope Sebastian found a new vehicle," Gabriel murmured under his breath.

He had what looked like a rug burn on the side of his face, his lip was split, and tiny cuts freckled his face and neck. Once on the elevator, Gabriel pushed up the service hatch on the top. "There is no cell reception down here. I want you up top until we know it is clear."

I followed orders, still in shock. They pushed me up through the hatch on the top on the elevator, and I waited literally on top of it in the shaft. When we reached the bottom floor, I heard the doors open and the sound of a diesel engine rumbling nearby.

"It's safe," Ian said, just loud enough for me to hear.

I pulled up the door and swung myself down, landing lightly on my feet. I was a little proud of my agility on that one. I walked out to be surprised at our form of transportation. Sebastian was in uniform behind the wheel of a police van.

"I thought we didn't want to mess with law enforcement in this country?" I asked as we moved towards the vehicle.

Gabriel shrugged. "He is the boss."

We sat on the floor as Sebastian drove us out of the underground garage. Sirens from the distance were growing louder. Sebastian made a series of turns, maneuvering us farther away from the hotel.

"Where's Uriel?" I questioned, alarmed.

"She'll meet us back at base," Sebastian replied.

Gabriel said, "Plan C then," under his breath.

We pulled under an overpass and parked behind a nondescript beige sedan. Sebastian hurried us out of the van, stripping off the police hat and shirt that he'd worn over his other clothes. He had a splatter of blood on his blue dress shirt from that morning. Sebastian handed a slip of paper to the man who'd been helping us.

"William will meet you in ten minutes. *Na, dann, viel Glück!* *(Well then, good luck)*" the man said, as he patted Sebastian on the shoulder and pulled away in the police van with a stoic expression.

We went in the opposite direction in the sedan. It was a quiet trip. Nothing was spoken save a few directions. We arrived at an airport on the outskirts of Stuttgart in the late afternoon after switching vehicles two more times. The hangar we pulled into was fairly dark, and the drone of a small plane engine could be heard from our side of the building.

A broad man with meaty hands and sandy-colored hair greeted us. "Sebastian, old friend, the need must be great to contact me."

Sebastian pursed his lips. "Trusted people seem to be a valuable commodity."

"I still owe you," the broad man replied, a tired smile on his face.

"Thank you, William."

"The Cheyenne is ready to go. If you want to fly under the radar once we hit water, it will take us longer. We will have to avoid shipping routes."

"Yes, we need to be as invisible as possible."

"I'll have you in Ireland in a little over four hours. This way." He motioned to the back door. We grabbed the few belongings we hadn't shed on our journey and boarded the plane.

Once airborne, the strain we were under eased. We hadn't yet stopped long enough to give Ian proper medical attention, and he was looking rather pallid.

"Ian, can I look at that now?" I asked.

"I'm fine."

"Of course you are. Your vampire-chic skin tone is really becoming."

Gabriel cut in. "I want you patched up before we land. Let her help you, and then get some rest."

Ian complied and unwound the bandage we had hurriedly put in place, then carefully pulled off his shirt. I had always thought he just had a sleeve of tattoos on each arm, but they continued onto his shoulder blades and chest—sayings in Latin, flourishes, angels, swords, and all manner of things swirled into a masterpiece of body art over his lean, muscular frame.

To get my attention, Gabriel whistled and tossed me the medical supplies we had. Then he moved to the back of the plane next to Sebastian, where they carried on a hushed conversation. From the intense expressions they had fixed on their faces, I was glad I had something to distract me, even if it was patching up a friend.

"This is a bullet wound," I said, a little surprised. For some reason, I had thought it would be from a knife. We had trained with guns, but until today, I had never seen one used in the field —or anyone actually get shot, for that matter.

"Yeah." He arched to the side, examining it. "It went all the way through. I wasn't too worried," he said calmly.

The bullet had passed through the love-handle area—not that he had an ounce of fat on his body. He was training to be a combat operative to assist Slayers in the field.

"You say that like it happens all the time."

"Nope, first time being shot." He had the same matter-of-fact way that Gabriel accepted inevitable injuries.

"You feel okay? No nausea? No abdominal pain?" I dug through the bag of supplies and took a mental inventory.

"No, I think I lucked out." He reclined in his seat and turned on his side so I could examine it.

I pulled on some gloves, and as gently as I could, probed to see the extent of the injury. Besides the damaged muscle and tissue, it didn't look like the round had punctured anything vital. He broke out in a sweat from my examination, though.

"How much do you weigh?"

"200."

The bottle of local anesthetic had an attached chart that listed dosages. I figured out how much he would need and filled a syringe, thankful I wasn't flying blind this time.

When he saw me coming at him with the needle, he opened his mouth to object.

"It's just a local, and we have four hours until we land."

He closed his mouth, his jaw set in a scowl. *What is with these men wanting to be tough and take the pain for no good reason?*

"As far as I can tell, there isn't any internal bleeding, but I'm not an expert. You want me to stitch you up? Or just tape it and have them stitch it when we get back? I won't be offended either way."

"Stitch me up. I think I'd feel worse off if this was anything other than a flesh wound."

"I figured." I shrugged and gently put pressure around the wound. "Can you feel that?"

"Barely."

"Okay, if you feel pain, let me know." And with that, I started stitching. It didn't take too long. I bandaged everything and gave him an antibiotic. "Let me grab you a new shirt." I slid between the seats and rummaged through his bag, pulled out a black thermal shirt, and tossed it to him. He gingerly pulled it on.

"Thanks," he said as he reclined in his seat, his eyes glassy.

"I think I need to thank you. I have a few memory gaps, but

I'm pretty sure I'd be in the trunk of a car heading to France if you hadn't been there."

"Oh, they would've let you ride in the back seat," he winked.

I rolled my eyes.

"Pretty sure you saved me too," he replied.

"Maybe."

"Not maybe; the guy next to Snaggletooth wouldn't have missed."

I chuckled. "Snaggletooth—I was calling him Crooked Teeth in my head. Yours is better...more apropos."

"I guess the vamps' minions don't get good dental coverage."

I smiled and suddenly felt exhausted, the last of the adrenaline burning off. My head hurt a little. I reached up and felt my forehead and discovered a small goose egg bump. "Ouch," I exhaled.

"Sorry, I didn't get to you before you fell forward. You kinda fell on your face. Your cheek is a little scratched too."

I felt the scrape, but it didn't hurt. "I guess I should invest in a helmet if I insist on passing out all the time."

"Am I allowed to ask what the passing out is all about?"

"I don't know." I bit my bottom lip. "It's not my call." I looked over at Gabriel and Sebastian. They were still in deep conversation. I started to overheat and shrugged out of my hooded sweatshirt.

"Your arm," Ian pointed.

"Oh." I'd bled through my shirt and there was a reddish-brown oval on the fabric. I was thankful I had a tank top on and pulled off my outer shirt. The wound started bleeding again. I cleaned it, but it was just deep enough that it was pulling open. "How are you with medical glue?"

"Awesome," he said with faux superiority. He knelt in front

of me on one knee and firmly held my forearm while he sealed the graze with a steady hand. "This isn't from your fall."

"Nope. A graze."

"Ah, not the only one to get shot today."

"Couldn't let you go home with the only cool battle wound." I looked over at Gabriel and then back to Ian. "Do you know what happened to them?"

Ian moved to the seat across from me. "In a nutshell, the minions pinned their vehicle and rammed it. They told me to get you to the hotel and meet up with Uriel.

"I don't know what happened after that. I carried you to the room where I found four dead men, all with the mark of the French coven. Uriel was gone.

"I worked with three of the local assets to get you out. We put you in a trunk, since carrying an unconscious girl around Munich would look a little suspect. We had almost made it to the service elevator when we were ambushed. Two of the locals were killed. You met the third, Dietrich. He was the one who got the sedan for us and took the police van."

"I guess saying the day didn't go as planned is an understatement." I paused. Ian looked exhausted. "You should try to nap."

"No argument here." He smiled, leaned back, and closed his eyes. Within a few moments, he was breathing deeply.

Leaning back in my seat, I looked over at Gabriel and realized the rug-burn-like marks on his face were airbag burns, and the cuts must've been from the glass of the car windows.

I rolled my head to the side and looked out the window. It was dusk. We were still over land. City lights were starting to dot the landscape as the blue hues deepened. It felt like midnight. My lids were heavy. I noticed Gabriel stand up, so I sat up a little. Sebastian walked through and went into the cockpit, and Gabriel sat down next to me.

"How are you holding up?" he asked, his voice quiet as to not wake Ian.

I didn't give my standard response. Instead, I paused for a long moment. "I've never actually seen someone die before."

"I am sorry. I wish..." He stopped short.

"How many people did we lose because of me?"

"Do not blame this on yourself."

"Why not? I dropped the ATM card so that man could ID me *and* blacked out in the middle of the sidewalk. Ian got shot..." My mind started to jumble up.

"Did you not notice what happened? They were waiting for us. They knew we were coming. You think there were twenty-one French coven lapdogs there by happenstance?"

"Twenty-one?" I blinked, thinking about the overwhelming odds against us.

"Yes. They knew."

"There's a mole," I whispered.

"Yes. We were careful with the flow of information on this. We have a short list of suspects. We will need to tread lightly."

"Weren't they all human? How do you know what coven they belong to?"

"The tattoos. They all had the same one. Either on the forearm or shoulder."

"Thought I saw one." I mumbled. "How many did we lose?"

"Three deceased, one in ICU. They lost seven at the hotel and five where the first attack took place. Who knows what Uriel will do with the one she is tracking."

"It seems like such a waste."

"It would be a waste if we had not learned anything or if we had lost you. We did neither," he reassured.

There was a long pause. "I didn't ask. *You* doing okay?"

He looked like I had taken him off guard. "Yes." He reached

over and squeezed my hand for a moment. "You never need to worry about me."

"I never worry," I lied. And he knew it was a lie—I always worried.

"Get some rest."

"Yes, sir." I brought my hand to forehead and saluted him. He shook his head at me.

"And tomorrow, I want you to tell me about what you saw before the blackout." He glanced over at Ian as if to finish his statement by saying, "When we have more privacy."

Nodding, the knot in my gut returned. I had a horrible feeling about that vision. A hush fell over the cabin; I think we all fell asleep. I woke enough to hear Sebastian return from the cockpit and drift to sleep himself. I couldn't wait to get back. I regretted that my last words to Joshua hadn't been: "I love you." I thought they'd been something like, "Sounds like a plan." *Lame.*

I drifted off to sleep, praying that I wouldn't have a nightmare and that there wouldn't be an ambush waiting for us at the airport. Something needed to start going right.

16

LAST WORDS

A ding over the plane intercom woke me. We were headed to a private airstrip in absolute darkness. I couldn't see lights on the runway at all. I wasn't even sure if the plane had its landing lights on.

Apparently, William had cut off all light in the main cabin once we hit international waters. I wondered why it had sounded like Sebastian would only call him as a last resort. The word mercenary echoed in my head. I wondered how many laws we must've been breaking flying dark and low over the water.

Glimpses of light like pinpricks started appearing on the horizon. We'd been in the air for well over three hours, so I judged that we must've been close to Ireland.

Nervousness tore at my stomach. I didn't like situations like this; too many unknowns. I couldn't handle the stress anymore. "How is he going to see to land?"

"The landing strip was sprayed with a chemical that can only be seen with special lenses. It will stand out like a beacon," Sebastian answered.

I swallowed hard and held onto the armrests even though we wouldn't be landing anytime soon. I hated flying. I'd managed to stay pretty calm on the way over, but this...

William's voice came over the intercom a few minutes later, his tone very unruffled. "Lady and Gentlemen, it seems we have attracted some unwanted attention. This will be a fast landing. I will stop long enough to let you disembark, then I will immediately take off. You have three minutes to pack up your things before you strap in."

We immediately popped up and shoved anything we had taken out back into our packs. I stuck mine between my legs and gripped it with my knees. I concentrated on the muscles in my legs, trying to distract myself.

All of the creaks and groans in the plane seemed to grow louder. The familiar sound of tires on tarmac were heard as we returned to the earth, but this landing was faster than those I was used to. We slowed to a crawl, and William immediately turned the plane around and stopped. The cockpit door opened and William entered with a small police scanner in his hand.

"Police are on the way. You should have four minutes on them. Hopefully your ride is here. The words *smuggling* and *arms* have been in the chatter. Good to see you, Sebastian." And with that, he turned on his heel and returned to the pilot's seat.

"Thank you, William," Sebastian replied, then shooed us off the plane.

The second the last of our feet cleared the steps, they retracted and the roar of the engine increased. The plane was off the ground faster than I would've thought possible.

We stood there in the moonless night for a moment. Once the scream of the plane engine dimmed, I heard the growl of an automobile engine approaching. A black van without lights on rolled to a stop. I didn't recognize it, but was elated when the sliding door opened.

"Sorry, I didn't want to be too close to that landing." We jumped aboard as Joshua slid back into the driver's seat. The van immediately plowed down a dirt road.

Josh sped away with the headlights off. I looked out the back window; the lights of the police vehicles had almost reached the far end of the runway. We made a turn, and I lost sight of them.

"Do you think they saw us?" I asked anyone who would answer.

"Leslie says we are clear. Ian, she wants to talk to you." Joshua plucked the ear bud from his ear and held it up.

Ian moved forward to retrieve it, then returned to the back of the van and spoke to her.

No one was in the passenger seat. I pulled my hood up to hide most of my face, belted myself in, and twisted sideways to avoid any traffic cams that might've been lurking about once we emerged in the city.

"How well can you see? It's pitch black out here." The only thing I could make out were black shapeless things against more black shapeless things.

Joshua thought for a second. "It looks like there's a full moon to me. There's still darkness and shadows, but I don't need the lights. They're nice, but not necessary."

"How long till we get back?"

"About twenty more minutes of country roads and thirty into the city."

"Mmmmm."

"How bad was it?" he asked, his voice low and hesitant.

I let out a gust of air and closed my eyes. "Did you feel it?" I asked, knowing that he would've been able to feel how scared I'd been.

"I can't express in words what it is like to know you are in danger and not be able to do anything about it."

"I'm sorry."

"You always apologize for things that aren't your fault."

"It kinda is," I muttered. I had force fed him my blood in California, creating the blood bond between us. "Would you rather not know?"

He got a pained look as he stared at the road. "It'd be torture either way."

We didn't say anything for the rest of the ride back. His words lingered though. As if he weren't tortured enough.

We parked in an alley a block over from the secret entrance to our hideout. We cut through the pub and slipped inside with not so much as an errant glance from the patrons in the drinking establishment. Everyone was too focused on their beers or their conversations to notice the battered people trudging through.

Once in the common room, we stood in awkward silence for a moment, not sure what we should do. Sebastian rubbed his beard as he often did when contemplating something.

"Go ahead and get cleaned up. We will debrief in the morning. Hopefully, we will have heard from Uriel by then. Good night, everyone." He brushed past me and headed to his office. Ian and Gabriel moved towards the stairs.

Joshua turned towards me. "I have to meet with Sebastian for a few minutes. I have to fill him in on some things that happened while you were gone."

"Is everything okay?"

He smiled and gently tucked a strand of hair behind my ear. "Nothing for you to worry about."

I noted his careful choice of words, nothing for *me* to worry about. He'd not said that worrying was not warranted. When I started to open my mouth to ask another question, he placed his index finger on my lips.

"Get cleaned up. I'll meet you in your room afterwards."

"A shower would be good."

"Take your time."

"How about you hurry?" I smiled.

"Do my best."

"Go ahead and come in when you get to my room: I'll dress in the bathroom."

He gave me a kiss on the forehead and seemed to disappear. I plodded upstairs; it seemed like I'd been gone for a week, not a day.

As I showered, I found bruises I didn't know I had on my knees and shoulder, probably from falling onto the pavement. Then, cleaned the area around my new bullet graze being careful not to tug at it too much. After, I poked at the pink line on my other arm from a couple of weeks ago and wondered how many scars I'd end up with. I shook off that train of thought. The events of today had been horrifying enough without thinking about my death. Hopefully that'd be a long, long time in the future.

It seemed an effort to pull my clothes on, like they weighed more than they should. When I got back to my room, I'd hoped Joshua would already be there, but my room was empty. Just a faint smell of cedar and dust; I hadn't stayed there long enough for the room to smell like me.

I wriggled under my blankets. I was freezing, probably because of my wet hair. I wanted to wait for Joshua, but I felt sleep pulling me under. I fought it, but it was of no use.

This was a dream. I was in an alley sharply divided by dark and light. I looked up, and it must have been mid-afternoon, the sun's heat warming me from high in the clear sky. The shadow from the awnings in the back third of the alley was dark; it felt cool even from a few yards away. The light in my eyes kept me from seeing into the shadows.

Something was wrong with the shadows. I started to run towards the street, but a sound stopped me, and I turned towards it—something familiar. I pushed hair back from my face and caught a few strands in my ring. When I drew my hand away to pull them out, I realized I wasn't me.

I was looking at the same ring and long slender fingers that I'd seen in an earlier vision. The hairs caught were long and blonde. There was a gap; I didn't know how it'd happened, but I —no, *she*—had ended up in Tyran's clutches again. I felt his breath on her skin—her fear—her courage—and her acceptance that she was going to die. I fought to wake because I didn't want to feel her life drain away again.

Breaking from the dream, I sat up screaming. It felt like experiencing her death would kill me too.

"It's okay," Joshua whispered, his arms already around me.

I sat up the rest of the way, closed my eyes, and took in a few jagged breaths as I nuzzled under his chin. My heart rate slowed. I was able to breathe normally after a short while.

"You want to talk about it?"

"I had another vision yesterday. This was the same thing. Tyran..." I realized that I *didn't* want to talk about it; I was going to have to dredge it up for the debrief in the morning anyway. "Can we just talk about something else?"

He was obviously curious, but he let it go. "Anything you *do* want to talk about?"

"Whether or not global warming is really happening.

Ummm. Existentialism and its impact on the modern psyche. Orrrr..." I reached for more absurd topics.

He leaned away a little so he could see my face. "You..." He laughed.

I looked at him doe-eyed and innocent like. "What? Those are important things that deserve serious discussion."

"Are you sure you don't want to tell me about the dream?"

"I can't relive it yet."

"You want to tell me why you were so frightened yesterday?"

I didn't even know where to begin. "I'm not trying to keep anything from you. I just feel so exhausted from yesterday. Like it frayed all my nerves."

"You need to get some rest." He ran his finger over the circles under my eyes.

"Please don't go."

"Just letting you lay back down; not going anywhere."

I reclined again, and he pulled the covers up under my chin. "You always make me feel like I'm home," I whispered, knowing it sounded cheesy.

"I could say the same." He stood and started to move to the couch.

"Would you stay over here, please?"

He looked at me a little warily.

"I promise not to attack you. No breaking the rules."

He grinned and came back. I scooted over so he could have half the bed. He lay down on top of the covers and faced me, running his fingers through my tresses.

"Mmmmm." I closed my eyes.

A few minutes later, I met his gaze and asked about something that'd been troubling me. "Does it bother you that I'm aging?"

He didn't so much as flinch, his eyes soft. "Not a bit. I will always love you. No matter what."

I frowned, rarely feeling insecure, but the thought of him staying with an eighty-year-old didn't seem possible. Not that I'd live that long. "It doesn't bother you that I don't want to be turned?"

"I would never wish this on anyone."

I believed that. "I know you wouldn't."

"And besides, your mom is still totally hot." He tried to keep a straight face, the corner of his lip twitching a little.

I pulled the pillow out from under his head and hit him with it. "I can't believe you just said that." Okay, I could.

"What? I'm joking, but kinda not. Tell me your mom isn't."

I chuckled. "She is," I admitted.

"You never have to worry. Have I ever cared what people think?"

I contemplated for a moment. "No."

"If you were a little older, and I wasn't," his voice hitched. "What I am. I'd probably be ring shopping for you and thinking of some elaborate way to propose."

"Really?"

"Yeah, really. We've known each other almost our entire lives. I guess part of me has always known you were special. But, you were just enough younger than me that I hadn't thought about you that way until recently."

"True. I never allowed myself to have a crush on you. You were always unattainable."

A crooked grin lifted the corner of his mouth. "Can I break the rules?"

"I guess you get one free pass."

He cupped the non-scratched up side of my face and pressed his lips to mine. I grabbed onto his side and pulled him closer, but I kept myself in check this time, though I wanted to lose myself in his kisses.

"I love you," he murmured.

"Love you too. I regretted not saying that to you before I left yesterday."

"You didn't?"

"No," I sighed.

"Don't worry; it's always implied."

"I know, but if something ever happens to me, I want those to be my last words to you. Not 'see you later' or 'it's a plan' or anything else."

"Please don't speak like something's going to happen to you." His voice broke a little.

The corners of my lips pulled down. How could I tell him I'd seen Tyran on a rooftop running me through with a blade? Despite all my hopes of growing old, of spending all my days with him, I didn't think I'd ever have the chance. My life had accelerated.

"Sorry. I'm sure everything'll be fine," I lied.

He pulled me to his chest; it was as if I could feel his worry. I didn't think I needed to tell him about the dream with Tyran. He could sense that our time might be limited.

At some point, I fell asleep again. It was dreamless sleep this time. And I was in the only place I wanted to be.

17

MOTIVES

I had the horrible sensation of falling, then started to wake. Whatever I'd been dreaming about eluded me. I stiffly rolled onto my back and was delighted to see Joshua still there. *This was a first.*

"Good morning," he whispered.

"What time is it?"

He lifted his head to see over me. "6:32."

"How long 'til sunrise?"

"I have one hour and four more minutes with you." He blinked his eyes contentedly.

"Mmmmm." I wiggled over towards him, he extended his arm, and I rested my head on it and gazed at him in the green glow of my overly bright alarm clock.

He gently ran his finger under my right eye. "You look like you took on the school bully."

"Is it worse?" I gently ran my finger over the goose egg. The lump was almost gone.

"Your eye blackened over the course of the night."

"Lovely. Now I must look smokin' hot."

"It's kind of sexy. Makes you look tough." His eyes smoldered.

"I can't believe you stayed all night."

He ran his fingers over my cheek. "I started to leave when I knew you were asleep, but you got this pained look on your face. I just couldn't will myself to go after that."

"You are so good to me." I took his hand and kissed it, then pressed it to my cheek. The coolness felt good against the bruise.

Now the pained look was in his eyes. "What's wrong?"

"Nothing. Nothing is wrong," he said softly.

I let go of his hand and traced over his jaw with my fingers. He closed his eyes, and I touched his brow, his lids, his cheek, and his lips, enjoying the intimacy of the moment.

"You are good to me. I don't think I deserve you sometimes."

He opened his eyes. "I don't think you always see things clearly, love."

I took a moment to organize my thoughts. "I asked Sebastian if the French coven would have found me, if all of this hadn't happened. You know what he said?"

"No."

"He said it was 'almost a certainty.' He said that both Watchers and vampires monitor medical facilities for precisely my type of 'ailment.' That's how Seers are often recruited. And honestly, with how bad the dreams have been getting, and once the visions had kicked in, I would've sought help."

"He said that?" I could see him mulling this over.

"This thing hanging over you—all this guilt. You can let it go. It appears that a genetic destiny of sorts won out over free will in this case."

For a flickering moment, it appeared as if his could let some of it go, and then the weight reappeared. "I don't—"

"No don'ts. Can't you see? You saved me. Can you imagine what it would've been like if I didn't have you and Sebastian and Gabriel to help me? I have exactly what I need *because* of you."

I pulled myself closer and pressed my head against his chest. He wrapped his other arm around me and held me tight, though he didn't say anything. He repeatedly kissed the top of my head. I breathed in his scent; it seemed to attach itself to my soul. We stayed like that until dawn threatened to spill into the room. This time, our last words before parting were, "I love you."

As I walked down the steps to Sebastian's office, I heard the first peals of thunder. Well, I more than heard them. I *felt* them. The building seemed to shift and retreat from the sound with shudders and groans.

When I entered the room, a crackling fire was in the stone fireplace that cast a warm glow about the room. I loved the smell of it. The curtains were drawn, blocking out the almost nonexistent morning light, but I could make out rain hitting the windowpane. Both Gabriel and Sebastian looked over and nodded in greeting.

I sank into a chair, and when asked, started speaking. I ran through all of the events from my perspective, starting with my walk to the bank. The man with the crooked teeth had made me feel so uncomfortable, even though he was very polite and welcoming.

Then the inevitable question: "What happened in your vision?"

I drew in a long breath. "I tried to stop having it at first, but that seemed to make it worse. Last time, I was able to talk through it. When I tried to push this one away, it was crippling.

And it was different–I was seeing it through someone else's eyes."

"Do you know who it was?" Sebastian asked.

"No, but I felt her die. If I don't figure out who it is, I won't be able to stop it. Tyran is going to kill her." I then proceeded to tell them every vivid detail.

"But there's more. I had a dream last night that was almost the same as the vision, with just a few more details." This seemed to surprise both of them. I asked, "Is there anything in the material about having both a dream and a vision on the same subject?"

"We haven't found anything yet. But we will continue searching," Sebastian answered.

Gabriel added, "The Nexus is supposed to have some unique abilities. Something beyond that of the rest of the Lux. We may have more insights about the dreams and visions once the prophecy is fully translated. Winslow said he is almost done."

"More info would be nice. If you could give me the ability to stop a vision when it comes at a bad time, that would be awesome. I'd prefer to avoid breaking my face in the future." I meant it to sound lighter than it seemed to come across.

They both looked at me blankly. Something was definitely off. We talked for a few more minutes, and then I was released to go.

After the meeting, I went to the common area, but no one was there. The room was only filled with the sound of pattering rain. I went upstairs. Leslie's door was open, so I popped my head in.

"Hey."

She turned. "Ouch! Was your eye like that last night?"

"Nope. I knew the goose egg was going to bruise, but this is way worse than I thought."

"You all got beat up, didn't you? I guess Sebastian broke some ribs. He was getting taped up after you headed to bed."

"I had no idea. I noticed he seemed stiff when we got off the plane, but he never let on. I couldn't help grunting and groaning when one of mine was broken a few months ago."

"He's pretty tough."

"Apparently so."

She waved her hand in a welcoming motion. "Take a load off."

"Don't mind if I do." I grinned. "Where is everyone?"

"Peter and Gentry are doing the grocery shopping. Ian is having a clean dressing put on his wounds. Michael and Raphael were both called away yesterday. Not sure about everyone else."

"So we're down to one Slayer, eh?"

"Looks like it."

"Any word about Uriel?"

"I overheard Gabriel speaking with her on the phone last night; he left the room, so I wasn't able to hear anything."

"That Gabriel, leaving rooms to have a private conversation. The nerve of him!"

"I know. So rude." She laughed.

A huge gust of wind pounded the window, and we both glanced over at it, then returned to our conversation.

"Just curious. How much more training do you have before you are a full-fledged Watcher?"

"Not much. Should be done this summer. I'll be put on assignment somewhere. I'm hoping to stay with Sebastian and Gabriel though. Them heading up the academy was only temporary. I was lucky to be there. Legendary."

"They were strictly in the field?"

"Being on their team is like being assigned to the Enterprise under Captain Kirk."

"Wow. That *does* put things in perspective." I raised my eyebrows.

"Knew you were a closet nerd."

"Oh, wait. Captain Kirk who?" I asked, feigning ignorance.

"Nice try."

"So, does that make Gabriel Spock?"

"Yes, but our Spock can kill people by raising an eyebrow." She rolled to her side and plucked something from the nightstand. "Hand, please," she said reaching out.

I hesitantly extended my hand. She shook something in her left hand. I realized it was nail polish. "Makeover time?"

"I like to keep my hands busy. Have you ever noticed all the doodles all over my notes?"

"I guess I hadn't thought about it."

She shrugged. "It's just my thing, like Ian and music."

"How long have you guys been friends?"

"Our whole lives. Our parents are best friends. We were sort of born into this life. They all teach at the academy outside of New York."

"You didn't want to be there?"

"Our parents have basically been training us since birth. We both felt it was time to stand on our own."

"Have you two been more than friends?"

"No, not really. He's my best friend. I don't know…maybe… not now. He knew me when I was hideous. I think it's hard to go out with anyone who knew you when you were thirteen."

"I don't know. There's something nice about them knowing your history. Knowing all your layers, being able to finish each other's sentences, seeing through all the garbage."

"True, very true," she agreed as she finished my right hand.

"Did you know Gabriel before this summer?"

"I met him a couple of times. But he scared the crap outta me. I was too afraid to speak around him. He and Michael both have that off-the-charts intimidation thing going for them. All warrior, no warmth."

When I thought back, that'd been my first impression of Gabriel too: menacing.

"He seemed off this morning in the debrief. I mean, he often seems solitary, but he was somber."

She popped up from her chair, shut the door, and plopped down on the bed next to me sitting cross-legged.

"I studied Gabriel's missions before all of you came last summer. They were flawless. Like I said—legendary. I'm just guessing, but a lot of things have not gone according to plan. I don't know what happened in California, but I'm guessing something bad prompted all this. Then, all of you were pretty beat up when you got here after evacuating. And, of course, there's yesterday…"

"Not rocket science, I guess." I sat still, not sure what to say.

"Gabriel is different with you. There is this…extra level of protectiveness."

"So I've been told." I thought of Winslow's comments.

She finished the last nail. "Perfecto!"

"Thanks, darling. I can't remember the last time I had purdy nails."

"I picked up some mud masks too. We'll have to do a spa night with Gentry soon."

"Absolutely."

She stood and stretched. "Well, I have to get downstairs. I'm supposed to help with dinner tonight. Peter and Gentry should be back any minute. We're making lasagna."

"I'll wear my big pants."

Leslie snorted a laugh and headed downstairs.

After a workout and shower, there was a knock at my door. "Come in." I spun around on my desk chair. It was Leslie.

"Sebastian wants you."

"Really? You know what it's about?"

"Sorry, no. He just ducked his head into the kitchen and asked me to run up and get you."

"Okay. I'll head down now." I tucked my pen into my journal.

Another crescendo of thunder rocked the building, but it didn't seem foreboding anymore. I skipped down the steps, feeling light, my battered appearance no reflection of what I felt on the inside. I felt good for the first time since the evac.

Sebastian's door was ajar; I let myself in without breaking stride. Two steps into the room, I froze. A chill raised the hairs on the back of my neck. It was Crina Rousseau—a powerful member of the Conclave.

I'd been introduced to her in California when I met with both sides of the Concilium. Her dark-red hair was still cut into a perfectly angled bob, and her skin was still shockingly pale. Part of me wanted to growl at her; she was the one who was still rallying to have Joshua eliminated, despite the rest of the Concilium's ruling.

Rousseau was seated crossing her ankles in the wingback chair, leaning back with a confident smirk. I swallowed hard— her presence was jarring. Her large, dark eyes were fastened on me with such an intensity that she made me feel like I was the crown jewels she was planning to steal. Her thin, painted lips held a pleasant look, but I wondered what was going on in her head.

"So good to see you." She smiled with that cat-like grin.

"Nice to see you too," I responded, my manners kicking in to cover up my contempt.

"I see you had some trouble there. Tisk-tisk, Sebastian. How could you allow such a face to be marred?" she chided. I couldn't tell if she was serious or joking. Everything about her seemed to be a contradiction. What could she possibly want?

"Are you in town for long?" I said with my sweetest voice.

"No, a couple of days," she replied.

Days. I cringed internally. *I was hoping for hours or maybe minutes or for teleportation to be possible. Beam her up, Scotty!*

"Nice. I am enjoying Dublin. They're very friendly here." I was reaching for something—anything to say.

"I hadn't noticed," she said in a distracted manner. She motioned to the seat across from her. "Aleria, please have a seat." I took the chair next to the one she indicated.

The kettle dinged on the buffet table. Sebastian started to get up. Now that I knew he had broken ribs, I noticed his slight wince.

"Don't be silly, Sebastian. I'll get it." She rose from her seat and maneuvered through the overstuffed room. "Sebastian, what do you take in your tea?"

"One sugar, please. Thank you."

"Aleria?"

"The same, please."

You could hear the clink of the cups being placed on the saucers. Rousseau turned and served each of us with gracefulness, though she didn't seem accustomed to serving anyone. Her feigned benevolence put me even more on edge.

She gave me a cup with a tea bag and poured the boiling water into it while I held out the cup. I eased back into my seat with the steaming liquid and tried to relax. She returned to her seat next to Sebastian and stepped out of her high heels, removed her dress jacket, and curled her legs under her body. I recognized what she was doing. She was making the atmosphere more casual, attempting to make me trust her.

"I've heard you're doing well in your schooling."

"As well as can be expected; I'm doing a little catch up."

"She is a natural," Sebastian complimented.

"So how did you end up with the facial trauma?"

Sebastian caught my eye and shook his head, almost infinitesimally. "Oh. Uhhh. We were out, and I took a spill. The sidewalk was slick, and I couldn't get my hands out in front of me fast enough. I felt pretty stupid."

"That's too bad. And your friend, the one who came with you?"

"Peter?" I had a hard time believing she didn't know his name.

"Yes, how is he adjusting?"

"He loves it."

We continued to talk in this round about manner, like we were family members that hadn't seen each other in years. This closeness she was trying to manufacture felt awkward. Sebastian gave me the occasional nod or shake of the head, advising me. I couldn't figure out what she wanted with any of this. Gentry knocked at the door after a little over an hour.

"Sorry to interrupt, but dinner is ready." She noticed Rousseau. "Oh, hello. We'll set an extra place if you would like to join us."

"I would like that. My colleague will be joining us momentarily. Two extra place settings would be nice."

"Aye, they will be on the table in a tick."

We filed out of the room. I bulged my eyes questioningly at Sebastian. He returned the look. He had no idea. *This is not good.*

And who is this colleague of hers? Then it hit me. I knew exactly who it was.

The dining room smelled of Italian food, and my mouth immediately started to water. I was going to do some serious eating. Once the food was served, all that could be heard was chewing and the clinks and scrapes of flatware on porcelain plates. Everyone was hungry. Halfway through the meal, Phineas entered the room, and no one really seemed to take notice, but I sighed.

Phineas put some parcels on an empty table, then sat down. He filled a plate without saying a word and started eating. He held his fork in his fist instead of his fingertips. It made him look like a kid. After most of us were done, Phineas circled to Rousseau's side and sank to his haunches. She whispered to him, and he took the paper shopping bag he'd put on the other table into the kitchen.

Rousseau stood and addressed us. "I've been impressed with your adaptability. I have been visiting the relocated academies and wanted to let you know that your efforts have not gone unnoticed. I was in Belgium this morning and brought something special for you."

Phineas emerged a minute later with ornate chocolate truffles on plates. He placed a paper plate with two truffles in front of each of us. For some reason, he avoided eye contact with me, even though I repeatedly tried to catch his eye. He finished serving everyone and sat across from me with a plate for himself. He finally met my gaze, but didn't say anything. His expression was odd. If I had to label it, I would say he looked lost, not angry like usual.

He looked down at my untouched chocolate and sighed. "I didn't do anything to them," he muttered.

He traded our plates and started eating. It was possibly the best chocolate I'd ever had in my life, and judging from the silence, everyone else thought so too.

I was worried that Joshua would run into our new guests, so I dismissed myself afterwards to find him. On my way to the staircase, I noticed that the deluge of rain had stopped and prayed it was a good omen.

Joshua's door was open. He was sitting on his tiny bed, reading. "Do you know who is here?" I blurted.

"Yes. Sebastian sent me a text and warned me to keep clear until he assessed the situation."

I closed the door in case there were prying ears in the hall. "I just had the strangest meeting with her. We talked about nothing for an hour and a half. No real questions. I couldn't get a read on her. And Phineas just showed up, too."

"Fantastic. Two of my favorite people."

"It makes me wonder about that first vision. I wonder if it will happen. Maybe he needs to be watched."

"Or it already happened," he conjectured.

"Hadn't thought of that." I sat down heavily next to him. "For about ten minutes, I actually felt worry-free today."

He put his arm around me and pulled me to his side. "That's ten minutes more than yesterday."

I chuckled. "Oh, you glass-is-half-full person you."

"Nice nails. You had some girl time today?"

"Yeah, hung out with Leslie for a while."

"I'm glad."

"You have to go out tonight?"

"For a few hours. Should be back just after midnight. Gabriel is monitoring those out of town vamps right now. We are going to swap soon. We have another crew taking over at twelve. I actually need to get going."

"I'll wait up for you," I smiled.

"No, get some sleep."

I grumbled, knowing he was right.

"I'll be there if you wake."

"Okay, but you are welcome to wake me." I hated that we were on opposite sleeping schedules.

I leaned over and gave him a soft kiss. He knotted his hands in my hair and gave me another kiss that I felt in my toes. I let out a gasp. His lips curved into a smile.

"I love that I can do that to you."

"Mmmmm, me too."

"Okay, I really have to go." He stood and pulled me up with him.

"I love you."

"Love you." He gave me one last peck on the forehead and vanished.

I walked up the stairs slowly, that kiss still lingering on my lips. I didn't know where Rousseau and Phineas had gone, but I found all the recruits were in the common room about to watch a movie. I wedged myself onto the couch between Leslie and Peter. There wasn't enough room for all of our shoulders to be side-by-side, so Peter put his arm around me. About halfway through the movie, I started to get really overheated. I leaned forward and tried to cool down.

"You okay?" Peter asked.

"Yeah, just really hot. I'm really tired too. I feel odd. I think I should just go to bed."

Leslie squeezed my arm. "I hope you feel better, sweetie."

"Thanks," I murmured and headed upstairs.

My forehead felt clammy, and I was exhausted. I supposed it had been a long day. I struggled into sweats and crawled into bed; it seemed an effort to get under the covers.

The rain started again, and light flashed through the crack in the curtains as lightning split the sky. I fell asleep really hard despite thunder rocking the building.

I couldn't help thinking there was something wrong. Some sort of danger, but I couldn't keep awake long enough to figure out what it was.

18

ACUTE

I was looking out a window, gazing at the silhouette of a statuesque woman on a veranda below. She turned to greet someone. When the torchlight revealed her face, I was startled to see it was Queen Agrona. She looked different than when I'd last seen her. Her almost white-blonde locks cascaded in waves to her waist. Her beauty was only matched by the cruelty in her eyes.

She held out her hand to the new arrival. I knew without seeing his face it was one of the twins. He reached out, took her hand, and kissed her cheeks in greeting. She spoke into his ear and pressed something into his hand. He put whatever it was in the inside breast pocket of his coat and immediately walked back into the building.

My curiosity burned with the desire to know through whose eyes I was seeing. It was a man this time, judging by the hands that gripped the windowsill. He was suddenly on the move. Within seconds, he was down two flights of stone stairs and in a grand hallway. Then the twin that I'd seen downstairs entered the other end of the hall. He saw me, or him, and approached, his grin wicked. It was Tyran.

"Hello, brother. Join me downstairs?"

I cringed. I was seeing through Bowen's eyes. "You know I have no taste for that."

"We need to feed, or are you fasting again?"

"I just prefer mine not to struggle," Bowen replied. I was surprised by the amount of disapproval he was feeling.

"It tastes better that way," Tyran mocked.

"What are you and mother up to?"

Tyran started to walk past Bowen, but Bowen grabbed Tyran's arm and squeezed. Tyran whipped around and drove a small knife into Bowen's abdomen and held it there. Bowen pushed Tyran backwards into the wall, the knife still in his gut, but Tyran clung to him.

"Is this how it's going to be?" Bowen hissed through the pain.

"When you stop pining for the thing you are *obligated* to destroy, then you will be privy." Tyran twisted the knife.

Bowen clenched his jaw and reached inside his brother's coat, ripping the inner pocket clean out. A metal tube clattered to the ground. "What is that?" Bowen asked.

They started to struggle, but I was torn out of the dream by my own blinding pain. I tried to scream for help, but nothing escaped my mouth other than a whimper. I attempted to crawl out of bed and get to the door. My legs gave out, and I fell hard as I crumbled onto the floor. I noticed the clock: 11:00 P.M.

I clutched the inside of my right hip, the same place Tyran had stabbed Bowen, and curled into a fetal position. The pain was so sharp I vomited over and over. Each time I stopped, my belly cinched up again until there was nothing but bile coming up. I did my best to wiggle away from the puke; the smell was making me want to throw up again. I clawed my way a few more feet towards the door, but I was too weak to get any closer.

I started to shiver as the sweat that had beaded up all over me started to run down my body. Joshua wasn't going to be back until after midnight, and no one would think of checking in on me. I didn't know if I would make it another hour or more. Something was seriously wrong with me.

My mind raced. *Could my dreams actually kill me? Or was there something in the chocolate, after all?* I wondered if anyone else was ill.

None of my theories mattered. I was in trouble. I wished I could pass out. I sucked in a breath. Another wave of pain seized me, and tears involuntarily sprang from my eyes. I heard something in the hall...hurried footsteps.

My door burst open. Gabriel had a phone clutched to his ear. "Ali! You were right," he said, then dashed to the floor next to me, dropping the phone onto the floor. He must have hit the speaker button; I could hear Joshua's voice.

"Is she okay?"

"Uhhhh." He tried to pull my hands from my hip gently, but I fought him. I couldn't help myself. "She is burning up. Well over a hundred. She has been vomiting. Ali, you need to let me see."

I cried in pain. He pried my fingers away and pulled down the waist of my pants just far enough to see where I was grabbing. "There is swelling on her abdomen." He pressed down on the area gently.

I screamed.

"Maybe appendicitis. We need to get her to a hospital. Our medics are with Michael and Raphael."

I felt him pick me up and cradle me to his chest. He made

long strides down the hall. "Meet me at the teaching hospital. There are observation rooms above all the O.R.s."

I started losing parts of what was going on. I had to concentrate on breathing. Gabriel called for Peter.

Just keep breathing, just keep breathing.

I heard a van door open and glanced at Gabriel as he hunched over and maneuvered inside. He sat down, but continued to hold me. The engine started, and we peeled out at breakneck speed. Gabriel was giving directions. I felt another wave of pain, but I was too weak to tighten my stomach muscles. I had a wad of his shirt in my hand, and now the fabric was damp from sweat.

The van came to a halt, and there was a flurry of motion. Fluorescent lights...a gurney...nurses...doctors...I grabbed Gabriel's hand and held onto it like I would surely die if he let go. He obliged me and held my hand just as tightly, easing my fears.

Someone tried to pull me out of the pretzeled position I was curved into, but I fought whoever it was. I knew I shouldn't, but the agony was too great. Something cold pricked my arm, then the pain ebbed almost immediately. I was able to relax. They rolled me on my back and probed my abdomen with their fingers. I saw many sets of worried eyes.

Someone said, "Prep O.R. 2, stat," and I was rolled down a long hallway. I still had Gabriel's hand, until they forced him to stay outside. After some arguing, he was told to wait in the observation room overlooking the OR.

Within minutes, I'd been dressed for surgery and transferred to an operating table beneath a mammoth light. It was rounded and reflective, allowing me to watch them finish getting ready. All of this seemed to take a very long time, but maybe it hadn't;

my head was swimming. The nurse seemed agitated that the rest of the surgical team wasn't there. I wished Gabriel was still holding my hand.

I noticed large plate glass windows above us—the observation room. The words "teaching hospital" came back to me. That's why we were here. Gabriel could watch me, and there he was. He was standing with both hands on the handrail, leaning forward and examining every movement, his brows knitted together. Two rows of stadium seats loomed behind him.

He looked to his left, and Peter and Gentry entered. I hadn't realized she was with us. Next to me, the nurse made a huffing sound, drawing me back.

"I'll go light a fire under them, honey; back in a tick." It sounded like something Gentry would say.

Soon, I felt the first twinge of pain again and swallowed hard. My mouth was pasty, making it almost impossible to completely swallow. The delightful substance they'd given me was wearing off.

The doctor and nurses finally entered, but they were oddly silent. I was feeling more distressed now that my pain level had increased. I glanced back upstairs just as Joshua appeared. My lips twitch upwards in relief. He placed his hands on the glass and stared down at me.

"Okay, Emily, I'm your anesthesiologist. I'm going to start your pain meds. I'm not going to put you completely under, but you may fall asleep. Just relax." I wondered who Emily was, then I felt stupid: that was one of my aliases.

The anesthesiologist wrapped an oxygen tube around my face and gently pressed it up under my nose. "Can you wiggle your toes for me?"

I did. At least, I thought I did.

"Can you wiggle your fingers?"

I thought I did. My arms were tucked up next to me, and I could hear the sound of Velcro.

"We are ready, doctor."

A tickling sensation tugged at my abdomen followed by some pressure. I looked over at Joshua and Gabriel. They were both locked in the same position. My lids started to feel heavy. I felt so, so tired.

Someone walked in front of me, blocking my view of the observation room, a doctor or a nurse, his back to the windows above. I lazily looked at him.

He had a scar that looked like a checkmark above his right eyebrow. It was silvery and left a fairly deep indentation. It looked like he was smiling behind the surgical mask, then his eyes started to glow a muddy green color. He must have seen the alarm in my eyes.

I sucked in a breath, ready to shout.

He placed his hand over my mouth, then realized that the drugs had robbed me of all my fight. He stroked my forehead with his other hand, his fingers cool. There was no aggression in his stance, but it was obvious he was here for a reason.

Straining, I continued to look toward the observation room, but to no avail. The man wasn't moving. He nodded at the anesthesiologist, and the sluggish sting of more drugs moved through my veins. I stared at him as long as I could, but it wasn't long. I was helpless.

The beep of the heart monitor bled into my consciousness. I wondered what was real. Snippets of scenes flashed by, but I had a hard time focusing. Things melded together: Bowen.

Tyran. A metal vial. A knife. Chocolates. Eyes—glowing, muddy, green eyes. They were what I needed to remember.

Fingers were laced through mine. And there was the breath of sleep. Opening my eyes into slits, I could see that the weight against my leg was Joshua's head. He appeared to be dreaming; his brow was furrowed.

Movement caught my attention on the other side of the room. With effort, I rolled my head to see that Peter was asleep in a chair, shifting in his seat. For some reason, he looked very young to me. A shadow passed by the window on the other side, so I rolled my head the other way again.

Pink blinds with some missing slats hung three quarters shut. The shadow passed by the other direction, and I could make out that it was Gabriel pacing back and forth, probably on sentry duty.

I felt so weak. It was a strain to simply move. I squeezed Joshua's hand, and he immediately raised his head and gave me a worried smile.

"Hey," I rasped. I tried to swallow, but my mouth was too dry. I coughed, and then moaned. There was a horrible pulling sensation in my abdomen.

He popped out of his seat and poured some water into a beige, plastic cup, then placed a bendy straw into it. I took a tentative sip. I worked the liquid around my mouth before swallowing and coughed again. After I took a few more sips, I waved it away. He placed it on the tray table and sat back down. He ran his hand over my forehead and cupped my face with his right hand.

"Your fever is almost gone. How are you feeling?"

"Not sure yet." I took a deep breath without moving my abs and tried to assess. My voice was a little better after drinking the water. "I feel weak. My throat hurts...and it feels like someone kicked me in the gut with steel-toed boots."

"I was so worried."

"What did the doctor say?"

"Gabriel was right: appendicitis."

"Are they sure?"

"Pretty sure. They removed it."

I concentrated hard. I was trying to remember something, but every time I got close to it, I ended up looping around to something else. My mind was still foggy from whatever they had given me, but my pain level was increasing. "Who talked to the doctor?"

"Gabriel and I. What is it?"

The pictures started cycling through my mind again. "I had a dream before the pain started. I need to talk this through. I feel fragmented."

"You want Gabriel to hear this?"

"Might be best."

Josh stood and went over to Peter. "Sorry to wake you, but would you mind swapping with Gabriel?"

Peter sat up and stretched. "Nope." He noticed I was awake. "Oh...you're up. How ya doing?"

"Alive." I gave him a tired grin.

He squeezed my foot on his way out the door.

Gabriel stepped into the room, his expression unreadable. "Are you in pain?"

I hesitated for a split second. "I'm fine." His eyes tightened. He started to reach for the nurse call button attached to the side of my bed.

"No. Wait. I need to think clearly."

He cocked his head to the side, watching me.

I was still trying to make sense of the images. They were

starting to resemble a film instead of a series of snapshots. But my mind was acting like I had tried to start driving in third gear instead of first. It lagged and threatened to stall.

"I was having a dream when this started. I was in Bowen."

Both of their faces were fixed in shock. "You're sure?" Josh asked.

"No mistaking it. I was inside the lair of the enemy. I saw... or he saw Queen Agrona give Tyran something. He tried to question Tyran and find out what he was up to. They fought, and Bowen ripped the item from Tyran's pocket. It was a metal tube just like the one I saw being given to Phineas. Things aren't good for Bowen. Tyran stabbed him...here." I pointed to my incision.

"You think the dream did this to you?" Joshua questioned, his voice rising.

"I..." I thought for a moment. "I don't think so."

"It could be coincidence. Sometimes people do just get appendicitis." Joshua's tone was hopeful. *If I can be hurt to this degree through dreams—game changer.*

"Did the doctor say it could be anything else? Or if he had an idea of the cause?"

The corners of Gabriel's mouth pulled down as he spoke. "He did not go into any detail. He was very abrupt. He gave us the facts and said he had another surgery to get to."

"He may be done with the other surgery. I'll see if we can talk with him." Josh was gone before I could open my mouth.

I looked at Gabriel. "Thank you. I actually thought I was going to die."

His lips pressed into a thin line. "No more talk of death. I may have to install some type of monitoring device on you." He smiled a little, but he was probably half serious.

Joshua returned. "There wasn't another surgery. They are

trying to find someone from the surgical team. They'll send someone in to let us know." A knot formed in my stomach.

We waited. About ten minutes later, a nurse peeked in through the door. "Sorry, sir. We can't locate anyone from the team that performed the operation."

"Thank you for checking," Josh said politely, but I could sense his anxiety rise. He and Gabriel exchanged a suspicious look.

I bit at my bottom lip. "I'm going to ask something. I need you to both hear me out." I looked at Joshua warily. "I...I want you to taste me. I–"

"No. Absolutely not," he cut me off.

I tried not to get flustered. "I don't think this was the dream. I think this has to do with the metal vial. You remember what my blood tastes like? Could you tell if there was something in it?"

"Do it." Gabriel said flatly.

Joshua looked like he was going to object again, his jaw in a scowl, nostrils flaring. He looked at Gabriel pleadingly.

"This is the fastest way. I do not like the fact we cannot reach any of the doctors or nurses. Do it. I will not let any harm come to her."

Defeated, Joshua sat down in the chair by my side. He picked up my arm; the situation felt oddly intimate. Gabriel must've sensed it, because he walked to the window and looked into the hallway, turning his back to us.

Josh put the back of my hand to his lips and kissed it, then gently turned my hand the other way to expose my wrist. His eyes began to glow, and his teeth unsheathed. He drew my wrist to his lips. The initial bite hurt as it had in the past, then all my pain was gone. Not even my incision hurt any longer. He took a few long pulls and paused. He took a couple of more, and then disengaged himself. He licked the wound and leaned back in his chair. He was in complete control.

Gabriel rejoined us.

"She's right There's something bitter…it's faint. But it could be the drugs. I'd need to taste what they gave her to be sure."

I sucked in a surprised breath as the epiphany struck. "They know I'm here." I finally remembered what had been eluding me. "In the operating room…a doctor…his eyes glowed. He blocked my view, so I couldn't see either of you."

Two doubtful sets of eyes looked at me.

"Are you kidding me? Do I not seem completely lucid? A vampire was in that room with me. They must've sent someone who can cloak their vampireyness." I couldn't think of better words. I felt exasperated that they were both doubting me. I got the fact that a vamp being in that room would've reached a new level of brazenness—to be literally under their noses.

"See if there is a doctor with a scar above his right brow in the shape of a checkmark."

Gabriel was out the door as I finished the last word. I looked at Joshua with some disapproval.

"What?" he shrugged.

"Nothing," I grumbled.

Gabriel came back a few minutes later, his jaw tense. He spoke to Joshua. "Peter and Gentry are pulling the van around to the back. We are getting her out of here now. No doctor with a scar above his brow."

"You think it's okay to move her?"

"And the alternative?"

Joshua grabbed the bag of my clothes out of the closet.

Gabriel turned towards us. "You carry her out. They will not see you. I will follow at a normal pace. It may give us a few minutes before they sound the alarm."

Gabriel opened the door, and Josh scooped me up. Then, everything became a blur. The only noise I heard was the flapping of my hospital gown. We were down the stairs and inside the van before I could've walked to the end of the hall. Joshua eased me next to him on the back bench seat.

Gentry slid the door shut and sat down on the seat in front of us. Peter was in the driver's seat with the engine idling. Through the tinted windows I could see Gabriel casually exiting the building. The van rocked a little as he climbed into the passenger seat. Peter was off before Gabriel had his seatbelt buckled. The emergency exodus actually felt a little anticlimactic, like vampires should have been dropping from the roof and sailing through the air, blades in their hands.

"Are we headed back to the house?" I asked.

Joshua looked out the back door. "I doubt it. They may be tracking us now. They may want us to lead them to the others. Clean us all out at once."

Almost on cue, we turned north and headed away from downtown. His words didn't make me feel comforted at all. He put his arm around me.

"I think there is a motorcycle back there. It's been with us for a while," Peter commented, sounding very calm.

"Turn up here." Gabriel pointed to the left.

We watched. The motorcycle mimicked our path. My heart started to race so loudly, I could hear it like I had my hands cupped over my ears. We proceeded to make turn after turn, each time a little faster, each time the motorcycle getting a little closer. It finally came up alongside our van. It had the same markings as the motorcycle I'd seen in my vision.

Joshua crawled to the other side of me, placing himself in between me and the bike. The rider kept looking over at us. It was as if he could see through the tint. Then, he swerved onto a side street and disappeared. *Was he just waiting for someone to take over? Or is he just toying with us?*

I overheard Gabriel telling Peter to continue north until we hit the M50, then to go south. There was a place to do a car swap in Cherry Orchard. The name reminded me of many of the street names around my house in California. Back when my life was simple. I felt like I was a million years old. Or maybe I had just traveled a million miles since those days.

We swapped vehicles and downsized to a silver sedan with tinted windows. I sat in the middle between Joshua and Gentry. Gabriel took over driving. The air of exhaustion hung over us like the storm clouds. We cleared Dublin and entered a more rural area. The swarm of city lights dwindled to a few, dotting the landscape here and there. I read the road signs as we went. We arrived in a small town named Enniskerry in the foothills of the Wicklow Mountains. I couldn't see much in the dark.

We hadn't seen any traffic around us in a long while. We pulled up to a dark home close to St. Patrick's Church. Gabriel said there was a windowless panic room inside where Joshua would be able to stay.

The house was a small structure with three rooms, not including the panic room. Josh carried me into a room that had two twin beds where Gentry had her bags. Gentry pulled down the covers on one so Joshua could tuck me in. She went back into the living room to see what supplies we had.

He knelt on the floor next to me and pressed his forehead to mine. "How are you doing?" he murmured.

"Hangin' in there." I didn't think "fine" would've cut it.

"Are you in pain?"

"No…as long as I don't move." I lied. The pain had been back for a while. I felt like the doctors had twisted up my insides, and the incision throbbed. I smiled as best I could. "I love you."

"I love you. Get some sleep." He kissed me on the forehead and the cheek and was gone.

Gentry came back. "Hey, darlin', found somethin' you'll love." She handed me a toothbrush with the toothpaste already squeezed onto it, then a paper cup with some water, so I could brush without getting out of bed. It reminded me of camping.

"Thanks, much better."

"Went through the place: doesn't even have aspirin. Sorry. I'll head out first thing and get ya somethin' for the pain. You must be goin' mad about now."

I tried to look light. "I'll manage." I smiled weakly. "Ummm… are there any clean shirts around?" I was sure the clothes in my bag had puke on them.

"I think I saw somethin' in the back." She walked out. I could hear her rummaging through something. She emerged a minute later with an argyle sweater. "Sorry, love. Best I can do, unless you want wool. Thought this wouldn't be so scratchy."

"It's great. Thanks. More concerned with the smell, not the fashion. Of course, Leslie would probably rather be put before a firing squad than wear this."

"Leslie would probably look dashing in it," she said matter-of-factly. "Let me help you."

Every tiny movement seemed to pull at my insides, but she had me in clean clothes in a few minutes.

"Thanks."

"Anytime."

"Do you think everything is okay back at the house?"

"Gabriel has already spoken to Sebastian. Besides Rousseau being there, everything seems to be normal."

"Good," I said sleepily.

"Try to get some rest."

"Glad you're here, Gen."

"Me too. Beats just hearin' the stories," she winked.

I pulled the blankets up almost over my head. I tried to concentrate on breathing and relaxing my muscles instead of the raw, gnawed on feeling in my gut. I must've been more than exhausted, because I was out in minutes.

19

PRESSURE

I was in London, riding the Underground to see the Tower of London, the souvenir map neatly folded in my hand. The doors opened, and the announcer's voice rang over the crowd, "Mind the gap. Mind the gap."

So I did; I stepped over the gap and onto the platform. Then something felt off. I looked around at the bustling crowd. They all came to a halt and seemed to melt into the ground, pools of blood left in their stead. There was so much that it started to run together and flow in my direction.

I backed up towards the train car again, when I heard a screeching sound of twisting metal and shattering glass. The train doors opened wide, but they looked like a horrific mouth with shards of glass for teeth. Flames licked at the car from beneath and blood ran from within, making it look like the mouth of hell itself.

Following a sign, I turned towards the stairs and tried to break into a sprint, but the blood was viscous and slippery. I lurched forward, falling to my hands and knees, and started crawling up the stairs towards the exit. More blood seemed to bubble up from the edges of the cement.

My mind was in chaos. I heard snarls behind me, coming from multiple sources—dogs—no, wolves. Shadows moved across the walls from the beasts. I tried to move more rapidly, but I kept slipping in the blood. I grew more panicked, gasping for air as I clawed my way upwards. Every time I looked down to keep from sliding backwards, it seemed as if flights of stairs were being added.

Finally reaching the top of the steps, I saw hope for the first time. Rays of sunlight blazed down from above, illuminating what looked to be an angel. Immense white wings spread like a fortress.

Relief. It was Gabriel, but with wings and the scar on his face healed. He reached down and grasped my hand, then he shuddered, and the color drained from his skin, darkness springing from behind him.

Black smoke churned and blotted out the sun. The white of his feathered wings turned black and ran with blood. He grew taller, and the lean muscles became more bulky. This wasn't Gabriel. He pulled me up, even though I tried to slip from his grip; he was too strong.

When he drew his face close to mine, a painful recognition took place—it was Moloch. I clawed and kicked and scratched, but he just smiled at me, that same wicked grin Tyran used when he knew he had gotten to me.

He pressed his mouth to my ear. "I'm so close." Then he reared back, fangs ready to pierce my skin.

My screaming reverberated in the room as I woke. And I kept screaming and screaming. I jolted up, and then moaned from the pain. In my terror, I'd forgotten about the surgery. I tried to lie back down, but it hurt too badly. So I sat there, tears erupting from my eyes.

I looked over at Gentry's bed, but she wasn't there. Gabriel entered the room within seconds of my scream; he was calm. He seemed to know the commotion was from a dream. He looked exhausted.

"I'm so sorry, Gabriel. Please go back to sleep. I'm sorry." A wave of guilt crashed over me. I bit down on my bottom lip to keep it from quivering.

"What was the dream about?" he asked, running his hand through his hair.

I shook my head. "Nothing that won't wait. Please get some sleep."

He started to turn to leave and go down the hall, but noticed Gentry wasn't there. He paused, then entered the room and crawled into the spare bed. He didn't say anything. There was no need.

When I was able to take the pain, I lowered myself onto my side again and went back to sleep. But I felt haunted; this dream had been different. Something was wrong. I had no control. I felt like there was pressure. I couldn't put my finger on it. I started to analyze the dream, but decided a dream like that might be better off as a mystery.

Gabriel's presence didn't keep the demons away this time. As soon as I fell asleep again, I was in a strange landscape. It was somewhere I'd never been, but was so real, I knew it must exist.

I was standing on a stone platform a couple of yards above the ocean. Waves crashed against it. The spray of the ocean moistened my skin, and the smell of the salt quickened my senses. A sheer cliff was behind me. It was so sheer, it looked as if God Himself had sliced it with a sword.

When I took a closer look at the ocean, blood bubbled up from a single location a few feet away from the platform. In the distance, it sounded as if there were screams, but when I listened, all I could hear was the cry of gulls hovering in the strong winds.

It was sunrise. Light made its way across the waves. I looked out at the horizon, and something huge hit the water not far from the rising blood, but I missed it. I stepped forward, trying to see what it was. Something dark moved underwater towards the platform, and then disappeared, as if it melted into the cliff's side. Sun started to bathe the platform in light. When I looked back at the ocean, all of the blood had turned black, like a volcano was spewing ash into the water.

Then I felt that same odd energy. This time it reminded me of being on a plane when the cabin pressure changed too rapidly. I noticed that the platform was slowly tilting towards the sea—but there were no stairs, no ladder to hold onto. I started to slide towards the water. My boots scraped at the rock as I tried to keep myself from going into the water.

Suddenly, the waves erupted with sea life; frenzied sharks nipped at one another and looked hungrily at me. I willed myself to wake up, but whatever that force was, it tried to suck me back into the dream. I concentrated and was able to it push back. I tried to wake again. I opened my eyes warily, wondering if I was really awake.

Gabriel was sitting up, looking worried.

I exhaled in a gust. "I'm sorry."

He shrugged. "I see why Gentry moved to the couch." He smirked.

"I'm not going to go back to sleep. I can't take another one of those. Please go ahead and go back to sleep."

"You need to sleep to recover."

I rubbed at my eyes. "I can't...I just can't."

"Then talk." He pushed himself farther onto the mattress and leaned against the wall, ready to listen.

I described the first dream in detail, then hesitated.

"What about the dream has you so rattled?"

"It felt different than any other dream I've had. It had this... Salvador Dali feeling. This surreal, nightmarish aura I've never felt.

"The second dream started out feeling like my prophetic dreams." I described everything that'd happened. "When the platform started tilting towards the water, I felt the same pressure that I'd felt throughout the first dream. Only, the first half of the second dream felt normal, after that, everything else just felt wrong. It took all my power to wake up."

Gabriel was peculiarly silent. He'd listened and hadn't interrupted me once, not even with a single question. A frown pulled at his lips.

When he didn't say anything, I finally asked, "Any insights?"

"The pressure you described, would you say you felt manipulated?"

I leaned my head against the wall and looked at the ceiling. "Yes. Something forced. It's hard to describe."

"I do not want you to try to sleep until sunrise. It is only another half hour or so."

"Okaaay," I replied, a little confused.

"Just a theory; do not worry about it. We will be safe here for another day or two. I want everyone rested up before we try to go back to the city."

"You aren't going to give me a hint?"

"You sleep better in a dark room? Or does it not matter?"

"Dark. I have to cover the light on the alarm clock half the time to sleep."

"It looks like Joshua is going to have some company." He

picked me up and carried me to the panic room; the door was still open as sunrise was still a little ways off.

Joshua was reclining on a cot reading. He looked up, surprised.

"I want to reverse her sleeping schedule to test a theory," Gabriel mentioned as he sat me down on the small couch in the corner of the tiny room.

"Thanks for the lift."

"I will see you in eight hours." He turned to Joshua. "Make her sleep as soon as the sun crests."

"Will do."

He left and shut the door behind him.

"What theory?" he asked.

"I don't know. He wouldn't say. I just had two horrible dreams back to back."

"Prophetic?"

"Part of one. The rest...I don't know what they were. He asked if they felt manipulated. Then next thing I knew, he was carrying me down here to test a theory."

Joshua got the same quiet look that Gabriel got. "What?"

"You look tired."

"Nice diversionary technique. What?"

"He said he wasn't sure."

I felt like he was holding back. Then I noticed that he seemed to be staying as far away from me as he could. He looked even more pale than normal. His lips looked dry, and his cheeks more hollow.

"Do we have any *supplies* for you?" I asked apprehensively.

His eyes tensed a little. "No, but I'll be fine."

"You don't look like you're doing fine."

"Thanks."

"You know what I mean."

"Yes. I do," he admitted.

There was a long silence. "Use me."

"No."

"Please, listen. It's going to be worse eight hours from now, right? You will have more control now. And who knows if they have a supply in town that can be bought or pilfered."

He became quiet. He seemed to be considering it. "Are you strong enough? You just had emergency surgery."

"I didn't lose much blood. The pain I'm in is because of the incision. I should be fine. I'm sure I can spare a pint. And now that the pain meds have worn off, I'm curious to see if you can still taste that bitterness."

"They've worn off? Do we have more?" His voice was alarmed.

"No. The van hadn't been restocked."

He didn't need to ask if I was in pain. He could see it on my face, as much as I was trying to hide it. He furrowed his brow and placed the book he'd been reading on the floor, *Paradise Lost*. I wondered if he'd had it in the van or if he had found it here. The cot creaked as he sat up. He walked the four steps it took to cross the small space and sat on the floor next to me. "Are you sure?"

"I *want* you to…really."

"I can't believe I am doing this. I promised myself."

"You want my arm? Or neck?" I felt awkward all of a sudden.

"Wrist. Neck might be too much for me. I don't want to get distracted." He swallowed.

"I can see that." I smiled and hung my right arm off the side of the couch.

He gently took my wrist and ran his fingers over my hand and forearm, giving me chills. He kissed my palm, the heel of my hand, and then my wrist. He took a few short breaths through his nose as he rested his mouth on the pulse point. He opened his mouth and fed on me willingly for the first time.

I wanted to run my fingers through his hair, but I was afraid to cause any lapse in concentration. I felt that same rapturous sensation I'd had in the warehouse when I'd force-fed him. That he could've taken every drop, and I'd be glad to give it. After he was done, he licked the wound, and it immediately started to heal. The pain in my belly had subsided too. I felt like I could breathe again.

He held my hand against his cheek and sat with his eyes closed for a long while. I finally broke the silence. "Are you okay?" I asked softly.

His eyes smiled. "Yes," he whispered almost inaudibly. "Are you?"

"Mmm hmm." I paused. "How much do you drink a day?"

"It varies on activity level." He still hadn't opened his eyes. He ran his nose up and down my forearm, giving me the occasional kiss.

"Can I sustain you till we get back?"

"Probably. If I reserve my energy. But not on a regular basis. Not without wearing you down. You wouldn't be able to recover fast enough." He opened his eyes and rested his head on the edge of the sofa, our faces close.

"If we aren't able to get any supplies for you, I'm yours."

"Thank you," he sighed. "The sun is up. We should both try to get some sleep."

"How do you know?"

"Trust me, vampires know exactly when the sun is going to rise and set. Kinda like the way my dad always knew the rain was coming. Feel it in my bones."

Standing up, he dragged the cot over and butted it up against the couch. He grabbed a couple of blankets off of the industrial-looking shelves next to the door and covered me. Afterwards, he reclined on the cot and rolled to face me. It was so squeaky, it sounded like two squirrels chirping at one another.

"I thought vampires were supposed to do things silently?" I teased.

"I don't think Dracula could keep this thing from making noise."

"Sure he could; he would just turn into mist and hover above it to sleep."

"Wouldn't that be a nice trick?"

"Yeah, Dracula could go out in the sunlight too. That would be nice." I felt bad after I said it. My mouth had taken off before my brain engaged.

He sighed. "I would love to see you in the sunlight again. See the strands of gold in your hair. Feel the warmth."

"I'm sorry."

"You have no need to be sorry." He took my hand in his and closed his eyes. He fell asleep quickly, and I soon followed.

OF THINGS PAST

I woke with my hand in Joshua's. He was still sleeping heavily. I didn't think he'd slept much in a couple of days. I had questions buzzing in my head. I sat up and suddenly felt like the muscles in my abs had worn thin and were no longer able to contract. I had to remain motionless for a while to recover from sitting up like that. I wondered if I should still be hurting this much, but I had no basis of reference. Josh started to stir. He yawned and stretched himself awake.

"Morning," I cooed.

"Morning." He smiled.

"What time is it?"

He pulled the phone out of his pocket. "4:00 P.M."

"Wow, the day is seriously almost gone," I said, a little surprised.

"Welcome to my world...though I usually don't sleep this long."

"Must have needed it." I spied some duct tape on the shelf next to the door and thought of a solution to my current dilemma. "Soooo, I really need to use the little girl's room, but the sun is obviously up. Would it be safe for you if we taped these blankets over the door so I could slip out?"

"That should work." He rolled off the cot, and it made all sorts of noises again. We both laughed a little as he slid it out of the way. Then he taped the blankets up, overlapping them securely so I could slide through the middle.

He pushed the shelving unit over just far enough that he could stand in the niche it created. "I'll stand here, so if any light bleeds in, you won't have to worry." He walked over to me and offered his hand to help me stand up very slowly. I stood on shaky legs, but was able to shuffle forward. I remained slightly hunched as I still didn't feel like I could stand up all the way.

"Off to the races."

"I'll see you in a bit." He stepped back into the corner as I hobbled out.

When I opened the door, I could hear birds chirping outside. I kept the opening as small as possible and slipped through, none too gracefully.

I proceeded with turtle-like speed straight to the bathroom. Afterwards, I went to the living room. Gentry was in the attached kitchen chopping something. Peter was hunched over some papers spread out over the coffee table, examining them with utter concentration. He didn't notice I'd entered.

"Hey, love. How ya feelin'?" Gentry asked in her cheerful style.

"Better. Got some good sleep. Don't remember the last time I slept for that long."

"Aye, you were a trifle fitful when we first arrived."

"Sorry, didn't mean to drive you out of the room."

"Wasn't tryin' to make ya feel bad. Just worried about ya is all."

"Where's Gabriel?"

"He wandered out 'bout a half hour ago." She walked over to the window and peered out. "I think that's 'im down there, in the graveyard next to St. Patrick's."

I shuffled over to the window. I thought I could see where he was. I opened the backdoor and wondered if I would be able to make it. The ground was fairly flat leading to a gently rolling hill, not much of a decline. I turned to Gentry. "Were you able to get any pain killers?"

"Oh, sorry, love. I did." She picked through a shopping bag on the counter. "It's not pharmaceutical grade, but it should help."

"Thank you so much." I downed them, and then I realized I'd never asked Joshua if that bitter taste was still in my blood.

I made my way to the back door and was able to traverse the steps if I stood sideways and took them one at a time. The sun was growing drowsy in the sky; it bathed the hillside in beautiful amber light, the orange hues inviting. I loved this time of day. The trees and shrubs that still had leaves looked like they were hung with gold. I continued my journey, drinking in the light. It seemed like it'd been raining forever.

Gabriel's back was to me. He was sitting amongst the gravestones, motionless. "What are you doing out of the house?"

"I see my stealth abilities have been impacted too."

"Dragging your feet while walking over gravel is always effective," he replied with some humor. "How did you sleep?" he asked without moving or turning to see me.

"Better."

"No more strange nightmares?"

"Not-uh-one."

"Good."

I finally reached him. He moved over on the stone slab bench on which he was sitting. He sat straight, with his hands resting one on each thigh. I carefully lowered myself halfway down and plopped the rest of the way to his left.

"Are you going to tell me your theory?"

"Not yet. Give it another day, then we will do another experiment."

"You know the secrecy thing isn't very comforting."

"I want to limit the variables in the experiment."

"Great. Love being a lab rat."

He smiled, but I could tell his thoughts were elsewhere.

I looked at the gravestones around us. Many of them were so old that the writing carved into them was worn. Stone that'd probably been smooth at one time was weathered and rough, with moss etching into the surface. Some of the grave markers were simple rectangles, others peaked arches. A handful of ornate ones added variety to the cluster of stones.

One drew my attention: a glossy, grey stone newer than everything around it. It was square, where almost all others were rectangular. There was an angel atop it, its wings arched protectively in a C shape above the stone.

The angel's face was turned to the side, eyes closed as if it was waiting until the end, for death to strike, making one last effort to shield his ward. So much emotion and beauty was in the carving, I was mesmerized. It was the way I had felt seeing some of Waterhouse's paintings in person for the first time—absolute awe.

A single name was on the stone with a month and day. No year. My stomach sank. *This is why Gabriel knows this place.*

The tombstone read "Laylah—March 8." I looked at Gabriel, his eyes somber as he looked at the angel. I put my hand on top of his and squeezed a little. He didn't pull away.

"This is the one place I visit every year."

"It's beautiful here." I didn't know what else to say.

"She liked it. It was one of her favorite places. We used to horseback ride in the mountains here. There is an old lighthouse not far away. You can see all the counties of Dublin-from-it."

"Sounds nice."

"Maybe someday I will show you."

"I would like that." I let go of his hand and picked up a leaf that had fallen onto the bench next to me. I slowly broke it to pieces at each of the vein marks. I'd been wondering something for weeks, and thought I might actually get an answer today. "Gabriel, who was the woman in Gloucester? The beautiful one, with the tattoos."

He exhaled through his nose. "I knew you would eventually ask me."

"I'm that predictable, huh?"

"Chlöe Rogers," he said, his voice soft...full of kindness.

"Rogers." I repeated. I'd heard that last name somewhere, but I couldn't place it. "How do you know her?"

He was quiet for a long moment, perhaps picking his words carefully. "Shared grief." He looked into the distance. In fact, I didn't think he'd looked at me once since I'd arrived.

I refrained from asking the barrage of questions that popped into my mind, as that didn't work well with Gabriel.

"It is ironic that we are here." A long pause. "Her brother was on Winslow's team. He was killed when..." He nodded at Laylah's grave. *Shared grief.*

"So you were close."

His thoughts came out in phrases, his voice sounding of regret. "We were. For a long while, but she wanted out of the Watchers. To cope, she pulled away. Wanted to work as an Asset...have a normal life. I worked more. She wanted me to leave with her. Deep down she knew I could not. This is what I am." He sighed with so much sadness. "I hurt her. I did not mean to, but I did."

"Do Slayers ever leave?"

"No. At least, it has never happened. We are hard-wired for this."

"What do you mean?"

He looked over at me for the first time. "I am not entirely human."

A light bulb went off. "In the warehouse last June, Tyran called you 'Semideus.'"

He nodded. "It is almost dark. I want to get you inside." I looked up. The sun was about to drop beneath the horizon. I'd been so absorbed on what he'd been saying, I hadn't realized so much time had passed.

"You're killing me here."

He smiled. "Let us get inside and get some food. Then you can have the history lesson."

"Phew. You had me worried there."

He stood and offered both his hands. I stood up like a ninety-year-old woman and started shuffling back towards the house. He walked along side me, or inched along would have been more exact.

"We will not make it before sunset at this pace." And with that, he scooped me up and walked faster than I could have walked when I was well.

When we reached the top of the steps, he placed me upright, and I entered the house under my own power.

The five of us ate together—well, Josh just sat with us. After cleanup, Gentry and Peter went to bed, as they'd been up since 5:00 A.M., and Josh went to walk the perimeter.

The wind picked up, and the house dropped in temperature; it was a damp cold that seemed to sink into my bones. I was anxious to get my history lesson while Gabriel started a fire. It crackled and hissed, like it wanted to be part of a conversation. It was the only light in the room. The rest of the lamps were kept off so we would have better visibility out the windows.

Before leaving for sentry duty, Joshua had dropped the copy of *Paradise Lost* he'd been reading on the coffee table. Gabriel walked through the room several times and finally sat down to send some text messages. I patiently waited for Gabriel to explain the significance of the word Semideus and what he meant by "mostly human." It was a challenge, since unlike everyone else, I didn't have anything to do.

Gabriel looked up from his phone. "You look like you have a question."

"Am I allowed only one?"

"You want your history lesson?"

"Still dyin' here."

"I am in a holding pattern anyway." He held up his phone.

I tried to pull my legs up and cringed. I kept forgetting not to strain my abs. He stood and picked up my legs and swiveled me onto the couch so my legs were elevated.

"Thanks," I said with a breath.

"I will need to start at the beginning, well before Slayers or vampires existed."

I nodded eagerly.

"There was a group of angels who were commissioned to watch over humanity, two hundred in total. They decided to turn their backs on God and rebelled."

"Like in *Paradise Lost*?"

"No, that was the first rebellion, when Satan was cast out. Unlike in Milton's story, Moloch and Dagan were part of the second rebellion; they actually fought against Satan before revolting themselves much later."

"How many rebellions have there been?" I asked curiously.

"Just the two. The second rebellion took place during the time of Noah, a couple of hundred years before the flood."

"Why did they rebel?"

Gabriel arched a brow.

"Sorry, I'll be quiet." My curiosity was bubbling.

He grinned, then answered, "Envy, lust, among other things. They had been asked to watch over humanity, but they gave up heaven to indulge their desires. Ironically, they were called Watchers, but they turned evil and corrupted humanity.

"God told them not to mate with humans, but they did. Their offspring, the Nephilim, were out of control. They consumed everything around them. They brought magic and evil into the land and eventually started cannibalizing humans, drinking their blood, despite being half-human themselves. They couldn't be satisfied. They corrupted everyone and everything."

"Did they corrupt *all* of humanity?"

"That is part of the reason God sent the flood. To destroy the evil they propagated."

"All except Noah's family?" I asked.

"Correct. God sent Uriel, the angel not the Slayer, to warn Noah's family. Michael, Gabriel, Raphael, and Uriel were the angels that pleaded with God to send judgment. He gave each of them a task. The flood was one part of what happened."

"Did the flood destroy the Nephilim and all the fallen angels?"

"God sent Raphael to imprison Azâzêl, the leader of the two-hundred. Gabriel was dispatched to deal with the Nephilim. Michael was sent to bind the other fallen angels after their offspring had been destroyed. The flood came soon after."

"How do you know all this?"

"Some of it is in the Bible: Genesis 6 and Numbers 13 make references. The Apocrypha, which was not canonized and put in the Jewish or Christian scriptures, has some information in the Book of Enoch. It embellishes the story a little, but we have other references that have remained safe in one of our repositories."

"So how does this lead to you?"

He shifted in his seat. "Moloch and Dagan were both members of the defunct Watchers, angels from the two hundred that rebelled. They and a couple of others escaped their prison and started to live amongst humans. Moloch may be Azâzêl and Dagan one of the lieutenants."

"So people were worshipping fallen angels?"

"Yes. They were gods to them. As you know, God cursed Moloch and all his worshippers to darkness, and they were bound by the blood they worshipped. They became the first vampires. Dagan was there, but he was not cursed in the way the others were. We do not know why; it may be that he did not take part in the blood rituals.

"After that, the Angels of the Four Corners, Michael, Gabriel, Uriel, and Raphael asked to be sent to earth to train up protectors. They became known as the Sentinels. They gave up their wings and immortality, but not all of their abilities, and started the new Watchers.

"With God's blessing, they married and had children. Their offspring were not the monsters that were created before, the Nephilim; they were the first Slayers—half-human, half-angel, or as Tyran put it: Semideus or demigods."

"So you guys are named after those angels—the Sentinels?"

"Yes. Every few generations the name is used again. It marks the line from which we originate. But the last time all four names were used simultaneously was a millennia ago."

"Let me guess: something horrible happened then."

He took a deep breath, but didn't answer.

"I'll take that as a yes."

Joshua came in through the front door. "I set up the motion detectors and ran the perimeter a couple of times. It's quiet out there."

Gabriel's phone chimed. "Excuse me." He stood and started speaking with someone as he glided out of the room.

Joshua sat on the edge of the couch next to me and tugged on a lock of my hair. "How're you doing?"

"Good. Just learned a lot of info. Still processing."

"Is everything okay?"

"No. No…fine. Learned some of the history is all."

He took my hand and held it to his mouth, kissed it, and closed his eyes.

"I meant to ask you. Was the bitterness still in my blood?"

He opened his eyes. "Yes, it was."

I frowned.

Gabriel came abruptly back into the room. "Blackthorne showed up at the Dublin house."

"That is out of character."

"Precisely."

I was glad I wasn't there and wondered why Blackthorne, the leader of the Conclave, would drop by the Dublin house unannounced? When I'd met with the Concilium in California, I'd found him very unsettling. I looked around and realized that I'd missed part of the conversation Gabriel and Joshua were having.

Gabriel was talking to me. "Sorry. What did you say?" I asked, trying to refocus.

"How is your pain level?"

"Okay. I thought I'd be feeling a little better by now. My

neighbor had appendicitis on a Monday, and she was back at work on Wednesday."

A strange look crept across his face. He held his finger up to silence me as he dialed his phone with the other. "Sebastian. Did you ever get in touch with any of the doctors at the hospital?" He listened for a moment. "Get back to me."

He walked with purpose into the kitchen. He looked through the duffle on the counter and pulled a handheld device out of it. He powered it up. It made a small humming sound, and then went silent.

"I already swept the place," Joshua commented, looking a little confused.

"Did you check her?"

Josh's eyes bulged. "No. Did I need to?"

Gabriel walked over and slowly moved the device over my belly. Afterwards, he sat on the armrest and rubbed his temple with his left hand. You could see the wheels turning in his head. When Gabriel didn't say anything, Joshua took the device from him and did the same.

Joshua's voice was solemn and confused. "It's ours."

"Yes."

"But it's not transmitting," Josh added.

Then Gabriel added, "Not yet."

I felt like my blood had turned cold.

A message came through on Gabriel's phone. He read it aloud. "None of the doctors or nurses who performed the surgery reported for work today."

"What does that mean?" I asked.

"Sebastian is going to send scouts to some of the medical staff's homes. We will know soon."

"What did they do to me?"

Gabriel placed his hand on my shoulder and tried to extend

some sort of comfort. *Violated* was the only word that I could conjure up to express how I felt. I sat there breathing, shallowly, but instead of feeling sorry for myself, I decided to hold onto the anger I felt.

"What do you want to do?" Joshua asked.

"We need to leave," I said. "We don't want to burn this safe house." I looked up at Gabriel. I wanted him to be able to come back here and be able to visit his sister.

"Wake Peter and Gentry."

Josh left the room immediately.

Gabriel dialed a number. "Jess. Yes. I need you to meet me. Bring a surgical kit and the portable ultrasound machine. Yes... now. Yes. Forty minutes." He hung up.

All traces of our stay were scrubbed from the room within minutes, the motion detectors were removed, and I was carried to the van. Even though I had slept the entire day, I wanted to close my eyes and sleep, to avoid my current reality.

It was going to be a long night.

I sighed as we pulled away from the house.

It started to rain–again...

A long, long night.

21

RATS

W e rumbled to a stop not far from an office building and waited in the vehicle for a couple of minutes. A single dim light could be seen through the blinds in one of the back windows. Gabriel pulled a pair of gloves and a flashlight out of the duffle.

"Gentry, acquire a car. Peter, I need you to catch a rat. I need it alive."

"Like a rodent? A real rat?" he asked, making sure he'd heard correctly.

"Yes." Gabriel handed him the gloves and flashlight. "There is a pub a few doors down; check around the dumpsters. This area of town is infested."

"Woo hoo," he said facetiously.

"Text me when you are on the way. We will let you in the side door."

Gabriel raised his phone to his ear. "You there?" He paused. "Arrival in thirty seconds."

Joshua plucked me from my seat, and almost instantly I

found myself at the side door to the office. Gabriel knocked, and it clicked open.

The hallway was dark; I could only see that the person who opened the door was tall and wearing a white lab coat. We walked into the office. A desk had been cleared and prepped with a plastic tablecloth. Joshua put me down next to the table. I tried to stand up straight, but then decided that wasn't the brightest plan and leaned against the desk instead.

The person in the lab coat who ushered us in turned around. She was beautiful—and tall—and perfect. She had that sweet, fresh faced, girl-next-door look, like she should be on an advertisement for the latest facial scrub. Her straight, dark blonde hair was swept back into a chignon; a couple wisps hung at the sides of her face, framing her sparkling blue eyes. *Yup, pretty sure I hate her.*

"Thanks for meeting us, Jess."

"I'm always here for you, Gabriel." She was an American. "Joshua, nice to see you again." The way she smiled at him told of something between them.

"And you," he replied softly. I felt a twinge of jealousy.

Joshua put his arm around my shoulder. "This is Aleria." He said my name with affection. My stupid jealousy melted away. *Okay, don't hate her.* There seemed to be some acknowledgement between them. Like I'd been a topic of discussion in the past.

Gabriel spoke, "She has a transmitter in her abdominal area. She had an emergency appendectomy yesterday."

Jess smiled shyly at me and tilted her head down a bit. "Okay, let's get you on the table and have a look."

Josh helped me get into position.

"We'll need to roll the top of your pants down," Jess said as she helped me push them down to just above my pelvic bone, so my whole abdominal area was showing. She twisted around and turned on the portable ultrasound machine that she had on a mail cart next to her.

"According to the signature, it is a 200 series," Gabriel informed her.

"We haven't used those in a while," she replied.

Gabriel walked over to the window. "We think they may have poisoned her and caused the appendicitis, or the appearance of it."

She pulled over a stool and sat next to me. "Well, let's see what we can see. This is going to be a little cold. You'll feel some pressure." She squeezed some clear gel onto my belly and pressed the ultrasound wand just below my belly button. She moved it in small circles.

"Okay. Let's take a general look first." She talked us through what she was looking at. I strained to see the monitor, but it really wasn't of much use. I didn't understand what I was seeing. A grey blob followed by another grey blob.

"Your insides look pretty healthy. Uterus...ovary... intestines... It does look like the appendix is missing. Let me double check." She moved it around in smaller circles again. "This isn't the highest resolution machine, but I don't see an appendix."

She pressed a little too hard on my incision, and I sucked in a startled breath.

"Sorry." She pursed her lips. "Not used to post-op patients."

"What do you do?" I asked, trying to distract myself.

"I am an ultrasound tech for a few clinics. Mostly baby stuff. Couldn't get the work visa to do anything else. I'm at Trinity College for the year. Taking a few classes. This pays my way."

"Mmmmm."

"And here's the transmitter. It looks like it is nested against the bone inside the right hip."

Gabriel stepped back over. "We need to remove it."

"I figured." Jess stood up and pulled out some more supplies. "If you can hold the ultrasound to guide me, I can open up less of her incision."

"Will do."

"Okay. You can wash up over there."

Gabriel strode over to a kitchen area in the corner and started the water.

"I'm going to give you something for the pain. Do you want me to put you out?" she asked me.

"No. I would rather be alert." I guessed I was taking after Gabriel.

She swabbed my arm and injected it. I relaxed almost immediately. Joshua moved around closer to my head and held my hand. Jess made a couple smaller injections around my incision.

Gabriel returned and put on some gloves. His phone chimed on the desk. He bent to read the text, then looked at Josh. "Peter is back."

"I'll get him." Joshua disappeared into the hallway.

A minute later, they both returned. Peter was holding a very well-fed rat in his hands. It struggled and thrashed, then relaxed, and then repeated the process, its whiskers twitching incessantly.

"Let's keep that over in that half of the room," Jess requested. She placed her hands on my abdomen. "You feel that?"

"Just the pressure," I answered.

"And this?"

"Same."

"Okay. We're ready." I felt what must have been the reopening of my incision. "Okay, I need you to..." Gabriel placed the scanner thing on my belly. "Okay. Move it." She paused. "Hold up." She put her hand on top of his, but I couldn't see what they were looking at. They ran the scanner back and forth, almost to my left hipbone and back again. I saw them look at one another, but they didn't say anything verbally.

"What?" I asked.

"Nothing. Just making sure there was only one transmitter." A lie. She wasn't telling me something.

They went to work on removing the transmitter. "We're going to need to open this up the rest of the way. I keep hitting something that shouldn't be there."

I got worried. *What had they done to me in that hospital?* I started breathing harder as my mind started coming up with completely absurd scenarios, everything from scenes from the first *Alien* movie to my insides liquefying from a delayed reaction to the poison.

Joshua squeezed my hand and started running his fingers through my hair with his other hand. I focused on that. His eyes smiled, but there was worry in them.

"You get past it?" Gabriel asked.

"They stitched these muscles together. Have you felt a pulling?" Jess replied.

"Yes, I haven't been able to stand up straight."

"I think whoever did this was trying to make it so someone would have to go into the wound again. You see this?" She showed Gabriel something.

"So the doctors may have been coerced."

"This is something only a surgeon could do. No damage done, but she would go back thinking something was really wrong. A trail right to the transmitter." She held up something between long tweezers. "And there we go. How long do we have?"

"Ten minutes until the fail-safe goes off."

"Not a problem."

I felt some tugging.

Joshua stopped her. "Just do some loose stitches. I have an idea. He let go of my hand and grabbed some gauze. He turned his back to me. "Try that." I felt something being swabbed on my belly.

"That will work," she said, her voice surprised.

"Peter, we need the rat," Gabriel called.

Joshua picked me up, making room for the rat on the table, and sat me on a desk chair. Peter walked over, cupping it. Jess soaked the back of its neck with alcohol and made a quick incision. Gabriel picked up the transmitter. She aptly inserted it into the rat and sealed the incision with glue.

"Perfect." She smiled.

"Joshua, would you be so kind as to set this rat free a couple blocks from here?"

"As you wish." He looked pleased as he picked up the rat and disappeared from the room. Gabriel's phone chimed on the counter.

"Gentry is in the vehicle outside. Exit in five," Gabriel ordered.

Everyone started to pack things up, while Jess came over and looked at my incision again. I had been so interested in what they were doing with the rat, I forgot to look.

"Remarkable," she commented.

The incision looked like it had been healing for weeks. *Saliva...Joshua's saliva.*

Joshua returned to hear Jess give instructions.

"You need to remember you are not healed up on the inside. Take it easy, but walk as much as possible. It could take you another four to six weeks to feel one hundred percent."

"I thought the recovery time for appendectomies was two weeks?"

She stammered a tiny bit before answering. "It varies; this may take a little longer...with the tracker, and the muscles that were stitched."

"I thought you said there was no damage from that?"

"No *permanent* damage."

"Sorry. I didn't mean to question you."

"It's totally okay. It's good to pay attention to detail."

"Are you a Watcher?"

She smiled. "Yes, I worked with Sebastian and Gabriel in Philadelphia when they needed a medic. I was in medical school there."

"Is that where you met Joshua?"

"They called me the night he was attacked. He was unconscious and had a fractured skull, leg wound, and the bite on his neck. I patched him up as best I could, but it was soon apparent that he was going to turn, and it was going to be slow. He was only exposed to a small amount of his sire's blood. If he hadn't been turned, he wouldn't have survived the night."

She thought for a moment; her words were always deliberate. "Sebastian fought for him from the beginning. He said he knew he was different. I officially met Joshua a couple of days later. I had a connection in the hospital and was able to get donated blood for him. I brought it a couple times a week." She looked over at Josh, who was discussing something with Gabriel. "He's a good man."

"The best. But didn't it bother you that you were helping a vampire?"

"I trust Sebastian."

"Yeah, me too." I confirmed that the boys were still talking. "Was Gabriel so easily swayed?"

She smirked and chose her words carefully. "He was *cautious.*"

"Gabriel? No!" I said jokingly.

I was about to ask another question, but the guys were already on their way over.

"You want to walk?" Gabriel asked.

"I'll try."

Jess put her hand on my shoulder. "Start the exercise after she rests in the car." She looked at Joshua. "Lots of walking, but low activity level for a few days."

"Got it," he replied as he picked me up again.

"Where are we headed?"

"To catch a rat," Gabriel responded ominously. "Jess, I want you clear of here. We never saw you."

"I'm at the movies right now," she said, pulling out a ticket stub.

"Good girl."

"Until next time. Nice meeting you." She gave my arm a squeeze as she passed with her gear.

We lingered just long enough to make sure she got to her car. As soon as she started the engine, we met Gentry in our new vehicle. We drove back into the outskirts of Dublin and checked into a small hotel, renting a mini-suite. The room was on the back of the building and nearest the exit. It didn't seem the safest room to rent, like we were more vulnerable to intruders, but Gabriel had to have had a plan.

The suite had a bedroom with two full-sized beds and a small sitting area. It had a large walk-in closet and a bathroom equipped with a huge bathtub. I had yet to see a "loo" like this in the British Isles. I was thrilled and hoped I'd get the chance to use it.

Joshua moved the rollaway bed into the closet. It then occurred to me: we needed this place for him. When Josh returned, Gabriel looked up from the device he'd been staring at.

"Are you ready?"

Josh nodded. "Yes. Was it activated?"

"Two minutes ago."

"Is it still in the same place?"

I wondered what they were talking about.

"More or less."

"Let's do this," he said, drawing in a breath.

Gabriel's phone buzzed. He pulled it out and stared blankly at the screen. "Wait. I need to contact Sebastian."

Joshua rocked back on his heels. I quietly went to his side. "Can I talk to you for a moment? Privately?"

He looked at Gabriel. His body language told me it was going to be a few minutes. Peter and Gentry were already sitting on the couch discussing something.

"Sure," he replied cautiously. He followed close behind me. I went to the closet, pulled the cord to the light, and closed the door behind us.

I spoke very softly. "Are you going out to track the rat?"

"Which one?"

"Ha ha." I rolled my eyes.

"Yes, we are hoping whoever put the tracker in you will show up. The tracker was activated a few minutes ago."

"Are you going alone?"

"Yes. We can't leave you unprotected."

"What if there are a whole bunch of them?"

"I'm just going to observe them. No confrontation."

I knew I wouldn't win the argument, and we did need to know who the traitor was amongst us. My voice had gotten a little loud, so I lowered it to a whisper once again. "How much or often, do you normally feed each day?"

"I'm good."

"You said you had to keep your activity level low. You would have fed already tonight. Wouldn't you?" I let my eyes bore into him.

He pursed his lips. "Yes."

I pulled my sleeve up. "You—sit." I pointed at the portable bed. His nostrils flared, but he did as I said. I listened; I could still hear two conversations going on in the other room. I sat next to him and handed him my arm.

"Ali…" he hesitated.

"Is it so horrible to drink from me?" I asked. For some reason, his reluctance felt like rejection.

"I like it too much. I'm just afraid I'm going to hurt you and you just had surgery."

"I want you strong. I want you to come back to me and I already feel better than I did after the last surgery."

And so he drank, but not much. I held still as to not distract him, but it seemed like it was easier this time. He made small circles with his thumb on my arm. He drank less than before; I'm sure he did it because he didn't feel I was strong enough. He sealed the punctures, then sat there holding my hand in silence, with his eyes closed.

"You are okay with this?" He stroked my wrist lightly.

"I've already told you. I want you to."

He nodded.

"Won't it make it easier…when we are close?" I asked.

"I think so; it was easier to stop this time."

"I really want to kiss you right now, but I don't think I can twist to the side."

He let out a little laugh. "That sounded a tiny bit pathetic," he teased.

He dropped to his knees in front of me and placed his lips on mine. I couldn't help but make a small gasp. I felt him smile a little. He cupped my face with his hands and gave me one last kiss; I wished I could freeze time. He leaned back and took both my hands in his. "I love you."

"And I you," I whispered, somewhat hoarsely.

And then the closet door was open, and I was alone. I sat there in silence for a while. I could still smell his scent on me. I finally stood and made my way to the bathroom. I lifted my shirt and hooked my thumb in my pants to examine my belly.

There was an agitated pink line just inside my hipbone. It was going to leave a scar, but it wouldn't be bad. I still felt sore, but there was no more extra pulling inside, and the fact that the incision area was no more than tender was a welcome differ-ence. Of course, I wouldn't want to be running for my life or anything. I meandered into the living room only slightly hunched over.

Peter sat on the couch, remote control in his hand, but the television was barely audible. He looked over at me and grinned. "Done with your alone time, princess?"

I looked around. "Where is everyone?" Then I paused and realized he had called me princess. I picked up the tissue box on the table next to me and hurled it at his head.

He batted it away and raised his hands in surrender. "Stop, I don't want Gabriel to break my leg for getting you riled up and hurting yourself."

I stuck my tongue out at him. "You didn't answer my ques-tion. Where did everyone go?"

"Gabriel is just outside, something about reception. He sent Gentry out for something. I guess grand theft auto was only her first act."

"I didn't realize she was so talented."

"She's full of surprises."

I sat down next to him on the couch. "You realize the last time we were on a couch together, Gentry ran in, and we had to evacuate."

"Seems like a year ago."

"Yeah."

He propped his feet on the ottoman. "You know I had a crush on you in eighth grade?"

"You did? I didn't even know you back then," I said surprised. "Weren't you still in public school?"

"Yeah, but Robert and I were friends. I visited one day. What'd they call it?"

"Shadowing."

"Yeah, I shadowed him for a day. I pointed you out. He said he didn't know you. That you were in the honors classes."

"Mmmmm, junior high. Great days. Yeah, not really."

"When I started at your school freshman year, I was pretty mad that he'd asked you out."

"That was kind of messed up of him."

"I don't know if he remembered."

"Robert never forgot anything." He seemed to deflate a little, so I quickly added, "But I don't know. Maybe he did forget." *No, he didn't forget.*

He shifted to his side so he could look me in the eye, and something changed. The vibe between us became awkward, and his eyes serious. "How long?"

"How long what?"

"You and Joshua."

"Oh." The air went out of my lungs. "Since..." I hesitated. "Since before we came here."

"Like Dublin?"

"No, like California." I felt ashamed.

He rubbed his palms on his pants like they were sweating.

"Peter, I am so, so sorry. I just. We just..." I slumped my shoulders. "I should have told you." I couldn't look at him anymore, but I could feel his eyes on me.

"It's okay. I mean, it's not like you've ever been available."

"When Robert and I broke up, and you told me that you couldn't hang out with me, I was devastated. I honestly mourned the loss of your friendship, even more than I did the loss of Robert."

"Mourned—really?"

"You didn't," I took a breath. "You didn't come here for me, did you?" I felt horribly embarrassed asking this, but I had to know. I could feel my face burning. It felt like I had swallowed cement. If he had, I would be the worst person on the planet.

"Maybe a small piece, but I really came to protect my family. And I really do love this life."

"You know I love you, right?"

"I know. I've always known that." We sat in silence for a few minutes. "I've actually been feeling a little guilty the last week or so."

"About what?"

"I felt like I was betraying you, because I started feeling something for someone."

"May I ask who? No, wait." I thought through some things I'd seen over the last couple of weeks: whispered conversations, dancing together with eyes closed, trips to buy groceries, chores together. "Gentry."

He smiled. "I've felt a little confused by it actually. But she's just so amazing."

"And the red hair and adorable Irish accent doesn't hurt."

He got a goofy grin. "That would never hurt."

"You should go for it."

He smiled.

"And Peter, I'm sorry. You are my best friend, and it was never that I didn't trust you. We didn't tell *anyone*, though some have figured it out recently."

"Do you…"

The door crashed open, shattering the calm in the room. Gabriel and Joshua were carrying a man—or vamp—into the room. There was a heavy black bag over his head.

Gabriel looked at me. "Stay back."

They bustled into the bathroom, lurching back and forth as he tried to kick free. We heard a few crashes, and then it was silent. Gabriel reentered the living room. "I need you to do an identification."

"Okay." I scooted to the edge of my seat and carefully stood up.

"Peter, pull her out if things go south. I am not sure she can move fast enough."

"Of course."

We entered the bathroom. The visitor had chains around him that raked against the porcelain tub. He panted and grunted from the struggle. Joshua was standing in the tub next to him with his foot in the middle of his chest. He was thrown back slightly when the vampire bucked.

Joshua pulled out a Durateus dagger and came down hard in the middle of his chest. The vamp's legs scuffed the tub as they straightened out, and then all movement stopped. He was paralyzed.

Gabriel bent over the tub, ripped the dagger out, and pierced him again next to the heart. Joshua repositioned himself defensively. The vamp moved a little, but he wasn't resisting. Gabriel tore the hood from his head. The prisoner looked around wildly, but when he took in the Slayer towering over him and Joshua ready to strike, he calmed back down.

"Ali, is this the vampire you saw in the hospital?" Gabriel asked.

I crept around Gabriel's side, my stomach aflutter, and peered at him. Muddy green eyes locked onto mine. A smile twisted across his face, narrowing the checkmark scar above his brow. It was the same look I thought he'd had in the O.R., but this time, I could see the gap between his front teeth.

With a taunting smile, he said, "*Bonjour.*"

"Yes, that's him," I confirmed. I clutched at my belly; the sight of him made me feel sick.

"What were your orders? Who do you report to? And do not lie to me; my friend here can sense your deceit." Gabriel's tone was harsh as he motioned to Joshua.

The vamp smiled at me with a disturbing amount of calm, like he was the cat that had caught the canary.

"Peter, get her out of here," Gabriel commanded.

Peter immediately put his hands on my waist and ushered me back into the living room and onto the couch. In the bathroom, someone turned on the rattly exhaust fan to cover some of the noise. Muffled screams and other noises I didn't want to hear made me cringe. Peter clicked on the TV and raised the volume this time. He put his arm around my shoulder, and I leaned against him.

While I could still hear the questioning in the other room, it seemed like hours ticked by. I fought for my lids to stay open. I knew I wasn't supposed to sleep at night, but physical and mental exhaustion were crushing in on me. Despite the horror it entailed, sleep came for me nonetheless.

22

BETRAYAL AND TRAGEDY

I was outside of myself and watched as Tyran knocked Peter and Joshua to the ground, everything moving in slow motion. To my left and I was there, trying to get a clear shot at Tyran. Recognizing that this was in the past, I wondered why I was watching this moment. This was my own experience. Joshua launched himself and flew through the air, tackling Tyran from behind. He cinched his arm around Tyran's neck and thrust a blade into his heart through his back.

Peter, who was still lying on the ground with his arms wrapped around his torso, was screaming. He'd seen Bowen go for me before I had. He'd yelled at me, but I didn't hear him, his eyes full of horror as Bowen locked his arm around me, pinning my arms to my sides. He had a blade under my chin and pressed it hard enough to draw a little blood.

Joshua pushed Tyran far enough away from himself to allow Gabriel to take Tyran's head. Bowen's voice thundered as he yelled, "Stop!" *Why am I here? What is so important about this moment?* I had been ready to die at that moment. I'd yelled for Gabriel to "Do it!"—to take Tyran's head, even if it meant my life. Standing at this new angle, I could see Tyran's face as I yelled it. He appeared to be shocked.

Gabriel was right: Tyran and Bowen were something different. Despite being paralyzed by the knife in his heart, he could still make facial expressions, and I could see his fingers and toes twitch. The others could do nothing but move their eyes. Joshua, sired by Tyran, could blink.

Tyran didn't look at Gabriel, who was about to take his head; he focused on his brother. I turned and looked at Bowen too. At that point, he had begged me not to make him hurt me. Then I remembered wishing I could see his face with my next words. I had tried to persuade him and said this was his "chance to be free." I remembered his breathing became rough, he pressed his cheek against mine, and then he buried his face in my hair.

I watched as the other me spoke the words. Bowen squeezed his eyes closed and looked wholly lost...and when he pressed his cheek to mine, he was truly tempted by my offer to be free. Then I got a sick feeling and spun around to look at Tyran. I couldn't see him while it was really happening. *Tyran saw Bowen's indecision. He saw that his brother was tempted to let him die, no matter how brief.* I looked at Bowen again and realized something—*he loves me.* There was no mistaking it. When he told me his real name and spoke to me in Latin, unfeigned love poured from him. I looked back at Tyran—he had seen it too.

Glass showered from the skylight as Uriel was thrown through it, but before I could look at anything else, I felt that horrible pressure again and struggled to breathe. I looked around and the scene was no longer progressing as I remembered it. A chasm opened up in the floor, and a hellish light emanated from it. The floor started tilting towards the abyss much like the platform next to the ocean in the other dream. I screamed as I watched Peter slide in and fall to his death. Joshua was the next closest. He clawed at the ground, but there was nothing with which to stop himself.

I managed to get to the stairwell that led to the office and grab onto the banister. A presence...maybe more than one became apparent. Scanning the warehouse with every bit of concentration I had, one of the pillars seemed to change shape for a split second. That's when the pain started—I was onto something.

All of my focus went to the pillar. My head felt like it might explode—my temples throbbed. I felt a droplet of liquid on my chest followed by another. The floor was at almost a forty-five degree angle and it was getting harder to hold on. Glancing down, I caught sight of my shirt: it was blood dripping on me. I hooked my leg into the railing and wiped at my face. My nose was now gushing blood. Someone grabbed my arms and shook me, but I couldn't see anyone. So I closed my eyes...*wake...I need to wake.*

I woke to Peter shaking me and screaming my name.

Looking around wildly, I said, "I'm awake," but it came out slurred and garbled. I pressed the sides of my head and moaned.

"Look at me," he said urgently.

My head was swimming. I focused on his face but was distracted by the scarlet stains on his shirt. I put my hand on them; they were wet. I took a couple of deep breaths, and my thoughts started to clear. It was that horrible feeling when you are torn out of a dream and can't figure out what reality you are in. "I fell asleep," I finally said with some effort.

"Lean your head back," he ordered.

I was still confused.

"Do it. Your nose." Then it finally registered. My nose was bleeding in both the dream and reality.

When he was confident that I was lucid, he hurried towards

the bathroom. I heard him apologize for going in. They must've still been in with that vamp. I wondered how long I'd been asleep. When he returned with a towel in his hand, he wasn't alone. Joshua was on his heels. Peter placed the towel over my nose with his right hand and put his left behind my head. I closed my eyes and tried to relax. It wasn't like I could will my nose to stop.

"What happened?" Joshua questioned.

"I don't know. We were watching TV, and she fell asleep I guess. Next thing I knew she was mumbling incoherently, and blood started surging from her nose. It was almost impossible to wake her. She would start to come to and then it was like something would drag her under." Peter paused for a moment. "Are you okay to be around her?"

Joshua made a sound under his breath. "I'm fine," he barked.

"Okay, just..." Peter didn't finish.

I looked through the slits of my eyes. Joshua's apprehensive eyes were glowing. He held his mouth shut in a way that told me he was covering his fangs. He took a step back.

"I'm okay," I whispered. "Just a nose bleed. Go. Help Gabriel." Josh lingered for a moment and slipped out of the room. All I wanted to do was go back to sleep, but that would probably not be in my best interest. I placed my hand over Peter's and took over attending to my nose. "I got it."

"You sure?"

"Yup," I replied in my plugged nose voice.

He sat back. My eyes were closed, but I could feel him looking at me.

"What?" I asked without looking.

"What were you dreaming about?" Peter asked.

I took in a stuttering breath. I felt like I'd been crying. "I was back in the warehouse where we were held captive. But it was like in *Christmas Carol* when the Ghost of Christmas Past brings Scrooge back in time, and he watches events unfold. I could walk around and see things from different angles."

"I couldn't make sense of most of what you said, but you said 'he saw him' over and over. Who saw whom?"

I got that same sick feeling. "Tyran saw Bowen. It doesn't matter…" I tried to blow it off. I opened my eyes.

He wanted to know more. "Why did you say my name?" Peter asked.

"Something is wrong with my dreams. Everything changed. I watched you die and there was nothing I could do but watch."

"Oh, well that kinda sucks."

"Yeah, don't go dying on me, okay?"

"Do my best." He shrugged. If it rattled him, he didn't let on.

Gabriel walked into the room. He noted the bloody towel I held at my nose but didn't say anything. He flipped open the smoke detector and flicked the batteries onto the floor. A minute later, the aroma of something burning wafted out. I'd smelled it before, when Gabriel had burned the body of the ugly shoe vamp in the train station—the questioning was obviously over.

I locked down the horror inside me and pulled the towel from my face. "Is it still bleeding?"

Peter assessed for a moment. "Looks like it stopped."

Blood was smeared on my face. I wanted to clean up, but the bathroom seemed to be off limits for the moment. I grabbed a wad of tissue, dunked it into the watery remains in the ice bucket, and wiped up as best I could in the reflection of the framed art.

Turning to Peter, I asked, "Did I get it all?" Bloody water was dripping down my forearm from the over wet tissue, so I grabbed another tissue and blotted it up before it reached my shirt.

Peter walked over and took the tissue. He bent his index finger and placed the side of it under my chin and gently pushed my head up. "You have some here." He wiped until it was gone and released my chin.

I inspected him for a moment. He had my blood smudged on his face and hands, and his shirt was ruined. He hadn't thought twice about getting my blood all over him. The image of him sliding into the abyss hit me…the crimson trail his body had left as he clawed at the smooth floor trying to catch a handhold.

Wrapping my arms around his torso, I hugged him. He jerked back a little in surprise, and then hugged me back. His whiskered chin pressed against my temple as we stood there. After a few long moments, I pulled away turning my back to wipe the tear that was threatening to streak down my face.

The tissue box was nearly depleted, but I grabbed the few remaining and dipped them in the water handing them to him. "You have blood on your face and hands."

He looked down at his hands. "That dream shook you up, didn't it?"

"I'm fine. Sorry. Got a little sentimental there for a moment."

"Ali, I'm not going anywhere."

"I know," I smiled, but my voice betrayed me. "We need to get rid of the towel for Joshua and…" I looked at him.

"And my shirt," he finished my thought.

"Do we have any extra clothes?"

"Not sure. I'll ask when they come back out."

I heard the water in the tub start and stop a few times. Gabriel emerged from the bathroom. He walked through the room and out the door without a word. He came back a minute later with a spray bottle and towels and went back into the bathroom. The water turned on and off several more times.

I sat back down on the couch and changed the channel. The news came on; I leaned forward to watch. When the preview of the lead story flashed across the screen, I dropped the remote on the floor with a crack and sat frozen. "The medical team. They're dead." I looked at Peter.

He turned to look at the screen in disbelief and backed up a few steps. He knocked on the bathroom door. "Guys, you're gonna want to see this."

Both Gabriel and Joshua joined us. The smell of smoke billowed into the room until the door was shut, the exhaust fan still chugging away. The news story played out. I looked at Gabriel. "If they did what he wanted, why would he kill all of them? Doesn't that just draw attention?"

"They may have figured out what he was. They do not leave witnesses. Regardless, they are escalating. Something so public. Police involvement..." His voice trailed off.

I noticed Joshua standing back, his eyes still aglow. Then I looked back at Gabriel, who was deep in thought. "Do we have any extra clothes?" I cocked my head towards Peter.

"We will. Gentry is on her way back with supplies." Gabriel's thoughts seemed to drift again, but I came sharply in his focus not a minute later. "Why did you go to sleep? I thought I asked you to stay up tonight?" His tone was the harshest he'd ever used with me.

I stammered as a knot lodged itself in my throat, "I... I'm sorry. I didn't mean to." my voice choked off.

He placed his hands flat on the table; anger seethed from him, his muscles taut, mouth pressed into a hard line. It seemed as if he was trying to reign himself back. Intellectually, I didn't think any of the anger was actually directed at me, but it didn't *feel* that way. Maybe he did want to rid himself of me.

Tears pricked at my eyes, so I composed myself as best I could and stood from the couch. I said, "I'm sorry. It won't happen again," in an emotionless voice and walked into the bedroom. I knew he would head back into the bathroom again, so I decided to go into the closet. Shutting the door with only the softest click, I leaned my cheek against the cool surface. It smelled like wood polish with orange.

The knot in my throat seemed to grow larger until the tears erupted from me. I didn't allow myself to sob, because I didn't want anyone to hear me. I felt humiliated enough that I had to leave the room to cry. *I need to be stronger than this. Everyone's nerves are worn thin.*

I felt around until I hit the rollaway bed and sat down. A large part of me still wanted to sleep and the dark room didn't make it easier to stay awake, but I did. My ears strained to catch bits of conversation, but as far as I could tell, everyone was silent, though the exhaust fan may have covered the sound of hushed voices.

A long time passed. I wanted to rejoin everyone, but I felt embarrassed that I'd been in here so long. The fan in the bathroom was turned off. All of the burned vampire stench must've been evacuated. The light in the bedroom was turned on, followed by a soft knock at the door.

"It's me, love, can I come in?" Gentry asked cautiously.

"Enter," I replied somberly.

"I brought you some fresh clothes. Thought you might want to get cleaned up."

"Where is everyone?"

"Avoiding Gabriel."

"So, Mr. Cranky Pants is taking a bite out of more than me."

"Aye, come on, love." She grabbed my hand and pulled me to my feet. "I brought a late supper too. Peter is about to get a shower. You can go second."

"Isn't that kinda weird? Didn't they just kill someone in that tub?"

"Best not to think about what's been done in hotel rooms."

I thought for a second and decided I probably should take her advice. I followed her into the living room. Gabriel sat at the table with his head leaning on his hand that masked his eyes. It looked as though he was reading a message on his phone. *Probably some encrypted file that just came through.*

Peter was digging through a bag of clothes. He looked up and winked at me. I looked around for Joshua. Peter read my mind: "He went out to patrol for a minute. Blood wasn't helping him."

"Aye, well tick tock; let's clear it all out then." Gentry pulled the liner out of the trash can and gathered up all the tissue we had used to mop up my nose. "Shirt, please."

Peter reached behind his head, stripped his shirt off, and tossed it to her. As she turned to move to the door, I caught a glimpse of her expression, and I couldn't help but smile. It seemed the sight of a shirtless Peter might've been pleasing to her. She went outside to dump the soiled items or more likely to burn them.

Peter started towards the bathroom. "Be in the shower."

I slumped onto the couch to wait for my turn. Gabriel was taciturn, but I decided to risk speaking to him. "Did you find out anything useful?" I asked softly.

He looked up at me like I'd torn him out of a deep sleep—obviously consumed with something. He put his phone down on the table and fastened his eyes on me with such a penetrating expression that it made me shift in my seat. Then, he closed his eyes and pinched the bridge of his nose. "I am sorry. I should not have been upset with you."

It felt weird having him apologize to me. "It's okay. I can be a pain." My voice was still low.

"It seems that no matter what I do, they keep coming at you." He clenched his fists and shook his head. "We will figure a way out."

I fixed my face with something pleasant and nodded, but in my head I thought differently. *Sometimes the good guys don't win.*

A knock at the door followed by a key made me hold my breath and listen. Gabriel pulled out a dagger and stood in wait.

Joshua entered, wet hair plastered to his forehead and clothes dripping wet. Gentry followed behind him. He snatched a towel that was hanging over the back of a chair. "It looks clear. Think we're safe through the night."

Gabriel nodded.

Gentry spoke to Gabriel. "I'm gonna catch a few winks, unless you need me to do anything else."

"No, go ahead," Gabriel told her.

She winked at me as she went into the bedroom.

"Do you think that vampire was working alone?" This was my second attempt to find out what had happened in the bathroom.

"Yes and no. We just identified him." He held up his phone displaying a picture. "His name was Lazare. He works alone, but he obviously had inside help. I was hoping to flush out the mole, but whoever it is…" His thought was left incomplete.

"Gabriel, what else did they do to me? In the hospital."

"Took some of your blood."

That seemed benign for the worry on his face. "Was that it?" I questioned, thinking about the odd look that he and Jess had exchanged.

"There is nothing to worry about."

Then his previous comment hit me. I sucked in a sharp breath and put my hand over my mouth with the epiphany. I looked at both Joshua and Gabriel through bulging eyes. "My blood. The Oneiroi. That's why you wanted me to stay awake."

"Yes. From what we know, they can only invade dreams when they are at peak strength during the night."

All the pieces fell into place. That horrible pressure—it was the force of their invasion into my mind.

"But you sense when they are altering things?"

"Yes. When I got the nosebleed, I felt something was inside a metal column, and when I tried to push and figure out what it was, my head felt like it was going to explode. My nose was bleeding in the dream, as well as outside of it."

"Did something physical happen in the dream to cause the bloody nose?"

"No, I think it was my concentrating and fighting their illusion."

"If it happens again, don't fight it; just try to wake."

"But what if I can learn—"

"No. This is an order." He pounded his fist on the table.

"Yes, sir," I said respectfully.

"Imagine the damage they could inflict on a seer if you didn't feel their presence."

I pulled down the corners of my mouth. "You could be driven mad."

The words "driven mad" seemed to linger in the room. "Yes. Did they have control of the entire dream?"

"No. The dream was different than any other I've ever had." I explained how I was able to dissect an entire scene of my life and look at things from different angles. The only thing I left out was my realization that Bowen actually loved me. It felt awkward to say with Joshua being there.

Joshua mused, "I can see why the Lux were hunted. You are truly a danger. Insights into the past and future. And the fact that you saw *through* Bowen..."

"I wonder what is unique to me and what the other members of the Lux had the ability to see."

"Hopefully we will find out soon. Winslow is in Ireland," Gabriel informed us.

"He finished?" I asked.

"He said he hit a stopping point. But he wanted to pass on what he had."

"Is he coming here?"

"Joshua is going to meet him."

"Can't we stay together? I would like to be there," I said with an edge of pleading.

Gabriel contemplated my request. "All right. But we will send Peter and Gentry back to the house. I want to be able to move faster."

"Thank you."

"One condition," he said sternly.

"Okaaay..."

"If he begins speaking too much about your future and I ask you to leave the room, you do it, without as much as a sigh."

"Don't I have," I caught myself. "You have my word."

"If it is danger you can avoid, you will know it. I have found it is best not to know too much about the future. It puts too much pressure on the present. It makes people question their decisions and hesitations can get you killed." He turned away.

"Okay...thank you."

The water in the bathroom shut off and I could hear Peter

humming something cheerful. A minute later, the bathroom door opened up.

Gabriel turned back. "Ali, get cleaned up. Joshua, please keep her up the rest of the night. I am going to try to get a little sleep."

I wished him good night as he stalked out of the room. I went through the bag of clothing Gentry had procured and pulled out some sweats that must have been meant for me. Ironically, the sweatshirt was from Trinity College. I took a long shower despite the fact I was still creeped out about Lazare being extinguished in it. There was only a small yellow stain left behind. When I was done, I tiptoed through the bedroom, trying not to wake anyone.

Gabriel was sprawled across one of the beds. It looked like Peter and Gentry were sleeping back-to-back. Peter was on top of the covers and looked cold; he was curled into a ball. I went into the closet and grabbed the spare blanket and covered him before going to the living room.

Joshua sat, remote in hand, legs stretched across the coffee table. He smiled as I approached. "Feel a little better?"

"Mmmmm, you going to shower?"

"Yup, just waiting for my turn. You gonna be able to stay awake for fifteen minutes?"

"No, I plan on becoming narcoleptic in the next two minutes."

"Good, let me know how that works out for you."

He vanished, followed by the sound of water. The hotel didn't get very many channels. I settled on *Hamlet,* as I couldn't handle anymore news, and I was sad to see that infomercials seemed to have found their way to the U.K., too. It occurred to me that I hadn't bought anything with money in months. Yet another step away from the real world. My mind started to drift to my family and friends back home but I stopped myself.

The wheels in my brain were spinning. Some elements of *Hamlet* struck me as I watched. I already knew the play, so there was nothing I hadn't seen before, but this time, some of Hamlet's characterization reminded me of Bowen. His feelings of loss and betrayal...not knowing who to trust...being disconnected from his own world. And for the first time, I felt like I understood Ophelia. I'd never been able to connect with her. I'd always written her off as weak.

Joshua interrupted my brooding when he returned, smelling of soap, and sat next to me. "I see you are in for some light-hearted viewing."

"Yeah, nothing much on. Makes me miss cable."

"Nothing like eight hundred choices."

"I like this though," I motioned to the screen.

"It's such a waste."

"What?"

"All those people didn't need to die." He watched as they carried in Ophelia's body.

"There has to be death in a tragedy."

"Guess I'm not a fan of tragedy."

"Come on, I thought your favorite movie is *Braveheart?*" I looked at him.

He twisted his mouth to the side and met my gaze. "Parts of it..." But he didn't finish his thought. I nudged him, but he got an indefinable look on his face and refused to comment.

I looked back at the film. "I understand Ophelia a little more now—or the madness part. She was swallowed up by the chaos around her. She took on the grief of others until it broke her." It made me wonder if I was stronger than Ophelia. Tyran had said he was going to break me.

"Whoa! That is not a character I care for you to identify with."

I looked at him again, his face set with worry. "What?"

"What do you mean, what? She killed herself!" His tone was incredulous.

"I would never. I mean I don't think..." I became tongue-tied.

He looked at me so intensely, I thought he might be peering into my very soul. His eyes moved like he was searching me for something. Then he took my hand in his and eased back a little. "Let's concentrate on happy endings. There's enough tragedy in real life."

"Agreed, Ferdinand." I smiled at our secret names for each other from months ago.

He finally smiled. "Thank you, Miranda."

"You can sense my intentions. You should know that I don't intend to end it all."

"What worries me is that you *intend* to protect everyone but yourself."

"Is that so bad?"

"Only when it leads to tragedy."

23

THE FAITHFUL THREE

With dawn came the time for sleep. My insides still ached, a dull throb that never seemed to completely dissipate. I don't recall ever being so happy to know that I would soon be in bed, though spending hours of uninterrupted time with Joshua was bliss. My body was screaming for rest.

"I need to get back to my cave," Joshua murmured.

"Do you think I should wait a bit before I try to sleep?"

"You should be fine; it's not like you're going to fall asleep instantly."

"Unless I managed to catch narcolepsy," I joked, wagging my eyebrows.

He rolled his eyes at me and stood to his feet, offering his hands to help me up. He kept one of my hands and led me into the bedroom. We paused; everyone was still sound asleep. Gabriel must have been dreaming, as he kept furrowing his brow. Gentry had her face buried in Peter's back. It was quite obvious that a bed would not be available anytime soon. I clearly wasn't the only exhausted person.

Josh bent and spoke in my ear. "Looks like you're with me. You can have the bed," he said, leading me into the closet.

I sank onto the mattress, my entire body so heavy that it seemed to tingle and hum in the anticipation of sleep. Joshua settled onto the floor next to me. I pulled the pillow from under my head and dropped it onto his. Rolling over a little more, I hung my face over the edge of the bed so I could see his expression.

He whipped the pillow off of his face and opened his mouth to object, so I gave him the stink eye.

"If I get the bed, you get the pillow."

He snapped his mouth shut, realizing that he wouldn't win this battle. "Thanks."

I reached down, picked up his hand, and kissed it in response. "Thanks for helping me stay awake. I wouldn't have made it."

"Reversing your sleep schedule is going to take a few days."

"Yeah." Sighing, I gazed at him; he wasn't looking so good. The way he swallowed made me believe he was struggling. It'd been several hours since he'd fed, and he hadn't been reserving his energy. He'd run patrols every hour and tracked and brought in Lazare.

It might have set me back, but it was more important for him to be able to get me out of here if we needed to move quickly. I released his hand and pushed up my sleeve. "Here." I offered him my arm.

He looked at me like I was torturing him.

"Unless you are going to go wake up Gabriel and tell him your blood supply is depleted." I looked at him like it was a dare.

He hesitated yet again, but then relented and took my arm into his mouth.

I was more lightheaded when he stopped than the last time. I didn't know if it was from the extra blood loss from my bloody nose, or if he'd taken more. It didn't matter. I had time to sleep and recover.

After a while, I asked, "At the office building, I know Jess lied to me. Did you pick up on anything?"

He was quiet for longer than comfortable. "Just like Gabriel, her intentions were those of protection." He paused for a couple beats. "Everything is fine. Sometimes you have to let things go."

Is this advice? Or does he know what they lied about too? Did Lazare break in the interrogation?

"Just get some sleep," he said peacefully as he kissed my wrist. I couldn't have argued if I had wanted to. My lids started to close involuntarily, and I was out.

Gabriel was on his haunches at my side, gently shaking my shoulder. I peeked at him with sleepy eyes.

"Hmmmm?" was all I could manage.

"We need to go," he said softly.

Confused, I looked around the room. The doorway was open and clearly flooded with light and my arm was still hanging off the bed. Rolling onto my back, it started to tingle as the blood rushed back.

"Where's Joshua?"

"In the van already. Move it." Now that he knew I was awake, his tone was no longer gentle.

Rousing myself, I stumbled behind, straight to the van, bed head and all. I didn't recognize the van. He opened the back door. It had been setup like the van they had in the States. I shut the outer door, and then opened the inner door to get into the back compartment and not crispify the love of my life.

Josh smiled brightly at me. "Morning, sleeping beauty."

I pointed at my eyes, and then at him. "Laser beams—you're dead." I made an exploding motion with my hands.

"Love you too," he said with sickening sweetness.

I moved to the bench seat that ran along the wall and laid down, closing my eyes, still so tired. "How long did we sleep?" I groaned.

"I slept for five hours. You, for over seven. Gabriel wanted to get to Winslow while it's still light out."

"How did you get out here?" I asked.

"A trunk," he responded flatly.

"Niiiccceee. Bet you loved that!"

"Better than the alternative."

"True."

"Peter and Gentry get back okay?"

"They should be back any time. They had to change disguises more than once and use public transportation. Just in case."

"Mmmmmm. Any chance there are real clothes back here for me?"

"Gentry left the bag in the corner for you."

"How long till we meet?" I asked.

"Prrrrrobably an hour."

"K." My mouth felt pasty and horrible. Gabriel hadn't even let me brush my teeth. Something was definitely weighing on him. I changed clothes in between the inner and outer doors, and then sat in the captain's seat next to Joshua. "Did you sleep well?"

"As well as could be expected." A smile played at the corners of his mouth.

"I'm sorry. The floor couldn't have been comfortable." I felt guilty for taking his bed.

"No, no, no. I was fine on the floor. Just trying to make some decisions."

"Can I help with something?"

"Not yet. I may ask something of you later."

"Now you have me curious." I gave a hesitant grin.

He smiled, but he was definitely preoccupied. I wondered if this was the same burden with which Gabriel seemed to be grappling. I wanted to know what had happened in that bathroom with Lazare.

Sometime later, the van rolled to a stop. The cab door closed, and voices outside the vehicle drifted inside. I wondered if it was safe to get out, or if I should wait to be retrieved. I was eager to hear what Winslow had uncovered.

"When is sunset?"

Josh looked at his phone. "Forty minutes."

The front doors opened, and the van rocked slightly as two people climbed inside. We drove for five more minutes and came to another stop. The front doors opened and closed again, then a much louder metallic clunk followed. I got a concerned look on my face as I listened.

"A gate or industrial door," Josh explained.

I nodded and leaned back.

The side sliding door popped open. "Okay, kids," Gabriel summoned. He seemed a little more chipper.

We stepped out into a long narrow room constructed with very old stone. There was a set of weathered, barn-style doors closed at one end, and small yellow lights every ten feet or so. The dirt floor felt compressed and hard enough to be stone.

"Where are we?" I asked.

"A church. This is the attached garage. There is a basement where we can meet," Gabriel replied.

"Is Winslow here? I thought I heard someone else."

"He went down already. He needed to get his notes."

We circled to the other side of the van and entered a small alcove that looked like it might be used as a mudroom. We entered the main building and went down a staircase leading to the basement. Benches lined one of the walls, along with dilapidated boxes that had browned with age, and hooks with dusty tools dangling from them. I followed Gabriel and Joshua as we descended the steps to the lower level.

It opened up to a large room that echoed from the sound of our feet. Large pieces of slate tiled the expanse. The walls had been plastered and painted with warm tones. There were five doors and a large dark fireplace in the far corner, with a carved wood table a few feet away from the hearth. Wide square stools were tucked neatly underneath the table. It was nicer than I thought it'd be, judging from the condition of the garage where we'd parked.

Winslow, carrying a leather messenger bag, came out of one of the doors. He smiled as he walked to the table and placed his bag on it.

He took my hand in both of his. "Ah, a pleasure to see you again, Miss Aleria. I hope you have been well."

"Nice to see you again, Winslow," I said, squeezing his hand.

"Ah yes, you must be Joshua. Nice to finally be acquainted. I have heard much about you." He reached out and shook Joshua's hand earnestly.

"Nice to meet you," Joshua replied.

He smiled at Josh, and then addressed everyone: "Ah, well, the layout. The water closet is there." He pointed to the door nearest the fireplace. "The other doors are to bedrooms. They have been used time and again during troubles in this country. The entrance to the basement was once hidden."

"And now we meet secretly," I added.

"Very true. Yes, yes, well, please have a seat." He swept his arm towards the table.

We followed him over and assembled. I sat next to him with Joshua on my other side. Winslow reached into his bag and spread four small notebooks before him. He placed his hand on the pad the farthest to the left. "This is most of the information you already know." He picked it up and thumbed through its pages.

I leaned in a little closer. It looked as if he'd written the line to be translated at the top in thick black ink. Below it were translation notes in blue ballpoint with the sources noted in parenthesis. He'd also detailed cultural aspects, as well as definitions, and possible variations. At the bottom, he'd written his translation of the line in red.

"You will need to forgive me. It would take a year to properly translate all of this. There is some beautiful poetry to it that I simply didn't have the time to infuse into my translation. They are very terse indeed."

"Last time we were together we had translated the following,

> The Nexus will be 'A member of the Lux
>   Casta.
> In a new age, a presence will unify,
> that which was once divided.
> Of humble life and noble origins of thee
>   derive
> A marked star will appear,
> when the need is great
> Weighted with dreams of a seer

Eyes of amethyst
Vision of dark and light
Pure heart able to withstand (not be bent).'

Joshua had some of the same questions we'd had when we first heard this section of the prophecy. Winslow was delighted to answer all of his inquiries.

Then Winslow turned towards me. "I do have some good news for you. Tragedy already averted. It says:

If the Nexus remained 'Undiscovered,
her flame would be extinguished,
she would forever be lost in delusion.'

And then there was something about the Sentinels that I have yet to be able to translate."

I smiled with an odd mixture of relief and alarm. Somehow a confirmation that I would have gone insane if I hadn't been swept up into all of this made my mouth go dry.

"Repeatedly it says you will be both a *'light'* and a *'catalyst'* for what is to come.

"It says, *'Constant in placement yet three lives will live'.*" He started to move on, but I politely interrupted.

"What does that mean? Three lives?"

"Ah, yes, well we often think of our lives in three parts: childhood, adolescence, and adulthood. It could be much of the same."

"But if that's what it meant, why say it? I mean if my life is like everyone else's?"

"Ah, maybe normal life, that of a Watcher, and that of the Lux Casta?"

"Maybe," I said softly. I looked over at Gabriel, his face reflected the unsettling feeling I had in my gut.

"There is a series of prose that could have several meanings...*The Nexus will:*

> Draw forth worthy from the lost,
> Will watch the darkness divide and grow,
> Two will become one, one will become two,
> The divided cursed will find purpose,
> Allegiance that of torment,
> The unbeating shall beat,
> Bringing new power and desire..."

He continued on, but admittedly I found it dizzying. I could read into any of it and give it a dozen different meanings. I wasn't sure if what he was sharing was useful. I looked at all three of them; they seemed focused. *Maybe I have ADD.* I caught the word "mate" and snapped out of my contemplation. "I'm sorry, Winslow. I missed the last part."

"Ah, yes, yes. It speaks of *'rival mates',*" Winslow said excitedly.

Gabriel cleared his throat. I peered at him to see if he was stopping Winslow from saying something, but I couldn't tell. Gabriel asked, "In your message, you had said you found something especially interesting?"

"There was a reference to something I have only seen a few times. It says she is *'The sole one to reach the Fallen.'* The context is interesting. It seems to be referring to both a single entity and a group."

"Who are 'The Fallen'?" I asked.

"The word used refers to someone who deliberately turned their back on God or a group that did so. There are many to which it could be referring. But it is something of importance. It was offset and had a symbol written off to the side."

Winslow flipped the page to a drawing he'd made. It was a diamond with an eye off-center surrounded by swirls. There was a string of symbols on two stripes to the left and words in an ancient language on the right.

"Do you know what this means?" Gabriel inquired.

"No. Sorry, something to do with The Fallen I would assume."

Gabriel flipped to the next page, and there was a list of three items.

I pulled the pad closer. "What is this?"

"The Paths. Three, to be specific," Winslow clarified.

"Like a map or the roads I will travel?"

"More like a three-way fork. We already know that one will never come to be."

I started to read the list:

Three Paths

> 1. Undiscovered…leads to insanity and
>   death

Gabriel reached over and removed the pad. My mouth dropped open, and I was about to protest. He looked at me in warning, so I closed my mouth.

When Winslow read number two, it was clear why he thought it might be best for me not to know.

> "2. Through agony she will rise to lead.
> In loss she will defy the false gods
> and offer release."

There had to be more.

"No pressure," I muttered and wondered why words like agony and torment had to be so prevalent. I closed my eyes and asked, "Do I want to know number three?"

> "3. If [she is] sacrificed, the increased power
> of the Devourer will end the reign of
> man."

Joshua took my hand under the table. My heart was pounding so hard I felt as if I was shaking with each beat. The only word I could conjure was Armageddon—and that I would be responsible for it. Maybe that was too grand, but vampires leaving the shadows and ruling humanity seemed equally dismal.

"Ali," Gabriel said gently. "It is time."

I nodded; I was actually grateful. I didn't want to hear anymore. He left the table and opened up one of the doors. He flipped on the lights and entered the room, but only stayed for about three seconds. I stood, ready to be sent to my room, but he reemerged and went to the next one, repeating the process. I stayed behind Joshua and rested my hands on his shoulders. He leaned back against me a little.

After Gabriel had inspected the three vacant rooms, he returned to the doorway in the middle. "Ali, I would like to have a word alone with you. Winslow, please show Joshua the section about the rivals."

Winslow cocked his head questioningly at Gabriel, and then looked over at me. The epiphany was clear on his face when his eyes ran over Joshua and me. "I didn't realize. Ah, yes. Of course."

Joshua reached up and squeezed my hand before I walked

THE FAITHFUL THREE | 271

into the bedroom. They were furnished with two twin beds, a trunk, and some extra bedrolls in the corner. Very spare, but the beds themselves looked comfortable.

I turned around. Gabriel closed the door and walked straight over to me. He picked up my right arm and pushed up my sleeve. Nothing. Then he did the same with my left arm. Two faint pink marks dotted my wrist that could be written off as anything, but Gabriel knew otherwise.

"How many times?" He must have sensed a difference in our physical relationship. I groaned internally, so much for discreet.

"Three. Please don't be angry with him. He—"

He held up his finger. "I am not." He sounded tired, but not agitated. "I know him well enough to know that he would never ask you. And that you are stubborn enough to insist."

"I was afraid for him if he didn't feed with all the extra patrols."

He shook his head. "It is fine. I knew in the hospital when you asked him to see if you had been poisoned that he could handle it—and that it was inevitable. I realized this morning that we never picked up additional supplies for him." He walked over and sat on one of the beds. "I need to tell you that there is renewed interest in expelling Joshua from the Watchers."

"Why? That doesn't make any sense."

"I am not sure, but I do not like the fact Rousseau and Blackthorne are sniffing around. You also need to know that Joshua is in the prophecy."

"The rival thing? There is no rivalry."

"Just because a lady has chosen her suitor, does not mean the other interested parties stop pursuing."

I walked and sat on the other bed across from him. "I guess," I said glumly. "So you knew about the rival thing already?"

"Yes. We translated some of it in York while you were sleeping."

Gabriel looked towards the door. "You are good for each other."

"Pardon?"

He gazed at me. "You…and Joshua."

"Yes. He makes me a better person."

"A year ago, I feared that I would have to end him."

"You'll never have to."

"I know." He exhaled slowly. "I forget how young you are sometimes."

I grabbed a pillow and hugged it to my chest. "Then why do I feel so old?"

His eyes were distant. "I believe one of the partial translations of the *Nexus* is in the hands of a member of the Concilium. I believe for some unknown reason, they have Joshua in their sights. And once they figure out who you are, I do not know what will happen."

"You don't think that is the person who had me poisoned?"

"No, I do not think the mole knows who you are."

"Why do you think that?"

"Later." He was quiet, and I couldn't follow his train of thought very well. It seemed like he wanted to tell me something. "I am surprised Winslow did not tell you this right away. It seems you have Slayer ancestry."

"Really?"

"It seems that Michael the Sentinel married a Seer. Their daughter was the first Lux. She did not have the physical prowess of her brothers, but her sight, resistance to mind control, and so on are now the stuff of legend."

"So I am distantly related to the current Michael?"

"That would be correct."

"You know, the accelerated healing would have been helpful."

He let out a single laugh. "Yes."

"And the ability to fly, maybe heat-ray vision."

"Now you are getting greedy." He stood up and looked at me, his crooked grin melting from his face. He became deadly serious. "You will not be sacrificed."

"Can I have that in writing?"

He started to leave the room. He turned and tossed a deck of playing cards onto the bed next to me. "It does not look like this place has cable."

"Thanks."

He turned and shut the door behind him. I could hear their muffled voices through the door. I ran my fingers over the box of cards and decided a wicked game of solitaire would suit me. What more could I ask for, me against fifty-two foes.

I crawled to the middle of the narrow bed and shuffled the cards more times than necessary. Somehow the slap of the cards was relaxing. But, my boredom became overwhelming after I lost the fifth game. I practiced cutting the deck with one hand and played War against myself. I decided that was probably my lamest idea.

My legs started to fall asleep, so I marched back and forth until the needles stopped. I imagined myself as a caged tiger wearing the floor of my cage thin as I paced back and forth. *How long were they going to talk?*

It was time for a trip to the bathroom before I went crazy. I opened the door and stepped out into the room. The conversation stopped. I felt an odd sort of tension in their absorbed expressions. I pointed at the bathroom and made my way through the room.

Once inside, I took my time. I washed my face with the bar

soap, which I would probably regret later. I ran wet fingers through my hair and calmed down some of the chaos. I found a pair of fingernail clippers on the ledge above the sink, so I perched myself on the edge of the toilet and trimmed. I couldn't conceive of anything else to do, so I washed my hands a second time, then started back.

Gabriel stood when I entered. "We are done for the night. You have the run of the room."

"Cool," I replied nonchalantly.

"Goodnight, everyone." Gabriel exited.

Winslow did the same. Joshua remained at the table. I strolled over to him and used the stool to step up and sit on top of the table next to him.

He didn't look at me. He leaned his head down and rested it on my knee. I ran my fingers through his hair and rubbed his shoulders a little. He let some of the stress go, and reached under the table and massaged my calves.

"Was that whole conversation about you?" I asked curiously.

"No," he said serenely without looking up.

"Was some of it about me?"

"Yes."

"Did you discuss non-prophecy related items?"

"Yes."

"Are you going to say anything other than yes or no?"

"Yes." His hands ceased to move on my calves. He stood abruptly and cupped my face and kissed me.

"Are you okay?" I whispered, my voice a little husky.

"Yes." He pushed my hair back and kissed the hollow under my cheek.

"You're starting to worry me a little."

He pulled back and looked into my eyes, that same unreadable expression.

"You know when you said if things were different you would probably be ring shopping? I wish we could get married and disappear together." I felt my face flush.

"You would marry me, even though I'm..."

I looked at him like he was a lunatic. "Mr. Copeland, do you seriously have any doubt?"

He smiled and ran his thumbs over my cheekbones. "No, Miss Hayes, I guess I don't. But I do have that rival lover to deal with."

"There is no rivalry," I glared. "I would be yours if your skin turned green and you sprouted antennae. I love what is here and here." I pointed to his head and placed my hand over his unbeating heart. "And..." I shrugged and continued, "I'm not gonna lie—you're a really good kisser."

He genuinely laughed and pulled me against his chest and hugged me. "The church is locked up. The sun is down. Whadaya say we go exploring?"

"Brilliant idea."

We walked upstairs and into the side door of the church, pausing in the doorway. It was utterly silent. The floor plan was that of a cross, like so many of the churches in Europe and the U.K., but not as large as a cathedral. There were enough pews to seat maybe three hundred and plenty of space to add more if they wanted. There were large stained glass windows on every wall, more than I had seen in any of the other buildings.

"This must be beautiful in the light," I commented.

"Winslow said it is often referred to as Angel Church. During times of trouble, people would seek refuge here. All of the panels depict scenes in the Bible where angels intervened."

We walked around, examining each one for a while.

"This is my favorite." I could just make out the words *The Faithful Three* on a banner on the lowest part. It depicted an angel wrapping its wings around three men who were all looking upward, as flames tried to devour them.

"Shadrach, Meshach, and Abednego. You didn't prefer the Angel of Destruction obliterating an entire army?" Joshua teased.

"Ummm, no. I like that they were faithful and were spared. They never gave up their beliefs, even when faced with death."

"It's comforting, although I think I would have preferred *not* being thrown in the fiery furnace to begin with."

"There's always that. Wish we could see them better."

"Yeah, too bad the full moon isn't for another week."

I nudged him. "Guess we'll have to come back next week."

"Ah, the days when we were in charge of our own schedules," he sighed.

"Someday...maybe."

"You wanna head back down?" he asked.

"Yeah," I paused and looked at *The Faithful Three* one last time. "I hope I have their strength."

He stood behind me and looped his arm around me. He kissed me on top of the head. "You do. I have no doubt in my mind.

24

VALUES

I woke to the sound of heated voices in the other room, but I couldn't make out what they were saying. I staggered over to the door and cracked it open. I heard the last half of a sentence.

"...just bed her then," Winslow said angrily.

Whoa.

"It's not that simple!" Joshua retorted.

"It *is* that simple. Don't you love her? Then spare her—spare the world the possibility—"

"So you would have her betray her beliefs?" Joshua snapped ferociously.

"No, but antiquated beliefs in this situation are absurd."

"I can't believe someone your age is calling it antiquated."

"I think there should be an exception in this situation, my dear boy."

"That's not how either one of us were raised. I respect her stance, and I happen to agree with it."

"It is the best thing you can do," Winslow argued.

Winslow must have looked at Gabriel for help. "Keep me out of this," he said a little too calmly.

"Have you met her? You really think she would back down on something that matters this much to her?" Joshua asked.

"Maybe the choice shouldn't be hers," Winslow responded.

"Are you insane! She is living her life like a prisoner, and now you think she shouldn't be able to choose who she sleeps with or when?"

"I'm only asking that you reason with her."

I missed whatever else Winslow said. My heart started beating feverishly. I didn't know how to feel. Mortification was the most prevalent emotion. And I was shocked by Winslow; I had thought differently of him. *Maybe he is just voicing what most people would think in this situation. Am I being selfish?* I had heard enough; I stepped out into the room. Gabriel was the first to see me. He had tipped back a stool and was leaning against the wall. He raised his eyebrows at me and shrugged.

I took a breath and cut Winslow off. "Josh, why don't you just take me out back and *do* me. If it makes Winslow feel better."

Winslow whipped around. "My dear, I'm sorry. I didn't mean—"

"Yes, you did. I know exactly what you meant."

Gabriel stood up and moved towards Joshua, whose rage had not abated since I'd started speaking. "Time to cool down, buddy. Let us take a look at that hand."

Josh looked down at his palm. He had crushed something, and blood was running from his hand onto the floor. Gabriel pushed him towards the bathroom.

"No, I—" he started to protest.

"Ali can take care of herself. This is an order." Gabriel clamped down on his shoulder and pushed him along.

Then I was alone with Winslow, whom I did not respect much at the moment.

"So I'm chattel now?"

There was a very awkward silence—for him. I watched him squirm and felt no compulsion to let him do anything but burn under the heat of my stare.

He's lucky I don't have heat-ray vision.

He was flustered. He tried to smooth his clothes and readjust his glasses. Probably a stall tactic. "I don't believe you are property or a slave for that matter. But holding onto old-fashioned ideals seems reckless considering the circumstances. It doesn't warrant such a cacophony of discontent."

"So you are saying it's no big deal?"

"Yes."

"And if I was your daughter? No big deal?"

He faltered.

"Exactly. You actually respect the virtue, but you're too— what? Scared?"

"Don't you think it best to—"

"It's a possibility. Not a guarantee. It is a big deal to me. I'm obviously not going to get the life I'd planned on. Why would you suggest I be robbed of this, too?"

"The danger is too—"

"Don't we all live with danger every day? And did you actually suggest having someone besides Joshua," I couldn't say it.

He looked ashamed. "Yes," he replied, the defensiveness drained from his voice.

"Who? Who would do me this 'great' honor?"

"I simply suggested a friend, if Joshua was afraid he couldn't keep his bloodlust under control."

"A friend." I didn't know what to say.

"Peter. He seems fond of you."

"You know what? I don't want to know what you were thinking. The answer is no and no and no. And if anyone finds out who I really am, I will blame you. No one else who knows would even consider what you suggested. I'm not a violent person by nature, but..." Gabriel reentered the room, his timing a little too perfect.

"Winslow, I think this would be a good time to go upstairs."

He walked towards the entrance. He turned and looked like he wanted to say something, but then thought better of it. His lanky figure disappeared up the staircase.

I plopped down on a stool and clenched my fists, trying to calm myself. I had too many emotions raging in my body.

"You okay?" Gabriel asked.

I sat there, shaking my head, unable to utter anything at all.

"He will not suggest it again."

I sucked in a breath. "Not if he values his life."

He sat next to me and rubbed his thumb along his scar.

"Do you agree with him?"

"No. Our values are what set us apart."

I exhaled in relief. I unfurled my fists and looked at my still trembling fingers. "Great way to wake up," I grumbled. "Where's Josh?"

"I asked him not to come out until his hand healed up. I prefer to keep you from any accidental exposures."

"Guess that would be best." I thought for a long moment. "If the Concilium found out, they would think the same thing, wouldn't they?"

"Some of them."

"Do you think Winslow will say anything to anyone?"

"Not if he values his life." He grinned, but his eyes didn't smile. He stood. "Stay away from that," he said, pointing to Joshua's blood on the floor. "I am going to find some bleach."

"K." I didn't feel like moving anyway.

He went upstairs for a few minutes, returned with a jug, and washed away the scarlet stain on the slate. "I will be back shortly. I think some food would do you good."

"And coffee?" I smiled pleadingly.

"And coffee. Do not let him get to you. He does not want any harm to come to you." Gabriel squeezed my shoulder and left for the food run.

A few minutes later, Joshua returned. I was still sitting on the stool, a little shell-shocked. I mustered up a smile. "How's your hand?"

He held up his palm; only a purplish-pink slash remained.

"Thanks for defending my honor," I said, my tone infused with sadness.

He pulled a stool next to me and sat so our arms were touching. "Are you okay?"

"I'll be fine. I should've expected it, I guess. It just seemed so…"

"Cold, dehumanizing, unfeeling, demeaning, debasing, humiliating, dirty, and all other synonyms."

I chuckled. "All of the above. Of course, I feel like a hypocrite."

"Why?"

"I did try to seduce you." I dropped my head in my hands.

"Temporary insanity," he replied and rubbed my back.

"If you hadn't kept your head…"

"I didn't want to. But when it happens, it will be for the right reasons. And, I didn't have as much control as I do now. I could have…"

"Can we just forget about that night?"

"Done."

I sat up again. "How long did I sleep?"

He checked the time. "Nine hours."

"Wow. It didn't seem like that long."

"Did you dream?" he asked.

"Not that I can remember."

"We'll take that as a good omen." We sat in silence, arms intertwined, until Gabriel returned with food. He had a serious look when he entered. Something was definitely up.

"Sebastian wants us back at the house. Blackthorne and Rousseau are gone, at least for a couple of days. I am going to take Winslow to his transportation. Be back in an hour. Eat and get cleaned up."

"Is everything okay?" Joshua asked.

"I am not sure. I will be back soon."

I wolfed down the ham and cheese sandwich he'd brought me and happily sipped on my heavenly, heavenly coffee. Afterwards, Josh and I both cleaned up for the trip and had forty-five minutes before Gabriel was going to be back. I walked into my room, but realized I had nothing in there but the deck of cards Gabriel had tossed to me. I sat on the bed and fiddled with the flap on the box.

Joshua came in and sat on the bed across from me.

"Do you think everything is okay at the house?" I asked.

"Hard to say."

I nodded and examined him; he looked extra pale. "You should feed."

He closed his eyes and sighed.

"Well, I feel like a piece of stinky cheese."

He laughed quietly, then moved in front of me and dropped to his knees. But instead of presenting my arm, I twisted my hair to one side and offered my neck. He bent down farther and laid his head in my lap.

"Ali," he whispered.

"If you don't want to, it's fine."

He rose abruptly and knotted his left hand in my hair. I relaxed and allowed him to move my head to wherever he needed it. His fangs penetrated my flesh, and I was careful not to move much. I kept my breathing steady and resisted the urge to comb my fingers through his hair or do anything else to distract him, which took significant effort. Within seconds, all the pain in my body leaked away, and the bite—it just felt so good.

He pulled away and placed his head back on my lap. I stroked his wavy locks as he rubbed his forehead back and forth just above my knee. He wrapped his hands around my calves and gently squeezed. I wondered what he was thinking. He sat up abruptly once again and kissed me urgently and whispered, "I can do this."

"Do what?" I murmured back between kisses.

"Control this."

"You won't hurt me. It's not in you."

He smiled at me, and for the first time since he'd been turned, I didn't see worry lurking anywhere in his eyes.

Gabriel returned, and we departed for the house. Once we were safely back, a meeting was promptly called. I looked at Gabriel questioningly. "Do you know what this is about?"

He shook his head "No." He appeared calm, but I knew him well enough to know he was concerned.

Sebastian entered the room, his face solemn. "I have received some news." He paused. *This is not going to be good.* "Michael has been killed outside of London." The room was silent. A Slayer had lost his life, and not just any Slayer—one of the four. I didn't know Michael very well at all; he'd been at the Academy for a while. He'd also lived in the first Dublin house. I swallowed hard. The new knowledge that we were distantly related made the news especially poignant.

I bowed my head and said a prayer—for Michael—and for all of us. Sebastian didn't provide many details. The news hit some very hard. Some cried, while others sat in shocked silence. I was one of the latter. Sadness fell over the house like I'd never seen, and there was no consolation for this type of loss.

Later, when the crowd had dispersed to deal with their grief or anger in their own way, I wandered to Sebastian's office. He was sitting by the fire with a weighty, leather volume in his lap, but he wasn't reading. Loss held him in his chair like mortar holds bricks. He looked up at me with weary eyes.

"Sebastian, I just wanted to say I'm sorry. I know you were close. If there's anything I can do to help." Though I felt helpless myself.

"Thank you. Please shut the door and have a seat. How did your meeting with Winslow go?"

"Oh, sorry. I didn't mean to interrupt you."

"It's fine. Distraction can be a good thing."

I shut the door and drifted to the loveseat. I curled my legs beneath me. "So?" he asked, prodding me when I didn't start speaking.

"It went fairly well."

"You seem as if you are being polite."

I bit my lip. "We had a disagreement. Maybe Gabriel should fill you in about it." Just thinking about it made me feel both angry and embarrassed.

He must have been tired, or he sensed how uncomfortable I was, because he didn't press. The fire flared up, intensifying the light in the room for a few moments.

"It seems the Lux began with the line of Michael the Sentinel," I finally offered. He combed at his beard and looked at me expectantly. This seemed to be new information. "He told Gabriel. He said that Michael married a Seer and their daughter was the first to have the abilities I have."

"Interesting," he murmured.

"Did Michael have any children or siblings?"

"No, no he didn't."

"So that's it? His whole line was wiped out?"

He heaved a breath and rubbed his brow with the ring finger of his right hand. "No. After Laylah, Gabriel's sister, was killed at such a young age, precautions were taken to keep that from happening in the future. All Slayers and Council members with special abilities have genetic material stored in a facility. We have already lost several Slayer lines, and we thought the Lux had been extinguished before modern science gave us the opportunity to preserve the lines."

"Like clones?"

"No, nothing that elaborate." A smile flickered on his face. "We can use a surrogate. Just like thousands of people who struggle with infertility."

"Oh...oh," I said a second time when my mind caught what he was saying.

"So, yes, I guess the answer will be. He *will* have children."

"I thought there were only four Slayer lines?"

"To begin with. Eventually, other angels joined the original four Sentinels. There were forty in total."

"But the original four are different?"

"They were the most powerful of the angels. Favored by

God, often called the Four Corners, because they held up the four corners of the earth. They were the ones who begged God to judge the two hundred who were corrupting the earth."

"Gabriel told me about that."

"And because of that, Moloch has special grievances with each of them, especially Gabriel's line."

"Why Gabriel?"

"Gabriel, the angel, was responsible for destroying the children of the two hundred, the Nephilim. They swore vengeance. When a few of them escaped, they adopted different names. Moloch, who we believe to be the leader named Azâzêl, renewed that vow. He murdered some of the Sentinels, but he was never able to wipe out all of their children."

We talked for a while longer. He asked more questions about the prophecy. I answered the best I could, but I again referred to Gabriel since I hadn't heard much of the conversation. And then he must've had a second wind because he decided to press about the aforementioned politeness. "What weren't you saying before? Was there tension of some sort?"

I closed my eyes, wishing I could teleport myself to another room. *Yet another handy power that would be nice to have.* "I came in the middle of a conversation. He had made a suggestion to Joshua that was not well received."

There was a knock at the door. "Enter," Sebastian said gruffly.

Gabriel filled the doorway, and at that moment, he was my savior.

I stood. "I should let you meet," I said, trying not sound like I wanted to bolt out of the room like my hair was on fire.

"No," he said firmly. "I would like to hear about this disagreement." I sat like a scolded child; it took everything in my power not to huff and roll my eyes. I looked at Gabriel; I could swear there was amusement behind his eyes.

"What suggestion was not well received?"

As I looked at Gabriel pleadingly, he walked in and took a seat. "Sebastian, you can let her go. I could hear her opinion with perfect clarity." He looked at me and grinned.

I guess my volume control in that particular conversation was broken.

Sebastian relented, and I all but ran from the room. *Note to self: I owe Gabriel one.*

Staying up all night was supposed to get easier, but when everyone else retired for the evening I wanted to follow suit. The confrontation this morning had left me feeling ragged. I hadn't seen Joshua since the meeting, so after I showered and put on some fresh pajamas, I padded down the hall in my slippers in search of him. He wasn't in his room or in the common areas, but he was gone. Plan B was to watch television. I sank into the couch and started to flip through the channels.

I remember looking at the clock around 4 A.M. My eyes felt dry, and I just wanted to close them for a minute. Just one minute to moisten them.

Then I was standing in a cavernous room lit only by torches that gave off black smoke and created a haze. Dark, chiseled stone walls heavy with soot towered four stories above. The damp walls extended into the distance, topped with a walkway that was interrupted with cages, or perhaps, prison cells. Moans and screams underscored the horrific feeling that permeated this place. I was standing on an elevated slab and looked out over the floor in front of me. It was a maze—larger than a football field. Eight giant pillars kept the roof of the immense structure from folding in on itself.

There was some type of horn or gong that rang out, and something moved behind me. I scrambled off the slab and ran into the maze as fast as possible, my lungs burning from exertion. I hit a dead end and spun around, my feet sliding out from under me. Picking myself up, I started running again, but something had changed. The way I came in was no longer there. I rounded a corner, and there was a long pathway. There was a gargoyle perched on top of the wall just ahead, and three large stone blocks stair-stepped up to its location. And then the pressure started again. I was lucid enough to know I should try to wake—Gabriel's orders. But I was so close; he was right there. I knew it.

I ran towards the gargoyle and clutched my head as I progressed towards the stone blocks, each step growing more painful. I pushed back at the sensation as hard as I could. My legs faltered. I crawled the last few feet, grabbing onto the step and pulling myself up; when I glanced down, I watched my blood splatter onto the ground. I wiped at my nose with the back of my hand and could feel it ooze and run down my arm. Feeling for the next step, I pulled myself up, and then onto the next stone.

When I reached the top and grabbed the foot of the gargoyle, it was no longer stone. He reached down angrily and grabbed me by the back of the shirt, raising me up with one hand. My feet scraped the top of the wall.

"I can see you," I said.

What was remaining of his disguise melted away. He was tall, broad, and his jet-black hair fell in long waves to his shoulders. His eyes were the grey of storm clouds; it was like there was light behind them.

He put his other hand on my throat and started to squeeze. I tried to wake, but instead, the pressure increased. Concentrating, I pushed back. He faltered. To my surprise, I realized it was working. He looked stunned. I tried to wake again; someone was shaking me, but I wasn't sure if it was in the dream or real life. The pressure receded, and I opened my eyes.

Joshua had my shoulders.

"Hey," I said, but my voice came out really slurred.

He pushed the hair back from my face, but some of it clung and felt wet. I tried to sit up more, but I started to swoon.

"Just sit still." His voice was racked with worry.

I focused on his face; his eyes were like beacons of emerald. I wiped at my cheeks and raised my hand. Blood ran down my fingers, over my palm, and down my arm.

"Humpf. That's a lot of blood," I mumbled. My shirt felt like it was sticking to me. I felt my chest, and it was soaking.

Then I heard footsteps. Gabriel entered with towels in his hand and pressed one to my face. He sat on one knee next to me. His eyebrows were pinned together, and he looked rather angry. The dizziness started to pass. I put my hand on Gabriel's and took over putting pressure on my nose.

"You did not try to wake up, did you? You went after them in the dream."

I darted my eyes in his direction, and then away, not answering.

"This is not a time for you to be stubborn. Follow orders. We do not know what this is doing to you," Gabriel fumed.

"I'm sorry."

Josh clarified. "I'm-sorry-I-won't-do-it-again, or just sorry?"

"I'm sorry. I won't do it again. I didn't mean to scare either of you."

"Scaring isn't the problem. You bleeding out on the couch or them doing something to your brain is," Josh reprimanded, his emotion barely reigned back.

I hadn't thought of the bleeding out part. I pulled the towel from my nose. I didn't feel it trickle. "Did it stop?"

"It looks like it," Josh breathed, his eyes still glowing.

I leaned forward a little and looked down at myself. So much blood had run from my face that it had soaked the top of my pajama pants, run down my hips, and onto the couch. "Wow," was all I could manage.

"Can you handle helping her clean up?"

"Yes, get some rest. Thank you," Josh replied.

"You need to stay up for another two and a half hours. See you in the afternoon," Gabriel grumbled.

"Good night, and I *am* sorry," I called as Gabriel stalked off. I looked over at Josh. "I think I need another shower."

He nodded, but was still visibly upset.

I tried to stand, but that didn't work out well. He ran his arm around my waist and helped me upstairs. He pushed the door of the bathroom open with his shoulder and helped me sit on the counter. I leaned against the mirror and shivered. Each of the showers was set up for a co-ed existence, with a changing area in front of the shower that was curtained off. He started the shower.

"I'll get you some clothes."

I kicked off my slippers, the rubber soles thumping onto the tile floor.

He returned and steadied me as I walked to the shower. "Can you do this?"

"Yeah, there's a rail if I get dizzy." I stepped into the changing room; he tossed the new pajamas on the bench and closed the heavy curtain. I stepped into the shower fully clothed to rinse all of the blood out. It took a while.

"You wanna tell me what you were thinking?" he asked, his tone a little harsh. It sounded like he was sitting on the counter across from the showers now.

"I wasn't," I admitted.

His sigh was audible, even in here.

I slid onto shower floor and let the water run over me, watching the crimson swirl down the drain. *What use are my abilities if I can't use them?* When I felt a little stronger, I forced myself to stand and clean up. After I was dressed in my fresh pajamas, I pushed the drape to the side. Joshua was sitting in silence, his eyes no longer glowing. He slid from the counter and followed me to my room. We sat on opposite ends of the couch. He still hadn't said a word.

"Would you say something?" I pleaded.

He closed his eyes, taking in a slow breath.

I pulled my knees to my chest and rested my head on them. "Josh, I promise not to try it again, not without approval."

"Thank you," he said. He obviously hadn't believed me the last time.

"Where did you go this evening?"

"I met with Gabriel before and after he met with Sebastian."

"About Winslow?"

"No. Something I started speaking with him about the day before we met with Winslow."

"Oh." I wanted to ask him more, but it seemed like he was being deliberately vague. I decided not to irritate him further by prying.

He reached over and grabbed my foot and started massaging

it. "As payment for your absence, you must continue this for one hour."

"Cute," he smirked.

"I really am sorry."

"I know," he replied gently, and with that, I was forgiven. I just hoped I could keep my promise.

25

JOY

It was light outside. I rolled over, pulling the covers over my head. Then I realized I wasn't alone. The pages of a book were being turned from the vicinity of the couch. My dreams had been horrifying, but the Oneiroi hadn't invaded them. Peeking from beneath the covers, I checked the sofa.

"Mornin' sunshine," Gentry chirped way too cheerfully.

I pulled the covers back over my head and groaned: a babysitter even while I slept. It wasn't Gentry's fault, so I tried to keep my attitude in check. It was actually my own dumb fault. If I hadn't gone after that Oneiroi in my dream, I wouldn't need one.

"Ya have ta be gettin' hungry by now, love. Why don't cha get up, an I'll fix ya somthin'?"

I pushed the covers back down and took a gander in her direction. "What time is it?"

"3:00 P.M., sunset in a little over an hour and a half."

I filled my lungs with air until they burned and stretched my body. The ache in my abdomen was only dull. I was healing. "Sounds good. Anything happen while I was out?"

"We planned a memorial of sorts for Michael. We'll be goin' out tonight to pay our respects."

"All of us?" I asked, curious about whether or not I was allowed out at night.

"Aye, all of us. Raphael came back. Rousseau and Phineas will be here shortly."

"I thought Rousseau and company were gone for a few more days?"

"Somethin' changed," she shrugged. "Blackthorne is coming back too, but not for another few days."

"Ah…" I really didn't want to see anyone from the Conclave, but I kept my grumbles internal.

I followed Gentry to the kitchen and happily partook of the food she made. A short while later, we gathered and departed in small groups for the vigil, each using a different route and different transportation.

We met under a bridge somewhere on the outskirts of Dublin. I wasn't sure by which river or under which bridge. It was older than most of them. No steel; just a natural-looking stone streaked with age. A staircase was near it that led to a walkway next to the river. It reminded me a little of Paris and the walk along the Seine, but only for a short stretch before the walkway disappeared.

All of us, about twenty, stood in silence under the shadow of the bridge, sheltered from the glare of the street lamps. It was a crystal clear night, and without the cloud cover, the evening was especially cold. I peeked up at the sky. The stars blazed against the velvet night, almost as if they were saying goodbye, too.

Leslie descended the steps with a few bundles of flowers. Gentry opened up a box and had Peter pass out some straw disks with a hole in the center. She in turn passed out tea lights to everyone. Sebastian said a few words; his speech was short and very moving.

And then people started filing past Leslie, taking a couple of flowers and stringing them through the hole in each disk. The candle was placed in a divot on top so it wouldn't easily slide off. I copied what I was seeing. Leslie sidled up next to me to explain; I must have looked confused. Peter came alongside to listen.

"The candles represent how the flame of life illuminates us and how that light shines in the lives of others. It also represents the human soul. Flames, like our souls, breathe and grow and change. They fight back the darkness, and ultimately, they are extinguished."

Then she referred to the flowers. "These represent life. The white chrysanthemum is for truth, poppy for eternity, and magnolia for dignity. The white carnation and rue are for remembrance, marigold for pain and grief, and finally, geranium for comfort."

It hit me, the Vitae, Veritas, Aeternitatis, and Dignatio on the tattoo that both Slayers and Watchers get: life, truth, eternity, and dignity. All of those were represented in the flowers.

One by one, we lit the candles and set them adrift on the river. We watched as the current slowly took them away until the flames looked like tiny stars in the distance, and then finally disappeared. Silence enveloped everyone.

Hardly a word was spoken after we returned to the house. Rousseau was eyeing me, so I used Gabriel as a screen and slipped away before she could get to me. If she wanted me that much, she would have to track me down. I headed upstairs to grab a book and find somewhere other than my room to hang out. I rounded the corner completely preoccupied and almost knocked Peter and Gentry over. I was immediately mortified when I realized that I'd interrupted a kiss.

"I am so sorry," I sputtered, feeling my face burning like it was going to go supernova. I couldn't look at them. In fact, I think I literally shielded my face as I tore down the hall away from them. I heard Gentry say something, but the words didn't register.

I rushed into my room, spun around, and leaned against the door as if it would shield me from my embarrassment.

"Hey." I heard a voice. I was so startled that I opened my mouth to scream, but nothing came out but a rasp of air. Then I felt Joshua's cool fingers on my mouth keeping me from really screaming. Reality caught up with me. "Sorry, I didn't mean to scare you."

I pulled his hand from my mouth. "No. It's all me. Too preoccupied." I mumbled something else incoherent. I didn't even know what I was trying to say. I took a deep breath and tried to regain my focus. "Let's start again. Hi. What's up?"

He had a mixture of confusion and amusement in his eyes. "Umm," he paused awkwardly. "Would you like to get away for a couple of days? We would be with Gabriel."

"Let me see, time with you and get to avoid Rousseau. Do you really need to ask?"

He smiled. "Okay, go ahead and pack a few things. We will leave in two hours." He seemed a little off, happy, and nervous maybe.

"Is everything okay?"

"Everything is perfect." He kissed my forehead and gently pulled me away from the door so he could exit. He stepped into the hall and listened for a moment. "Speaking of Rousseau, she is downstairs asking where your room is."

"Did I mention I love your hearing?"

"Leslie just went into her room."

"Thanks," I said as I slid past him and rushed to her room. I knocked softly and let myself in. "Hey, you mind if I hang out for a bit?"

She was digging through a drawer. "Not at all. Please." She swept her arm towards the bed. "I was just about to go down and get some tea. You want some?"

"Yes, please."

She plucked a tin out of the drawer she'd been searching. "Back in a minute."

I pushed myself back on the bed and leaned against the wall. I pulled a lock of my hair around from behind my ear and made a small braid and repeated until I had three perfectly even ones.

A dull thumping sounded at the door. I jumped up and opened it cautiously. Leslie had two cups of tea and a box of shortbread cookies under her arm. I let her in and shut the door behind her.

"Rousseau is lingering in the hall outside your room."

I rolled my eyes and returned to my seat on the bed. "Josh said he heard her asking around for me. How long do you think till she checks in here?"

"Uhhh. She eyed the two cups of tea. Just a minute." She left the room and returned with Gentry. "Two bodies... two cups of tea." She pulled a chair over and twisted sideways, dangling her long legs over the arm.

"Aye. Am I part of a conspiracy now?" Gentry prodded while she sat next me.

"The avoiding Rousseau kind," I answered.

"Why does she want to speak with you?" Leslie wondered aloud.

"I don't know. But when she looks at me, I feel like I need to shower afterwards."

"She does seem to be very aware of you. I noticed her watching you at the vigil tonight," Leslie added, sounding suspicious.

"At least I know it isn't all in my head."

"Love, ya are a bit touched," Gentry said teasingly to me. "Just not about Rousseau. Never cared for the woman."

"Speaking of crazy." I leveled my eyes at her. "Someone seems a little crazy about you." I wagged my brows.

Leslie looked at her with a knowing grin. "And who might that be?"

A flush of pink colored Gentry's porcelain face. She covered her mouth as she grinned uncontrollably. "I prefer to keep it a mystery," she giggled. I'd never seen her like this—positively giddy. She opened up, and when she spoke about Peter, there was awe in her tone. She said that she'd liked him since we'd arrived. I felt an almost uncontainable joy for them.

I checked the clock; it was late. An hour and a half had ticked by, and I needed to pack. "Thanks for letting me hide out. I need to go pack a few things." I dragged myself from my cozy spot.

"You leavin'?"

"Yeah, leaving with Gabriel and Joshua in a half hour. Not sure where we're going."

"Be safe," Leslie said.

"Is Peter still up?" I asked.

"He turned in early tonight," Gentry replied.

"Say goodbye for me?"

"Course, love. See ya in a few."

I opened the door and peeked into the hall. It was quiet. As I turned to shut the door, I poked my head back in. Maybe it was the memorial. I suddenly felt choked up and sentimental. "Love you guys." I lingered just long enough for them to see I meant what I said, and they returned the sentiment.

I cantered to my room and stuffed a couple of changes of clothes and my toiletries into my backpack. I started to leave, but decided to bring my journal and favorite pen; maybe there would be some down time when I could actually write. I headed downstairs.

Ian was parked on the couch watching TV. He looked up. "They're at the back entrance."

"Thanks." I headed down the back stairwell. Josh was leaning against the wall next to the door with a bag slumped on the ground next to him.

He gave me a crooked grin. "You ready?"

"Mmm hmm." He picked up his bag and reached for mine. He looped it over his shoulder and placed his hand on the small of my back as he led me out the door. Gabriel sat in a van with the engine running. He nodded as we walked past and crawled into the back. When the door shut, we were in motion before we could take our seats. "Are we in a hurry?"

"Nope."

"Where are we headed?"

"Kilkenny. Gabriel needs to plan an assault to test some new tech. There's a cottage there where he can spread out and avoid the prying eyes of Conclave members."

"What kind of tech?"

"Some new toxin that works on vampires at a cellular level. Not sure. It's called Aurora."

"Isn't that the name of a goddess?"

"Yes, the Roman goddess of the dawn."

"Mmmmm. You're not going on that op are you? I would

prefer you be very far away from anything involving toxins and the dawn."

"Gabriel already told me I'm not going on it."

"Where are we going?"

"To do nothing related to work."

"Like a real break?"

"Unless you call moonlit walks down the river Nore work?"

"I'm not going to be locked away in a tower the whole time?" I fluttered my eyelids.

"There is a tower." He cocked an eyebrow. "Promise, no locking you away in it, though."

The two days that followed were the best in my life. This was not a spur of the moment trip. Joshua, with Gabriel's consent, had meticulously planned every detail of the getaway. Gabriel did plan the assault like Joshua had said, but that was not the focus of the outing. There was no talk of vampires, Watchers, Slayers, Seers, angels or any other related item. I wished it could last forever. For two days, I did not have a night terror, or day terror as it would be, and no visions of an imperfect future.

We returned on Wednesday just before midnight. Blackthorne was going to be arriving on Thursday evening. There was a meeting scheduled for 7:00 P.M., Joshua walked in ahead of me with the bags.

I hung back for a moment, and when Gabriel got alongside me, I whispered, "On the way back, something occurred to me. Blackthorne is coming here for a reason, isn't he? He wants to use me again."

He put his hand on my shoulder as we stepped through the door. Through downturned lips, he answered, "Yes."

I stopped walking and looked up at him. "You don't agree with whatever they're planning."

"Everything will work out fine," he replied, his hand dropping from my shoulder as he sped upstairs. I decided to worry about tomorrow when tomorrow came.

I didn't catch up to Joshua until I reached my room. He sat on the couch and looked at me, his eyes still warm and worry free from the last two days. I went to him, sat on his lap, looping my arms around his neck, and pressed my cheek to his. We sat for much of the night in silence, just enjoying being with one another, enfolded in our own world.

Just before sunrise, I walked him down to his room, our fingers laced together. "I guess it is really back to reality," I sighed.

"We'll get away again soon."

"Not soon enough." I pressed his hand to my cheek.

"Agreed." He reached around my waist and pulled me close for one last kiss. The same kiss that made my head spin and my body feel like a network of sparks every time.

I took two stairs at a time, feeling stronger today. Stopping in the kitchen, I made myself a huge sandwich and devoured it before heading to my room. Now that my belly was full, I was ready for sleep, so I proceeded upstairs.

Gentry stumbled into the hall heavy with sleep, on her way to the bathroom. She shuffled over and gave me a hug. "You're back," she cooed. "How was your trip, love?" She pulled back and looked at me through heavy lids.

"It was perfection," my voice dreamy.

"Aye, sounds like there are stories to tell."

I smiled coyly. "There are always stories."

"We are planning to go to a late lunch. A band Ian knows is doing a practice set. You want to go?"

"Did you clear it with Sebastian or Gabriel?"

"Sebastian agreed when Uriel said she would attend. And we'll get you back well before sunset."

"What time?"

"We are leaving around 1:00."

"I think I can handle a little sleep deprivation. Would you mind waking me at noon?"

"I have the 10:00 A.M. shift, so no problem."

"Seriously, formal babysitting hours?"

"Leslie has the first shift," she grinned.

I gave her another hug and kissed her cheek. "See you in a few."

She quickly plodded to the bathroom, and I made my way to my room. I sunk into my bed, and my dreams returned. I wasn't safe from them, despite the Oneiroi's apparent inability to reach me in the daylight hours.

A prophetic dream tore at my consciousness. I was strapped to a stone slab that remained cool despite the heat in the room. Iron cuffs were cutting into my wrists and ankles as I tugged to free myself. I looked down my body: there was a thick leather strap holding down my torso.

I was wearing nothing but a thin, gauzy, white dress, making me feel even more vulnerable. Torches lit the room. Frantically, I examined my surroundings. A fire that had gone to deep red embers glared at me. The heat made sweat bead to the surface of my body and drip down my sides in salty streams. I examined the fire once again. Thin metal rods rested on a ledge, and I felt a familiar presence.

A man dressed in a black robe entered and removed one of the rods from the fire. He stepped towards me, the glowing tip moving ever closer. I screamed as he lightly pressed it to my flesh, writing the first symbol on my right foot. He replaced the first rod and removed another from the fire. He moved to my ankle and started the next. I tried to endure the pain without screaming, but I couldn't bear it. I cried out over and over while sweat poured from my body like blood.

I woke screaming out in pain and frantically tore the covers off and pulled up the pant legs of my pajamas, still feeling the burning flesh. Nothing there. Then I realized Leslie was sitting next to me, looking kinda freaked out. I made eye contact, then squinted my eyes closed while I felt the sweat trickle down the sides of my face.

She rubbed my back trying to comfort me. "Is there anything I can do?"

"Just a bad dream." I noticed her book splayed open on the floor. "You can go back to reading. I'm fine." I gave her the most confident smile I could. She eased off the bed and picked up the book reluctantly.

"Some dream," she commented, her eyes bulging.

I flopped back down. "Yeah, I don't do things halfway."

I pulled the covers up over my head. I could swear that the symbols were still burning on my leg all the way up to my hipbone. I debated on whether I should let myself fall asleep again. But the debate didn't last long.

Someone was running fingers through my hair. I looked through slits to see Gentry gently waking me.

"Heard ya had a rough night of it. It's noon, darlin'. Ya still up to comin' with? It'd be lovely."

I rubbed the sleep from my eyes. Some strands of hair had

dried to my face from my profusion of sweat. My skin felt oily, and just like the dream, I could smell the salt on my skin. I managed to sit up, everything still a little blurry. "Yup, be fine after a shower."

While standing under the hot water, I composed a journal entry in my head, though it was more of a letter to Joshua. One I didn't necessarily intend to give to him. I finished getting ready and disguising myself for our outing and still had fifteen minutes, so I decided to write my thoughts down. After completing the entry, I carefully removed it from the journal and sealed it in an envelope. In calligraphy, I scrolled Joshua's name on the outside and tucked it back inside the book. Should something happen to me.

Gentry burst my door open, eyes aglow. "You ready for our hot date?"

"Always ready for you, baby."

"Brilliant! Meet Uriel and Ian at the back. The rest of us are going out the front." And then she was off, leaving the door wide open.

I shoved my journal under my mattress to keep it out of sight while people like Rousseau were around. Giggling echoed outside, so I stepped out into the hall. I could hear Gentry retrieving more troops for the outing. I stood there in a complete daze, my thoughts drifting. Someone abruptly grabbed my elbow from behind, and I screamed like a little girl. I swung around my hand clenched in a fist.

Peter jumped back and laughed, with his hands up in surrender. "Didn't mean to scare you," he said with faux sincerity.

"Yeah? Then why the stealth mode on approach?"

He twisted up the corner of his mouth mischievously,

coming up short. "Um," was all he said while attempting an innocent look.

"That's what I thought. Busted." I punched him in the stomach teasingly, but hard enough to make a point.

"Sorry, I couldn't resist."

I rolled my eyes. "Fine. What's up?"

"You're actually coming?" he asked in disbelief.

"Yup." I turned and shut my door.

"Really?"

"Is it so shocking?"

"Well, kinda. The few times we've gone out, you've said no."

I grinned crookedly. "I just want to make sure you appreciate my presence when I do come."

"Oh, I see how it is, milady," he said, dramatically bowing. He stood and put his arm around my shoulders and ushered me down the hall to the stairs. We parted at the bottom and headed to our separate exits.

A small lunch crowd was at the pub only a block away. Musicians were setting up on a diminutive stage in the back right corner diagonal from the front entrance. Ian headed over and spoke with them cordially and helped them unpack the rest of their gear.

Booths lined the left and right walls with a freestanding bar in the front third of the space; there was one booth in the back corner separated from the rest and directly across from the stage on the same wall. Leslie and Gentry were already seated there.

Dark blue walls with framed pictures of the sights in Dublin were surrounded by an abundance of cherry wood paneling.

Each booth was made of the same deep red wood with clear stained glass dividers between them.

I trailed behind Uriel to sit with the others. Peter came out of the hall that ran to the left just before the booth. He looped his arm through mine and pulled me into the booth with him. I couldn't stop smiling.

It had been just shy of a month since all of us had been out together, although Joshua wouldn't be able to join us this time. Emotionally, I was in a different world though. I could say I was happy—truly happy.

The band started their practice set while all of us picked at the food we ordered. Ian, in his element, drummed on the table and occasionally leaned over and spoke into Leslie's ear. Peter pulled Gentry close. Uriel, on my other side, kept texting someone between scans of the area.

After the band finished their session, they packed up their gear and loaded it into the back room until that night's set. None of us wanted to leave, so we ordered some dessert. The place cleared out. Only our waitress and a bartender remained until the dinner crowd. The waitress perched herself on a stool at the bar and chatted with the bartender while we consumed the last of our desserts.

Leslie headed to the bathroom, and I decided it was time to visit the little girl's room, too. I followed not two minutes later. When I entered, she was washing her hands. I glared at the speaker in the ceiling; it was piping in music a little too loudly.

"I know. It's not like it's evening, huh," she yelled, overcompensating for the noise.

"Um, yeah."

"How'd you like the band?" she asked.

"Great. Does Ian know them well?"

"He used to jam with the bass player sometimes." She had

removed her rings when she washed her hands and picked them up off the counter and started sliding them back on her elegant fingers.

I stopped cold in the middle of asking her another question and walked over to her. I took her right hand in mine and looked at her ring. The blood drained from my appendages. It was the ring from my dream. It was on her hand, clawing at Tyran as he drained the life from her.

"When did you get this?" I asked breathlessly.

"While you were gone. A couple of days ago," she said, a little perplexed by my odd reaction.

The ring had stones of green and purple in a large free form silver setting that looked like nebula. She didn't know about my visions; as far as she was concerned, I was troubled with horrible dreams stemming from my past.

"We need to go."

"Okaaay. You're kind of scaring me here."

I mustered up a little smile. "It's daylight; we're fine. I'll meet you out front in a minute." I really did need to use the restroom.

While I was washing my hands, what sounded like a tray of glasses dropped to the floor outside. I opened the bathroom door and saw blood spattered on the wall in front of me. My heart started beating painfully hard, hammering against my chest with such force, I was afraid it would jump from my chest.

I ran towards the booth and stopped short of the main room. The waitress was in a small heap on the floor, a bullet hole between her eyes. I could only assume the bartender was in the same condition on the other side of the bar. I took a few more steps inside. Everyone was gone. Some chairs and tables had been knocked over, and a spray of broken glass littered the wood floor.

I spun and looked to the front door. Four motorcycles were

parked out front. There was a large clump of hair that could only be Uriel's near the entrance. Another motorcycle pulled up. The rider had the same gear I'd seen in my vision.

Pivoting on my heel, I dashed into the hall towards the rear exit. The front door jingled behind me, quickening my pace. I heaved the door inward, light flooding into the dark hall, blinding me. I glanced back at the approaching figure and ran forward outside, tripping over something. I fell hard on my belly, knocking the wind out of me. The heavy metal door closed on my foot, and I struggled to free it. When I did, it closed the rest of the way with a loud clank. I sucked in air, trying to catch my breath again.

Rolling onto my side, I realized I was half on top of a body. "No...no...no...no..." I moaned, tears springing from my eyes. I pushed the hair back from Leslie's face, her lifeless blue eyes peered at me.

I wiped my nose with my sleeve. There were punctures on her throat. I placed my head on her chest with the faint hope I would hear something, but there was only silence. It suddenly dawned on me; there was still a vampire inside. I pushed myself onto my feet, not wanting to leave her, but I had to.

I scanned the alley. There was a motorcycle at the mouth of it. I looked the other way. There was a massive faded canopy over a large roll-up door that was open. It was pitch black inside. Then I noticed a ladder leading to the sunlit roof. I opted to keep in the light.

Scurrying over, I jumped up, catching the second to the bottom rung, and walked up the wall. It was hot from the direct sunlight, but not hot enough to burn me. I managed to get my foot on the bottom rung. I heaved and got my right hand to the third and pulled myself up. I put my foot on the second rung and heard something just inside the roll-up door.

"Leaving so soon?" Tyran called from the opening.

I froze. He stepped out of the deepest shadows into the shade where I could see him. He had the same gear on, minus the helmet. I started shaking. In his left arm, he had Peter in a headlock, and in his right hand. He held Gentry out slightly in front of him by the neck.

I grimaced and looked away, pressing my forehead against the brick, and then looked back. Gentry looked at me and mouthed the word, "No."

Tyran grinned icily. "You, for them. You have three seconds."

I squeezed the ladder and glared over at him as I felt the sunlight protectively bathe me. I was about to step to the lower rung when he made one quick movement; Gentry's neck made a dull popping sound and the light went out of her eyes.

He tossed her into the wall, and she dropped like a ragdoll, eyes open, half her face smashed from the collision with the bricks. I shrieked and dropped to the ground, my feet stinging from the impact.

Peter yelled out and struggled against him. "Ali, run! Leave me!" Tyran shook him, and he stopped yelling, but Peter pleaded with his eyes.

He moved Peter to his right hand.

"Please. No...no," I begged and dropped on my knees. "Please don't kill him, please."

"You for him," he confirmed. He was enjoying this.

"You won't kill him. You—or any of your people," I amended.

"Agreed."

I stood and walked on trembling legs towards the shade.

It was Peter's turn to beg. "Ali, please don't do this."

Tyran allowed me to hug Peter. I pressed my lips to his ear. "I love you. Please tell Joshua I'm sorry."

Then Tyran knocked him over the head. He went limp, and I

fell with him, keeping him from cracking his skull on the ground.

"You said you wouldn't hurt him."

"I said I wouldn't kill him," he replied shrewdly.

I pressed my head to Peter's chest. His heart was still beating strongly. Tyran ripped me away, grabbing my hair and twisting me around to look at him. He smiled and pulled me close.

He nuzzled my neck and whispered, "You broken yet?"

And then he bit me. It hurt. He drank until I lost consciousness.

But I knew this wasn't the end…

I wasn't broken

…yet.

26

CAGED

I had flickers of memory. Being carried through sewers, being belted into a seat on a plane, and then I really came to. I slowly opened my eyes. I was in a car. I looked around.

Correction: I was in a limousine.

I tried the door handle, and I heard someone make a derisive sort of laugh under his breath. I cast my eyes in the direction of the sound.

Tyran sat perfectly composed next to me, crisp and clean like he could be on his way to be photographed for a magazine ad. He had on a blue, striped dress shirt and faded designer jeans. The blue in his shirt brought out the color of his eyes.

I raked my eyes over myself—different clothes, a finely ribbed, fitted plum sweater and black denim jeans. Even my shoes were new: black leather, rubber-soled boots with side zippers. I was too drained to feel violated.

My hands no longer had the rusty smudges from the ladder I'd started climbing. When I thought of Leslie and Gentry, I had to turn my face away from him and fight the tears that pricked my eyes. I wondered if Uriel or Ian were alive. There'd been a minimum of six vampires judging from the motorcycles I'd seen. And they'd had the element of surprise. I fiddled with the hem of the sweater.

"Promise I didn't look," Tyran grinned widely. "The decoy looked fetching in your clothes."

My nostrils flared.

He reached over, took my hand, and gently pushed up my sleeve, running his nose along my skin like he was breathing in a fine wine. It was all I could do not to recoil, but I knew that would only please him. I steeled myself and tried to clear my mind of the flood of emotions that fought to drown me.

"Your Slayer did well, considering," he mused.

"Did she survive?"

"Maybe. She and the boy took out five of my team. It was impressive."

"So you don't know?" I desperately wanted to pull my arm back.

He shrugged. "We jammed your phones, but Gabriel knew somehow. We had what we needed, so…"

They had retreated! And I knew exactly how Gabriel knew: Joshua. He must have gone crazy when he couldn't follow me. Emotion started to well up inside of me again, but through considerable effort, I pushed it back down.

"What are you going to do with me?" I asked, knowing full well what was to come.

"Sacrifice you, of course. Fear not, we'll have some quality time first. We still need to gather a few things for the ceremony, but they are easy to come by. You, my darling, were the rare ingredient." He kissed my wrist and spoke lightly.

"How long do I have?"

He ran his finger down my arm with his free hand and pursed his lips. "Days. Weeks."

I swallowed, but it was like trying to swallow cotton, my throat was so dry.

"I can smell him on you."

"Who?"

He smiled and ran his finger over the barely visible puncture marks on my arm. I wondered how obvious they were to him. I could barely see them, and I knew where to look. I couldn't take it any longer. I pulled my hand away and folded my arms over my chest. *I may have to chop that arm off later.*

A minute went by, and I had to ask, despite the fact I was sure I knew the answer. "You had Daylight gear with you. Why did you negotiate? Why didn't you just abduct me the moment I entered the alley?"

He smiled—a cruel smile—and looked into the distance like he was reliving the moment. "And miss the look on your face when you discovered your friend and when I killed the other in front of you?"

"It was more than the look, wasn't it?" I paused, remembering him feeding on me in the apartment. "The blood bond. You wanted to feel my pain." My voice was more calm than expected.

"It was worth letting your pathetic little friend live, just to have that moment."

We sat in silence for the rest of the journey. The vehicle slowed as we pulled off the main road. It was a clear night, and the terrain was visible. We rounded a hill, and a monstrous castle rose in the distance. It was on an elevated bluff with four towers at its corners, two round and two square. There was a sheer rock cliff on two sides, with the ocean below.

We advanced toward a long stone wall that protected the land approach. As we passed through the guarded gate, I noticed the wall was thick enough to drive a car down the top of it. We passed another check station with another gate that had a secondary fence, which extended to each cliff's edge. *I guess no tourist would accidentally wander up this hill.* We pulled onto a roundabout that ended in front of the main entrance. There was a beautifully lit fountain gushing in the middle.

The vehicle stopped in front of grand-looking steps. Several footmen were immediately at the car and opened both the doors. I stepped out into the night air. An icy wind clawed at me as I stood shivering, looking at the castle. I don't think I could have felt more insignificant. Almost immediately, Tyran's iron grip wrapped around my right bicep. He pulled me along as we traversed the steps towards the entrance.

We reached the top, and there were more guards who swung open the arch-shaped doors. We entered the lobby, which was large enough to be a grand ballroom. Alternating cream and grey marble tiles glistened underneath magnificent rugs. The stone had been plastered over and painted with frescoes that rivaled the Sistine Chapel. On a normal day, I would have spent hours getting lost in them. Carved marble pillars three stories high ran the length of the room. A sweeping staircase swirled its way to an upper level on the left.

We walked past the staircase and through a grand arch at the room's end. It was the most opulent thing I'd ever seen. Red velvet curtains covered a massive window that had the same coating I'd seen on the windows of the cars and motorcycle helmets. On the floor, black and white marble tiles ran at angles that drew the eyes to a single location: the throne.

Queen Agrona sat perusing some papers. She stood, her rail-thin body clad in an elegant business suit, and descended the steps, stopping at the bottom. As Tyran strolled towards her, tugging me along with him, she looked quite pleased. We stopped a few feet from her. He bowed, and she moved forward and kissed both his cheeks. She spoke in French. *"Tu as bien fait, mon fils.* (You've done well, my son)*"*

"Merci, Maman, (Thank you, Mother)*"* he replied.

She glided in front of me and grabbed my face. She turned it from side to side and looked at me like I was an animal she was inspecting. I half-expected her to check my teeth.

"Emmène-la aux cages et on parlera. Bien fait. (Take her to the cages, and we will talk. Good work.)*"* She kissed him on the cheek again and glanced at me one last time. She had the same greedy expression Rousseau always had on her face when she looked at me.

"Oui, Maman, (Yes, Mother)*"* he answered, and then I was escorted out.

We walked through a corridor behind the stairs and through a series of rooms, sitting rooms, ballrooms—more than I could count, each equally grand. We entered one that smelled like paint, and I saw a tall, lanky figure painting a new mural in what looked to be a dining room.

I wondered why they would need a dining room.

We finally came to a massive wood door that didn't fit the finery of the rest of the property. Tyran yanked at the huge iron ring that hung in place of a doorknob. There was a small landing and steps that disappeared below. The walls were no longer plastered; they were old stone like those in the medieval castles I'd visited in England.

We descended deeper and deeper into the bowels of the castle. It smelled like salt, metal, damp earth, and suffering. I tried not to jump from the screams echoing off the stone walls. We passed by a series of cells before we went through a narrow, tunnel-like hall that was rounded at the top.

Then, judging by the acoustics, we stepped out into a massive room. I couldn't see past the cells on each side. When we reached an open spot where I could survey everything, my bones felt hollow as I took it in, and my knees gave way enough that Tyran had to take on some of my weight or let me slump to the ground.

I was looking at the maze from my dream. Everything was here: the cavernous room lit by torchlight, the prison cell cages that were dotted along the top walkway. I half-expected to hear the horn-like gong shatter the air. This was where I'd been hunted in my nightmares. I blinked, recognizing the reality of it.

It seemed so much *more* than my dream. The massive pillars were larger than those in front of the Vatican. We rounded the first corner and came to a sitting area where vampires could watch the hunt.

There were three male vampires seated, ready to watch like Romans at the Colosseum. Two of them were smirking at me like they knew me. Then I laid eyes on the third.

He didn't look as amused. In fact, he looked at me with what seemed to be a mixture of hatred and confusion; he seemed familiar. I stared at his wavy black hair and grey eyes and remembered. He was one of the vampires invading my dreams. I was in the presence of the Oneiroi.

We stopped. I looked up at Tyran, and he still had the same satisfied expression on his face. "I believe you know the sons of Nyx: Morpheus, Icelos, and Phantasos."

I swallowed. "Morpheus. I thought that was just a Sci-Fi character."

Tyran grinned. "He is the reason they gave that character the name. Morpheus is the god of dreams."

I looked at Morpheus; he didn't seem to be pleased by Tyran's gloating. His two brothers chuckled under their breath. I looked away, thankful when we moved on.

We rounded the next corner and walked the other long length of the maze. Tyran stopped in front of the second to last cell, pulled out some keys, and unlocked it. He walked me in and pulled me to him by the waist. Everything in me wanted to fight him, but I didn't want to give him the satisfaction. I was determined to save my energy for something I could win.

He ran his thumb over my lips. "I will see you tomorrow." He pushed my head to the side and sank his teeth into my neck again. I prayed to pass out, but he only drank until I felt weak, then let me topple to the ground. The door clanked shut, and I was alone.

There was an elevated area in the back corner. I crawled over and hoisted myself onto the stone slab of a bed. There wasn't even straw to pad anything. I looked around my new home. Bars ran the full length of one wall with the door. The side walls each had a window into the next cell with a metal grate inset. The back wall seemed to have a vent at a downward angle so as not to let in any direct sunlight; I could smell salt air coming in through the opening. I doubted I could get any more than an arm through it.

Without warning, I started to sob. I muffled it the best I could, but it was welling up from deep within me. I rolled over and faced the wall, making myself as small as possible. I grieved for Leslie and Gentry. I wondered if I'd given myself up faster, if I could have saved Gentry. *Had Tyran even counted to three?* He was punishing me—breaking me.

Gabriel had been close enough to cause the vamps to retreat. I pictured him running down the street and finding nothing but bodies. *If I'd just been able to stall a few minutes longer. Then maybe...No. Peter would be dead too.*

I prayed that Uriel and Ian had survived. And I hoped that Joshua would forgive me for trading myself for Peter. I sobbed until I slipped into oblivion.

I woke to someone clanking the bars of the cell next to mine, the last one in the row.

"Food," an impatient voice spat.

I sat up and watched his shadow move in the torchlight towards my cell.

"Food." He held a metal tray with divided sections through a slot in the bars.

Hurrying as best I could, I took it. "Thank you."

He was older and filthy, like he'd been living down here for a long while. He licked his lips when he looked at me.

I was almost sorry for thanking him and cringed away with my meal. I sat in the far corner with my food, not taking my eyes off of him until he moved on.

I examined what he gave me. A crust of bread and some sort of shepherd's pie maybe, a mush of vegetables, potatoes, and bits of beef. I smelled the food, and my mouth watered, but I was afraid to eat it.

A timid, female voice came from the cell next to mine. "It's safe to eat. They don't poison their food."

I realized by "food" she meant me.

After debating for about thirty seconds, I soaked the bread in the mixture and took a bite. It was actually good, though shoe leather might have tasted just as good in my current state. I finished the plate and sat for a moment, feeling sick from gorging myself after not eating for over a day.

My eyes went to the grate connecting my cell to hers. I wanted to talk her, but I wasn't sure what to say. I walked over and peered inside; it was so dark. I couldn't see much. The cell was laid out like mine, and she was sitting on the slab in the far corner. She appeared to be small, but I was only seeing a darkened silhouette.

"What's your name?"

"You don't want to know my name." There was a long pause. "Most people don't last long here, unless they need something from you. It's better *not* to know." There was hopelessness in her voice.

"How long have you been here?"

"Years. I think…"

"My name is Aleria," I offered.

"Beautiful name." Her voice sounded dead.

"Thank you," I paused. "Please. What's your name?"

I heard her sigh. "Neka."

The name was familiar; I liked it. I stood, trying to make the connection in my brain. I pressed my fingers to my temples. My voice trembled when I asked, "Neka Rousseau?"

There was a startled intake of breath. "How would you know that?"

"I'm a Watcher," was the best I could do without going into too much detail. I added, "I know your aunt."

She dashed over to the grate and latched her fingers into the holes. I could see her pale skin and red hair. And how fragile she looked. Her bones poked beneath her skin like dry twigs. "Is she all right?"

"Yes, I saw her a couple of days ago."

"Do they know I'm here?"

I hesitated. "No. Neka, they think you're dead."

I didn't have it in me to give it to her softly. And then I had the most dreadful revelation. Someone does know she is alive—the mole. I thought of the greedy look that always enraptured Crina Rousseau's face when she looked at me.

She finally had something the French coven wanted: me. But

when she gave me up, she didn't know she was also giving up the last member of the Lux—a double-edged secret, both protecting and destroying.

But it wasn't the only secret I kept that would do the same. Then I doubted my theory. If Crina Rousseau was the mole, then why was Neka still here? Wouldn't she have been released? Or had the vampires not held up their end of the bargain? Or was I only part of the bargain? I forced myself back to the present.

She let out a shaky breath. "I thought as much," she finally said.

"I'm sorry." I didn't know what else to say.

"Who is your Keeper?"

"Sebastian."

"So you work with Michael?"

"No, Gabriel."

"I thought—" she stopped short.

I didn't want to talk anymore. And I didn't know how much I could trust her. She'd been here for years. Who knew what they'd done to her or where her loyalties lay. I didn't know if I should tell her Michael was dead.

"They reorganized. I'm sorry, I need to sit for a little while."

"Yes, rest," she said quietly and moved back to her stone slab.

I did the same. I had information and no way to get it to anyone. I leaned my head against the wall and wiped an errant tear from my cheek when I pictured Peter's face the moment Tyran snapped Gentry's neck.

Glancing up, I noticed Tyran leaning against the bars watching me and wondered how long he'd been there. His smug expression told me that it had been a little while. He'd seen me cry. I turned my face away, and I heard the squeak of the metal door open.

He grabbed my arm and hoisted me from my seat like I was five. We walked down the corridor to the cages that were more open. They had bars on all sides and overlooked the maze.

"I have a treat for you," he whispered into my ear, letting his mouth linger next to my cheek.

I controlled my revulsion and didn't reply.

He yanked open a cell in between two others and shoved me in and locked it. I looked up to say something horrible to him, but he was already gone. I sat alone between two empty cells.

A while later, two vamps escorted two hooded males to the cell next to me. They ripped the hoods from their heads and shoved them into the cell. The guards had backpacks with them, the kind hikers use. They started going through the bags and tossing their contents onto the floor.

The shorter of the two yelled, "Hey, that's my stuff!" and started charging over to the guard. The guard raised his hand to strike.

"Stop!" I yelled at the new arrival. The guy looked at me like I was crazy, but he did what I said. "You won't be able to stop him. It's just stuff. Let it go."

The guard sneered at me.

"But—" He looked over at me.

I shook my head in warning.

The vamps confiscated a multi-tool and anything else that could be used as a weapon. The door was shut, and before they could speak to me, another vamp showed up holding a small jar with a handle.

Two different guards stood in wait while he unlocked the door and stepped in. He pulled what looked like a paintbrush out and slapped purple paint onto the front of each of them. Then he pulled out a marker and made a symbol on each of their foreheads. When he seemed pleased with his work, he left with the others.

I walked to the other side of my cage and surveyed the maze. I remembered Bowen's words to Tyran: "I prefer my food not to struggle." I looked over at them and felt only sadness. Not ten minutes later, two girls were brought into the cage on the other side of me. The painting process was repeated. The blonde girl was crying.

All of them looked to be around my age, the boys maybe a little older. One of them placed his hands on the bars between our cages. He looked like he was going to ask me something, but a guard walked by, and he stopped.

He had light brown, close-cropped hair and large blue eyes. His slightly olive skin was indicative of someone who spent time in the sun, probably playing sports. His friend had a similar look, but his hair was blond and his skin more pale.

"How did you get here?" I asked.

"These dudes just grabbed us. We were camping in this totally awesome spot, then wham! They just pulled us out of our sleeping bags, grabbed our packs, and shoved us into the trunk."

"What's your name?" he asked.

"Ali," I frowned, but I didn't ask his. I knew now why Neka didn't want to know. I looked out at the maze below and knew the horrors that were before them.

"I'm Nick. This is Codie."

"Hey," I replied and looked over at Codie.

"Your accent is American," Nick noted.

"Yeah, from California."

"Us too." He seemed pleased by the connection.

I looked over at the girls. The redhead was sitting next to the blonde with her arms around her crying friend. The crying one had her knees pulled tightly to her chest. She was rocking back and forth slightly to soothe herself.

Codie stepped over to the side of my cage and grasped the bars. He spoke to the crying girl and her friend. "What are your names?"

The red haired girl looked up, her pale eyes terrified. "Samantha. This is Rachel." She paused for a long moment. "We were with her parents. A car ran us off the road. We ended up in a river. When they pulled us from the wreck, we thought they were saving us."

Rachel started to sob. My guess: the parents didn't make it. Or they were left to cover the accident. Maybe it would be assumed that the girls were swept away by the current. The vampires were taking people in an inconspicuous manner— hikers go missing and car accident victims drown in rivers. I tried to swallow, but couldn't. The knot in my throat wouldn't allow it.

Two guards came back, and one indicted me. "She supposed to be painted?"

"No, the Prince said hands off." They continued on.

Codie made a "psst" sound.

I looked at him.

"Prince? You know where we are?"

"France."

"No," he whispered. "*Where* we are?"

I debated what to say. "In a castle...about to be hunted by vampires."

He laughed and made a joke.

I didn't.

Do they have a better chance if they know what they are dealing with? I doubted it. I slid down the bars with my back to the maze. "I'm not joking." I let out a single morbid laugh. "I wouldn't have believed it either."

They broke into smaller conversations, obviously thinking I was a loon. Guards came back with plates of food. I took mine immediately and started eating. I needed to get my strength back. *For what?* I wasn't sure.

The boys looked at their food suspiciously like I had. After seeing me eat, not so delicately, they delved in. Samantha ate hers, but Rachel only picked at her food.

There was a sharp edge on the handle of my spoon. I rubbed my forearm until it started to bleed. I let the blood trickle down my arm. *Maybe I could die of a staff infection before the sacrifice.*

"What are you doing?" Nick asked, still looking at me like I was crazy.

"Watch the guard's eyes," I murmured.

A few minutes later, the filthy one I'd seen earlier returned for the trays. I walked over to hand him my tray, and faster than I could react, he grabbed my arm and yanked it through the bars, smacking my face against the iron. His brown eyes glowed and his fangs were about to rip into me. He was ready to partake of my blood when he caught himself and ran off, mumbling something.

I rubbed my forehead. *Okay, not the best plan, but I think I made my point.* All four of them sat in stunned silence as I walked over and plopped on the ground with my back to the maze again.

Samantha asked, "They're gonna kill us?"

I dropped my head into my hands. This was a no-win situation. I doubted *I'd* have a chance, and I'd had training. "A stake through the heart will paralyze them, but it won't kill them. In order to do that, you will have to take their head." I waited, letting the information sink in.

Rachel, the blonde girl with the innocent-looking blue eyes, spoke for the first time. "Take their head? Like...as in, cut it off? I can't do that."

"Then you'll die," I replied matter-of-factly. Feeling it was better they know the truth.

"Hey," Samantha said, scolding me.

"They are faster, stronger, pure evil. And are planning to eat you," I retorted and felt like a jerk.

"We need to hear it," Nick said. "Anything else?"

I told them what I could, but it wasn't much. I stood and looked over the maze. I noticed that there were caches of weapons throughout. I guessed it wouldn't be a real sport if there weren't some danger.

I took a slow stuttering breath and looked at all four of their innocent faces, feeling grieved. Hating that I already liked them. Hating the castle and everything it represented. Hating Tyran even more. I sat defeated, squeezing my eyes shut, completely powerless to do anything but pray, part of me wishing I could die now so I didn't have to watch them be hunted. Morbidly, Shakespeare's words popped into my head. This time, I felt I understood them:

> "Death, death; oh, amiable, lovely death!
> Come, grin on me, and I will think thou
>   smilest."

27

BIT BY BIT

Maybe an hour had passed, I could hear more voices echoing in the large space, and I could feel the energy that seemed to charge the air. Something was going to happen soon. Four guards came and marched off all of my new companions.

They were led to one of the narrower ends of the maze. There was a long, steep staircase leading to the platform I remembered from my dream. The guards poked them with swords, forcing them to descend the steps. When they were halfway down, the steps collapsed and turned into a slide. They all slid to the bottom and reminded me of the children's game Pick Up Sticks; their bodies straight and piled haphazardly on top of one another. They stood, and Codie tried running back up, but the incline was too steep. He slid back down and landed at Nick's feet.

That gonging horn went off, and I could feel it in my chest. A voice rang out announcing: "Your goal is to reach the cage on the opposite side. Survive three times, and be rewarded." Another horn blast.

They took off running, staying together like I had told them. They navigated quickly through the first quarter of the maze and picked up weapons, but I hadn't seen a single vampire. The moment the lack of vamps occurred to me, I watched two approach the slide. One of them was Morpheus, still looking like he was in a foul mood, or maybe that was his permanent state of mind.

The other was a woman, actually the first female vamp I'd seen besides the queen. She was tall and lean, but still had some curves. Shiny, deep auburn hair fell in waves a few inches short of her waist. She had full lips painted red and huge doe eyes. I couldn't see their color from such a distance, but judging from the olive undertone to her pallor, they were probably dark.

They both moved forward and stuck out a foot, landing lightly on the steep surface and sliding down on one foot while extending the other gracefully in front of them. They alighted at the bottom, took a few steps forward, surveyed the maze for a moment, then moved so quickly I couldn't follow. The four humans were almost halfway through when the maze changed shape. Halls turned into dead ends and vice versa. Samantha was cut off from the group. I could hear screams from both of the girls. I watched as Nick and Codie dragged Rachel on until she got a hold of herself.

The female vamp caught up with Samantha, but only knocked her to the ground before disappearing. She did this repeatedly, dropping from above, ambush after ambush. Each time, Samantha moved more slowly; exhaustion was setting in. I couldn't watch. I turned my back and sat down. I heard one final scream, and then there was nothing.

I heard one of the boys yell out. I grimaced, not wanting to look. Then I heard Rachel scream Nick's name. I put my hands over my ears. I couldn't handle it; I turned and sat on my knees.

Somehow, all three of them were still on their feet. The boys were helping Rachel, who was limping. Morpheus sat on top of a wall one pathway over, watching them struggle through the last section of the maze.

The female leaped up next to him like she was hopping up a single step. She danced from one wall to the next using a perfect grand jeté split jump. Morpheus vaulted one more wall over; he didn't look like he belonged in a ballet, but his movements were still graceful. They both crouched and smiled at one another, their eyes glowing.

I turned away. Tears pricked my eyes when I heard the screams. Then it was silent. I pulled myself together. I was sure Tyran would be back soon to gloat, pleased with himself for making me watch that. I heard what sounded like an actuator. I looked over my shoulder as the cage from the maze was rising to the upper level.

It looked like someone was in it. There was a clanking sound when it reached the top. Soon the guards returned and threw Nick back into his cage. He crashed against the wall in between us and landed with his back to me. He didn't move, but he was breathing.

I crawled over to reach through the bars and put my hand on his shoulder. "I'm sorry."

He wasn't crying, but his voice was choked. "She just ripped his throat out right in front of me. Ripped it out," he repeated in disbelief. "The man had Rachel, and I stabbed him, like you said, but I couldn't get to Codie. She—"

"There was nothing you could've done."

I heard a giggle and looked toward the walkway. The female was walking slowly, strutting like a cat. She ran her hand along the bars. Her face was fixed with a wicked grin. She stopped in front of Nick and wiggled her gloved hand at him. When she got in front of my cage, she continued to smile, but dropped her hand, then moved on.

"I can't do that two more times," Nick breathed. There was a long silence. "How do you know so much about them?"

"This wasn't my first time being kidnapped," I exhaled harshly. "Long story that I can't tell."

"Are they going to send you down there?"

"They have other plans for me." He shuddered.

"Yessss. Very special plans." Tyran unlocked the door. When I didn't move, he stepped in and yanked me to my feet. I surprised him by flailing my arms, and I slipped from his hands.

"Don't touch me! I can walk myself," I exclaimed, sounding like a child throwing a tantrum.

"Seems something upset you," he said in syrupy faux concern. He turned and touched my elbow. I yanked my arm upwards, but he didn't let go; instead, he pulled me close again.

The thin bands on my restraints slipped. I hit him in the face and screamed, "I hate you! I hate you! I hate you!" Then I pounded on his chest.

He didn't like being hit in the face; his expression darkened.

"I would behave, or your new friend might have something extra painful happen to him." He shoved my face against the bars, forcing me to look at Nick, his eyes wide with terror.

I relaxed and stopped fighting. Tyran escorted me back to my original cell, but he was seething. He removed my restraints and made a gesture in the air with his hand that sent a pulse throwing me into the back wall. I struck my head on the stone. I'd forgotten he had that ability. I gritted my teeth, trying not to express the pain I was in as I crumpled onto my hands and knees.

He grabbed me by the throat and lifted me from my prone position before he pinned me against the wall. He drank, but this time I feared he might actually harm me. He twisted my arm behind my back until I whimpered.

"I *will* break you," he whispered. The darkness in his tone unnerved me. "Not even my brother will want you."

I sucked in a breath. "That's why you hate me so much," I croaked, wishing I hadn't uttered it aloud.

"I can do anything to you short of compromising the sacrifice. We merely need you untainted and alive. Your mind is mine."

"He chose you. He saved *you*."

Tyran looked me in the eye and wrapped his hand around my neck. His desire to crush my throat was evident. His eyes glowed in the dim light as his mouth twisted into a snarl. His rage was barely contained.

"Do it," I managed to choke.

He pressed harder on my throat. I started seeing stars in my peripheral vision, and then everything went black as I was swept into a dream.

I could sense Morpheus, Icelos, and Phantasos prowling around and pressing me deeper into the hellishness of the dream. But I didn't have any fight in me. I watched everyone I loved running through the maze and dying over and over as they toyed with me in my sleep. I kept repeating, "This is a dream," to myself like a mantra.

The next day, I was dragged to the maze again. I held my necklaces, placing my locket in my palm and rubbing the North Star charm as if it could transport me somewhere else. Nick was painted with blue this time and a different symbol scrolled on his forehead.

The new arrivals were shoved in the other cell and painted with purple and the same symbol from the day before. I realized the paint indicated the number of times they'd been through the maze for the spectators. Purple for the first, blue for the second, and I guessed bright red for the third, judging from the paint smudges on the stone walls below.

I watched Nick die that day—horribly. That was the last time I talked to any of the prisoners. After that, I curled up on the floor and feigned sleep. When the hunt started, I covered my ears to quiet the sound of screeches.

Neka tried to talk to me whenever I was returned to the adjoining cell, but her words only floated into the air, as if I weren't there.

This became my life. I was fed twice a day, and each evening I was dragged out to the maze. Afterwards, Tyran brought me back and fed on me. I locked myself up tight inside, my only companion the sharp rock I'd managed to palm. My time was spent honing it against my bed as I watched the vent in the corner of my room change color with the moving of the sun and moon. Ten days passed, and Tyran was breaking me—chip by chip I was losing parts of my soul.

I went through my arrival over and over in my head, piecing together floor plans and weaknesses. I'd counted a dozen guards at each of the outer gates and that many again at the front door, plus the guards outside the throne room. Then there were all the guards down here. I must have seen over a hundred vampires, yet I'd only seen a fraction of the castle. And who knew how many human guards they had during the day.

I felt hopeless. Then, a thought occurred to me. The filthy guard that licked his lips every time he'd delivered my food; he lost control with only a trickle of blood. I wondered if I could totally break that control. I wondered if I could get him to kill me. That was the only out I could conjure. I was guarded too closely when I was moved. If I tried to bleed out, they would smell it and seal my wounds. I wondered if God would forgive me for attempting to end my life. I had no hope.

The next day, when the filthy one delivered Neka's food, I gouged a long cut into my arm and turned my back to the door; I couldn't watch him lick his lips one more time. When he got to my cell, I heard the tray hit the floor and the door creak open, and then he had me. I arched my back trying to keep my face away from his. I felt his warm breath spill over me as he pulled my hair away from my neck. In doing so, he tore off one of the necklaces Joshua had given me.

His head swiveled back and forth as he looked at the blood pulsing from my arm. "Just a taste," he growled, but there was little control in his expression.

I was ready to die. The room seemed to fill with darkness. But the filthy guard was suddenly ripped away in one motion, his upper and lower body landing on two different sides of my cell. I looked up at the massive being towering above me. He emanated power, as if he were humming like a transformer on the city grid.

It was Dagan in the flesh—an actual fallen angel. It seemed like our brief encounter in the warehouse had been another lifetime ago, and he seemed larger than in my memory. I swallowed hard. He had torn that vamp in two like he was breaking a loaf of bread.

His body was built for destruction. His strong, square jaw clenched, defining long cheekbones and an angular nose. His almost black hair shaded his eyes and thick brows. His large eyes were so dark, I couldn't distinguish the iris from the pupil. He grabbed my arm and turned his head towards the door.

"Zahra." His voice was deep and calm.

The fierce female vampire from the maze materialized in the doorway.

"Clean this up." He referred to the body. "And you are to deliver her food from now on. No males alone with her unless it is the Prince himself."

"Yes, General." She walked in and picked up the two halves of the body, and holding them away from her like they were dirty rags, she disappeared around the corner.

Dagan still had my arm. He pulled the sleeve from his shirt and wrapped it around the wound. All the while, it seemed, he didn't take his dark eyes off my face.

I opened my mouth and spoke, my voice sounding foreign. "How could you give up heaven for this?"

He had no reaction except a slight tightening of the eyes. Then, like vapor, he was gone and the door was shut, even faster than a vampire's exit. No blur of movement; I blinked, and he was gone.

I sat in shock. I didn't think I could be stunned anymore. I wasn't moved to the cages that day, and Tyran didn't visit. Three good things in one day: filthy vampire dead, no hunt, and no Tyran.

Maybe there is hope.

Zahra delivered my meals, but she would drop the tray onto the floor. She didn't flip it over. It fell flat on the stone ground and the impact would cause half the food to splatter off. *Apparently waitressing irritates her.*

Two more days of this ticked by, making it thirteen since I'd arrived, maybe more. I was starting to get hungry enough that I considered eating the floor food; she would stand there, probably hoping I would. I'd dropped enough weight that my bones were grinding into the stone when I tried to sleep. I was so weak I had to crawl to the plate, which was humiliating enough.

And I was so close to eating the food that splattered on the floor. I didn't know how much more I could take.

I was curled in a fetal position in the corner for a long while. Counting the stones on the opposite wall, trying to ignore my hunger, my pain, my helplessness, when I was jarred from my daze.

There was a commotion down the corridor, and a voice said, "Sire, please. No one is allowed down here."

"She's here, isn't she?"

"Prince, please, we were given strict orders!"

And then, a body flew by the door and crashed into the dead end, followed by another, and then another. The door was wrenched from its hinges.

I didn't think I would be happy seeing him, but I was. Bowen entered, his presence the opposite of his brother's. He lifted me into his arms and carried me from my place of darkness. I latched onto his shirt like it was my lifeline. I closed my eyes and allowed myself to feel safe.

ALL I ASK

B owen placed me on something soft. I opened my eyes and realized I still had his shirt knotted in my hand. He placed his hand over mine and eased my grip, then helped me lean back. I relaxed enough to notice I was on a chaise lounge in an opulent room as large as the house in which I grew up. He took my face into his hand and gently looked me over as he ran his fingers over my neck. Judging from his downturned lips, it wasn't good.

He lifted my arm and noticed the knot of fabric underneath it. He peered at me for permission. I nodded. He drew up my sleeve, revealing the field-dressed wound. He gently untied the cloth and looked at the gash.

"Did you do this or someone else?"

"Suicide by vampire didn't work out very well for me—or the vampire."

He made a huffing sound through his nose. "Self-preservation is not your strong suit."

I couldn't think of a reply that didn't sound pathetic or whiny, so I simply turned my head away and said nothing.

"Have they fed you at all?" I stared up at him again. He was still holding my arm. Looking at my wrist bones, which were, admittedly, protruding out more than normal. In fact, everything looked remarkably thin. My clothing draped on me loosely. In the light, I could see how utterly grimy I was.

"Some," I replied.

"How long have you been here?"

"A couple of weeks, maybe more." Time seemed irrelevant.

He stood up abruptly and walked through an interior door of the room. I could hear water running. He reemerged into the room, the sweet smell of oils trailing in his wake. He walked to an armoire intricately carved in the French tradition and painted with a pastoral scene in blues, matching the motif in the room. He yanked open the doors, slid open a drawer, and pulled out some clothing. Then he returned to the other room.

Several minutes later, I heard the water cut off, and he returned. "Are you strong enough to walk?"

"Mmm hmm," I said, but I honestly wasn't sure. I stood on shaky legs.

I'd been dragged back and forth by the guards and Tyran, and because of that, I hadn't realized the degree of weakening I had actually undergone. I'd already lost weight before my abduction with my erratic schedule.

I proceeded slowly, balancing as if I were on a tightrope, trying to move in the direction Bowen had indicated. He walked next to me, his hand almost touching my elbow, ready to catch me. I passed through the doorway into a vast bathroom. The steaming tub was the most welcoming thing I'd ever seen.

He pointed at some clothes on the counter. "They won't fit, but they're clean and here's your towel. I won't come in unless you call. Take your time." He had the kindness in his eyes I remembered from when I'd first met him at the coffee shop.

I thanked him and moved to the edge of the Roman-style tub. He closed the door firmly. I sat to gather my strength and wondered what was in store for me next. I unzipped my boots and kicked them off. My clothing literally had to be peeled off. I rolled it all into a ball and weakly tossed it to the far side of the bathroom to get the stench away from me. Now that I was out of the dungeon, I realized how putrid I smelled.

I didn't care how hot the tub was; I plunked myself inside. The bubbles tickled my chin. I found a rounded shelf under the water on which to recline. I leaned my head back and listened to the bubbles popping and the sound of my own breathing.

The ceiling was painted with clouds and a sunrise above the door, gold filigree at its borders. A painted tree branched out, extending from the edge of the gold borders of the sky, making me feel like I was outdoors. Even the bathroom had pillars, and there was a mass of highly polished marble everywhere in varying tones of beige. It felt like I was in the Maxfield Parrish painting *Daybreak*.

I disappeared under the water and ran my fingers through my hair, the oils leeching from me and floating away. While I dipped under water, I pictured Peter's anguished face again, and then my thoughts quickly went to Joshua and what his face must have looked like when he found I'd been taken.

Surfacing, I sucked in air for my silent howl of pain. Then, I became distracted by voices in the other room; they were calm, and I may have even heard a giggle. My head eventually cleared, and I felt a little stronger. I dragged myself from the tub, wrapped the plush towel around me, and sat again on the ledge. I was trembling, but I didn't know the cause: food, exhaustion, fear, despair, loss—all of the above.

A dark pair of drawstring pajama pants were on the counter, they were so long that I had to fold them over four times to keep them from pooling on the floor, a black tank top and a black, long sleeved shirt. I rolled the sleeves up since they ended mid-thigh. It reminded me of sleeping in Gabriel's shirt after I'd stood in the rain. And I had thought I'd felt helpless then.

I caught sight of myself in the mirror. I already knew I looked terrible, but this was worse. I saw no beauty in my reflection whatsoever. My face looked brittle and angular, the hollows under my eyes looked bruised. Those purplish hues were the only color I had in my face. My lips were pallid and dry, threatening to peel from dehydration.

My neck had masses of finger bruises in varying stages of healing where Tyran had grabbed me each time he'd fed, punctuated by twin scabs in different locations. Not once had he sealed the wound. Not once had he eased my pain during the process. Scarring me had been just one more thing he could do to break me down and make me feel violated. I clenched my fists and tried to compartmentalize my anger. At least I felt good enough to feel anger instead of the indifference I'd felt for days.

I stood in front of the door, my hand on the knob for several minutes before summoning the courage to exit, my wet hair hanging like damp vines down my back and soaking my shirt.

I'd spent the last five months hating Bowen, the man who'd obviously broken rules to remove me from my confines. When I entered, for a brief flash I saw the look he had in the warehouse during my vision—unbridled affection. He quickly composed himself, his face pleasant and concerned. He ran his hand through his blond hair.

"Did that help—a little?" His voice faltered, like he didn't know what to say.

"Yes, thank you." I didn't know what to say either.

I glanced around, taking in the rest of the space. It was a

corner room with grand windows in two directions, coated with that vampire-level UV protectant. They were framed by royal blue, satin curtains that must've been fifteen feet in length and embroidered with gold flourishes. Elegant Aubusson rugs at different angles, all in blue tones, covered most areas of the expanse.

There were two sitting areas, one with the chaise lounge that he'd placed me on when he'd carried me in. It was now covered with dungeon filth. I felt like I'd walked into an article in *Architectural Digest* on classical French homes of the sickeningly rich. The marble floors on my bare feet were cold. I stood there, shivering my only movement.

"I'm sorry," he said. He was suddenly across the room and opening a cabinet. I blinked. Then, he was wrapping a blanket around me. "It's cold in here. It's snowing before I even notice." He shook his head, but it looked like he was berating himself. "Please sit. I have food coming."

I walked towards the settee and sat, curling my legs beneath me to warm my now frozen toes. I pulled the blanket up around my neck and ears and pressed my nose into the fabric, trying to warm it too. He sat in a chair opposite me, looking like he wanted to speak.

I finally did. "Have you been here this whole time?"

"No. I returned yesterday."

I nodded, then bit my tongue when the only things I could think to say were unkind.

"I...I knew something was about to happen when Tyran left a few weeks ago with a dozen of his men. I have never seen him leave with so many. I finally found someone you knew. I was going to try to get a message through that your new location must have been compromised, but then I realized something had already gone wrong. I came home immediately. When I arrived yesterday, there were too many whispered comments and side-long glances."

"Who did you find?" my voice hoarse.

"Your friend that Tyran captured."

"Peter," I whispered.

"Yes."

"Did you speak with him?"

"No, I didn't need to. He was sitting alone on a rooftop; he looked inconsolable. I was going to, then Joshua appeared. When I saw him—I knew."

"He looked…"

"He looked like I would, if you were mine, and I never thought I would see you again."

I felt as if my heart might actually break; I clenched my jaw and pressed my fist over my heart, driving my knuckle into my ribcage. Bowen stood and walked over to the window, probably to give me some space. I didn't expect him to be so open or so vulnerable. *I guess if your time is limited, there is no need for posturing.*

There was a knock at the door. He opened it, and a sweet waif-like girl stepped inside with a tray of food. She didn't notice I was there; she only looked at Bowen. He took the tray from her and balanced it in his left hand, then placed his right hand under her chin, gently raising her eyes to meet his, saying, "*Merci, ma petite. Tu n'etais jamais ici.* (Thank you, my dear. You were never here.)"

She looked dreamily at him, and then disappeared down the hallway.

He returned with the tray.

"Is she human? Did you just alter her memory?"

He pursed his lips. "Yes and yes; I don't want her to be punished for my actions if she is questioned." He placed the food next to me, and I promptly popped a grape into my mouth, followed by another and another. I felt the natural sugars in my bloodstream almost immediately.

My mind was suddenly flooded with the memory of one of my visions. "Did your brother stab you a couple weeks back?"

He looked startled. "Did he tell you that?"

I continued to pick at the tray of food. "No. He actually hasn't mentioned you once. Too busy plotting evil I guess."

He didn't laugh. "Then how?" his voice trailed.

"Trying to help me has cost you."

"Killing and inflicting pain is as natural to my brother as salt is to the ocean, trees to the forest, or ice to a glacier. I've changed, and he can't comprehend that; he's been less than gracious."

"I'm sorry," I said with a sincerity that surprised even me. I sat holding a piece of cheese in my hands, feeling self-conscious.

Bowen spoke softly, but firmly. "You are not responsible for my family. You have nothing for which to be sorry. Now, how did you know?" he pressed, not allowing my comments to divert his question.

I didn't want to lie to him. "I saw it...in a dream. I saw him stab you here." I placed my hand over my incision.

He frowned, his voice almost sounded ashamed. "Later, he said he got to you. He was simply showing me what was done to you." I still wondered if that was all that was done to me.

"Poison, pain, appendectomy, tracking device, blood for the Oneiroi, people inside my head. Good times."

"I see the food is helping."

I cocked an eyebrow.

"Sense of humor," he replied with a hint of a smile.

We talked for a long while, easily falling into old patterns. I remembered why I'd enjoyed speaking with him so much before. I never lied, but I did protect myself as much as possible.

My gut told me I could trust him, though I didn't know if I ultimately could with my life. Tyran had said Bowen was "obligated to destroy" me. Would he? What tied him so strongly to this situation? Why didn't he walk away?

I became quiet for a long moment. "Is Tyran here?"

"No."

To my surprise, tears welled up in my eyes and spilled down my cheeks. I guess I'd been expecting him to burst through the door and grab me by the hair and drag me away.

"How long?" I asked, wiping the tears with my sleeve. He leaned forward slightly, like he wanted to reach out and console me, but instead eased back, pressing his fists into hard balls. Since carrying me in here and looking over my condition, he hadn't so much as touched my hand.

"A couple of days, maybe more."

The stress drained away, though it was temporary. I had at least a few days to be safe.

"I won't let him take you."

"Until I'm sacrificed."

He grimaced and looked away before I could fully read his expression.

"Why does Tyran want this so much? Why does he want to raise Moloch? I just don't understand."

He looked up at me again, his eyes locked on mine. His voice hollow. "Moloch, he's...our father."

"Your father," I choked out, Gabriel's voice echoing in my head—*they are something else.*

The food I'd just eaten threatened to come back up. I wanted to run for the bathroom, but I didn't think I would make it. There was a flash of movement, and the trashcan from the bathroom was suddenly in my hands. I wretched. Without ever actually touching me, Bowen carefully pulled my hair back, when it was in jeopardy of sliding off my shoulders into the can. I pitched forward and almost fell off the couch. The undulations from my stomach were so great that he quickly pulled me back, then released me. As soon as I stopped vomiting, he took the trashcan and returned with a damp cloth to wipe my face.

He voice sounded rough. "I guess I should have broken that to you a little differently."

"It's fine. Just a bit of a shock. The man who's been giving me nightmares for months is your father. The one I'm supposed to be," I sighed, "I guess that would explain your brother's obsession. But you?"

"Don't want him to come back."

"Why?"

"I've never felt comfortable with the world my mother and father created. I don't want to return to that, even if it means having to live life in the shadows." He looked at me. "You should sleep, unless you would like to try eating some more...or again."

I looked over the food, but my stomach felt raw. I shook my head. "Where are we?" I asked, wondering for the first time.

He sounded hesitant. "My room." He must have seen the alarm on my face, but of course it was *his* room. I was wearing *his* clothes.

"You sleep in the bed. I won't. I won't." He didn't finish, but he didn't need to.

My lip quivered. "Thank you."

He pulled the covers back on the bed. I walked to it, my legs barely holding me. I lost my balance traversing the steps up to the bed, and my body pitched backwards. He caught my elbow and righted me, then immediately let go like I was a poisonous. He pulled the heavy blankets over me after I crawled in.

Curtains ran around the grand canopy. He drew them shut to block the light from outside.

Before he closed the last one and disappeared from sight, I half chuckled, "My friends used to joke that the only sign of a true friend was if they would hold your hair back when you threw up." The sides of my mouth twitched upward.

"I hope to be a true friend to you, Aleria Hayes." And with that, he closed the curtain.

29

NO TEAR-FLOODS

It didn't take long to fall asleep, for which I was thankful. When I woke, I ached everywhere. I don't believe I'd moved once while I slept. I drew back a curtain; it was still light out.

Bowen was asleep on the settee and appeared to be rather uncomfortable. He looked so innocent. I'd forgotten how beautiful he was since I found Tyran so revolting. Though identical, he was different. There was no cruelty in his features; he had that same vulnerable look he'd had when he'd mentioned Joshua.

His blond hair was swept to the side. His eyes, fringed with thick, dark blond lashes, twitched in his sleep. His hand contracted and released a pillow he had clutched to his chest. His skin looked more translucent, the map work of veins under the surface more prominent than before. He needed to feed.

Placing my feet on the floor, I carefully tested my ability to stand, then eased off the bed. My legs were too shaky for the steps, so I sat and slid down them. Once to the base, I pushed myself up, padded to the bathroom, and shut the door quietly.

I used the facilities and splashed my face with water,

hooking my elbows in the sink to keep me upright. The hollows under my eyes were slightly improved.

The quiet was shattered with a panicked call of my name.

"I'm here," I answered. I turned and could see the shadow of feet on the other side of the door.

"Are you all right?"

"Yes, thank you." I emerged from the bathroom a moment later. "Sorry."

"No. I just thought."

"That I'd been snatched away."

"Yes, I shouldn't have slept."

"You can't stay awake 24/7. How long did I sleep?"

"Over a day. I worried that you might not wake at all," he said with his brows pinned together.

"Then it was good you slept."

"You should eat." He ushered me over to a fresh plate of food, more cold cuts and fruit. I sank into a seat and slowly ate to make sure my stomach could handle it. After I was finished, I wanted to ask him something.

He looked thoughtfully at me. "What is it?"

I shuddered. I'd forgotten how well he could read me. "How did this start? Why were you the one at the coffee shop? Why not your brother?"

He drew in a breath and looked at the ceiling for a moment. "Tyran saw Joshua one night on the East Coast. It had been almost two years since the night Joshua was turned. A rage welled up in him, the likes of which I'd never seen. He used familiars to track him. He searched his apartment and found a picture with Joshua and three others. He thought the girl was his sister. After investigating, he found that Joshua's parents were dead and that he had no siblings. He became obsessed with finding the girl—finding you.

"I was worried he was out of control, so I agreed to travel to California. And in fact, he was out of control. He drained three girls he thought might be you. I had to clean up his mess over and over."

He hunched down and rubbed his face. "He agreed to let me go to the coffee shop. I'd convinced him he couldn't draw any more attention. And then I met you. Everything changed. I wanted to know everything about you. I wanted to spend every moment with you. I kept telling him for weeks I wasn't sure.

"In all my years, I have never met someone that truly had power over me. And, I was more than a little shocked it was someone your age."

He was quiet for a few long moments. It appeared as if he was weighing his words. He finally sat up and looked me in the eye. "Tyran left early one night. The sun had barely set. I didn't know where he'd gone. I went to the coffee shop to meet you. When I walked in, the boy behind the counter gave me a puzzled look and asked if I'd forgotten something. He seemed irritated. The worst sense of dread imaginable came over me. I checked the path you normally took home. Nothing. That same sense of dread came over me again when I went to the apartment we'd been using. I found the door smashed in and droplets of your blood on the couch.

"I tracked him to the warehouse he'd been preparing while I'd been with you each evening. He said it was simply a backup since the apartment location was blown. I went back to your home and watched as Gabriel carried you into the house. It was the first time I'd ever been thankful to see a Slayer, even one to which my family had sworn vengeance. Joshua paced outside like he would shatter into a million pieces if he stopped.

"Just before dawn, I went to look through your window and make sure you were all right. Days later, I checked on you again,

I realized I could enter, that Tyran must have been invited in somehow."

I stopped him for the first time. "You didn't have to be invited, too?"

"No. Identical twins—same DNA."

"I know that Tyran attacked me and left me the flowers. Were you the one in my room after my trip to the beach? Who fought with Joshua?"

"No, that was Tyran as well."

"I thought…"

"The idea to turn you, it was mine."

I swallowed hard.

"I convinced him it would be better than killing you. I'm sorry. I didn't want you to die. After whatever occurred in the apartment, his rage increased. Whenever I would ask him what happened, he would only give me this smile. He had never kept secrets from me before, but he knew I was hiding my feelings for you. I think he knew before I did that I had them.

"He said if you chose me, he would accept that. He agreed to make the offer. We argued for the first time in a century. I wanted to speak with you; he made it a race. I tried the coffee shop first and missed you a second time. Your team of protectorates saw me and pursued. I caught up with my brother at the warehouse again. He said you rejected his offer and that, next time, he would end 'this thing.'"

I shook my head. "Of course, he didn't tell you *how* he presented the offer."

He closed his eyes. "We fought for the second time that day. I told him that if I didn't get to speak with you, we would part ways permanently. That he would no longer be my brother. So he took you from your school, along with your friend, to make you more manageable." He opened his eyes again. "The fact that you rejected the offer of immortality—royalty—all of it, only made me care for you more."

I thought about the warehouse, how it seemed as if he'd never touched me. "At the warehouse…"

"He brought you in. Later, I lost myself for a minute and embraced you. That was the first time I had allowed myself to do anything other than touch your hand. My brother had tainted everything. He called Mother days before without my knowledge to force my hand. Nothing happened as I wanted it."

"So that kiss…"

"I'm sorry. I thought if just once…" He shook his head. "If you hate me, I understand. What I feel for you is real. But I don't expect anything in return. Except, that someday you'd forgive me."

He looked at me with his clear blue eyes—broken. He'd always been confident, almost to the point of arrogance.

"I'm sorry. I have spent months hating you—both of you. I…" I hung my head. "You saved my life and the life of all my friends a few months ago. For that, I will try."

A shadow of a smile crossed his face. "And that is all I ask."

I wondered if my honesty would cause a rift, but it didn't. I started feeling better. I was sleeping well and able to eat for the next couple of days. Bowen must have threatened Morpheus and his brothers to stop infiltrating my dreams. I woke on the third day to see Bowen looking out the window that overlooked the terrace and driveway. He heard me get up.

"There is movement outside. I suspect my brother may arrive later."

I exhaled in a small gust and felt sick. "He'll be back," I

rasped. My knees felt weak, and I sat down hard on the steps to the bed.

He walked over and knelt in front of me. "I won't let him take you."

I smiled sleepily and touched his hand. He looked down surprised, and I quickly took my hand back. He seemed exhausted; the veins in his face were even more prominent now.

"When was the last time you fed?"

He frowned. "I can't leave the room. I can't leave you unguarded."

"Then feed here."

"No. Not in front of you."

I sighed and rolled my eyes. "Really? How old are you? I'll go in the bathroom. If your brother is coming back..."

"Definitely getting back to yourself, I see," he commented, giving me a crooked smile. If I weren't taken, it would probably have made me melt.

"What, bossy and temperamental?"

"Feisty."

I pushed him and laughed. It was probably the first time in weeks. It felt good.

A few minutes later, he made a call for a familiar. When there was a knock at the door, I escorted myself into the bathroom. He was right. It would have been way too awkward to watch him feed.

When he was finished, he tapped on the door, then sat on a chair in the far corner where he'd been reading the day before. He looked amazingly better. I could hardly see the network of veins beneath his skin, and the dark circles under his eyes were gone.

I nodded in greeting and walked to the windows on the ocean side to look out at the cove. On the other side of the water, there was a plateau that rose to about the same height as the one on which the castle was built. There were no buildings there, and it was thick with trees. I imagined myself free to walk amongst them, a soft breeze blowing through my hair, and the smell of the ocean comforting me.

My gaze went back to the water; it seemed calm, but the horizon was dark, like a storm could be approaching. I had awakened with Joshua's words on my mind this morning: "You survive. I will come for you."

I looked out at the darkening sky. At barely a whisper, I said, "Please don't come for me." Then I bit my lip and quoted, "'So let us melt, and make no noise, No tear-floods, nor sigh-tempests move'." *I'll find a way to end this.*

"He will come for you," Bowen murmured.

Cursed vampire hearing. I cringed and turned to meet his gaze. "He can't. It's impossible."

"It wouldn't stop me, not even the 'trepidation of the spheres' could," he said, using another line from the poem I was quoting—not even the shaking of the entire earth would stop him.

At that moment, the door burst open. Instantly, Bowen was at my side as Tyran prowled towards me.

"Well, well. I see you found my precious jewel, dear brother."

"I've always liked shiny things," Bowen replied as he stepped between us.

"But I don't intend on sharing this one with you. I think it's time to put her back."

"I'm afraid I will have to disagree with you."

Tyran slowly circled to the side, and my heart started hammering in my chest. Bowen backed up until his shoulder blades were almost pressing up against my face.

"What are your plans? Steal her away one night?"

Bowen squared his shoulders. "Of course not."

"If you do, you are not long for this world."

Bowen made a scoffing sound.

"Hope if you save her, she'll love you back? What you feel isn't real. It's the blood of the Lux Casta calling to you." He looked around Bowen's arm at me, his eyes glittering with a contemptuous light. "You need to come with me, darling."

"No. You have nothing here to threaten me with," I replied.

"That is where you are wrong. Our informer left your precious few friends today. We are free to clean out the rest of them at sunset."

The blood drained from my face; I reached out and gathered the back of Bowen's shirt in my hand. "And that, is for you, brother." I wondered what he meant by the last phrase.

Bowen's voice was rough. "Leave her here. I will fight you."

"I know. Enjoy your time together." He waved at me, wiggling his fingers mockingly. "Just remember, brother. She stays vertical," he snarked and was gone.

I stood there clutching Bowen's shirt. I leaned forward and rested my head just beneath his shoulder blades. He reached behind him and gently took my hand, disentangling it from his shirt, then he turned slowly. I let him hold me, my heart still beating painfully.

A minute later, I asked, "Why did he say 'for you brother'?"

He tensed slightly.

And then, the horrible weight of it dawned on me. "Joshua." I would never love him while Joshua was alive. His brother was in a sick way doing something for him while accomplishing his own plans.

"My brother's gesture is double-edged," he said. "Strengthen our bond only to make my pain two-fold when…"

He pulled me closer for a moment and, then, all at once, he let go. I tottered from his absence.

He picked up the messenger bag that was slumped by the chair in which he had been reading. He rummaged through it, plucked something out, and then he was back next to me at the window. He pressed a phone into my hand.

"Warn them. Text only. It's secure. No more than eight or nine back and forths. Keep them short and vague."

"You would protect them?"

"For you."

I closed my fingers around it, looked up at him, and walked to a chair in the grouping in the middle of the room and sat. I reached back in my memory, searching for one of the secure numbers that were routed through multiple satellites. I typed in the number followed by a text to Gabriel. "Get out. House comp. Neka alive." I hit send and waited.

"Who is this?"

"Ali. Evac b4 sunset."

"Try again. Who is this?"

"Josh there? Tell him Miranda."

"U hurt?" The abbreviated words told me it was Josh.

"Fine. Leave me. No rescue."

"U survive."

"U too."

Bowen's hand was on mine. "That's it." He took the phone, removed the sim card, snapped it in half, and then crushed the phone in his palm.

"They believe you?"

"I think so."

"Then they will be fine."

"Thank you."

He smiled, but there was sadness in it.

I took his hand in mine. "I don't hate you." It was a strain to admit it. "I'm working on the forgiveness." He squeezed my hand in return.

"Thank you, that's all I ask," he repeated from before. "That's all I ask."

30

DOUBLY UNDONE

The storm came, and it seemed as if the winds were trying to tear the castle from its stony cliff. The building seemed to growl and keen at the attack as if it were alive. I placed my hand on the windowpane and felt it move with the pressure.

I was still worried about Joshua, Gabriel, Peter, and the others. I wondered if they were safe. My heart said they were, but I still yearned to know. Bowen had been quiet since I'd sent my message so many hours ago.

I wondered what he was thinking. He sat in the corner with a book resting on his lap. The occasional turn of pages made it appear he was reading, but the expression on his face made me think merely the act of turning pages was the action, not the reading.

The clump of trees on the plateau on the other side of the cove was backlit with the approaching sunrise. I decided to take my leave of the window and crawled into bed after I'd drawn the curtains. As I drifted off to sleep, my thoughts were on my last two days with Joshua.

He still made my heart sprint every time he touched me. I

thought of his cool hands cupping my face before our lips met and the feel of his body pressed against mine. And lying underneath the brilliant sky with the sense that the rest of the world had ceased to exist—that our love was all that mattered. My desire to be with him was palpable, as were the vows we'd made to one another.

I slipped from my reverie into fitful dreams of running and graveyards and cold and the blade of a knife. Despite trying to put the pieces together, I only saw flashes that would come apart with my efforts like two magnets repelling one another.

I opened my eyes and fear crept through my veins. There was a figure standing over me at the side of the bed. I met his eyes and held my breath. Dagan appeared to have been there a while, an indecipherable expression on his face. It could have been confusion, curiosity, contempt, or a list of a thousand other words. He didn't move when I met his stare. I sucked in a startled breath and sat up, partially looking for Bowen.

He was asleep unawares on the couch. I leaned back and stared at Dagan, who was still standing like a statue. His lips thinned to a hard line, then he vanished once again as if he were an apparition, but I knew he wasn't. When I glanced down, my necklace with the North Star charm that had been ripped from my neck was carefully coiled on the bed next to my hand. I gathered it into my palm and blinked in confusion, pulling the blankets to my chest.

Bowen stirred and groggily sat up to look over at me. I was still frozen in position. "Is everything all right?"

I held up the necklace and replied, my tone haunted, "Dagan just returned this. He was watching me sleep."

Bowen paled.

I paced the room—something was coming, though I had no idea what it was. Daylight faded into a coppery dusk, seagulls squawked eerily on the strong winds, hovering not far from the window. Night fell, and nothing happened except my nerves steadily unraveling. I meandered my way across the room and sat next to Bowen.

He had a new book propped on his lap. It was open to John Donne's "Valediction Forbidding Mourning," the poem I had quoted earlier. He tapped his finger on the stanza, "A love that does not depend entirely on the flesh, though apart, their souls are united. Like gold when beaten with a hammer it lengthens, expands, and never disappears no matter how thin." His lips twitched in a smile. "This is how you feel." A declarative statement, not a question.

"Yes."

"Yes," he repeated. His look was wistful.

My heart started pounding, the feeling I got when I needed to say something that made me uncomfortable. "Bowen," I hesitated. This was more difficult to say than it should've been. "I do forgive you. It' not that—'"

He put his cool hand on mine. "You don't need to say anymore. Thank you."

"I never hated anyone before all this."

"It eats you up."

I nodded, biting on my lower lip. "I need to let go of all of it. I didn't realize..."

"What other dungeon is so dark as one's own heart! What jailer so inexorable as oneself!"

"What's that?"

"Something Hawthorne said."

I walked back to the window again. The predawn light was beautiful on the water. The navy blues gave way to deep purples. If I had tried to paint it, no one would have believed it was real. There was a boat passing languidly, not too far from the cove. I wondered where it was going

"Do you normally sleep during the day?" Bowen asked.

"It was the only way I could avoid the Oneiroi."

He frowned. "I wish I had your heart for forgiveness. What my family has done to you."

"You said it eats you up. Even vampires need to let things go, right?"

The doorknob clicked and slowly turned. I looked over, alarmed. Bowen was instantly in front of me, and, at some point, he had drawn a dagger. A flood of both relief and horror washed over me when Joshua stepped into the room dressed as one of the guards.

He raised a Durateus sword at Bowen, who in response lowered his arms. I flew to Joshua, who kept his sword pointed in Bowen's direction.

"We need to go," he whispered.

Bowen cocked his head like he was listening. "They know you're here."

Joshua hissed something under his breath.

"You are alone, aren't you," Bowen said, a statement again, not a question.

"Almost. I was forbidden to come; it was the only way."

Bowen walked to another cabinet and pulled out a large duffle. "They will have covered all the conventional exits by now. I have gear; go through this window to the veranda. You can use the rope to rappel down the cliffs. You can use the Daylight gear once you get there."

"You just happen to have this."

"It's how I was planning on getting her out. Go."

Joshua ran to the window to open it.

I swung around and spoke. "Bowen, they'll kill you for helping me."

Bowen's jaw flexed. He looked at his dagger, cut his cheek and arm, tore his shirt, and handed me the dagger. "Through the heart."

I stood for a split-second, knowing any time I wasted could mean our lives, no time to argue. Almost like it wasn't myself, I pressed the blade into his chest, tears bursting from my eyes. He fell like a wave onto the floor, his body too heavy for me to control. Joshua grabbed me before I could think about what I'd done. He picked me up and jumped from the window.

We landed silently. There was a staircase leading to a lower terrace that appeared to hang over the cliff. We ran down the steps, Joshua pulling rope from the duffle.

Halfway there, he turned and pulled his sword from the sheath. I hadn't heard anything. The second he had it out, there was the terrible sound of steel upon steel, sparks flying from the blow. I stumbled backwards, Joshua keeping me behind him.

Tyran swung his arm around again for another overhead blow and another and another, each blow driving us closer to the edge. He came down one last time and didn't pull back to strike again; he bore down on Joshua. Their faces were close as Tyran slowly inched the sword towards Joshua's neck. I looked around in desperation. There were no other weapons I could see, and the terrace was bare.

Suddenly, guards were flooding the upper stairs, and one yelled from Bowen's window above. Bowen stumbled to the window clutching his chest and sat on the sill looking over the scene as he swiveled his legs outside.

"Tyran, you have them. Stop."

"This is your doing!" Tyran yelled venomously, not releasing an ounce of pressure off Joshua.

I screamed. "Please, I'll do whatever you want!"

"You will do my bidding regardless of this outcome," Tyran replied.

I stepped out from behind Joshua. "I beg you."

"That only works once with me, sweetheart."

I looked up towards Bowen just as he dropped from the window above. He stumbled uncharacteristically when he stood upright. The wound I had given him had obviously weakened him. I looked over at the staircase and felt paralyzed; Dagan and the Queen herself stepped onto the veranda. She had her hands on her hips and an icy scowl on her face.

Bowen suddenly had his hand on Tyran's shoulder; he didn't appear to pull at him. It was a calming sort of gesture. Tyran reared back and elbowed Bowen with such force that he launched Bowen into the air. He slid backwards, yards away.

Joshua swung his sword while Tyran was distracted and sliced him across the chest. Tyran cried out and made a couple slashing motions in the air, driving Joshua away.

I reversed until my spine was pressed against the wall. There was a large cutout next to me with a decommissioned cannon a few feet away, as well as a ledge maybe two feet tall and four feet wide. A gust of salt air threw my hair in every direction, blinding me momentarily.

Bowen stood back up. I turned as Tyran backed Joshua up onto that two-foot ledge next to me and made one last lunging slash at Joshua.

Josh shuddered, and his sword clattered to the ground. I started towards him.

Josh's eyes darted from Tyran to me, and he stood there motionless.

Tyran dropped his arm and took a step back.

Frantically, I turned my head back to Joshua just as a flood of scarlet poured from his neck. There was no break in the line across his throat—clean through.

I screeched with a sound I didn't think a human being was capable of making. I took two more steps, reaching out for him.

His eyes closed, and he fell backwards, the tips of my fingers brushing his leg as he went over the edge.

"Nooooo...Nooooooo...Noooooooo!" I continued to scream as I dove towards him.

He fell unmoving into the deep blue waters below, the ocean swallowing him up.

I would've gone over too if something hadn't caught my ankle. I kicked at it, wanting to join him. I looked down at the waters again. I thought there might be a chance until I noticed the horizon, the sun only minutes from rising.

I was dragged back towards the platform. I turned to see who had me. Bowen let go of my leg and grabbed my arm, hoisting me back onto my feet while he argued with his brother, keeping me behind him. I couldn't understand anything.

They were hurling French at one another with such speed I couldn't make out anything.

Tyran walked towards his mother saying something; he seemed to be asking her for something. Her eyes went back and forth between her sons, but she made no comment.

Then, Bowen said something, and Tyran exploded into action, striding towards both of us. I swallowed hard as I realized his expression was identical to the dream I'd had of him running me through with a sword.

I stepped backwards until my calves hit the low part of the wall. Bowen's back knocked into me, then he fell forward.

Looking down at myself, my knees went wobbly. I sat down hard on the wall while bringing my hands to my chest. I raised my hands and looked at them, blood dripping from my fingertips.

A gurgling sensation in my chest made me cough. Blood splattered on the stone next to me. I wiped my mouth with my arm. More blood. The shock staved off the pain for a minute, but not long.

I fell backwards, my head dangled off the wall. I rolled to my side and looked at the water. There was a dark spot in it where Joshua had disappeared beneath the sea. My other dream came flooding back to me. I noticed the stone dock that I'd been standing on in that vision.

I was dying.

Good, I thought. *Good.*

I coughed up more blood, my breathing ragged, my lung filling with fluid. I looked at the trees across the cove: a spot of light, like a prism, winked at me once. I concentrated on the spot, not blinking, wishing I could see what it was. The sounds around me came into focus. The queen's unhappy voice sharpened. She was giving commands.

I smiled. I guess her plans were ruined with me about to die and all. I would have chuckled, an evil chuckle worthy of a good villain if I could. But I just stared at those trees, my eyes getting dry in the wind that came howling up the castle wall, yet I didn't blink.

Then, Queen Agrona spoke in English. "Make sure he is finished." Then there was an extraordinarily large boot next to my head as someone stepped up to the edge.

I ran my eyes up the leg to the face of whoever was standing next to me. It was Dagan.

He stripped off his jacket and tossed it to someone. He extended massive black, feathered wings that sounded like the snapping of fabric. He looked down at me with that same indecipherable expression.

I managed to get enough air to mouth one word. "Please." I wanted to say, "Please save him," but that was all I could manage.

He grimaced, dove off the cliff, and sailed in a large plummeting circle, before he straightened out and dove into the water like a magnificent bird. *The bird in my dream wasn't a bird.*

I was dragged from the edge and picked up. I was trying to stay conscious. And then the argument registered. Bowen said, "*His* bite—*my* blood; blood trumps bite."

"And so it is written," the queen replied.

Tyran say something else, but he slipped into French.

I rolled the words over in my head...his bite...my blood... over and over. I was carried inside, and though my eyes were closed, I could tell by the sweet aroma that we'd entered Bowen's room. He placed me on the bed and sat by my side.

I tried to speak again, but only a gurgle escaped my lips. My lung was heavy, the pain of the entry wound excruciating. I looked at my chest and saw blood oozing from the slit in my skin next to my heart. It felt like a fountain of crackling heat, individual sparks; surely I was going to die.

And then I realized what was said earlier. Tyran's bite and Bowen's blood—*his blood*. Tyran's sword had gone through Bowen and into me. I was going to become a vampire. I was going to become an immortal now that all I wanted to do was die.

The thought of living forever, without Joshua. How could my soul survive without him? I choked on some more blood.

I grabbed onto the front of Bowen's shirt and managed to push out a few words. I begged, "Kill me, please."

His eyes, glowing like blue flame, were unwavering. "I won't."

I dropped my hands and squeezed my eyes shut.

"I can't stop the transformation, but I can help with the pain and accelerate the process. With the small amount of my blood you took in, it will take days. But if I..."

I met his gaze.

He pursed his lips and looked at me with tragic eyes. He held out his shaking hand.

I knew exactly what he was offering. I closed my eyes again, thinking. The fastest way through the transformation was to get rid of more of my blood and take in a large amount of vampire blood. It would only take a matter of hours instead of days.

Joshua had suffered for days when he'd been turned. Part of me wanted to suffer as much as my heart was, but was I really that much of a masochist?

I tried to speak, but could no longer manage it. Just a gush of blood came up. My eyes started to burn, and I felt the tears tumble down my cheeks.

He sat there deadly still, save his trembling hands, as he waited for permission.

After several long moments, I nodded in consent.

He didn't look any happier, his face a mask. He slowly shifted his position next to me on the bed. My hands were clutching my chest. I could feel my temperature dropping. I tried to relax my body so my teeth wouldn't chatter.

"Your body has pulled all of your blood towards your core, trying to combat the shock. Do you feel cold?"

I nodded, and a new torrent of tears streamed down my cheeks.

"I'm going to need to use your neck. There's hardly any circulation in your extremities."

He squeezed my cold hand in his warm one. *Not good.*
Suddenly, his face was very close to mine, his eyes blazing. He
reached behind my head, gently knotting his fingers in my hair,
just as Josh had done when he drank from my neck.

Bowen elevated my upper body a few inches. I coughed
again, feeling the bubbling in my lung, and he cringed.

I shook my head no.

He paused, looking confused.

I started to pant in small breaths, trying to speak. "Promise
me," I pushed out my voice with all the strength I had left and
grabbed onto his shirt. "Don't let me kill anyone. Promise."

He deliberated for a moment, his breath on my face. Then,
he finally answered. "I promise I will not let you take a life. I
give you my word."

I nodded and closed my eyes, waiting.

With his mouth against my neck, he whispered, "I'm sorry,"
then he sank his teeth in. It hurt for a split second.

Then, everything felt better, even my chest wound and the
cluster of painful sparks that were spreading. A warm sensation
of comfort coursed through my body as he deadened my pain.

He drank, and I felt myself growing colder. When he
stopped, I felt his tongue on my neck seal the punctures.

My lids were so heavy it was hard to look at him. He bit his
wrist, and my stomach turned in revulsion. He placed it on my
lips. I cringed.

"It's the only way." His voice was low and liquid.

I opened my mouth, and, after a few pulls, a shocking
hunger took control. I gulped it down greedily. I drank,
watching as the veins under the surface of his skin darkened
and the pallor of his skin increased.

His eyes dimmed. This was hurting him. I tried to stop.
Finally, I pulled his wrist from my mouth and watched as his

eyes rolled back into his head, and he fell backwards onto the bed unconscious.

A heaviness swirled through my veins, and I felt my heart falter and my vision darken. The only thing behind my lids was Joshua. I could hear the sound of his soft breath, feel the coolness of his skin, the scent of his hair. And I could see that last look on his face until he fell into oblivion.

My senses dimmed, and I felt myself being pulled under. My last human tear rolled down my cheek before the blackness took me.

> *Forever...*
> *Forever without him.*
> *I am undone, I thought.*
> *I am undone.*

EPILOGUE

"I can't do it," I protested hopelessly.

"You must," Bowen said with firmness. He was keeping his promise that he wouldn't allow me to take a human life. But, in this castle, there were no bags of donated blood for me to survive on as Josh had. I felt a pang in my heart the moment I thought it...*had, as Joshua had.* I lived each day haunted, no longer being able to feel the connection between us.

It was my tenth day as a vampire, and at each feeding, Bowen had to rip me off of the familiar to prevent me from draining them. But he never lost his patience with me. He was methodical and kind.

I found there was another way to kill a vampire, as I had almost killed him. Draining a vampire was different than one going dormant. He had risked being put to death by his own family and being drained by me, all in one day.

He sat next to me, his mouth close to my ear, whispering as if my conscience. I took the boy's wrist. He was an artist they had painting new murals in one of the downstairs rooms. I wondered if they'd wipe his memory when he was done or simply wipe him out. Or maybe, if he'd impressed them enough, they'd turn him. I never asked any of their names, the nights in the maze still lingering in my mind.

He nodded at me, giving me permission, looking at me with his large chocolate brown eyes and ridiculously full lips. His stylishly cut shaggy hair swayed with his movement. I sighed, refocusing, and started feeding.

"Do you hear his heartbeat?"

I nodded.

"You need to focus on that. It will slow slightly, strain. When you hear that, you have to stop. The more you drink, the more you will want."

I heard the slowing of his heart, but couldn't stop myself, and once again he had to tear me away like a rabid animal. My emotions went wild.

I thought I would feel differently as a vampire, but I was still me. If anything, my passions were stronger. It made me wonder if the coldness I felt in the other vampires was an act, or if any sense of humanity was worn away with the years, cutting it out like water cuts a canyon. Or maybe they had little to begin with.

Bowen sent the artist boy back to his painting.

"I'm sorry," I groaned.

He squeezed my shoulder. "It will come."

"You're going to want to trade me in for a pupil with some self-control." I walked to the settee and sat down, curling myself into a ball.

"Never happen." He winked and grinned at me, that same grin that made my insides go liquid when I had first met him.

I looked away every time he looked at me like that. I felt like I was doing something wrong, that I was cheating on Josh. My grief stuck to me like barnacles to a rock, forever attached to the surface. It was part of me.

Daily, I ran through my vision of the ocean and what must have been Dagan plunging in after him, wondering if there was some shred of hope. I looked back at Bowen; he was more honorable than I'd thought possible. It made me feel guilty accepting his kindness.

Tyran and the queen were up to something. The sacrifice had been postponed for a year. I wasn't sure if this was negotiated by Bowen or not, but I had the feeling that they had some alternate plan. I had no female relatives that could've carried the gene, and my mother'd had an emergency hysterectomy when my brother was born. Bowen was locked out of the inner circle; any inquiries he made were met by silence.

I woke on the first day of the third week and could smell blood as strong as someone could smell cookies baking in an oven. I tore the covers away and pulled back the curtains. A body lay unconscious on the floor near the door. It looked vaguely familiar.

Then, I realized he was the artist boy who was painting a mural the day I arrived. I looked frantically for Bowen, but I didn't see him. I latched onto the bedpost to hold me in place. My fangs unsheathed; I clamped my mouth closed, splitting my lip.

The boy stirred and sat up, rubbing his head, pulling his slender legs in front of him.

"What's your name?" I asked. The strain in my voice had to be apparent.

He looked up at me, alarm creeping its way across his features. "K-Kyle."

"Kyle, I need you to leave. Quickly, please." He stood and

propelled himself to the door, which made me want to give chase. He jiggled the doorknob, but it was locked.

He looked at me pleadingly.

"Kyle," I said his name again. "I need you to lock yourself in the bathroom. Try to stop the bleeding." His hand fluttered to his throat and caressed the shallow rent in his skin. He did as asked. Once the smell of his blood had cleared the room, my desire eased, but I didn't dare release my grip on the bed.

The weight of this came crushing down. Tyran's games with me were not in the past; the games had simply changed. And there was no hope of escape for the time being.

I had to learn to control my murderous nature before I could consider leaving. I wondered where I would go if I were to leave. I had no idea where to look. The Dublin location would by now be abandoned, along with the others I'd known about.

Slowly, something tickled the edges of my memory. The month of March emerged as if through a fog. I had to be better than this. I now had a deadline—three months. I knew exactly where I could find someone: Gabriel. I had until March 8th, the anniversary of Laylah's death.

Through an act of will, my fangs retracted and I let go of the bedpost.

I was going to get out or die trying.

THE SACRIFICE: CHAPTER ONE

A SNEAK PEEK AT BOOK THREE

n excerpt from chapter 1—AURORA

. . .

I didn't think vampires could get cold, which was yet another surprise. Standing in knee-deep snow, I wondered if it was too late in the year for this type of weather. Moisture was saturating the legs of my filthy jeans, and my shoes were hopelessly water-logged. My skin, a crisp 65 degrees, melted the flakes alighting on me.

I paced, hoping this would be my last night of waiting. Tomorrow was the anniversary of Laylah's death. I was pinning all of my hopes on Gabriel visiting his sister's grave. I knew of no other way to locate a Watcher or Slayer who wouldn't operate on the stake-first-incinerate-later mentality.

The sun was about to rise, so I trudged to the mausoleum and slid the heavy stone aside, replacing it once inside. Rats had been my only food for a week, and I hated the unpleasant musk that tainted their blood, the way their fur stuck to my lips. I curled up on the dank, granite floor, wrapped my arms around my torso, and prayed that Gabriel would come tomorrow and stay after sunset.

When I closed my eyes, all I could see behind my lids was Bowen's face. I choked back the guilt of not really saying good-bye, though he must have known I wanted to. In the months I'd stayed with him, not once had we engaged in more than a squeeze of consolation on the hand or shoulder. My grief for Joshua had crushed my heart.

I'd had two shocks my final day in the castle. The first was when Dagan had appeared in the room and handed me the means to my escape. He was the head of Queen Agrona's Royal Guard and the general over the army she was creating. Dagan was the most massive being I'd ever seen, a literal fallen angel walking on earth.

He'd peered down at me with his almost black eyes and had simply said, "Thirty minutes before sunrise," nothing more.

There was an escape route mapped out in the package, followed by instructions. I opened the door precisely thirty minutes before sunset to find the guards missing, and I followed his plans without wavering. They led me to London. I was able to get myself to the money and IDs that were stashed in Gloucester, and from there I'd headed to Enniskerry, Ireland.

My second shock was the way I felt with the knowledge that I might never see Bowen again. He'd entered the room not long before I was to leave. I was standing on the bottom step leading to the bed.

He gave me a crooked grin. If my heart still beat, it would have gone into a sprint. When I didn't say anything and continued staring, he did a double take and approached me slowly, a faint smile still on his lips.

"Are you well?" he asked, concern creeping onto his face.

I didn't answer, but held out my hands. He stood before me and placed his hands in mine, looking down at them. His hands were perfect, like everything else about him. He was tall and blond and had the lean musculature of an Olympic swimmer. I ran my thumbs over his knuckles and pulled him a little closer. He stepped forward, and I dropped his hands and cupped his face. *People had once worshipped him like a god...he looked like one.*

I traced my fingers along his high cheekbones, over his arched brows, and down his perfectly chiseled nose. We stood nose-to-nose, with the aid of the step, his blue eyes piercing and full of questions. *He must have sensed something.*

I ran my right thumb gently over his lips, and for the first time, I willingly drew his lips to mine. My impulse to kiss him was a surprise to even me. We'd kissed once before many months ago at the warehouse in California, but it was irreparably twisted by the actions of his twin brother. I'd kissed him because I'd had to, not because I'd desired it.

Bowen took in a startled breath at the last moment, clearly not expecting me to actually kiss him. His lips were soft and firm and tasted sweet. My lips moved slowly as I leaned into him. His hands found my hips as my arms encircled his neck. I pulled him against me, feeling the hard planes of his chest press against the softness of mine.

My kisses became more feverish, and I brushed the tip of my tongue across his top lip. They parted as he let out a gasp. I ran my fingers through his blond locks and grabbed on, hard, desperation driving me. His hands ran upwards, one accidentally catching the hem at the bottom of my shirt. I sucked in a shaky breath, feeling his hand on the bare skin of my lower back.

Kissing him was nothing like kissing Joshua, where I'd always felt like my body was a network of sparks leaving me breathless. With Bowen, I felt like I had an ocean raging inside me, undulating and pulling at my very core—waves of emotion colliding and collapsing on one another. Our breathing was ragged and fast. He pulled me closer, his arms enveloping me, my feet barely on the ground.

The barriers I'd so carefully built were chaotically crashing in on me. I wished I could tell him everything I was thinking. *I truly do care about you, but I have to leave. I can't be here. You are amazing, and if my heart wasn't broken, a part of it would be yours. Goodbye.*

I felt tears well up in my eyes as I pulled myself away. He looked at me in an awe-struck daze, and I caressed his face again. *So beautiful.*

I felt the warmth of a tear against my cool skin. I wiped it away with the back of my hand and caught a glimpse of its color. There was a tinge of red in it. "There's blood in my tears."

Bowen pushed some loose strands of my hair behind my ear. "Is something wrong?"

My voice stuttered from the onslaught of emotion I had broiling under the surface. "No matter what, know I care about you, and I never wish to see you hurt."

He straightened up slightly and held my face between his hands, wiping the next tear tenderly away with his thumb. "I love you, Aleria. I always have, and I always will."

A sob escaped my lips. "D-don't say that. Please," I whimpered and looked down.

I knew he loved me, but hearing him say it aloud for the first time—now—I'd been so careful to keep him at a distance. I pushed past him and locked myself in the bathroom.

He stood vigil at the door for a long while. He whispered my name and the words "I love you" again and again, as if I needed convincing of their truth. I anxiously watched the shadow of his feet reflected on the shiny marble surface beneath the door. When I finally exited, he was gone, and it was time for me to depart.

I sighed heavily as my thoughts returned to the present. I gripped the locket from Joshua in my palm and rubbed the North Star charm he'd given me, as was my habit to soothe myself.

With some effort, I was able to fall asleep, surrounded by the decay of ancient corpses in coffins. I had a dream that I'd dreamt before of graveyards, running, and a knife, but it was more fragmented this time. I woke a few hours later, my chest constricted. Though my bloodlust was under control, my emotions definitely weren't.

This time of year, days and nights were roughly split fifty/fifty. I'd been spoiled in the castle with its protective windows coated by something—something I could never pronounce. It'd made me feel like I was still human, being able to watch the sunrise and sunset. I certainly didn't need twelve hours of sleep, no vampire did. Dark and light, literally and figuratively, had become my eternal struggle.

I wondered how Joshua had been able to cope with the claustrophobic feeling of being trapped by day. *Joshua.* I gripped my chest and wondered how an unbeating heart could feel like this. I pressed my face against the cold stone and concentrated on breathing. The last thing I needed to do right now was cry.

If Gabriel did show, I didn't need watery blood dripping from my eyes. I looked at the watch Dagan had provided; it appeared the sun had just set. I carefully slid the stone to the side. The golden light of sunset was but a whisper in the air, the blues and purples of night washing away the sun's warmth.

I circled around one side of the mausoleum and was overwhelmed with joy when I saw Gabriel's large and lean figure sitting slightly hunched over on a bench near his sister's grave, not a hundred yards away.

His chocolate brown hair and olive skin looked darker in the evening light; the long fishhook scar on his left cheek was pronounced in the shadows, increasing the lethal image he always projected. But his grief was evident in his posture; at least, I knew it to be grief. Normally the silent warrior, I was one of the few people he actually talked to, and he'd become family.

Without thinking, I smiled and ran to him, approaching from the side; I was about to say his name, but something stopped me in my tracks. I looked down at my chest. There was a Durateus blade stuck there like my own personal gravestone.

I looked at him through wide eyes. Gabriel's expression of rage melted into horror when it registered. I fell backwards like a slab of granite, unable to move; his blade was straight and true and had found my heart. My paralysis was complete.

"Aleria!" he frantically yelled. I felt him slide up next to me on his knees. My upper body convulsed as he withdrew the blade.

"I'll heal," I whispered.

But he shook his head, the look of horror still fixed on his face. And then, without warning, I screamed out from a searing pain more horrific than anything I'd ever experienced. My chest burned like a thousand fires. I felt sweat bead to the surface of my entire body, a sensation I hadn't experienced since I'd been turned.

I was vaguely aware that I was being carried. I was loaded into the cab of a vehicle, maybe a truck. I curled my body inward on the bench seat next to him, wishing I could snuff out the blaze in my chest. I heard the tires screech as Gabriel accelerated out of the cemetery.

He was yelling into the phone. I only caught bits and pieces between my whimpers and moans, something about "training room…ice…antidote…and…NOW!!"

ACKNOWLEDGMENTS

Here I am, once again, trying to express an ocean full of thanks on a single page!

Of course, I need to begin with my better half. He has hung in there and given me the space and time to complete this second novel. You are more than I could have ever hoped for.

I need to thank three other people in particular who have helped me in ways more than I can express:

Katie Isaacs, you have amazing talent in both artistic and grammatical editing. Thank you for all the hours.

Alexis, thanks for being the repetition police and helping me with logic. I still think you are a rock star.

Rachel, thank you for your continued dedication to helping me with continuity. You are my go to girl when I need to brainstorm, vent, and hash out anything. I have one thing to say, "tone/mood?" ;)

And yes, there are still others: Judy, Anne, and Irene, for helping with translations. James Stewart, for trudging through the first draft and editing supplementary material. Judy, thank you for helping me with my Achilles' heel in my writing.

You-are-the-best.

Thanks to Chris, Lisa, Rebecca, Janelle, Rachel, Jessica, Becca, Jessie, Tamar, Amy, Beth, and Laura for giving me both feedback and encouragement. And to many of my students and former students, for enthusiastically being my focus group.

Vera Walker, for designing and illustrating the beautiful cover. And all the extra help you give me without a single complaint or eye roll. I know you want to sometimes.

And to Mom and Dad, for always being my cheerleaders.

BOOKS IN THE WATCHER SERIES

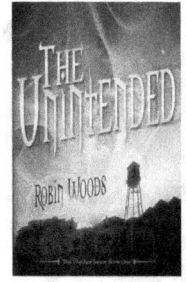   

  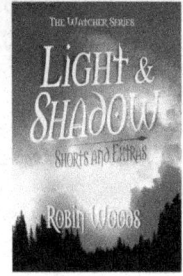

Fiction Books

Allure: A Watcher Series Prequel

The Unintended: Book One

The Nexus: Book Two

The Sacrifice: Book Three

The Fallen: Part One: Book Four

The Fallen: Part Two: Book Five

Light & Shadow: The Watcher Series Shorts & Extras

ALSO BY ROBIN WOODS

Creative & Fiction Writing Books

Prompt Me: Creative Writing Workbook & Journal

Prompt Me More: Workbook & Journal

Prompt Me Again: Workbook & Journal

Picture This: Photo Prompts & Inspiration

Prompt Me Novel: Fiction Writing Workbook & Journal

Prompt Me Sci-Fi & Fantasy: Workbook & Journal

Prompt Me Romance: Workbook & Journal

Prompt Me Horror & Thriller: Workbook & Journal

Prompt Me Reading Log & Analysis: Workbook & Journal

Coming Soon: Prompt Me Mystery & Suspense

ABOUT THE AUTHOR

Robin Woods is a former high school and university instructor with two and a half decades of experience teaching English, literature, and writing. She earned a BA in English and an MA in Education.

In addition to teaching, she has published six novels, eight creative writing books (and counting), and has multiple projects in the works, including writing for a Hollywood producer.

When Ms. Woods isn't chasing her two elementary school kids around, she's spending time with her ever-patient husband, or sitting in a coffee shop wondering how vampires like their lattes.

For more information, an extended bio, free writing resources, and free extra scenes, visit her website at www. robinwoodsfiction.com

www.ingramcontent.com/pod-product-compliance
Lightning Source LLC
Chambersburg PA
CBHW072110250626
47159CB00007B/2383

* 9 7 8 0 9 8 5 4 5 4 2 0 3 *